I0685372

A gifted archeologist.
A skilled social strategis

A rebellious teen romance.
A desperate need to be loved.

A naïve optimist.
A depressive alcoholic.

A hostile planet.
Thirteen children.

What could possibly go wrong?

Ancient

History

Even the Best stories have to start somewhere.....

The **Best Intentions** series

Best Intentions
Best Efforts
Broken Trusts
Best of Everything
Ancient History

Also available in e-book format

Best Intentions' first section titled "Ancient History" originally covered forty pages of the parent's backstory. Twenty-seven pages were edited out for space. Portions of the final *Best Intentions* text with the original cuts edited and restored are reprinted within this text for continuity's sake.

Best Intentions told the family's story from the children's point of view. Here is how the parents saw it.

This is an original work of fiction. Names, characters, places and politics are strictly the work of the author's imagination and are not meant to endorse any political viewpoints. Any similarity to persons living or dead is entirely coincidental.

Additional coverwork by Bob Staneslow

One

A ndrea-Marie Maximovna Ivanova stood firmly in the top quarter-percent of Earth's economic ladder, a fifty-percent owner in the largest net worth in the state of Byelorussia. Narkissa Rumel tottered on the one-percent rung. Narkissa's main home boasted nineteen rooms, seven bedrooms, and a full-time staff of eight. Andrea's main estate listed forty-two rooms with ten bedrooms, not counting her personal suite or the apartments of the handful of her forty-five staff who lived over the kitchen in the north wing, nor the outbuildings and guest house. Andrea's home bore a decorating scheme straight from Traditional Museum-Style Living For The Terminally Tasteful Connoisseur, from the color palettes to the art collection to the brass and marble crest inlaid in the polished floor of the cavernous foyer. Narkissa's home screamed nouveau riche, with computer-driven ultra-modern flash and fancy gleaming from every smooth bright surface. Andrea counted Narkissa as a friendly acquaintance, someone to hit on for charity events or when fishing for gossip, but in private considered her boorish and tawdry – which she was. Narkissa used Andrea as a source for tabloid publicity and as a spring to dredge for investment information, but behind her back called her arrogant and merciless – which she was. The fact Narkissa was thirty-seven and content to live like a parasite off her husband's wealth grated Andrea raw. The fact Andrea was ten years older, worked eighty-hour weeks, and looked not a day past thirty-five

5

without cosmetics made Narkissa furious. Neither would have given each other the time of day if their daughters hadn't been best friends.

Helina Rumel and Maryana Ivanova met as kindergarteners at the prestigious Leonov Academy for Excellence, Helina lithe and athletic, Maryana fifteen centimeters shorter and delicate as an orchid petal. Helina moved on to the Saint Euphrosinia School for Girls, the most highly respected boarding school in Byelorus. Maryana found herself sequestered at the Villovsky Academy in Moscow, a far more elite school where brains mattered, but financial accounts mattered more. Saint Eu girls became leading educators, scientists, or Presidential cabinet members. Villovsky girls married well, expertly groomed for executive management of corporations and estates, cultured social planners well-versed in art, music, and classical literature, with impeccable fashion sense to accompany their unfailingly slender physiques. Helina was never sure if she was supposed to be jealous of Maryana or sorry for her.

December pulled them back together for the six-week semester break. Helina's bedroom was adorned in pinks and greens, modern and sleek with glossy white walls and fixtures. Cabinets, closets and drawers were set invisibly into the walls, leaving the room airy and spacious. Strands of tiny accent lights criss-crossed the ceiling, giving the visitor a feeling of walking into an unexpected garden party. Mirrored accents around the room reflected the sparkle.

Helina swooned onto her bed, bouncing lightly before sitting up. "I'm so excited I could cry! I'm allowed a hundred guests! A hundred! Mum's letting me do all the planning, from the music to the menus to the decorations. I had to beg for half an hour, but Papa agreed to let me order real champagne for the toast. But only three cases, so no one has too much. My first New Year's party, and I'll serve champagne! I am *so* going to shine!"

Maryana smiled softly, a gesture that lit her face until the room itself seemed brighter. "Like a supernova! People will talk about it for years to come. No one will be able to top you. I hope it goes orbital for you."

Helina's glow evaporated. "What do you mean? You're coming, aren't you? You're like my co-hostess! You're so much better at that stuff than me. I can't do it without you."

Maryana plopped into a pink cloud chair, then leaned forward to free her long hair from behind her back. She bit her lower lip in a sulky glare, but instead of angry, the action rounded her cheeks and made her look childishly endearing. "Mamá's having the Graffias and the Kusharevs to dinner. She expects me to be there to entertain Emil Graffia, even though I already told her I was coming here. I can't stand him! His idea of entertainment is exploring topography – mine. I threw a proper fit, but now she wants Tomas to escort me."

"Escort?" Helina wailed in disbelief. "You're sixteen! I didn't invite your brother, I invited you! That's the last thing I need. He'll tell me I'm doing everything wrong, take over, and ruin the whole evening. He has a million friends at university; he doesn't need to be hitting on ours."

"Mamá's afraid things could get out of hand. I'd rather bring Tomas than Emil. Do you know the disaster that would be? I love Tomas, don't get me wrong. Sometimes he takes me places Mamá wouldn't approve and we have so much fun, but he's got a date with Stephania Yurgenev, so I know he'll be furious and nag me every minute to leave."

Helina waved her hands in a cutting motion. "You can't. You can *not* bring an escort. Tell your mother it's very tightly planned and you can't bring any guests. My parents will be here, along with the Pilarcheks and the Winewskis, hence no one is bringing an escort. That will destroy you socially."

Maryana gave a soft snort. "Don't I know that? Sometimes I swear that's what my parents are trying to do, ruin my life so they can take it over. It's like all they know how to do! I can only date boys from a list they've screened first. I can't go anywhere or do anything unless it's been pre-planned and a galactic task force has combed through it and given their approval. They don't trust me to do anything. 'Do this, Maryana! Don't do that! Maryana! People of our situation do not run around dressed like that! Maryana! Do not speak to the media! I don't care what Ivana Vankova's mother let's her do, young girls do not go around without an escort.' It's not like I've ever even done anything wrong! Tómas can do whatever he wants, that's okay, but I'm not allowed a single thought that's not pre-approved. Not that I've ever had a chance. Jupiter's moons, they just got rid of the nanny two years ago. Honestly, who has a nanny at fourteen?"

Helina pulled Maryana from the chair. "Tomas can't come home pregnant. Come on. Let's go back to your place and talk to your father about ditching Tomas. He's never said no to me yet."

"You've never asked him for anything."

"So he can't refuse me, can he?"

Zukash, the Rumel's chauffer, flew the girls across town to the Ivanov's. Maryana handed their coats to the man at the door, and they proceeded down the length of the house, through the massive foyer, to her father's study in the north wing.

Maryana knocked lightly before entering. "Just me, Papa. Me and Helina."

Fyodor Ivanov glanced up from his bank of computer displays. Stock numbers from around the known galaxy flashed in six subscreens of one; three others connected with various offices. Ivanov avoided standing whenever possible; sitting made him appear more imposing than 167 centimeters. He kept his hair dark whether it wanted to be that way or not, projecting an image that claimed experience, but not enough to be outdated. A warm smile broke across his face. "Little Bird! What are the two of you up to? You're not still planning gifts for the holidays that will bankrupt me?"

Maryana wrapped her arms around his neck and kissed his cheek. "No, Papa, but I still have my heart on those earrings at Verlovsky's jewelers. I'm sixteen now; I can wear diamonds. No. Helina and I wanted to discuss something with you."

"Is it about business?"

Helina spoke up. Her familiarity with the Ivanov household and Mr. Ivanov's height had long ago eased any intimidation over his wealth and reputation. He was just... Maryana's dad. "Well, sort of. It's something that's interfering with my business plans."

Fyodor spun his chair around to face them. "Ah! Then we must address it at once. If you correct a problem early enough, it will never be a problem at all. What can I help you with?"

"Well, I'm planning a rather important event, and I've taken care to provide adequate security measures, but there are those who feel my efforts aren't good enough and are trying to make changes that will have an adverse effect on those attending the event. As I want the event to succeed, I don't know how to prove my efforts are satisfactory in themselves."

"Well put, Helina. You've been developing your business sense. Your father should be proud. Now, what organization is trying to undermine your event, or are you trying to trick me into answering a schoolwork question?"

Maryana climbed onto Fyodor's lap and hugged him. "You are, Papa. You and Mamá. It's a teen party, Papa. Tomas is twenty, he's not a teen. You let him go out alone at sixteen. You didn't have a personal bodyguard at sixteen, and neither did Mamá. You let me go to Helina's all the time without an escort, so why not on New Year's Eve? Or is it Levan you don't trust?"

Fyodor wiggled the tip of her nose. "I trust my chauffer just fine. You are my only daughter, Maryashka. You are my greatest treasure, and you deserve protection."

Sarcasm tinged Helina's voice. "So what you're saying, then, is you don't trust my parents. There will be at least six adults there to supervise, not counting the staff. My mother's already said she's putting a guard on the stairs so no one can go up there. Please, Mr. Ivanov, sir?"

"Please, Papa?" Maryana snuggled up under her father's chin. Long lashes batted over large eyes of twilight blue. "If you loved me, you'd know I'm right."

Papa wrapped his arms around her. "I love you even when you're wrong. What did your mother have to say?"

"She hasn't given an opinion either way."

Ivanov chuckled. "Nicely put, Maryashka. You haven't asked her yet."

"Please, sir?" Helina said. "I promise, the only alcohol will be the champagne toast. You can check in with her whenever you like."

Ivanov sighed. "My Little Bird is growing up. All right. Being as it's Helina's, I will see if they mind an added security detail, okay? No one will know they're there for you, so your social standing will remain unblemished. Levan will be there to yank you out at my command, you can wear my wristcom so your mother can track you every minute, which should quell any objections on her part, and if all that comes to pass, I give my permission for you to attend alone."

Maryana squeezed him. "Thank you, Papa! Thank you! But only a tracker; a wristcom would ruin my ensemble."

"Stars forgive me! I wouldn't want to do that."

Helina shook his hand. "Thank you so much, Mr. Ivanov!"

"If!" Ivanov held up a finger. "Only if your mother agrees as well."

Maryana's shoulders slumped, and she slid off his lap. "Well, I'm a quarter-way there, at least."

The dining room sagged under the layers of decorations for the upcoming holidays; greenery and ribbons reflected in the curves of the silver like a carnival ride. Tomas breezed into dinner two minutes late.

Andrea Ivanov swallowed her reprimand for tardiness the second she glanced up. "What in God's name are you wearing, Tomas? Some sort of dressing robe?"

Tomas fluffed the short tails of his quilted velour jacket as he sat. "It's the latest fashion in Moscow, Mamá. Very cutting edge. This one's rather moderate, I'm afraid. The extravagant ones puff out five or six centimeters under the quilting."

"Taste and fashion are rarely cohorts."

Fyodor gave a brief nod. Debonair Tomas had princely good looks, in possession of a trim, athletic frame that made almost any outlandish costume look dashing on him, a fact Tomas knew too well. "That's fine for sporting about university, but don't let me see that in the office."

"Of course not, Papa. I know. I was thinking about wearing it for New Year's. I bought a wonderful shirt to go with it, ruffled Kandalusian silk with cuffs to match the jacket. Maryana will have to find something to match."

Maryana put down her waterglass. "I already bought my outfit, and Mamá approved. And you're off the hook, anyway."

"Speaking of which," Andrea interrupted, "Fyodor, Maryana says you gave her permission to attend the Rumel's party unescorted. At the very least, you should have consulted me first. We have no idea who might be in attendance or what media may be lurking about. Narkissa isn't nearly as vigilant as she should be. Maryana isn't used to fielding paparazzi by herself. There is no reason Tomas can't go along as an added hand."

"I agree," Tomas said.

Maryana dropped her fork with a clatter. "*Mat*, we've been over this! I know at least half the people coming. You know most of them yourself." She counted off on her slender fingers. "Tiana Grutsky, Liza Minarsky, Bartus Jurganis, the Shelikov brothers …"

"It's not the ones you know, Maryana," said Mamá. "It's the ones you don't."

* * *

10

Maryana sulked at her vidlink screen, deep in conversation with Helina, her head still spinning from Mamá's lecture on good girls versus bad girls. It wasn't the mortal embarrassment of listening to such a ridiculous talk, but the fact Mamá didn't believe that Maryana had no desire to become a bad girl that truly stung. Helina planned a tasteful New Year's soirée, not a Bacchanalia brawl, and Mamá had no business trying to twist it into something evil.

A brief knock sounded at her door, and Tomas entered.

Maryana scowled at him. "Later. I'm on the link, and you are not welcome in the conversation."

"Hello, Helina," he said to the screen. "She can call you again later. My turn right now," and he closed the connection.

Maryana's hands fought his for the controls. "Tomas Severyan! You had no business doing that!"

He waved her anger away and spun her chair toward him. "I want to talk to you, alone. As much as I have no desire to waste my holiday escorting you, I don't think you should be going to such a party by yourself. You and your cloistered fellow inmates have no idea what goes on at big parties."

"Drop dead, Tomas. I heard enough of that excrement from Mamá."

"No, you haven't," Tomas insisted. "Mamá hasn't been to a teen party since the last Ice Age. It can get ugly, uglier than you can imagine. It's not the alcohol Helina will be serving, it's what others bring with them. I'm not implying you're loose, I'd kill you myself, but there are those boys who won't take no for an answer." He lifted her hand, squeezing and stroking the soft skin. "They caress your hand and you think that's so sweet, but the entire time they're rubbing in a drugged cream that will have you flat on your back before you know it, and you won't remember a thing that's happened until you see the video on everyone's mail cache the next morning. You don't know what you're getting into." He released her hand with slight flick, as if it had annoyed him.

"Is that how you get your girlfriends?"

"Of course not. I prefer mine live and kicking, but I know others who have."

Maryana rose and tried to turn him to the door. "If that's what happens at your glorious university, maybe I'll attend somewhere else. I am not your damsel in distress anymore, Tomas. Helina is not planning that kind of party, there will be chaperones present, Papa is sending a field of undercover operatives to surround the building, and I not only like Helina's parents, I trust them. Did it ever occur to you I know what I'm doing? I'm not the baby you people think I am! It's better to stay here and let Emil Graffia check my sweater to see if I stuff it? I am going to that party if for no other reason than to escape him, and I am going *alone*."

Tomas fell silent for a pause. "Why are you so adamant about going alone? What have you and Helina got planned?"

Maryana stomped her foot in an attempt at fury. "*Arkh!* For goodness' sake! Mamá's paranoid enough without you joining her. I want to go alone because I'm sixteen and a half years old, I can be a legal adult in just five more months, diploma in hand, and I don't need a nanny anymore! I am perfectly capable of taking care of myself, thank you. Now leave me alone!" Tomas wasn't particularly tall or heavy, but it took considerable pounding and shoving for Maryana to push him out of her room.

"I'm going with you," he insisted as she shut the door.

Two

Zapoiniye Ribi, The Drunken Fish, was not so much a tavern as a divey little bar half-hidden by its location in the basement level of the Golumkov Dental Surgery building in the reclaimed section of Minsk. Its short little windows held blinking signs to advertise the brands of liquor available within, and a scroll board hooked onto the rail at the top of the stairs, trying its silent best to entice passers-by with the kitchen specials of the day. Few paid attention. Those on their way to see a dentist weren't about to stop for a snack on the way in, and food was the last thing on the minds of people leaving – though they sometimes stopped for a shot of vodka, or three or four. The decor had once been cheery: the ceiling beams painted in a folk-art style, quaint murals showing Minsk before and after the last reconstruction, the cozy glow of low-energy wall sconces lending an odd sense of serenity to the room. Years had faded the folk art, covered the photos with grease and dust, left the plastic tables wobbly and the chairs a mish-mash of whatever was cheap the year they were bought. Blocking the few windows with signs and the accumulation of dirt on the sconces left the bar in perpetual gloom, made worse when snow covered the windows in the long winter months. The day after Christmas, the weather was cold but snow hadn't yet covered the windows.

Piotr spread another dollop of seasoned sour cream on his blinchik, rolled it, and bit half off at once. "So I said, look Bitch, I slept with you once six months ago. Unless that baby's three months early, it's not mine, and that baby's four kilos on an empty stomach. I'm telling you, you gotta watch your back every second with some chicks."

"What do you expect, with the women you pick?" said Ivan. "You're ugly as a monkey's ass, so it must be your money they're after." The comment brought a round of laughter.

Ivan poked his friend with his elbow. "Can you imagine someone making that claim to Sash, here? They'd know by the bulge in the diaper."

Ivan and Piotr laughed, while Sasha managed a knowing half-grin as he spooned his soup. He was by far the tallest man in the bar, ducking through doorways and weaving around hanging lamps. His voice rumbled up from somewhere under the floor. "You should be so lucky."

"If we were all hung like you, you'd never get any women," Piotr said. He ignored the table's cracked ordering screen and waved a hand in the air. "*Officiant!* Bring us a round of your best. We will drink to paternity testing and the innocent man."

Sasha pulled the arm down. "I can't afford it this week."

"It's payday. Of course you can."

"It's rent week. Perhaps next Friday."

"Then this week is on me, and you can owe me next week."

Sasha looked no happier for the vodka placed before him, but he toasted politely and downed the shot.

Piotr licked his bottom lip and leaned in over his empty glass. "Actually, you want to get in on some good grub? Gourmet shit, expensive drink, maybe a pretty new bird? High-class tail?"

"I'm not doing time for a stupid heist," Ivan said warily. "You pick a fat pocket or something?"

"No, no, completely legit," Piotr swore. "My brother Misha got himself invited to a New Year's party over on the west side, very uppity, gated roads and everything. Total cosmo. I can copy his invitation, get us in there."

Ivan sat back in disgust. Piotr and his brother were separated by ten years and two different fathers. "Misha? They're kids! Every skirt there will be illegal. That's like walking through a liquor shop after hours and not being allowed to touch."

Piotr shrugged. "Not everyone, I'm sure. It's free food, better than any restaurant we'll ever afford. Eat, drink, and we'll go elsewhere to be merry."

Sasha turned the thought over in his head. "We'd have to dress right or we'd never get in the door. I haven't got anything that good."

Ivan examined him with a critical eye. "Paint your shoes black; no one will notice. For the sake of dear mother Byelorus, do your patriotic duty and take a bath. Find out where the circus is wintering, maybe they can lend you something."

14

Sasha's jaw seemed to clench for a moment; a sour frown flitted across his rough face. He lifted his soup bowl to his mouth to drain it, then scraped the last of the vegetables from it with his finger. "That explains where you get your clown suits."

Piotr gave a loud cackle and leaned across the table to slap Ivan on the shoulder. "Hey! He's pretty good, once he thinks hard enough, no? Faith, my friend. Five days from now, we'll be eating like the Tsar."

Three

T he Rumel's estate radiated a festive atmosphere; blaring music, holiday lights and the colored lights of the various vehicles crawling around the circular flyway advertised the merriment within. In turn, Levan slid the hovercraft to a stop at the entry. The parking gear deployed and the silver-blue vehicle settled with a hydraulic sigh until it rested thirty centimeters from the ground. He walked around and opened the door on the opposite side. Maryana nearly knocked him over in her eagerness to get out. He escorted her to the door.

"One a.m., Miss Ivanova. Please be prompt."

Maryana rolled her eyes. She wore the lightest of cosmetics; her beauty came naturally, more color would have looked garish. "I know! I know! Or Papa will have a fit. I've heard the lecture from both sides for the last two weeks."

A dour-looking man in a white-and-wine uniform opened the door. Levan placed the girl's hand in the doorman's and informed him, "Miss Maryana Ivanova."

The doorman bowed and spoke loudly over the noise pouring out the door. "Good evening, Miss Maryana. Miss Helina has been most anxious for your arrival."

"Thank you, Vaslav." Maryana paused to fasten a trinket of tiny bells and shiny ribbons to his lapel. "Happy New Year!"

Narkissa Rumel greeted her inside, kissing her on each cheek. "Maryana! What a lovely outfit, darling! Those colors are just perfect on you. I see you're wearing your new diamonds, too."

Maryana gave a happy twirl, making the silver threads of her leggings shimmer like rain. The bell-shaped sleeves of her sheer pink and blue shrug spun outward. "Isn't it gorgeous! It's a Tami Trevor original. I feel like a butterfly. And it's so much warmer than a dress."

16

"You look like one, too! You're always so practical. I wish some of that would rub off on Helina. Her mind is always in the clouds. How kind of your mother to allow you to attend; I was afraid I'd have to give her a piece of my mind. Come, come! The party's just getting started. We've got entertainment in the lounge every hour – I think there's a magician in there now. The buffet is at one end of the ballroom. Make sure to try the Centauri spice eggs; I had them imported direct." Mrs. Rumel leaned close to whisper, "Zuran will kill me! I thought the price was per dozen, not each."

A girl burst into the hall from a side room. "Maryana!"

"Nairi! Happy New Year!" Maryana gave her a hug.

"Ah! I should have known you'd know everyone. I'll go back to greeting," Mrs. Rumel said, and left them.

"Maryana!"

"Hey Maryana!"

"Maryana!" Maryana never took more than three steps without someone calling her name. She waved to some people and hugged others, both boys and girls. She knew the names of most of the Rumel wait staff scurrying room to room, and remembered to greet them as warmly as the numerous friends who called out. *Always acknowledge the staff; treat them politely and with respect. They will go out of their way to treat you well in return.*

She stopped in awe when she reached the ballroom, half the size of hers at home. Buntings and banners covered the walls. A forest of silver and gold metallic streamers rained downwards from the high ceiling; nestled among the glitter were a hundred shimmering fist-sized globes programmed to burst on the stroke of midnight, showering the revelers with confetti and small coins. Strobes and spotlights bounced off the swaying ribbons, sending prisms of light around the room. The circular banquet table held a vast array of traditional and exotic delicacies; an arched bridge of stars crowned a central ice sculpture of the numbers 2239, lit from below by electronics that flashed changing colors to the beat of the music blasting from a four-member band. Most of the boys grouped on one side of the grand ballroom, the girls on the other, and a few brave souls of both sexes danced madly between. Maryana wove through the crowd until she found Helina, regal in ruched purple Argosian silk and gold ribbons. Her hair had been professionally styled, and Maryana recognized her pink and white diamond neck bib as belonging to Mrs. Rumel.

"Helina! You look orbital!"

Helina hugged her with relief. "Thank God! You were supposed to be here an hour ago! Look! Look! I have my power heels on!" Her feet ran a flurry of excited steps in place.

Maryana glanced down. Helina teetered on ten-centimeter silver spikes, while dozens of shining diamondettes wrapped her feet on invisible strands to hold the shoes on. Mamá would have sneered, but to Maryana they twinkled like constellations in the night sky.

She had to shout above the music. "Like an Empress! You totally rule! I couldn't leave until after dinner. Even then, Mamá tried pawn Emil off on me. I had to play the no-added-guests card. She'll probably give your mother an earful tomorrow. This is fantastic! I can't believe how many people are here!"

"Tell me about it! Maybe not you, but half the others brought friends. My father will jump to Jupiter when he sees the catering bill. I hope there's enough champagne."

"What do you want me to do?"

"Mingle," Helina decided. "You're better at it than I am. Make sure everyone is happy. Direct them to the tables or the entertainment rooms. I'm trying to make sure I greet everyone. Reyka's here; she's working on it, too."

A red-haired girl in a tight dress rushed up. She grabbed Helina by the arms as she attempted to stop sprinting on high heels. "He's here! He's here! He's actually here! You won't believe it!"

"Who! Who!"

"Ar-kin Lar-it-sky!" the girl squealed slowly. "And he flew here himself in his brand new Sterling Sunset!"

Helina gasped. "Liza! You're kidding!"

Maryana grabbed Liza's arm. "Where?"

"There! He's just coming in now. Ooooh! Isn't he just the most gorgeous creature in the Alliance? Look how many girls are around him already! There's that witch Anya right next to him, too. You *knew* she'd be the first one to spot him. I'll bet you coined credits she'll dirty the back seat before the night's over. He's a superstar galactic cover boy now; he'll expect it. Helina, why didn't you tell us he'd be here?"

"I had no idea myself!" Helina exclaimed, delighted the most famous, handsome boy they knew was right there in her home. "Well, as hostess it's my duty to greet each guest personally. Here I go. Is my face okay?"

Liza adjusted the off-kilter necklace. Maryana assured her, "You're gorgeous! Calm and welcoming."

"Calm and welcoming," Helina repeated. "Oh, my legs are shaking! I hope I don't fall off my heels. Wish me luck."

Maryana gave her arm an excited squeeze. "You're beautiful and charming; you'll be fine."

"I know I'll say something stupid. Should I greet him with a kiss?"

"Go for it," Liza urged.

Helina gulped air and wormed her way across the floor.

"Don't they make a perfect couple?" Liza sighed. "Look at that face! Money, looks, inheritance – what more could a girl want?" She glanced at Maryana, and they giggled.

A boy approached from the side. "Maryana? Would you … wanna dance?"

He wasn't much taller than herself, his skin too smooth for more than a single hair on his chin, but Maryana gave his hand a squeeze. "Of course, Vanka. I'd be honored."

Maryana lost track of Helina. She caught part of a comedy routine in the lounge, avoided drinking the three glasses of punch she received from admirers, played a piano accompaniment for someone in the conservatory, and urged food on almost everyone she met. As she hunted the rooms for Helina, a scruffy fellow by the buffet table caught her eye. He was tall, more than a head taller than anyone else in the room, with shoulders enough for two. He hunched over a plate mounded high with food, guarding it as if he didn't want it seen. Dark eyes darted about to see if anyone was watching before he shoveled as much into his mouth as it would hold. His black hair fell across his eyes when he leaned forward, and he tossed his head between bites to flip it back. She didn't recognize him at all.

A group of girls pulled her away to gossip. When she returned, the man wasn't by the table. She scanned the crowd and found him slouched against a wall, unable to blend in. Broad from build, not weight, a few more kilos wouldn't have hurt him in the least. His hair was neat but came down nearly to his shoulders, framing a coarse face in dire need of a skin peel. Despite the holiday, his clothes were worse than business-casual, far sub-standard for her group of acquaintances. It wouldn't be like Helina to know such a person, let alone invite someone as shabby as that to such a grand affair. Perhaps he was a staff, or the son of a staff person, and thus she allowed him to attend out of graciousness. She found Helina at last.

"Who's that over there? Next to the red chair. I've never seen him before."

Helina made a pained face. "I couldn't do much to keep him out. His name's Sasha, some friend of Misha's brother Piotr's friend Ivan. I can't believe he had the nerve to show up. He's scum of the scum. Misha says he's got a devil of a temper."

"Shouldn't you have him leave?"

"Do you want that thing angry at you? Kjel and Dima said they'd keep an eye on him so he doesn't steal anything. As long as he doesn't start any trouble."

"Goodness' sake! Look at the *size* of him! He's got such sad eyes, don't you think? Like a big bear in a zoo. Perhaps he should be introduced to someone."

Helina eyed her warily. "Don't you get any ideas in your crazy little head, Maryana. He's bad news. If everyone ignores him, maybe he'll get bored and leave peacefully. Ooh, there's Tony." Helina waved across the room. "I'll catch you later, okay?" She disappeared once more into the pool of young people.

Maryana tried, but her head kept turning back. He was too easy to spot. Uninvited or not, it wasn't right for a guest to look that unhappy. It would disturb the pleasure of the other guests. Perhaps if he were able to find a conversation, he wouldn't be so miserable.

Liza came up behind her. "Helina told me to watch you."

"Helina's failing at hostessing," Maryana said. "It's not right to ignore a guest, no matter how difficult or uninvited they are. Helina may be that rude, but I'm not. I'm going to ask him to dance."

"You are not. We *want* him to be unhappy. We want him to *leave*," Liza said. She grabbed Maryana. "You can't be seen near that kind of trash! Your mother will never let you out again!"

Maryana pulled away. "Maybe if we annoy him, he'll leave on his own. It's only a single dance, Liza. If you don't tell her, she'll never know."

She felt Liza's sharp glare on her back as she walked up to him. "Hi!" she said brightly, and stuck out her hand. "Maryana Ivanova."

He pulled back against the wall as if she'd growled. *"Pri'vyet,"* he mumbled. Two overgrown fingers touched her hand for a single shake.

She waited, but nothing followed. "And you are?"

"Sasha."

"Nice to meet you, Sasha. I'm a good friend of Helina's. She throws a great party, doesn't she?" She phrased her words with thoughtful care. If he were ignorant of the hostess before, he could save face. "I didn't notice you arrive with an escort. Would you like to dance?" The idea seemed preposterous now; it wasn't until she was next to him that she realized just how big he was. Her head didn't reach his shoulder.

He scanned the edges of the room with his eyes, then tore himself from the wall with a nod. He didn't say a word, but moved with surprising ease. When the music changed, she begged him to stay.

"Ooh! This is my favorite! Would you grant me the honor?" He stayed.

Helina discovered them. She spun Maryana around by the arm. "Are you *crazy?*" she whispered. "What are you doing!"

"Think of it as charity," Maryana whispered back. "I'm keeping him out of trouble for you." She finished the dance, and two more.

With glasses of punch she requested directly from the caterer, she walked him to the sun porch, where a dozen people were cooling off. He said almost nothing, but Maryana kept the conversation light.

"Why did you ask me to dance?" he interrupted.

"You looked lonely. I thought you might enjoy it. Why?"

His eyes searched the walls. "Because every time someone ever has, it's been on a dare, and someone's laughing in a corner. I haven't seen who's laughing yet. Or are we on surveillance camera?"

"That's awful! Helina was rude for not asking first, but it's her first major party, and personally, I think she's a little overwhelmed. I thought I'd cover for her. Why would someone laugh? You dance as well as anyone."

"It doesn't seem odd the only person to speak to me is the smallest girl in the room? Are you twelve yet?"

"It's not polite to talk about age. I can't change my height any more than you can."

"Perhaps not. But you won't be arrested for being seen with someone that young."

Maryana understood. "No, but talking to someone isn't illegal, especially if they will be an adult seventeen next birthday."

One by one she knocked down his cautions, and he opened up a sliver more each time. Under his mistrust he was courteous and well spoken. His clothes were inappropriate to the occasion, in the light his massive shoes looked … like an old sport shoe painted black, but he was intelligent and articulate, not what she expected. The conversation began to flow two ways.

"I go to the Villovsky Academy in Moscow," Maryana chattered at his polite inquiries. "It's a very exclusive school for girls. I'm home on break for the holidays. I like art and music best, though I can't draw to save my life. I have a class in real cooking, too. I guess I love the feeling of accomplishing something without the help of a machine. Besides," she laughed lightly, "food tastes so much better when it hasn't been computer processed. What about you? Do you go to school?"

He shook his head.

"Not even university?"

"No."

The thought of school dragged up bitter memories…

Sasha slouched in the seat, the only way to fit his big knees under the desk. He eyed the director through the hair over his face.

"Look at yourself, boy! You couldn't even wear a presentable pair of shoes? No respect! That's what your problem is! All bad attitude, no respect. It's a good thing you didn't apply to a university, because I'd never have given you a recommendation."

Sasha glared back coldly. He was tired of being harassed at every turn – girls laughing, guys picking fights, teachers on his back. He'd lost a year for failing to show up for classes. He'd passed the tests, but they failed him for attendance. Yes, his shoe had a hole in it; it was the only pair he owned that fit his oversized feet. His shirt sleeves were rolled to his elbows to hide the fact they were fifteen centimeters too short. Eighteen years old and more than two meters tall, too big for school. Five years they'd kept him here, and they still didn't want to let him go.

"I watched you," the director continued. "I watched you real close, but I couldn't catch you cheating. How did you do it, Alexander? Find a copy of the test and memorize the answers beforehand?"

"I didn't cheat!"

"Then tell me how some good-for-nothing student, who in five years never pulled a grade above 78, managed to pass his Certificate of Education with the third highest score this school's ever seen?"

"I guess I'm just lucky," Sasha sneered back. "Maybe I'm not as dumb as I look."

"I don't believe that for a minute. Your performance in this school has been a waste of your time, a waste of my time, a waste of the faculty's time." The director slapped a computerized test pad in front of the boy. "You want your diploma? Ten questions, two from each major subject. I want them answered, right here in front of me. Every figure, every line, every thought, I want to see it. Prove to me you didn't cheat on that exam. Because I know you can't."

Sasha met the stare with disbelief. "I passed the exam. You can't deny me."

"Watch me."

Sasha fought the rage that boiled up. Nothing but deliberate administrative harassment. They couldn't hold back his diploma! He'd taken the courses! He'd passed the exams! Even when he toed the line The Man wanted to get him. With an aggravated sigh, he picked up the computer stylus and read the first question.

It took nearly an hour to answer the ten questions. The computer pad scored them when Sasha finished. All were correct.

The director tossed the pad on his desk. "I wouldn't have believed it if I didn't see it with my own eyes. You disgust me. All that brain, and you've never once used it. You'll never amount to anything in this world, Kirushenko, with an attitude like that. What a waste."

"Tell me something I don't know," he sneered. "Do I pass now? Can I graduate?"

The director nodded. "Take your diploma, because I never want to see you back here again."

"I never bothered about university. I work at the Ulitov museum."

"Really? So, if I went to the Ulitov, I'd see you working there? You'd be wearing a silly uniform and handing me a guide to the exhibits? Or would you take me on a tour, tell me more secrets than the holograms?"

He shrugged a massive shoulder. "I work behind the scenes. Set up, cleaning, maintenance, unpacking, whatever they need. We're not allowed to use 'bots to clean, in case they suck up something important. Sometimes I get to help with research projects. I study the paintings and things on my own when no one else is there. I read the notes they leave lying around. Did you know you can date bits of pottery just by the kind of clay they're made from, not even the design?"

Maryana broke into a smile. "No, I didn't, but it sounds like we study the same things – art and all. You must know so much about the displays. Would you show me around?"

The distrustful dark eyes measured her, toe to head. "You'd come there?"

"Absolutely. You've got me intrigued."

"I work at night. If you came to the back door, it's not alarmed, I could let you in, free. You could take your time, with no crowds to fight. I have the codes to the displays; you could touch things, if you wanted."

"I'd love to. Do you work later this week? Perhaps Friday?"

The blank face gave a glimmer of life. "I work Friday."

A blond man came up and slapped Sasha on the shoulder. "There you are. I never thought I could lose you in a crowd. Piotr's ready to leave." He gave Maryana a nod. "Now I understand. Hello. You look like you just fell out of a Renoir painting, did you know that? Don't worry, I'll rescue you from this bumbling slug. I hope he's behaved himself. He doesn't get a day pass very often."

Sasha seemed to fold up at the ribbing, shrinking behind his stoic veneer.

Maryana's hostessing charm surged upwards. "Of course. I've had a most wonderful time." She took Sasha's hand in hers. It was huge and callused, the nails rough and dirty. Papa's hands were always soft and smooth and perfectly manicured.

"I'm delighted to have met you, Sasha. I hope you enjoyed the evening as much as I have. May your New Year be like champagne: sparkling and full of joy."

Four

The mound of blankets and coats on the couch didn't move when the pounding sounded on the door in mid-afternoon. Aaron answered it, wearing his coat.

Ivan entered. "You have clothes on. I'm shocked."

Aaron flashed the long coat open to reveal his nudity beneath. "Heat went out last night. Our dog-fucking landlord says he doesn't work on holidays; he'll fix it tomorrow. Cooker works, though. I've got hot tea, hot soup, and hot toddies, if you'd like."

"What kind of soup?"

"Cream of something, and I threw in the leftovers I brought home last night – kielbasa, fish, peppers, and chunks of bread."

Ivan's breath steamed in the frigid room. "Sure. Food is food. He still asleep?"

Aaron brought him a small pan of soup and a cooking spoon. "This is all that's clean. Hey! 'Shenko! Get up, or I'll get someone to give you last rites."

The pile on the couch began to writhe, accompanied by a deafening blast of intestinal gas.

Ivan sat on the coffee table to eat his soup, as there were no other chairs. "Too late. He smells dead last week."

"More likely, he'll kill us with the stench." Aaron headed back to the warmth of the pots on the cooker.

Sasha sat up, pulling the blankets around him. "Any hot air is good air. *Kak dyela?*"

"Magar Lukacs got trampled at the Boyar's Club last night and broke three bones. He had tickets to the boxing match at the arena tonight; he gave them to Fadil Armetz, who gave them to me. So, do you want to go to the arena tonight?"

Sasha's tongue scraped at the pastiness of his mouth. "Yeah," he grunted. "If nothing else, it's warm there."

Ivan drained the last of the soup and picked out the remaining chunk of kielbasa. "After last night, I thought maybe you'd have a hot date."

Aaron returned, hands warming around a cup of hot schnapps diluted with tea. "I didn't hear about that. She put out? He needs to get laid."

"It was nothing like that," Sasha mumbled.

Ivan explained, "We crashed this party. Tiny little rich chick, looked like a fucking doll that fell off a chain, spent most of the night hanging on him. Looked like a midget standing next to him."

"Was she blind? Sasha the Troll didn't make her run off screaming?"

"He kept his pants up."

"Then she's mentally defective."

Sasha fell back on the couch and curled up in a fetal position. "Fuck both of you. I'm sure it was because she lost a bet. At least she wasn't a prick about it."

"Pretty?" Aaron asked.

Sasha sighed with a faint moan of longing. "I wanted to stay and watch her leave. I wanted to see angels descend and carry her back to Heaven."

"Uh oh."

"He's not exaggerating much," Ivan said. "Blondy-blonde hair down to a sweet little tomato of an ass, and huge blue eyes like some damned reindeer. Weighed about as much as a bottle of vodka. Dressed all high-class with manners and all, acting so important and friendly, like she was trying to sell you the damn party itself."

"Why did she do that to me?" Sasha asked. "Why would she tease me like that, talking to me like I was a welcome guest, the nicest anybody has ever talked to me, when you know she probably went back to her friends to make fun of me. It's not fair!" he bellowed into his pillow. "Girls like that shouldn't speak to people like us. Why did we go there."

"Did you get her link address?"

"No. And it's not like I have one to give her. Not that I would have," Sasha added. Aaron paid two-thirds of the rent; Sasha could afford only the remaining third. The expense of a personal comm account wasn't feasible, and he'd broken his one and only pocket com two years ago.

"Then what do you have to worry about?" Aaron said. "Forget her. You never have to see her again. She can run naked through your fantasies for years to come."

A look of blank terror seized Sasha's face, stealing his breath. "I think I'm meeting her Friday at work."

Aaron closed his eyes. "You stupid lump of shit."

Five

"I can't believe you!" Helina raged over the videolink the next day. "Arkin Laritsky! Of all people, *Arkin Laritsky* comes to my house and sits on *my* furniture in *my* lounge, and you go and pay attention to that monstrosity? Are you insane?"

"And if you had any grace, you'd realize the sacrifice I made," Maryana sniffed. "I kept him out of sight for you until he left. Arkin never knew he was there."

"Thank you, I guess, but you're too nice to waste such a night for me. I should have just had my father ask him to leave."

"Really, Helina, he was very shy but quite pleasant if you talked with him. You had nothing to worry about."

"Well, it won't happen again," Helina swore. "So, what did you think about the party? Did you get to see Arkin's Sterling Sunset? Did I tell you he kissed me in greeting? He said I looked pretty in purple! I nearly cried!…"

Maryana let her prattle on without interruption. Somehow she didn't think Helina would listen to more about the rough-hewn Kirushenko man. The idea of asking Helina to accompany her on Friday had crossed her mind, but now she kept her plans to herself.

Levan pulled the vehicle away from the theater. Maryana watched him leave through the glass doors. When she was sure he hadn't simply gone around the corner, she sprinted out and crossed the street. Two blocks down and one over sat the Ulitov museum. The building was closed; he'd told her to come to the back, a two-block walk around. Maryana stopped at the corner. This wasn't one of the main commercial avenues, but a side street of cafes, bars, and closed governmental offices. In the deserted rear access alley, the shadows far outnumbered the lights.

"You promised," she lectured herself. "To back out now would be rude." The longer she hesitated, the more she realized she was trusting far more than she should. This was exactly the type of situation she'd been taught to avoid. No one knew what sort of vile deviants lurked in the murky shadows. She shook off the thought. With a positive spirit, nothing bad could happen. And she had her handicom in her pocket if she needed it. She picked her head up and made herself move forward.

A light glowed above the door to the museum's service entrance. Silhouetted black, a tall figure paced beneath it. Maryana strode out of the darkness with renewed confidence.

"Hello!" she called out.

The figure whipped around.

"I'm sorry, I didn't mean to startle you. Hi!" She held her hand out. "Maryana Ivanova, from the Rumel party."

"*Da, da*," Sasha stammered. He gave her hand a quick shake. "I - I didn't think you'd come."

"Why wouldn't I? I'm sorry, am I late? Thankfully my brother had already gone out. My parents think I'm at the *kino* with friends. So, you work here?"

Sasha paused as if he needed to think about the answer. Maryana tried to catch his eye, but his gaze never left the ground. "Yes. I … Would you like to see it? The museum, I mean. We're closed, but I'm working. Inside, I mean."

Maryana laughed lightly, a tinkle of music in the cold air. "I'd love to. I've been to museums all over the world, but I've never been to this one in my own town. Isn't that silly? I've been to the Lovenberg at least four times."

Kirushenko pounded on the door. "That's just art. We have some of everything, and we get new exhibits every few months. History, anthropology, art, archaeology, natural history. Not heavy sciences, though. That's at the science museum."

"I wouldn't have guessed."

The door opened. A blond man let them in. "Hell-o, sweetness!"

"Nice to meet you," Maryana said, offering her hand. "Maryana Ivanova. You look familiar; were you also at the Rumel party?"

He took the hand and kissed it. "Yes, actually, I was. My name is Ivan, but I'm not so terrible once you get to know me."

Maryana laughed again. "Well, it's *great* to meet you, Ivan."

Ivan waved a finger at her. "Brainy, too! You're good!"

Sasha motioned toward a door. "Come on. The museum's this way."

Ivan shooed them. "Go! Get lost. If you want the lavatory, the first floor is clean. I'll be on the second."

Their footsteps echoed in the empty galleries. Now and then came the distant calls of the small night crew to each other. "I can't believe I'm doing this," Maryana shivered. "It's so creepy in here." In the dimmed lights of the halls, the statues and friezes glowed a ghostly pale, eyeless witnesses to everyone who passed. Many corridors were dark until their motion set off the sensors. She snaked her hand around his arm.

Sasha noticed. "They're just statues."

"I know. They're just so white. Did you cut your hair?" she asked as he pushed it nervously back from his eyes. She reached up and fluffed a stubborn wave into place. "It looks very nice."

"Yes. Thank you." Indeed, his shirt looked crisp and new, and the strangely painted shoes from the party were replaced with winter boots. "Would you like to see my favorite painting?"

Maryana's smile burst forth like a sunrise. "I'd love to. Goodness, we've seen so many beautiful ones already. There's more?"

"Sure."

He led her up a floor, where the hall turned a corner. "This one," Sasha sat on a bench before a table-sized painting. "This one's my favorite, I think." Maryana slid next him, close enough that her back leaned against his arm. He tipped his head closer until his nose was just touching her perfumed hair.

The long arm wrapped innocently enough around her shoulder as he pointed. "See the way the colors are blended at the edge of the focal image? It was a revolutionary idea for the time."

Maryana agreed. "Very impressive. I love the detail over there on the right. Have you ever read Benton's *Exodus of the Phoenix*? It reminds me of a passage he describes: the legions walking through the flames of Hell and all."

"I don't read much modern stuff. I prefer ancient epics – mythology and legends."

"Do you have a display on those?"

"Not directly. I could suggest it, though." He paused, then sat up straight, thinking of something. The spotlight caught his eye, reflecting a devilish sparkle in the blackness. "Do you scare easy?"

Maryana eyed him suspiciously. Despite the emptiness of the building and the potential for danger, he'd been pleasant company. If she encouraged him too much, he might get the wrong ideas. "I don't know. Why?"

He grinned with delight at her apparent interest. "Want to see something scary?"

"As long as you stay with me. I'd be lost in here."

Sasha led her through the corridors, past anthropological dioramas that seemed voyeuristically real in the darkness, past an actual Egyptian mummy, down an aging flight of rear stairs to a door marked 'Restricted Access - Employees Only.' He flashed his ID at the scanner, gave it a thumbprint, and entered the dark room.

The bad feeling crept up Maryana's spine again. "Where are the lights? I won't go in there in the dark."

"I'll get them." He waved at the sensor.

Maryana let out a shriek and grabbed onto Sasha's arm. Empty eyesockets glared from every direction, lipless grins taunting her as if they knew something she didn't. Racks of skulls lined an entire wall; some larger, some smaller, some misshapen with missing pieces. On several work tables lay more bones, with hand-held scanners and tabulations. In one corner lay a reconstruction in progress.

Her heart thumped through her chest even as he held her. "Oh, how awful! What *is* this place? Are they real?" *A morgue, perhaps? Or his own private murder hall?*

Sasha led her to a table. "Most of them. It's an anthropology study room. Sometimes I come down here and talk to the researchers. They show me what they're working on, and I ask them about other things in the museum." He used a specimen cloth to lift a vertebra, brown with age. "This is a neck bone. See the scratches here? Those were made by a knife of some sort, possibly stone by the deepness of the lines. This guy had his throat cut for some reason."

"You can tell all that from that little bone?" Maryana asked, afraid of this room that looked like the inside of a crypt, and of the little bone that had died a frighteningly violent death.

"*Da.* Look at this one." He returned the bone and scanned the skull racks. He picked one, checked the identification tag underneath, and held it out to her. "This skull is South American, at least three thousand years old. See this hole in the top? Whoever made it, however they made it, she managed to live through it. See this ring here?" He traced the hole with a thick finger. "That's all healing bone. The smoothness here tells you it belonged to a woman, and the way these seams come together? She wasn't more than thirty years old."

Maryana backed away from the skull. "That's – really interesting, that you can tell all that. You *like* all these dead bones?"

He replaced the skull on the rack. "I don't care for the bones as much. I like the stories behind them, the great kings, the civilizations built by people so primitive they had no writing systems but they built huge working cities. So many of the stories were believed to be just legends, yet we keep finding evidence they were at least partly real. They're mysteries."

Maryana glanced around the room again. "Could we go back upstairs? All those empty eyes staring at us …"

Sasha's face fell, but he agreed. "If you want."

Maryana couldn't stretch her time any longer. She had to get back to the theater before Levan. Standing in the cold alley behind the museum, she thanked him for the evening.

Sasha blew on his bare hands to keep them warm. "I'll call you. Perhaps there's another museum you would like to see. Are you on the videolink, or that new commlink system?"

"Please don't call me at home. My parents are very protective, and my brother is nosy. I'll call you here at the museum. That way if they trace the call, it won't lead directly back to you. I can simply say I had questions."

Sasha's face clouded with a sullen shadow. He backed up a step, pulling inward until it seemed as if he were retreating into a shell. "I understand. I know what kind of people live on that side of the city. I'm not one of them."

Maryana seized his hand. "That's not true! Believe me, they'd be upset no matter where you lived. I had a lovely time, but I go back to Moscow at the end of next week. I'm not allowed male visitors there, so I don't want you to be mad when I can't meet you." She thought for a second. "I'll tell you what: sometimes Mamá will let me walk through the park after church on Sundays. If you were walking there, perhaps you might see me by the duck pond."

"Bulganin Park? I know it." He unfolded again.

Since she couldn't hope to reach his cheek, Maryana lifted his oversized hand with both of her gloved ones and squeezed it. "I have to run. Sunday!" she promised, and took off down the block.

Six

"I know you, Maryana," Helina said. "You've got that look in your eye. You didn't talk to Arkin Laritsky, did you? I'll kill you if you're seeing him in secret! He called me twice this week, but nothing in three days. Maybe I should call him."

They sat on Helina's bed on Saturday morning, painting each other's toenails and applying swirling velvet decals. Maryana gave a snort. "No. He's an old shoelace, anyway. Have you ever really listened to him? All he talks about is his latest photo shoot. He's as vain as a parakeet."

Helina put a hand on Maryana's face. "Do you feel all right? You must be sick. Maybe you should lie down."

"I want someone who can converse about something. I mean, what happens if Arkin gets old and bald? Then what do you do with him?"

"That's why God invented hair creams."

"God didn't invent those, bald men did."

"So maybe God is a bald man."

"If he's God, he's perfect, and he'd keep his hair."

"Maybe God thinks bald is perfection and hair is for animals." Helina capped the enamel pen. "'Fess up, Maryana! Who are you seeing? That friend of Tomas's?"

Maryana's hand slipped and she painted Helina's knuckle. It was self-correcting polish; she paused while it faded from everywhere but the nail. "Bite your tongue! Ilya scares the daylights out of me. All his talk of hunting and killing. He can't speak a sentence that doesn't involve the words 'military' and 'weapon.' I'm not seeing anybody. Mamá's pushing me, but I've been thinking. Ideally you should marry for love, right? Let's say you agree to marry someone based on money and power and stuff, and figure you'll fall in love with them later, after you're used to them. What if you don't? What if you never fall in love with them? What if you think you will, but you wind up disliking them more every day?"

"It's called divorce, and it can set you up very nicely if you do it right," Helina said with great seriousness. "Look at my Aunt Zarya. She's set for life."

"But looks aren't everything, are they? What if they had a really bad accident that damaged their face? What if their eyes were nice, but their nose lumpy? Do you think you'd be able to love someone who wasn't perfect? I mean, if you really look at Ilya, his nose is so pointed he could poke holes in trees. He could roll over one night and take out your eye. Dima Shelikov has that twisted tooth, right there in the front. You could cut your tongue every time you kissed him. Emil Graffia… Akh! Just his voice makes my skin crawl."

"I don't know," Helina said truthfully. She chose a decal from the choices laid out on the bed and handed it to Maryana. "I mean, if you married Arkin Laritsky and he turned into some hideous monster, then he wouldn't be the person you married, would he? It's a breach of contract. No one could blame you for running. Imagine all the plastic surgery to put him back together. It would take years."

Maryana pressed the decal onto Helina's big toe. "What about fortune? Do people ever start out low and make their fortune later in life, or do you have to start out with large capital to get anywhere? How can you tell what a person's worth is? What if they're invested but have no sense of fashion? Or they're tight-fisted and live below means to hoard their wealth? How do you know?"

"You look it up in the financial registry, and examine their parents. Have you been reading too many romance stories? You're never this serious."

Maryana applied a matching decal to Helina's other toe. She gave a soft laugh. "Maybe I have."

Helina paused in horror. Her feet swished across the silky bedcover as she knelt up in Maryana's face. "Oh, Maryanka! You're not! You're not talking about that awful beast who crashed my party? How could you!"

Maryana put down the decal she'd chosen. "No! Of course not. Not the way you're thinking. I was being hypothetical. We picked on him so badly after he left, I felt sorry for him. I was just trying to figure out someone like that. I mean, people like that must still have lives, no? He sounded educated enough when I talked to him; he just – had no refinement whatsoever. I don't understand it."

34

"You don't understand science, either, but you don't spend time thinking about that."

Maryana hugged her knees and admired her toenails. "Science is irrelevant in daily life. What do I care about the physics of space travel, as long as it works? Let the scientists worry about that; that's what they're paid for. Culture is more important. You only get one chance at a first impression; you have less than two minutes to impress your client and persuade them to see your way. Address them in their language, know their customs, and you'll win." Her face pinched in thought as she sighed. "Perhaps no one ever told him that."

Helina snorted. "Your mother would never let you be a social worker."

"No," Maryana agreed. "Fund the programs, but never deal with the clients directly. Even when we visit the charities, we speak only with the workers. We never get to see the recipients. That's why all I can do is wonder."

Throughout the weekend, Maryana buzzed like a hummingbird, brightening hearts wherever she landed. She impressed the trustees at the tea for the Greater Minsk Historical Preservation Society, the old men all but fighting to speak to her. She remembered each by name, remembered their businesses and historical interests.

Dorek Zabel, a former Major in the army, nudged Fyodor Ivanov in the side. "Keep a tight eye on her, Fyedka. Marry her well. She'll get you more business than you'd get yourself in a hundred years."

Fyodor's chest puffed. "She's a natural, that one. Paired with Tomas's nose for investment, I can turn everything over to them ten years from now and retire in peace."

Saturday night was a benefit concert at the opera house, one of Mamá's pet charities. Maryana wore her Christmas gown, a blue strapless affair weighed down by a kilo and a half of pearls, beads, and sequins. Cameras and reporters formed a windbreak on the sidewalk; she resisted the urge to smile and respond to their calls. The less attention one gave the paparazzi, the more they paid for interviews.

"This is the most god-awful boring thing I've suffered this year," Tomas muttered between acts, himself dressed formally right down to gloves. "I believe I shall sneak a brandy during intermission."

Maryana beamed at him with a well-rehearsed smile. "It's the first week of January, dear brother. There's plenty of time for worse."

Sunday she wooed the ladies at church, remembering to ask about each of their families.

"Andrea, what a charming young lady she's growing into!" Mrs. Zaretsky exclaimed. "You simply must let her help on the fundraising committee."

Mamá gazed down on Maryana, a proud warmth in her eye though her face never changed. "She's still a bit flighty at times, but when she hits university this fall, it will settle her down. We'll have to see how much free time she'll have."

Maryana knew opportunity when she heard it. "Mamá? Since the sun is out and it's not so cold, may I walk through the park? I've done nothing but sit all weekend. I could use the exercise before Ludmilla's big dinner."

Mrs. Zaretsky laughed. "My dear, one blast of wind and you'll be blown to the Urals! You could use a big dinner."

Andrea gave her public smile. "Don't be long. Keep your distance from strangers, and Levan will meet you by the fountain after he drops us off."

"Of course, Mamá." She kissed her mother's cheek and skipped out of the church before Tomas could follow.

On Monday, Mamá sat with the house manager and caught up on the plans for the rest of the winter. Papa had a morning meeting in the back conference room. Tomas would have slept, but Papa forced him up at seven to instill a more productive work ethic. Maryana played tennis against herself in the gym, then lounged the rest of the morning watching fashion programs on the surround screen in the media room. After lunch, she and Helina planned to shop in the city.

"Tomas, you're late yet again," Fyodor said as Tomas slid into his seat four minutes after everyone else had sat for lunch. "Tardiness is rude; it projects disorganization and indifference. Once more and I will make you carry an alarm."

Tomas spread his napkin across his lap and nodded at the wait staff offering him baked squash. "I'm sorry Papa, Mamá. I just had a very interesting call from a friend of mine. Would you like to know what it was about?"

"Don't play games, Tomas," Andrea said. "Be direct."

"Ilya, whom you know, and Arman Saroyan were at Bulganin Park yesterday. They saw a tiny little blonde girl wearing a coat exactly like the one Maryana wears, and she was talking with an exceptionally tall man."

Mamá put down her fork. "Maryana? Did I not tell you not to talk to anyone?"

Maryana's shoulders sank. The world was her fishbowl, and she was a prized guppy. "I bought a handful of feed from the vendor and stopped to feed the ducks. A man asked me if I knew what kind of ducks they were – the ones with the lumpy red heads? I told him I didn't, we spoke for a minute, and then I moved on. It was nothing. Who is Ilya to speculate on my business?"

"Do you know who that man was?" Tomas snapped. "Alexander Kirushenko, and he's dangerous. Do you know what could have happened?"

"Nothing happened!"

Andrea paled. "What do you mean, dangerous?"

"You are certain of the name?" Fyodor asked.

"There's no mistaking him," Tomas insisted, flaunting the fact he'd done his research and could back up his facts. "He's one of the tallest men in Minsk. He once lifted more than 200 kilos to win a bar bet. He's older than I am, twenty-two or so, from a bad family. He's supposed to have a temper to rival a supernova. Rumor has it he once killed a man but never served time. The police know his name. Remember his face, and keep your distance from him."

Andrea clutched her chest. "Dear God! No more walking anywhere alone! He could have grabbed you and run off before anyone knew you were gone. Thank God for your friends, Tomas. How many times must I tell you two, you can't trust anybody these days. Not with modern surveillance. They'll track you from the front door with satellites and you'll never have a clue. Fyodor, make them do a test run with the security system, just to be sure."

Fyodor returned to eating. "I will make an inquiry with law enforcement, get a background check on him, just in case. Perhaps he's wanted for something else."

Maryana stared, dumbfounded. "For what? Talking to me? He never touched me, never said anything out of line. You people are blowing this out of proportion. He asked me about the ducks!"

"Like you'd recognize the subtleties con men use to put you at ease," Tomas chided.

"Excuse me, Mister Galactic Know-it-all. Next time I'll ask for social references before conversing with someone," Maryana shot back. "You're an absolute pig, Tomas, and your friends have no business in my affairs. If you want to investigate anyone, investigate Ilya! He's the one stalking me! But no, your friends are above that, aren't they. Don't be so trusting, Tomas, or when an underling shoots you in the back, you'll be the only one who didn't see it coming."

"Maryana! Enough!" commanded Mamá. Her gray eyes stabbed a sharpened steel glare.

No one could contradict Mamá when she looked like that. Maryana stood up. "I'm not hungry. I will be in my room."

"You will sit," Fyodor ordered quietly. "Now, now. What's done is done. The fact remains, you must be extra vigilant when in public. Because of who you are, there are those criminal types who would use you as ransom to get to me."

Maryana flapped her hands. "Ducks, Papa! The kind that say *krya krya* and leave feathers everywhere. Do we have a market exclusive in park ducks, too?"

"Irrelevant," Andrea said. "You will return to school in four days, and we won't have to worry about it again."

Maryana stewed. Mamá cancelled her trip with Helina, erring on the side of caution. How dare Tomas cause trouble for her, when she did nothing wrong! And the reports of the nice Mr. Kirushenko being a murderer... If it were true, he would have been locked up. If he were going to kill her, it would have been when they were alone in that horrid room of bones. Even Papa's investigators hadn't turned up any real threats. She had promised to be in touch again, and to break a promise was beyond rude. It was a mark against one's character, a permanent stain on one's name. It wasn't good business and it wasn't good manners, but until Friday she had to have an escort in public. Except...

Maryana found her loophole.

Seven

Helina shivered as Maryana pounded on the delivery door at the back of the museum. She followed up the steps to the loading platform, but she wouldn't step within five meters of the door. "I can't believe I'm out here freezing for this! You are the craziest person I know. I told you you were messing with fire. My mother finds out we're here, she'll skin both of us! Let's go, while we're still alive for her to do it."

"I just have to say goodbye," Maryana insisted. The door opened and Sasha appeared, pulling on his coat. He noticed Helina cringing back.

"Won't you come in where it's warmer?" he offered, holding the door.

"No, thank you," Helina stuttered. She backed up to the edge of the loading platform and glanced nervously at the dark street. "Our ride will be here any second."

"We can't stay," Maryana said. She pulled the sides of his thin jacket closer to fasten them, smoothing them when she realized they wouldn't reach. "I have to say goodbye. My brother found out about the park and told my parents. I can't see you again."

Sasha's face darkened. "What difference is it to them?"

Maryana stole a fast glance at Helina waiting at the shadows, and lowered her voice. "I told you, I have to keep up a proper appearance. Papa has considerable power and influence, and it wouldn't look good if his daughter is seen with a... a more... proletarian type."

He shoved her hands off his coat. "Is that what I am to you?"

"Of course not! But Tomas said so, and Papa believes him."

Sasha stared down at her for a moment, face expressionless. Without bending, he lifted the forty-two-kilo girl with one hand and rested her against the cold building.

Helina shrieked. She patted down her coat, searching for her pocket com. "I'm calling for help! Hold on!"

"No! Helina! Don't! Please wait!" The last thing Maryana wanted to do was frighten him into something foolish, or antagonize him further. This was her problem.

Don't panic, use grace, think calmly, she coached herself.

"Sasha, what are you doing? Put me down," Maryana protested. They were all alone in a dim alley. If he wanted, the man holding her could break her in half and pick his teeth with her bones, and there wouldn't be a thing she or Helina could do about it. She'd never thought for a moment he might harm her – until now. "Please put me down," she repeated.

His voice echoed like a thunderstorm. "I just wanted to look you in the face when you tell me to get lost."

Maryana met the dark eyes, hardened like polished marble against the inevitable rejection, and her heart melted at the depth of the sadness she saw. He looked like a little boy trying not to cry. "I never said *I* wanted you to get lost," she reminded him gently. "I go back to school in two days. I won't be here." From her glove, she drew forth a small slip of pink paper. She tucked it inside the open collar of his shirt and patted it in place. She whispered near his ear, "Wait a week, and you can contact me at this routing number."

His breath steamed thickly in the cold. "You mean it?"

Maryana nodded, and found herself on the receiving end of an impulsive kiss. She put her fingers over his lips and pushed him back. "Control yourself!" she hissed. "Not in front of Helina!" She gave him a chaste peck on the cheek. "Now please put me down. I really have to go, before Helina has a stroke."

* * *

"Sorry to wake you," Aaron apologized to Ivan over the public vidlink. His voice was low and serious. "You better come. I don't think I can handle him. No, no. I've never seen him like this. It's bad. I don't know what started it. The neighbors are getting upset. *Da.* Good." He raced back up the four flights of stairs from the lobby. Ivan banged on the door twenty minutes later.

"What's up?" he asked.

Sasha sat at the grimy kitchen table, a glass of vodka in his hand. An empty bottle lay amid the debris on the countertop; a half-empty sat before him. His thick hair stuck out in every direction, greasy with sweat. He sat, eyes glazed, staring into space, immobile except for the times he gave a loud wail and tears rolled.

"I managed to water that one down," Aaron whispered to Ivan. The apartment heated again, he wore only undershorts that fit like a second skin. "He's not using anything else, is he?" He flicked a finger against the inside of his arm.

Ivan shook his head. "Not that I know. Hey! What gives?" He sat next to Sasha. "You cracked a bottle and didn't tell me? Rude bastard! Now I have to catch up." He took a dirty glass from the table, checked for anything uninvited, and filled it half-full of diluted vodka.

Sasha gave a bellow that quivered the liquid in Ivan's glass. His forehead hit the table as someone next door pounded the wall. *"Z'gubil'vo."*

"Shto?"

"I ruined it!" Sasha sobbed. He sat up and took a gulp of his drink. "I coun't elpit. I shcareder. I coun't shtop 'self."

Ivan got serious. "You talking about that girl? Maria, or whatever her name is? What did you do? Sash! What did you do? Are the police looking for you? Because we can't get you out of here unless you can shut up and walk. What did you do?"

"I'ma fffuckup. Fuck, fuck, fuck, fuck, fuckup."

Aaron paled. "Shit. Rich bitches get lawyers. He'll be neutralized, and I'll be nailed for harboring him."

"I kisheder," Sasha slurred. "Coun't elpit. She stanning der... and th' light.... glowing, hair... Angel. I shoun't done dat... ARGH!" he howled, and cursing sounded through the thin wall.

"What the hell's he still seeing her for?" Aaron asked. "I thought she'd have dumped his ass by now."

Ivan shrugged and downed the rest of his glass. "Is that all you did? Kiss her? You didn't tear her clothes, even accidentally... Maybe not hear her say no until you were done?"

The big head swung side to side. "I thought she... fuck off, but no... Nummer... I look, an look... S'gone. So fuckn beau'ful!" The bawling took over for a moment.

Aaron frowned. "Did you get any of that?"

"She told him to fuck off and when he looked for her she was gone?" Ivan guessed.

"I warned you not to mess outside your territory," Aaron said with authority. "She's gonna wrap you around her little finger, fuck you up in the head, and then when the right person comes along, she's going to laugh in your face and tell you to fig off. She's already got you chasing shooting stars with this university crap. She's a pricktease. Don't let her do this to you. Don't do this to yourself."

Ivan agreed. "Look, don't let some high-class whore get your eggs in a knot…"

Sasha exploded. He shot out of the chair and hauled Ivan up by the front of his shirt. "SHE'S NOT A WHORE! She's not a whore! She's the most perfect creature ever to walk the planet! I never touched'er! I never should have kissed'er! I had no right! She gave me her number an' I los' it. Now she'll never come back." His entire body shook.

"No one cares! Shut the fuck up!" sounded through the wall.

Aaron grabbed the arm. "Easy, Sash. Let go. Down, boy."

"I'm sorry! I'm sorry! I've met her. You're right, she's not a whore," Ivan said quickly. "We'll get it straightened out, but we can't do a thing until morning. Why don't you lie down and wait for sun up, and we'll see what we can do."

Sasha released him. "Sorry." They helped him stagger to the sofa. Sasha fell onto it like a tree and began weeping again. "She'sh pure, like 'n angel."

"White as Siberian winter," Aaron assured him. He wiped the sweat from his forehead. "Man, he needs to get laid. He'll kill us yet."

Ivan waved it away. "Let him sleep it off. He won't remember it tomorrow. Poor bastard. He finally falls in love and it's with the Madonna. What the hell do we do when she breaks his heart?"

Eight

V illovsky was not the biggest private school in Russia, nor the most academically stringent. There were more selective science academies and technical institutes, more progressive art schools, more elite music schools. Instead, Villovsky was one of the most expensive private schools to be found for girls aged 12-18, and that made it one of the most exclusive.

Villovsky girls were no slouches. Those that couldn't handle the stringent curriculum and endless regulations had their enrollment revoked at the end of a semester, never to be heard from again. Of the two hundred girls, most came from homes where their name alone was a headline, and a quarter of tuition costs went toward security. No boys, except for carefully orchestrated events with their brother school, Northern Academy. No personal communication devices. No unapproved messages or calls. Grandmothers and great-grandmothers prowled the floors, sniffing out violators. Many a teen romance was crushed by the babushka squad reporting back to parents. Boys in a dorm room meant immediate expulsion. Drunkenness – expulsion. Security guards carried live weapons, several of them private hires by the families of the girls in residence. It was as guilt-free a place to dump a child as anywhere on Earth.

Relieved of Mamá's relentless scrutiny, Maryana found it freeing. Her kind manners and thoughtfulness made her a favorite among the babushkas. Strong grades and a positive attitude made her a favorite among her teachers. Humility and sincerity made her hard to hate among her classmates. As a senior, she enjoyed the privileges that went with the rank, such as later hours, more autonomy, and solo trips into Moscow proper. She went home every other weekend and every break, giving her enough time to make Papa miss her and to recover from Mamá's grueling schedules. Tomas attended university just across the river; he had visiting privileges, and she was allowed to visit him. Homesickness was never a problem.

"You were there when I said 'goodbye,'" she insisted to Helina over the videolink, and half of her hoped it was true. She was graduating in five months; she didn't have time in her life right now for pet projects like culturing a vagabond, nor did she wish to jeopardize her other relationships.

On the other hand, Maryana wanted him to call. He had frightened her with his strength that night, but in that instant, just for a second, she swore she'd glimpsed into his soul, and the loneliness she saw broke her heart. Perhaps he wasn't used to such kindnesses. He wasn't a bad person, she it knew in her heart, just incredibly sad. If he'd had any intention of harming her, he would have, but he didn't, and that proved everyone else, from Ilya to Tomas to Mamá to Helina, wrong as rain on Easter morning. She waited for the message light to signal on her computer, but Friday passed without a word. Saturday, Sunday, a week, and Tomas flew her home for the weekend. Only the knowledge that Sasha didn't work weekends kept her from sneaking away. A third week passed, and Maryana lost hope. Surely Tomas hadn't caused trouble for the man. Mamá hadn't mentioned a thing unusual, and if a lesson could be made from misfortune, Mamá wouldn't have wasted a minute exploiting it. Perhaps Sasha'd found a girl, one closer to his social standing – and his height. What could she expect? She hadn't known him but two weeks.

It wasn't as if she *loved* him or anything... She hadn't really decided yet if she even *liked* him. There was so much not to like, it was hard to think of anything encouraging. His kiss perplexed her – was it merely a gesture of thanks for being kind, or did it have deeper meaning? It wasn't the urgent, lustful, slobbering kisses Emil Graffia cornered her with, or the dry, nervous kissing she'd done with Giles Gerard last summer in France. It was rash, it was rude, it was ... almost brotherly. So what did it *mean*?

Friends and schoolwork kept her busy, and he slipped from her mind. She'd just gotten into bed one evening when her room's intercom gave a chime.

"Maryana, you have a visitor in the foyer!" the voice whispered urgently.

A visitor? This time of evening? Tomas might stop by, but never this late. She threw clothes on and ran for the stairs.

By the doors stood a tall figure, out of place and looking terrified. His unruly hair lay respectably cut and combed, his shaved chin curved smooth, and he wore a new, fashionable coat that fastened properly against the Moscow winter. He clenched a warm *ushanka* in his hands, along with a single scarlet rose. A smile rushed to Maryana's face before she could stop it. What a sight she must have been, with no makeup, damp hair, and leisure clothes!

She hurried up to him. "How did you manage to get in here? You were supposed to *call* me!" she whispered. "You can't *be* here!"

"I lost your access number. I had no other way to talk to you." The hand holding the flower shoved forward, his face as red as the petals.

Maryana glowed, breathing deeply of the blossom's out-of-season scent. "Thank you! You're too kind, but we're not allowed male guests, especially after curfew. If security sees you, we could both get in a world of trouble."

"I couldn't get here any earlier. The commuter flight took four hours. I just want to talk. Even for ten minutes," Sasha pleaded. He grabbed her hand before she might disappear.

Maryana yanked away. Touching would be suspicious. To sit in the open visiting rooms was suicide. To sneak him upstairs? Unthinkable.

"Come with me." She darted into a small side room used for study. A narrow window stole privacy from the door, but some was better than none. She sat across the study table from him, hands in her lap.

Sasha put his hat on the table. His breath came in nervous gulps. "I had to see you. I haven't thought about anything but you."

"Sasha, you shouldn't *be* here! This is a private *girl's* school. You don't exactly blend in. I guarantee you're on camera somewhere; if they report your visit to my parents, there's no telling what could happen. You don't want to cross Papa. He'll have you arrested – stalking, burglary, trespass, assault, *anything*. We can't be seen together here, either."

"Where can we be seen, then?" he demanded. "This isn't Minsk. You can't tell me there's no place in all of Moscow we can't sit and talk."

Maryana fell silent. Surely there had to be anonymity somewhere in a city of eighteen million people? Papa couldn't have eyes *everywhere*. How many security cameras could there be? "I'm here every other weekend. I can get out on a Saturday afternoon, perhaps, say that I'm going to a theater or shopping. As long as I stay on the privilege list, I can do that without an escort."

Sasha's face fell. "I signed up to take a class on Saturdays, just like you said I should. I took their tests and I exempted three classes. I chose beginning archaeology, and if I study hard I will need only three years for a degree. That's good, no? Sundays. Do they have commuter flights on Sundays?"

"Sasha, that's wonderful! I know you'll do well. I could clear time after brunch on Sundays," Maryana conceded. "Calling me is safer. There's a public videobooth outside the cafe; they can't trace the recipient." She fingered the cuff of his coat sleeve. "You look very nice tonight. Is it just for me?" His face reddened, and he nodded.

She reached up to touch his cheek, and saw the jewelry for the first time. "I never noticed your earrings before. They must have been hidden by your hair. You shouldn't wear hoops with hair that short, though – something smaller. A stone or something. A black stone, I think. And only one ear," she advised him. "Two makes you look like a pirate."

"Then I shall get one," he promised. She had removed her own earrings before she washed; he took the hoops from his ears and she endured his painful fumbling as he placed them in hers. His hands smelled of cologne, too sharp and cloying to be an expensive brand, but mixed with the scent of the new coat and his own personal odors, it wasn't unpleasant.

He leaned side to side to examine the effect. "They look bigger on you." Even without her subtle teen cosmetics, she radiated a natural beauty. He lunged across the table to kiss her, but this time she saw it coming and turned her head so it landed on her cheek.

"Not here! Goodness, no! Slowly, Sasha. There's a time and a place for everything, and here is *definitely* not the place. You must leave. I will call you tomorrow night and tell you the number again. Don't lose it this time." She squeezed his rough hand and kissed it. "'Til tomorrow night. Now run!"

After several video calls, Sasha met her two weeks later, at a large commercial center on the far side of Moscow. Maryana's heart melted when she saw the smaller, more subtle earring he wore, charmed by his clumsy efforts to impress her. Despite the inexpensive craftsmanship, she had yet to remove his hoops.

She brought him two pastries she made herself, watching him devour them as they sat on a bench inside the huge indoor emporium, out of the bitter winter cold.

"These are really good," Sasha said, stuffing half an entire pastry into his mouth. "You only made two?"

"You're supposed to buy pastry on a shopping trip, not take it shopping with you," she laughed. "Any more would have looked suspicious. They teach us basic cooking so we can know what the cook is doing and that they're not cheating us. It's a hobby thing, unless you invest in a business. I think it's fun. I feel like I know more than the computer."

He licked cherry filling from his fingers. "Can I kiss you yet? Is this place safe enough?"

"If you must. Wipe your face first. You're covered with food, eating like that." Maryana used her handkerchief to dab the corners of his mouth. She flipped her hair back and braced herself, surprised by the force of the long-awaited kiss.

It wasn't as animal as Emil, passionate yet controlled. Up close, he smelled of cherry turnover, cabbage and sweat, strange but ... fitting. The embrace seemed to last half of eternity before he pulled away, catching her eyes. His eyes were so dark! Like the new moon hiding in the night sky; as deep as the center of the universe. Maryana's insides gave a sudden heave, her heart banging against her ribs until it knocked the air from her. She turned her head before he could kiss her again.

"Easy, Sasha," she blushed. "You'll break me."

He sat back in defeat. "I'm sorry. You make me forget what a beast I am."

"You're not like that at all." Maryana gave his arm a reassuring squeeze. She reached into the bag she carried and held out a small package. "Anyway, I have another present for you."

His cheer dimmed, and Sasha eyed the gaily wrapped cube with distrust. "I don't need presents. I don't want your money. I just wanted to see you."

The words hurt. "Sasha! It's my money and I'll spend it as I please. It's rude not to accept a gift, even if you don't want it."

Sasha hung his head. His paw dwarfed the box as he accepted it. "I didn't mean it like that. I-I didn't bring you anything in return. I don't want anyone thinking I'm hanging around you because of your money. I work for a living. I pay my bills. I can take care of myself."

"I never doubted that. I wouldn't believe anyone who said that about you. You gave me the rose at the tram stop, so you're one up on me anyway."

Sasha picked the package open as if it contained something dangerous. Inside, he found a small gold earring – real elemental gold, according to the box – made up of his initials in small block letters.

"Spasiba," he mumbled. A boyish, lop-sided grin broke across his face, the first she'd seen.

"Do you like it? You gave me yours; I wanted you to have something in return," she said. "I would have gotten three letters, but I didn't know your middle name." She removed the jewelry from its box and placed it in his earlobe.

He felt the new adornment with his fingers. "Middle name?"

"You must have a patronymic?" *Everyone* in Russia had a patronymic!

Sasha hesitated as if the word could convict him of something. "Grigorevitch."

"That's a fine name!" Maryana said proudly. "Mamá insisted on giving us two first names. Papa didn't see the point of two names plus a patronymic; he thought it too dynastic, but Mamá's grandmére was a Frenchwoman and that's what they did there, so it started with her."

"Two? You have another name?"

"Natasha. Maryana Natasha, and my brother is Tomas Severyan. It takes forever to write the whole thing out, so many names. Maryana Natasha Fedorovna Ivanova...." Maryana signed it in the air with a flourish of her finger.

"Natasha," he repeated, rolling the name around. "I like that better than Maryana. Tasha. Sasha and Tasha." He smiled that endearing lopsided grin again, teasing her.

Maryana gave a lighthearted laugh. "That's silly. I don't want to be a rhyming word."

"Then I will be the one who rhymes. Tash and Sash." Sasha wrapped his arms around her, hugging her off the seat. He buried his face in her hair, inhaling the scent, then snatched a fast kiss.

"Stop that! Behave!" Maryana ordered, but the words had no conviction. "I talk about my family all the time. Tell me about yours."

Sasha shrugged. "I left home after graduation. I've got three sisters, all older than me, and I haven't seen them in years."

They had never been friendly with their stepsisters; Mother's daughters from her first marriage were twelve and thirteen years older than Sasha. He barely remembered them as part of his life at all. He hadn't seen his full sister Anastasia in person in five years. Even that had been a surprise – she was the only one who came to his graduation back in Sochi, she and her fiancé.

"I'm proud of you, Sash," Ana told him. "Sticking things out like that. I know how hard it had to be for you."

"You have no idea," he grumbled, though he knew she did.

Ana and Georg took him to lunch at an expensive restaurant. Sasha knew he was underdressed, but he had nothing better to wear. He hadn't meant to take advantage of his sister's hospitality, but he hadn't eaten like that since – he never had, ever. Ana knew it. She watched him with sorrowful eyes, and ordered him course after course. She handed him an envelope with a graduation wish. In it were five hundred new interstellar credits, cash.

Sasha did a double-take. "I can't take this!" He handed it back before he could lose it. He'd never seen that much cash at once in his life. It frightened him.

Ana pushed the hand back. "You can, and you will. I wish I could have done more for you. You can't tell me everything you own isn't in that bag in my flyer. Take it. It's a gift. Less than you deserve, but it will get you started somewhere. Don't party it away. Get a decent place to stay. Buy some clothes that fit. If you want, you're welcome to come back and stay with me."

"Ana, I can't..." he started, then said simply, "Thank you." He hugged his sister longer than was proper, unable to put into words how much she meant to him. Ana had been his surrogate mother. His Savior.

"Don't be a stranger," she said as she kissed him goodbye.

"How can you not know where they are? Don't you speak to them? What about your parents? What about holidays?" Despite differences of opinion, Maryana couldn't imagine remaining angry with her parents or Tomas. She had grandparents and aunts in France, a set of grandparents somewhere on Centauri, and more distant relatives spread about the country and planet. There was always someone to visit or entertain.

Sasha pulled her effortlessly onto his lap. "I'd rather not talk about it. Talk about us instead."

Nine

February turned to March, March to April. In April the snows receded and the pair emerged from the shopping arcades and into the parks. The sun turned warm but the cool air reeked of the abominable spring mud. Maryana's face lit up when she spotted him, waiting on a bench near the shuttle stop. Sasha jumped up, a smile chasing away the fear that she wouldn't appear.

Maryana twirled for him, her long hair spinning out in a fan. She wore a clinging pink sweater with a matching tailored skirt, and a strand of high-end Altairan weather-pearls whose glow mirrored her cheeks. "What do you think? I bought it last week over at Tretyakov's. It's from the Nadia Narinka spring line."

"I like it." He lifted her onto the bench, where they were almost eye to eye. His arms wrapped around her as they kissed. Maryana leaned in for a second one, holding him to it while she stroked his hair. Sasha's hand inched across her back, rubbing the warm fuzzy fabric of the sweater. It worked its way around to the front, exploring a softer place.

She pushed him away. "Sasha! We're in public! Control yourself. If that's all you've come here for, I'll leave now." She climbed down off the bench.

Sasha sat. "Why do you dress like that, then?"

Maryana frowned. "What do you mean? I bought it because it's spring and I thought it looked nice. I even found this matching shopping bag." Doubt seized her, and she gave her ensemble an anxious once-over. "It does match, doesn't it? Or should I have worn different shoes?"

"I mean it makes you all soft and squishy, and I want to squeeze you. It gives me a bad itch. Of course, you could be nice and scratch it for me... ." He pulled her toward him, caressing the warm curves of her backside.

"Sasha, stop." She pried herself loose with a coy laugh and sat on her temptation. "You'll make me itch, too. I'll think impure thoughts, and then I'll have to confess them at church."

Sasha tried to kiss her again, but it landed on her ear. "Who cares? Knock it off with the church crap. Why do you even bother? It's a waste time we could spend together."

Maryana pushed him back, aghast. "How can you say that? A soul is not a waste of time. Don't you believe in God?"

"Nyet," Sasha said easily. "It's bullshit. It's a myth invented by man to control his fellow man. We deny the ancient Gods of Rome and Greece, and a thousand years from now we will look back and laugh at all the current church nonsense as well. If there were such a kind and wonderful God, he wouldn't allow half the shit to happen that does. Why are there earthquakes? Why are people murdered? Why do people have to pick through garbage to find food?"

Maryana found herself speechless. Mamá attended services. You did what Mamá said, because she knew everything. If she didn't, Papa would. They hadn't created a financial empire through ignorance. If they said it, you believed it because it was true, and that pertained to quite a few influential people, not just her and Tomas. To question was… unthinkable.

"I don't know. Character flaws, I guess. God tests those whom he thinks need to rethink their path."

"Bullshit. What if you're a perfect person, never sins, never misses a service, and you take your child to the zoo and he's mauled by a lion. What does that teach a child with no face about God?"

Maryana wasn't used to thinking hard. Matching drapes to carpeting was difficult enough – exact matches or coordinating colors, textured or smooth, sheers or ruffles, patterns or solids – and then came accessories. Religion was like a successful business plan – if it worked, you didn't fix it. "How should I know? Stop it. I don't want to talk about it. Talk about something else."

"Why? Because you know I'm right?"

"No, because…. Religion is a personal thing," Maryana decided. "There is no right or wrong. God is God, no matter what religion you follow, and it's not our place to know why things happen. If it's going to happen, it will happen."

"That's not religion, that's fate. So, if religion is a personal choice, it doesn't bother you if I go to a church or not?"

"I guess," Maryana said without conviction. "But it's not fair to pick on me if I do."

"Fair enough. You deal with Heaven, and I will deal with Earth. Now, where were we? That's right. Earthly pleasures," and he landed another kiss.

Maryana passed Easter at home and saw Sasha the following weekend, bearing a basket of hand-dyed eggs, finest chocolates, and Easter bread. He gave her a rose made of candy glass in return. Finals closed in on him. Maryana proofed his research project but found little to question. He went into exams with the highest grade in the class. By Tuesday afternoon, home was not high on her mind when the teacher told her to report to the Headmistress's office instead of her next class.

The secretary let her in. Maryana stopped short as she entered. Inside sat her parents. Papa wore his normal *Kaplan Kouture* office attire, but Mamá's baby-blonde bun was pulled so tight her eyebrows seemed frozen in surprise, and she wore her navy Jacques-Pierre 919 suit – Mamá's undefeated method of intimidation through elite designer corporate-battle wear.

"Mamá? Papa? What's wrong? Has something happened?"

"It seems so," Headmistress Mirinova informed her. "We would, of course, like to hear your side of it."

Maryana sat, bathed in a glowing halo of innocence but terrified by the presence of The Suit. "What rule did I break?"

Mamá's face held a pinched line. Each word seemed to cause a toothache as she bit it off. "Mrs. Zaretsky came to Moscow last Sunday to attend the Bolshoi. She claims to have seen you with an exceptionally tall man, and you were quite familiar with him. Is this the same man Tomas told you to avoid last Christmas?"

"What? I went shopping last Sunday. In fact, Oksana went with me," Maryana insisted. "I don't go near the Bolshoi unless I have tickets. If Mrs. Zaretsky saw me, why didn't she say hello?" *Evil old Mrs. Zaretsky!*

"Yes, Oksana did leave with you," the headmistress said. "She also said you split up, and she didn't see you again until dinner."

"You are not a good liar, Maryana," Andrea said coldly. "You said it was a random meeting in a park. Obviously, you've been lying to us for quite some time."

Maryana's halo evaporated in a flash of Hellfire, and the truth sprang free. "That's not true! If you only *knew* him! Just meet him and

53

you'll see how wonderful he really is! He's *nothing* like Tomas claims!"

"Do you know anything of his background, Maryana?" her father demanded. "His mother's been treated for alcohol dependency so many times shops are forbidden to sell to her! Did you think of your own mother? How can she hold her head up when her daughter was seen kissing an indigent man in public? What about this school? They have a reputation to protect as well. Do you know what the press will do with that?"

"With *what*? I've done nothing to be ashamed of! Not a thing! How can you sit there and condemn a man for the crimes of his parents?" Maryana argued. "He had nothing to do with those things. He's not a drunk! You're making this all up! You've never even met him!"

"We didn't say *he* did them, but no one can escape a bad influence like that," Andrea sniffed. "It's in his genes. He has no money, no education, no future security, no social standing, and he's far too old for you. I didn't realize you were that naïve, Maryana. I won't think about what he has coerced you into. Although you've not broken the school rules directly, after conferring with Mistress Mirinova, we've had your things packed. You will return home. You obviously need greater supervision than the school can provide."

"*Home!* But Mamá! I *graduate* next month! I can't leave now!"

"You may finish your classes with a private tutor and return to graduate with your class. You can tell everyone that you've got an illness that requires several weeks of rest, and that's why you went home. That is the end of it."

"*Mamá!* You can't do this! Please! You don't understand! Twenty-three isn't that old! He isn't a vagrant! He works for a living! He attends university! He's always a perfect gentleman. He's not like you say at all!" Maryana cried. "Why won't you listen? Papa, please! Talk some sense into her!"

"No, Little Bird. This will stop here and now. If you truly care about him, you will not make me take action against him."

"Maryana!" Mrs. Ivanov's steely eyes flashed like a lightning strike. "Good girls don't argue. The subject is closed. You will not think of him again. *Comprendes-tu?*"

"*Oui,* Mamá." Backed into a corner, Maryana wept. Mamá spoke Russian when she addressed the hired help, or on the rare private occasions when she cursed. She used her fluent English when dealing with business and the press. The French was a private public warning to shut up and obey, or else.

Maryana cried for the entire two-hour flight home, curled against the window of Papa's big black Galaxian Airblade Esprit, as far away from the angry glares and huffy words of her parents as she could get. She cried most of the evening and more the next day, kicking angry feet into her innocent mattress. Poor Sasha! He would never know what happened to her. No matter how she tried, she couldn't summon the positive spirit that made everything work out right. Papa hired a security team to patrol the estate, keeping certain girls in and certain men out. He seized her private palmcom and set controls on the videolink, tracing calls and monitoring those sent by her. The Velikaya Estate was huge, her bedroom expansive, but no prison ever felt smaller or more lonely.

Tomas returned on Friday. "My goodness, Maryana," he said as she sulked on her bed. "I can't believe you. I was always the one in trouble, tying you to the trellis, using Papa's skis as ramps, backing the gullwing into the flythrough.... I think you've outdone me."

"If you've come to poke fun at me, Tomas, I would kindly ask you to drop dead," she sobbed. "They're insane! You have no concept of the amount of humiliation I've been through! He's a sweet, intelligent, thoughtful, ambitious, caring man. Not one person in this house will give him a single chance to prove I'm right."

Tomas conceded. "Facts are facts. You're not the first. They broke up Karlita Johansen and me in eleventh form, if you'll remember."

Maryana blew her nose on a germicidal handkerchief. "Her shorts were so short even the staff were talking. Fania said Mamá did it because Papa kept dropping things, hoping she'd bend over to pick them up." Fania had been their nanny at the time.

Tomas gave a hard laugh, but Maryana couldn't force a smile. "It's not funny, Tomas. I don't remember them forcing pregnancy exams on you."

"That would have been rather odd now, wouldn't it."

Maryana would have replied, but she choked on a sob and came close to vomiting.

He rubbed her back. "Easy. Breathe. Face it, Maryana. You don't know what you're getting into. Your pretty little head is full of champagne bubbles and sparkly rings. Stick to what you know."

"I know far more than you think, Tomas. I know I'm not a baby, and I won't have people choosing my life for me. I will die before I marry that Graffia wretch or any other of those toad-faced heirs Mamá keeps pushing on me. Laugh now," she cursed him, "because they could do the same to you."

Maryana sat through breakfast the following week pushing her food around the plate but not eating, silent and sallow in spirit. No girl ever graduated Villovsky more than two kilos over their ideal weight; not eating had become an unofficial sport. "I'm not hungry. Permission to be excused," she asked.

"If you show me a smile," Fyodor said.

Maryana stood up. A roaring filled her ears, and the table disappeared in a rush of black. She grabbed for the table, missed, and fell backward onto the carpet.

Andrea screamed. Fyodor reached his daughter seconds before his wife. "Call for a doctor!" he ordered the staff.

"Maryana, darling." Andrea rubbed her hand between her own. "What's wrong? They assured me she wasn't pregnant."

Maryana stirred. "Lie still, my Little Bird," Fyodor said, petting her head. "The doctor's on his way." He carried her to a sofa in his office.

The doctor's examination was brief. "Mrs. Ivanova, your daughter fainted because she weighs thirty-six kilos. She needs to eat."

"She's been under a great deal of stress, with her upcoming exams and graduation and things," Andrea said smoothly. "We took her out of school because of it. We've tried to make her cut back and rest, but she seems worse."

The doctor nodded. "I'll prescribe some tranquilizers. Sometimes if you take away the anxiety, the appetite returns. I'd recommend letting her resume her normal activities. Sometimes teens will work things out with their peers that they won't with their parents."

Maryana had her escape.
Doctor's orders.

Ten

"I don't get it," Sash mourned to Ivan during their dinner break. "How could they know? We were all the way up in Moscow. She barely let me hold her hand in case someone saw us."

"It was a sham, then. She wanted to see how far she could take you, and when she got bored, she left," Ivan said. "It's a very convenient excuse. She ever kiss you?"

"Yes. Not a lot; she was afraid of getting caught."

Ivan raised his hand in concession. "She ever put out?"

"I tried, but I didn't want to piss her off."

Ivan frowned. "Not even off the cheek?"

"No."

Ivan slouched back in his chair. "Mother! And you didn't think there was something wrong? That should have been a dead giveaway."

Sasha scowled. "She's better than that. I could have pushed, but if we broke up, I didn't want her to have regrets. She's into that religion shit."

"Do you hear yourself? She's brainwashed you. I can't believe what I'm hearing."

"Why did her parents pull her out of school, then? Why? It doesn't make sense. She worried about her father getting angry. If he hurts her, Ivan, I swear I'll make him pay, no matter how long they lock me up."

Ivan packed up his dinner bag. "You're talking like a whiff of shit. You don't seek revenge on people with money. They'll run you over without ever looking back. It was nice while it lasted. You got to fondle Money. Time to forget her, and get on with living."

Sasha couldn't forget. The mystery, and the lack of Maryana, ate at him. He thrashed restlessly at night, possibilities prancing through his head like so many leaping ballerina legs, legs that looked remarkably like Maryana's. No girl had ever stayed with him this long; why would she stay if she only pretended to like him? His mind wandered during his exams, thinking about all her initials instead. At the university study center, he printed out a list of all Fyodor Ivanovs in Minsk, but he didn't try the videolink routers. Not yet.

Leaving work at midnight at the back of the museum, he didn't see the figures emerge from the shadows until after the doors locked behind him. Six people, wearing winter balaclavas and carrying makeshift weapons pulled from the museum's recycling bins. Sasha never feared a good fight; he'd thrown the first punch in many a pointless argument, but six to one weren't the best odds even for him. Not against weapons.

A figure in military green stepped toward him. A length of packing wire snapped in his hands. "You've been straying to the wrong side of the city. Your kind of scum has no business over there. We're here to revoke your travel pass." A pebble stung Sasha in the side of the head.

Sasha protected himself, but did little to stop the attack. After he'd been dropped and wounded like a dangerous animal, the figure in green placed a thick-soled boot on his ear, pressing his face into the gravel beneath.

"Let that be a reminder, pig," his assailant warned. "Stay away from things you aren't meant to touch. Next time, we won't play so nice." He spat a steaming wad onto Sasha's face. "*Nu, tovarishchi!* Let's go." He twisted his boot and ground Sasha's head into the gravel one final time before they slipped silently into the darkness.

> *His mother beat him, almost daily it sometimes seemed. It didn't matter about what. Sometimes he fought with her 'boyfriends.' Once because he'd asked about dinner. Once the police brought him home, caught stealing from the local market. Mother hadn't restocked in a month, and the fresholator contained only coffee.*
>
> *Mother was a slapper, but she also hit with whatever was handy – her shoe, a belt, a coffee cup. Once she smashed a clock over his head. Vodka bottles were a tough weapon. Glass ones left wide bruises, and sometimes they broke. Ana had protected him, but she didn't like mother's men-friends either and often stayed out until long after dark. She felt safer sleeping in his room. Ana fled home when he was twelve.*

*He never hit his mother, but he often thought about it.
Father had drilled it into him, you didn't hit women.
Instead, Sasha fought with anyone who challenged him
and gained a bad reputation. At thirteen, he was a lanky
hundred and eighty centimeters; at fifteen, one ninety-
seven. At seventeen, he was detained in the death of a
known chem dealer. He found acceptance, if not kinship,
with a wild crowd who respected him for his underlying
core of anger, and because he'd never lost a fight outside
his home.*

Sasha lay in the dirt well after they left. Ivan discovered him
sitting against the building, shaken and bleeding, a half-hour later.

Three nights later, Sasha was leaving work – through a better-lit
side door – when a shriek split the dark. His heart nearly stopped, and
he stuffed his fingers in the door before it could shut all the way.

"You! You scared the life out of me!" cried Helina, clutching her
chest. "Maryana said back door. You shouldn't be coming out this
one. Here!" She held an envelope out as far as she could stretch. "I'm
– I'm supposed to give this to you."

Sasha eyed the shadows before accepting the envelope. "Wait!"
he called to Helina as she turned to flee. "Stay! Please! I don't bite.
Where is she? Is she home? How is she?" He fell to his knees in the
security light and tore open the letter, reading as fast as he could. The
page shook in his hands. It was real cloth paper, not the recycled
plastic sheets everyone else used. He took a deep breath to counteract
the tears that threatened his vision. The blushing pink paper even
smelled like her.

Helina shuffled a fearful step forward. "She's home. Don't call
her. They'll have you locked up before you can disconnect. Don't
even dream of seeing her. Security has orders to shoot on sight." She
took a step closer. "What happened to your face?"

Sasha looked up from the paper. He had a bruise near his eye and
a wire cut across his nose and cheek. He'd have a thin scar there the
rest of his life. "A warning from her task force." He scanned the
second page, then searched his pockets in vain. He had nothing for a
reply.

"Give her a message for me?" he begged Helina. "Tell her I'll
wait as long as it takes. Years, if necessary! Tell her not to give up.

Tell her… I'm thinking about her. Every minute of every day! Will you do that for me? Please, Helina!"

Helina nodded. "You don't know when to give up, do you? I'll tell her. Even though I think you're both crazier than a spacewalk in a swimsuit."

Eleven

Sasha sprawled in the apartment, unwashed, unshaven, wearing a sweat-stained shirt and an old pair of pants that wouldn't stay fastened. He needed to register for his next university class, but a thumping headache polka'd in his skull and he hadn't decided yet if he would actually do it or not. It had been a long night, and he didn't feel particularly well as a result. He debated if it was worth the effort of cleaning himself up when a knock sounded at the door.

"Put your pants on, someone's here," he called to Aaron, and pulled himself from the sofa to answer it.

He expected to see one of their friends from the party last night. Instead he found Maryana and Helina, dressed for the spring weather in pale colors and hats.

"Surprise!" Maryana said gaily.

Sasha yanked the pair into the apartment and locked the door. "Are you *crazy*? You shouldn't be here. Even I know ladies like yourselves do not go to a man's apartment alone. If you're caught here, they'll string me up by my balls."

Maryana shot him a glare of reproval, but it came across as an impish pout. "There's no need for such language. I thought you'd be happy to see me. We even managed the tram all by ourselves. Helina's my chaperone."

"Helina's not a chaperone, she's a partner in crime. Don't you think they might be watching me, too?"

Helina hung back against the door, afraid not only of him but of the dangerous section of city they were in. Trees wouldn't grow in the sterilized soil reclaimed from centuries-old radioactive wastelands. Only those desperate enough for housing, ignorant enough of science, poor enough to risk their lives would dare live on reclaimed land. "Trust me, I won't shut my eyes for a minute."

Sasha sighed, unsure whether to be angry or seize Maryana in his arms and never let her go. He gestured toward the room. "Well, come in. How did you find me?"

"My father's not the only one who can track someone down," Maryana replied. She glanced around the room with an uncertain expression.

Even a professional decorator would have been hard-pressed to imagine the tiny apartment made neat. Chaos ran across the dirty carpeting in so many rivulets. Overflowing baskets, boxes of clothes and papers and items were heaped in a corner. The long armless sofa, stained and torn, cowered under a grayed pillow and a blanket that might once have been striped. The small table before it flaunted several half-eaten meals, restaurant wrappers, and a heel of bread. A bottle of cheapest vodka lay on its side, not enough left to spill out. Empty beer and liquor containers lined the walls and littered the floor. Dirt, clutter, laundry and recycling extended well into the open kitchen. No curtains softened the two windows; the autoshade knob on the glass of one had broken at maximum darkness, keeping out the bright noon-day sun.

Maryana blinked her eyes at him, eyes the exact color of the oceans when viewed from space. "Did you miss me?"

"Miss you?" Sasha eyed her hungrily. He swept some of the garbage from the sofa table to the floor and lifted her onto the bare spot. She didn't protest the interminable kiss he ground into her lips. *Helina be damned! Let her see!* Sasha didn't care anymore.

"Sash! You ordered one for me, too." Aaron exited the bedroom, sandy hair sticking up, wearing only his skin-tights and a short, wildly colored satin robe tied so loosely it didn't cover much more than the low underwear.

He whistled. "So this is what's been making you cry yourself to sleep every night. I can see why." He eyed Helina with amusement. "And who is my Goddess from Heaven over here?"

Sasha broke off the kiss but held Maryana close as if to shield her. Aaron's edgy shock style and reckless sociability were a strong offset to Sasha's reclusive introversion. On most days Sasha found him amusing; right now he was nothing but an embarrassment. "This is my... roommate, Aaron Aronsky. This is my Tash, and our good friend Helina."

"Imagine! Charmed by High Society, right here in my own home." Aaron made a beeline for Helina. Helina backed against the wall on her toes, crushing drink cans as she stepped. Aaron dropped to one knee before her and seized her hand in both of his. "Fairest Helina, it is my greatest pleasure to meet you. I hate to see a woman alone. Why not take me home with you? I promise, I won't hog the covers."

Helina smiled painfully and pulled her hand back. "I'm afraid I leave town for the summers." Louder, she said, "Maryana and I can only stay a minute!"

"Come! Sit! Let the lovebirds have their quickie while I entertain you with my incredible wit." Aaron went over and tipped a kitchen chair to dump a dirty towel to the floor. He flung the offending cloth to a corner with his toes, then patted the seat. "Sit! Can I offer you a beer? Or does a lady like yourself drink only wine? Gin! Gin is a lady's drink. I think I have some in the bedroom. Will you help me look for it?"

"No, thank you, I'm all set. We really need to be going, Maryana," Helina said with exaggerated sweetness.

"*Please*, Helina!" Maryana begged over Sasha's shoulder.

"*You owe me!*" Helina hissed in return. "Five minutes, that's all! Don't you dare leave my sight." She forced a nauseated smile at Aaron and dragged herself to the kitchen.

"We have to stop this," Maryana said. "They're not going to let us see each other anymore."

Sasha helped her down from the table. He made a space on the couch, then saw the condition of the cushion. He took his winter coat from behind the door and spread it out over the sofa. With a wave of his hand, he offered her the cleanest seat in the apartment. Maryana accepted, and he dropped down next to her.

"Did someone stay with you last night?" she guessed, patting the piled blankets.

Sasha held his head up. She'd uncovered his living conditions; there was no point in pretending anymore. "This is where I sleep. The sofa is longer than a bed. My feet don't hang off. This is my area; Aaron has the bedroom."

"Oh Sasha! You poor thing!" Maryana ran a tender hand over the bristly cheek. Her finger traced the recent scar across his face. "Helina told me you were in some sort of fight. Please tell me you didn't start it."

Sasha swatted her hands away. "Start it? I wanted nothing to *do* with it! Six people jump me after work, beat the shit out of me, and tell me to stay away from you or they'll be back to do worse. I could have bloodied every one of them, but you know what I did, Tash? I *let* them beat the shit out of me! I didn't fight back because I didn't know if your brother was one of them, and I didn't want to take the chance of hurting someone in your family."

Maryana put a hand to her face in horror. "No! No! *Sasha!* I swear to you, Tomas was not one of them! Tomas is not violent! Mamá doesn't tolerate violence of any sort; he would not have done such a thing. You must believe me! I know who might, though. Tomas's friend Ilya. He's a self-sworn Stalinist Revolutionary. He tries to impress me, but he scares me instead. If anyone did something like that, look for Ilya."

Maryana leaned against his side and stroked his leg. "Oh Sasha! Why can't they just leave us alone! My parents found out about Moscow. Papa had you investigated. He told me things about your family… Terrible things I don't believe. I wish you had told me first, so I'd know Papa was lying."

Sasha leaned forward, elbows on his knees. His past was nothing he was proud of, nothing she ever needed to know. Now she would know what kind of person he truly was, and she would want nothing to do with him. Pain reared up, unexpected, and he let anger hide his embarrassment.

"What things? The part where I found my mother on the floor, so drunk she was passed out pissing herself for two days? The part where she never wanted to be married to my father in the first place but she was pregnant with Ana, and I happened six years later? The part where my father couldn't take it anymore and left when I was seven? What didn't you want to hear, Tash? That she used to beat me if I simply asked for dinner? See this?" He smoothed back the hairs on the inside of his arm to reveal several round scars the width of his finger. "This is what a heater coil does to skin. Have you ever smelled burning flesh, Tash? Especially your own? Which lie should I cover up?"

Maryana's eyes filled with tears. "Stop it! Stop it! That's barbaric! Why would someone do that to a child?"

He pulled her onto his lap, where the difference in height didn't strain his back, and he rested his cheek on her head. "I never figured out an answer to that. I'm sorry. It must have been nice to grow up with a whole family in that big house of yours, always happy. I never wanted you to know anything different."

Maryana sobbed on his chest. "I love you, Sasha! I don't want to say goodbye. Papa's opening a new branch on Mars, and Mamá wants us to spend the summer there overseeing the setup. I'll be so far away. The sun is just a dot out there. I hate artificial gravity. What if the biodome gets a leak?"

The words struck a particularly sensitive chord. He cradled her elfin face in his hands, afraid of what truth he'd find there. "*Do* you love me, Tash? Do you really love me?" In his entire life, he could only remember those words directed at him once.

She sniffed tears. "Of course I do. You know I do. You're so different from anyone else I know. You actually care about things. Real things, like plans and dreams. I wouldn't have risked coming here if I didn't. I'll always love you."

His next words came from some other reality, some other self in some other place, because he would never have had the nerve to say them aloud. They slipped from his heart without any thought, without any fear holding them back. "Then … Marry me! *I love you, Maryana!* I love you more than anything I ever loved in my life. I would rather die than give you up."

Her eyes reflected the seriousness of his words. "How can I? I'm not even supposed to be talking to you. My parents would never allow it, no matter how much I begged."

"I don't want to marry your parents. I want to marry *you.*" Sasha touched the tip of her perfect little nose. The concept terrified him, but it was too late to back down now. The more he said it, the more he liked the idea, and the more enthusiastic he became. "Must you always do what they tell you? You're going to graduate! Can't you make decisions for yourself?"

"Yes, but… I've always done what they say. They know all about success."

"What are you afraid of? What could they do? Tell you no? They've already done that. Throw you out of the house? You'd be with me, in a place of our own. I would take care of you."

The angel's face pinched up fretfully. "It would never work. They'd send me away somewhere. Papa has offices in America; he could move us there, or Mars, or anywhere else to keep us apart. If nothing else, he'll have you arrested on false charges. He has hundreds of friends in government and the business world. He will not be crossed."

Sasha began to believe his own fantasy. "We'll go somewhere else, then, far away! Somewhere they won't find us. We have the whole galaxy to hide in."

She stared at him in blank confusion. "What?"

He seized her hands. "Run away with me! We'll get married whether they like it or not. By the time they find out, it will be too late. They'll have to accept it."

"I just turned seventeen two days ago! Do you know what you're *saying?*"

Sasha bared his deepest soul in a whisper. "I'm saying I can't live without you. If you love me too, then marry me."

The most beautiful blue eyes in the universe gazed up at him, the long lashes beating out their uncertainty in time with his heart. "Do you think it would work?"

Sasha kissed her tiny hand and held it, afraid to breathe lest he wake from the dream. "Absolutely! People do it all the time. Tell me what you need. A ring? I'll get you one. An apartment of your own? You'll have it. When could you be ready?"

Maryana paused as the idea sank in. "I'd have to declare myself a liberated adult, and there isn't a judge in Minsk Papa doesn't know by name. And I really need to attend graduation; Mamá's planning a huge party to get my mind off things. She's put so much into it I couldn't disappoint her. At least three weeks."

"But you'll do it?" The hope in his heart rose up to choke him. "You won't back out?" *Would she? Would she?* His fragile new sense of self would utterly collapse if she changed her mind. Never had he trusted a girl like this. Never had he left himself so open for pain.

Maryana met his gaze, and she smiled like summer sun.

"Let's do it!"

Twelve

"Helina! Wait!"

Helina fled down the stairs half a flight ahead. She didn't stop until she reached the sidewalk, trying to remember the direction to the tram stop. She turned on Maryana.

"Don't you ever, ever! do that to me again! 'It's fine, Helina, don't be stupid, Helina!' I've never felt so soiled in my life! That is absolutely the most disgusting thing I have ever done, the most disgusting place I have ever been!" She rubbed her hands as if scraping off something foul. "How will we explain it when we come down with some God-awful disease? And that man! That naked, disgusting man! That is the most awful, frightening, horrifying situation I have ever been in! The two of them could have …. !"

"Sasha would never have allowed us to be harmed," Maryana insisted. "He's a perfect gentleman."

"I'm supposed to believe you? You *kissed* him! I saw you! That filthy, overgrown, stinking, hairy-as-a-yak buzzard with arms like a gorilla? What else have you been doing with him?" They arrived at the tram stop as the next car pulled in, and they boarded it. Helina grabbed a single seat at the back; Maryana was forced to sit ahead of her, kneeling backwards on the grimy bench to continue the argument in a restrained whisper.

"I've never done a thing beyond that kiss, I swear on Saint George! Helina, stop."

"No! I will not stop! First you told me you weren't seeing him. Then you told me you were saying goodbye. Then you had me running notes to him. I'm done! How can you sit there after being in that cave and say he's anything more than a peasant?"

"Peasants died out hundreds of years ago."

"Vagrant? Serf? What do you call something that low on the social scale? There isn't even a word for it. And you made me enter their den! I'll have to mention that at confession," Helina realized.

"I'll be doing penance for weeks. They'll wash my eyes with Holy water."

Across the aisle from Helina, an old woman tipped her head to hear better. She whispered to the woman next to her, who leaned to get a better view.

Maryana tilted her hat and turned away. One Mrs. Zaretsky in the universe was enough. "Helina, he loves me. What am I supposed to say to him? I didn't know he lived like that. He's had a terribly hard life, unimaginable. He's trying his best. Can't you feel the least bit sorry for him?"

"No, I can't," Helina snapped. "You want something to love you, get a little fuzzy dog."

"Mamá won't let us have a dog. They dig up carpeting and chew furniture. Sasha's housebroken."

"After seeing where he lives? I'm not so sure. If your mother knew …"

Maryana felt a sting of panic. She had only a few weeks to accomplish her plans before being dragged to Mars. If Mamá suspected anything, they'd be on a private charter tonight. "You won't say a word, will you Helina? Please! I won't ask you to do anything like that again."

"Doesn't matter, because I wouldn't. You so much as mention him to me and I'll tell your mother everything! I don't care if I get in trouble. My mother would laugh like hell about the whole thing because I wasn't the one letting a vagrant feel me up. She'd kill to be the one to tell your mother, just so she can see her face. What kind of low-class slut are you?!"

"He never touched me like that," Maryana replied weakly. Helina was too upset. It was time to tell the truth. A professional, business-type truth, the kind that placated angry associates without actually conceding a thing.

"You're right, though. I could never have imagined a place that filthy. No wonder he doesn't always smell nice. And his roommate was beyond rude, greeting us that way. I could never live like that. I'm sorry for making you go there, but I'm very glad you came. I felt much safer with you there. Thank you for staying with me. Please, promise you won't say a word, and I promise, on my honor, I will never visit him again, with or without you. You're right; I could never be a social worker."

68

Helina's attack eased, though she still glared. "Maybe now you'll listen. I won't tell, as long as you never mention him again. I mean it, Maryana. It's for your own good. You're too young to throw your life away. When you hit university, you'll see what I mean. Tomas will find you someone more suitable, someone you won't have to hide under a carpet. Someone invested, with two eyebrows and smooth skin and Franz Weber shoes who can shower you with the gifts you'll deserve."

"Someone who can buy me a Sterling Sunset."

"Exactly."

Maryana nodded. "You're right. That's what I was bred for." She slid down in her seat, face forward, and crossed her best friend of eleven years off her list of confidants.

Thirteen

*T*he *Drunken Fish* was busy, but they had the back corner table, granting them a small amount of privacy.

"What the hell did you go and do that for?" Ivan said angrily. "You're twenty-three! What the hell do you know about marriage?"

"She'll never let you back out of it," Piotr said as their vodka arrived.

"I don't want to back out," Sasha insisted. "I meant it. Isn't that the goal? To fall in love, get married, live happily ever after?"

Piotr hooted. "The goal, dear comrade, is to get laid as often as you can by the hottest babe around, and get away before she gets her claws into you. You failed the second half."

Ivan nudged him with an elbow. "He failed completely. He hasn't even taken a test flight yet."

Sasha grumbled. "Maybe I like a higher class of woman."

"She's too short to be higher." Piotr downed his shot and followed it with a slice of smoked fish. "You're mismatched in everything. One run at her with that battering ram of yours and you'll split her in half. She's a pixie! Put wings on her and she'll fly around the room. What is she, a hundred centimeters against four hundred of yours?"

Piotr's selfishness only served to irritate issues Sasha'd already considered. "It's a hundred fifty three to two hundred four. She's braver than you can imagine."

"She must be, to give up a life like that," Ivan said. "What else can you offer her besides sex? You don't own a thing beyond your textbook. She's going to want a big house, fancy clothes, holidays on warm beaches, meals in restaurants you can't afford a glass of water in. She won't last a month in our world. Where are you going to live? I'm sure she'll love Aaron wiping his prick on the furniture every day."

"She's seen my world. What makes you think we plan to live that way?"

The comment brought a round of laughter. Piotr slapped Ivan on the arm. "It's all those classes he's taking. He's going to become an important manager and draw boss's pay. Hah! Wait'll he farts in a board meeting and the chair bursts into flames."

Sasha brooded over the table. He downed his current glass of vodka. "Back in Sochi I used to enter the amateur boxing bouts. Some of the prizes were up to five hundred credits. There're eight different licensed amateur events in Minsk. I entered all of them. Four have prizes of five hundred credits, and one is a thousand. If I can win three or four, even six in the next couple of weeks, I'll have enough for a ring and a lease on an apartment."

Ivan looked doubtful. "Three years is a long time. You're out of practice. They'll be all over you."

"I'm working on it. In my weight class, the competition is mostly hot-headed punks who hit wild and wear themselves out in the first round. Three kilos, and I can drop another weight class. No one can touch my height. I can do it. Just don't tell Tash. She wouldn't approve."

"We'll come cheer for you," Piotr swore. "We'll put the word out, bring crowds to demand you. You'll get better offers."

"Bah, you know we were just kidding you before," Ivan relented. He poured another round and held his glass high. "To Sasha, who managed to land not only a rich girl, but the most goddamn gorgeous broad I've ever laid eyes on. I'm jealous, Sash, I admit it. May their lives be blessed, their joys be endless, and their children be many. *Za zhenshchin!*"

"To women!" echoed Piotr.

A smile nudged the corner of Sasha's mouth. He raised his glass with a nod. "To love."

> *It was the last person Ana expected to see on her videoscreen.*
>
> *"Ana? I need help," were her brother's first words to her in two years, still every bit the scared little boy she had raised.*
>
> *"Sasha! What's the matter? It doesn't have to do with the law, does it?"*
>
> *"No! Nothing like that. I've stayed clean. There's this girl I met…"*

"Oh, Sasha," Ana said sadly. "Please, at least tell me she's legal..."

"Ana! Please! It's nothing like that. I need you to do me a really big favor..."

Fourteen

Mamá had more spies than Papa had hairs on his head; keeping a secret in Moscow was hard enough, under her nose almost impossible. House staff and tutors never gave Maryana a moment's peace. She longed for Sasha's comfort and advice, to feel his powerful arms encircle her, forming a protective barrier from the world. Maryana longed to smell him, sometimes faintly sweaty, sometimes so strong it made her stomach queasy, but it was *him*. Her last weeks of classes were so boring and pointless compared to Sasha's discussions of his work, and she rebelled by refusing to write her required essays. She passed off her lapses of spiteful silence as a side effect of the tranquilizers Mamá forced upon her each morning.

Her graduation party the following week seemed no more than a debutante ball, an auction block for the sons of associates and partners and Tomas's most select friends, a rush to marry her off before she did something stupid. She endured the endless introductions and practiced plastic smiles, wearing the latest in Annekki Ruoko originals and the necklace Mamá would not yet let her wear in public, kept hidden in a biolock in the wall behind the electrical generators in the attic. Spike heels made her unsteady, but the added height made her look a little more her age and lot more sophisticated. She managed to keep her distance from Emil Graffia except for once, when he cornered her by the library.

His lips locked on hers as he pulled her against him; his crotch ground against her hip like a dog. "You're an adult now. Our parents have us practically engaged. I've got all but their written permission. You've never shown me what your guest rooms look like." His hand groped the front of her dress.

Maryana's Forensi stiletto happened to land on his foot as she twisted sideways. As Emil yelped, Tomas appeared out of the men's lavatory on the north wing hall.

"Carry on, children. More tongue, Maryana," he said wryly.

"No! Tomas! I've been looking for you," she said, sprinting after him on ballerina toes. She grabbed his arm and turned him toward the porch doors. "I have to tell you something."

When they were out of Emil's sight, she whispered, "You will keep him away from me the rest of the day, or so help me, Tomas, I'll … I'll… I'll put lipstick on you while you're asleep and send a photo to all your contacts!"

"What shade?" he inquired, but he stayed by her side.

She hoarded her money in the form of currency cards, always drawing more than she knew she would need for a purchase and carding the extra, so her accounts wouldn't look suspicious. After several shopping sprees, she had funded a small dowry. She traded some of her stocks around, selling off shares from her joint accounts and snapping up new speculations under her own name. Sasha might be too proud to use her money, but she wasn't, and Papa wouldn't know until the end-of-quarter statements, weeks away.

Acting normal was harder.

Papa noticed. "Little Bird, you're as jumpy as a Centauri caterpillar. You're not still upset, are you?"

Maryana sighed. A partial truth was more of a white lie, and white lies were a firm part of genteel life. "A little, perhaps. I feel like a princess in a castle. I bought a lovely new pair of summer shoes and if we go to Mars I'll never get to wear them."

Fyodor laughed. He put his arms around her and rocked back and forth. "My baby bird is bored, sitting in her nest all day. You find your very best outfit to match your shoes, let me check my schedule, and Saturday we will fly to Paris for the day, just you and me and your pretty new shoes. *Nous pratiquerons notre français.*"

Maryana hadn't expected that. "Really? Oh Papa! *C'est tres bien! Merci!*"

She shopped for her trousseau on Papa's account.

As the days wore on, Maryana convinced Mamá to toss the tranquilizers. Her stomach burned with the strain of her secrets, but she forced herself to eat lest she draw suspicion. Sasha's confessions of his childhood made her reflect on her own. Important people of industry and politics from around the known galaxy streamed through the estate like hotel guests. Life was a steady flow of royal dinners, charity balls, luxury travel, and more famous elbows to rub than she could count. There were meet and greets, ladies' teas, and ribbon-cutting ceremonies; art receptions, theater openings, and political fundraisers. Each event required planning, preparation, and dressing for the occasion, Mamá's greatest fortes.

Despite its size and intricate scheduling, home had always meant a cozy refuge from the world. Mamá could be gruff, but Maryana never felt unloved. That was simply how Mamá managed to run the household and keep up her part of the business. Alone together, Mamá would share stories of her own childhood, or cut loose unexpectedly with a witty rejoinder after a second glass of wine. Papa was Maryana's ally when Mamá said no. He would grant her anything she asked, or find someone who could. He'd attended every music and dance recital she'd ever had, no matter what his schedule, always in the front row and clapping harder than any other parent. She ached at keeping her secret from him. Tomas had been her best friend until he went away to school. He was a pest and a tease and drove Mamá to tears with irreverence, but he showed Papa's sixth sense for investment, and his gallant manners could outshine even Mamá. How she wished she could confide in him, gain his support. Tomas could win Mamá over.

Her hands glided over the cream-colored fabrics that draped her room, giving graceful curves and texture to the walls. Her favorite lamp, with the hand-painted roses. The marblesque replica of Sarentall of Altair's *Maiden in Morning*, her favorite statue. If she left secretly, she wouldn't be able to take everything with her. She stroked the laser-carved etchings on the headboard of her bed – a skillful rendering of the estate at sunset. A beautiful bed, yet poor Sasha couldn't fit in it without curling up. She would have to have all new things with a home of her own. *Cheer up,* she consoled herself. *At least you'll have Sash.*

Maryana checked the cache on her mail as she did every morning. A text message signal flashed, and she clicked on read.

There is a riddle driving us crazy:
History says a gift awaits, two away, three quarters the
dark. Does this make any sense to you?
Anastasia Grigorevna Kost

The address said Villovsky Academy, but she didn't recognize the name. Grigorevna was the right patronymic; Maryana insisted he use it as a code name, but who was Anastasia? A moment went by before she remembered he had a sister Ana. He must have sent it via his sister to the school, which would have forwarded it without raising a flag in the security system. How clever he was! The plans were set, two days from now. *Three quarters the dark...* She consulted the weather report. Three quarters through the night was 2:30 a.m.

She made a show of packing on the pretense of the Mars trip, stuffing her bags with all the things she thought she might need, including extra linens from the upstairs service closet. A man wouldn't think of such things, and Sasha didn't have a bed, anyway. She hid the luggage in stages, first in a closet by the servant's entrance, then, after dark, in the shrubbery over the wall of the estate.

She left a brief note for her parents on her bed:

> *Mama and Papa,*
>
> *I am doing this of my own free will. Please let me go. I wish we'd been able to resolve our differences without the need to dissolve the company, but I couldn't get you to a bargaining table for even a minute. Think of me as a new branch office, or a stock that has split. I'll be fine.*
>
> *I love you both.*
> *Maryana*

and another in Tomas's room:

> *Dearest Tomas,*
>
> *If you've ever been in love before, you will stall them for me. I didn't want to hurt anyone, but no one left me much of a choice. This is my decision, I know what I'm doing, and I will deal with the results. I love him Tomas, more than I can put in words. More than you or anyone else will give me credit for. Swear on your honor, don't rescue me this once. I'll miss you.*
> *Maryana*

Maryana crouched alongside her hidden luggage. The landscape lights had powered down at midnight; a sliver of moon gave a glow to larger objects, but she had no need to move about. She'd been sitting in the hedges across the street since 23:30, before the security system alarmed the perimeter, listening to a chorus of insects singing in the damp cool of the June night. With less than two weeks until solstice, summer night was a fleeting thing. Daylight and danger would arrive at 4:30.

Where is he? He promised he'd come. He'd better come!

She wasn't sure what her parents could do if they found her. Nightmare visions of Emil Graffia's puckered lips, or Jilt Van der Meir's lack of ambition to do more in life than race his sailboat loomed large in her mind. Dumping her in a convent on Mars or even Altair was not beyond Mamá's idea of punishment, and Papa's financial 'gift' would ensure it.

Maryana froze as a security patrol vehicle drifted by, but it continued onward, its sensors aimed at the Ivanov property, not the neighbor's where she hid; that would have been illegal. At five of three, the faint whir of a vehicle caught her ear. Running dark, it glided closer so slowly she could have outrun it with her petite legs. The hovercar stopped at the edge of the street path as if lost. Maryana clawed her way out of the hedge with a soft cry, running for the shadow.

The door opened, and with much grunting and tugging Sasha unfolded himself from Ivan's small vehicle. Maryana's heart swelled until her chest hurt with the force of her joy. She leaped for him; he caught her in his arms, kissing her.

"I missed you!" she cried, lost in his embrace.

His voice caught as he held her. "I was afraid you'd change your mind. I was afraid they'd be waiting to shoot me."

"The patrol passed twenty minutes ago. We shouldn't linger."

Sasha put her feet on the ground. "You're sure you want to do this?"

Any doubts had been erased just by seeing him. "I can't bear to live without you a day longer." He bent down and she kissed him again. Neither one broke away.

Ivan rolled his eyes. "If you want a bounce in the bushes, I'll take you to the park, but we can't stay here. Get in!"

Luggage crammed uncomfortably behind their heads, Maryana rode to the shuttle station on Sasha's lap. "Where's the present?" she inquired. "Your note promised me a gift. Or are you the gift?"

With difficulty, he twisted to pull a small package from inside his jacket. "Happy Birthday."

"Sasha, sweetheart! You shouldn't have! It was last month, anyway."

"Well, it's not like I could give it to you then," he rumbled. "Seventeen isn't as romantic as sixteen, but you're a free adult now, right? Go on. Open it."

Maryana's breath came out in soft giggles as she tore away the simple wrapping. She knew what came in boxes that size. She wanted it to be what she hoped it was with all her heart, but then she knew Sasha's financial constraints and idea of taste.

Ivan activated the interior lights. Maryana's jaw dropped as she opened the box. It was exactly what she'd hoped, and more beautiful than she'd dreamed.

Sasha pulled the tiny ring from its box and slid it onto the third finger of her left hand. "It's yours, Tash. If you still want it."

Maryana gazed at the ring, a natural ruby surrounded on each side by diamonds almost as large. It sparked and shone as she moved.

"It's the most beautiful thing I've ever owned!" she said, and kissed him once again.

Fifteen

L ydia knocked on the door to Andrea's suite and entered at her bid. "Madam, I found this in Miss Maryana's room. I thought you might wish to see it." She held out a piece of scalloped pink paper.

Andrea finished fastening a bracelet and snatched the page with an impatient snort. Her eyes scanned the page rapidly. "What is this? What does she think she's doing?"

"*Ni znayu, Madam.* It was on her bed."

"Where is Miss Maryana?"

"*Ni znayu, Madam.* She was not in her room. Her bed is not turned down."

Today's schedule began with a morning meeting of the Council for Galactic Research, which was looking for a grant, then a lunch meeting with the local business and industry association, an afternoon teleconference with the Ambassador to Rigel, a fast bite of dinner, and then a meeting of the Lady's Society at St. Nikolai's church, if she still had the energy. Andrea didn't have time for Maryana's lovesick teen drama.

"Fine. I want all staff in the foyer in five minutes. I don't care what will burn in the kitchen. Everyone. Someone has to have seen her. Maybe she went down to the sauna."

"I'll check, Ma'am."

The night security man insisted no person had left the house without his knowledge. He gathered all staff into one room and ran an infra-red on the house. No unaccounted persons turned up. Maryana was not in the house.

Andrea placed a call to her husband, en route to Moscow. "Fyodor, she's not in the house. They're checking the property now but the wildlife creates false positives. You don't think That Man kidnapped her, do you?

"Don't be silly. He couldn't have gotten onto the property. She's probably at Helina's. I'll turn around."

Andrea's shoulders slumped with relief. "Of course. She hasn't been over there in weeks. That's where she is." She called Narkissa, vitriolic words at the ready for a woman who didn't know her daughter was letting friends in at all hours.

"Maryana? She hasn't been here in ages," Narkissa swore. She bellowed over her shoulder, "Helina! Answer me! Is Maryana upstairs with you?"

Faintly in the background, Helina could be heard to say, "I haven't seen her since her party."

"I don't think they're speaking at the moment," Narkissa said. "Perhaps she went for a walk around your property. She might have gotten lost."

Andrea cut the connection without even a goodbye.

Fyodor arrived less than an hour later. "Don't panic," he ordered. "The last thing we need is investigators swarming the house. Someone will have a tabloid headline on the network within an hour." He called Tomas at the Moscow office.

"No, I haven't heard from her. Is something wrong?" he asked. "She can't still be seeing that Kirushenko man, can she?"

"Impossible," Fyodor said. "There's no way she could have contacted him."

"I'm leaving now. I'll put out a word."

* * *

When Tomas arrived, the house teemed with detectives. His father sat next to his mother in her office, patting her hand and answering an unending line of questions from various officials. Having spent enough time in courtrooms and boardrooms for one business reason or another, his father remained his collected self, knowing that if he maneuvered the maze of questions calmly and truthfully, he would win his case and Maryana would pop out of a closet somewhere, the grand prize of cooperation. It was not like his mother to be silent, however. Mamá bore strong opinions on all subjects. She commanded situations; the universe yielded to her. Habits that gave away personal feelings were an especially strong admonishing point of hers, yet she sat on the sofa, rubbing a fingernail on her teeth and pretending not to, and worrying her handkerchief back into fibers. That alone was enough to pull any cheerful banter from his tongue. Before Tomas could say a word of reassurance, he was escorted to an interrogation of his own.

Several hours passed before he had finished, spoken with his parents, grabbed something to eat, and slipped upstairs. His room, like the rest, had been scanned and videoed for clues. Tomas kicked off his shoes, dropped his jacket on a chair, and took off his wristcom. It fell as he placed it on the lamp table, landing under the edge of the bedcover. Bending down to pick it up, he noticed something pink next to it. He pulled out a piece of paper, unfolded it, and read Maryana's note.

Why, you little shit! were the first words that came to his mind, and the words to activate the house intercom readied to burst from his tongue.

You will stall them for me.

He bit his lip, restraining the words for the moment, and sat to ponder the issue. Of course he should say something immediately. The faster they moved, the sooner Maryana would return home and stop wasting everyone's time. Time was money, after all. Mamá was dreadfully upset, and that just wasn't right, either.

Swear on your honor

On the other hand, she demanded his complicity. He and Maryana annoyed each other like any brother and sister, but underneath they were close. He was happy to escort her anywhere; she was just as pleased to hang out with most of his college friends. She was obviously brainwashed by the sweet words of a predator; her very life could be in danger. She'd put him in one hell of a hard place.

He changed his mind a dozen times before he made his choice. He'd play her game – on his terms. He wouldn't mention the note, but he wouldn't deny it, either. It might buy her a day, it might buy a week, long enough for her to realize her mistake. In the meantime, he would put out feelers of his own, let his own friends and contacts do their work. Wouldn't Papa think highly of him then, using a social network to the best of its advantage! Wouldn't Mamá be proud when he did what the investigators couldn't! He activated the commlink and started his web.

* * *

By evening, the lead investigator called them together. "I must tell you, Mr. and Mrs. Ivanov, I'm not sure how much of a case you've got. Your daughter was declared adult on six June. We can file a missing persons claim, but if it's voluntary, there isn't much we can do."

"What do you mean?" Andrea snapped. "We didn't allow her to be liberated. That was the last thing she needed. She's not mature enough to make important decisions on her own."

"We have access to the documents, signed and witnessed at Uskhodni Public Court Three. It is fully legal."

"Uskhodni?! How would she get to Uskhodni? She has no pilot's license of any kind, and the chauffeur would not have gone there without notifying us."

Fyodor handed back the investigator's compad. "This has to be falsified. If not, it was by extortion of some sort. Maryana knew our wishes. She's a good girl, never gave anyone a bit of trouble until this man started manipulating her. Someone else had a hand in this. He has an arrest record; obviously he must have someone else working with him."

"No matter what arrangement you may have had with your daughter, sir, Declaration of Adulthood is a binding term, granting the person every right and privilege of legal adulthood," the investigator said. "She had every legal right to walk out of your house, with or without your permission. In my experience, there is no faster way to get a young girl to leave home than forbid her to see a boyfriend you don't approve of."

"Approval has nothing to do with it," Andrea said. "He's a known criminal, a violent criminal, and Maryana's very life could be at stake. She wouldn't have even a portion of the strength to fight him. She is in grave danger every second she's with him, which is why speed is of utmost importance. She could be dying this very minute!"

"And you've investigated how many runaways from this section of Minsk?" Fyodor inquired, though his tone was rather condescending.

"I'm generalizing, sir," the investigator admitted. "I'm not sure how many may have been from this area."

"Mind your words, then," Fyodor corrected. "Say only what you know to be true. Anything else is speculation."

Tomas steered them back on track. "What are you doing to locate the man she's with?"

"We've got a state-wide alert to detain him for questioning. They will check all flights out of state. We're trying to locate his last known residence, employment, friends, things like that."

Tomas nodded at the leads to follow, and kept his details to himself.

Sixteen

They departed at four am from the southernmost station in the city, where Sasha made her toss her handicom and any other traceable electronics into the marshes. A tram took them south to Stolin, then a private taxi deposited them over the border near Dubrovitsya. From there they caught a flight to Kiev, took another to Batumi, taking turns hiding in the restroom while the other paid the fares so they were never seen together. Their flight ended in Tbilisi, where his sister now lived. Ana stood a meter eighty herself, her lofty head crowned with soft brown curls that made her appear even taller. She hugged Sasha, kissed him, and fussed over his appearance like a mother. Sash squirmed like a little boy.

Maryana hugged Ana, then her husband Georg. "Thank you so much! You're the only people who have given us any blessings at all. You're so kind to do this."

Ana hugged her again. "It's the least I can do. I never thought I'd see Sash as happy as when he talks about you. It means the world to me. You're even prettier than he claimed."

"How did you do?" Sasha asked.

"Not bad," Ana replied as they loaded up the mound of luggage for the final leg of its journey. "There's a furnished two-room on the second floor next house over; it's clean, and the price is fair. When something opens in my building, you can have it."

Georg grunted as he hefted a suitcase into the taxi. "My God, what have you got in here, rocks?"

Maryana counted bags. "Close. Statuary. That one's got the art in it."

Sasha frowned at her. "I told you to take only what was necessary. You risked everything for art?"

Maryana shrugged. "Only my favorites. Some of them were graduation presents. I absolutely adore Sarentall. Three for clothes, one for household, and one for things I couldn't leave. It's nothing, really. I take more on holiday."

Sasha tried three times to get into the small bubble taxi. At last he managed to slouch into the front, twisted sideways across the passenger seat, Maryana, Ana, and Georg squeezed into the back. The taxi engine groaned and strained, well over its load capacity. The rough streets offered an even rougher ride.

"Can you wield an arc blade?" Georg asked. "I asked the boss about getting you in where I work, but he really wants an arc slicer. Have you ever done demolition work? You sweat in metal and wall dust all day, but it doesn't take an astrophysics degree to do it. Pay's decent."

"I can do anything you show me," Sasha swore.

"What about you?" Ana asked Maryana. "What are you looking for?"

It was a question that had never been mentioned. Maryana shrugged. "I don't know. I've never worked before. I'm good at hostessing, maybe bookkeeping, and Mamá said I did a wonderful job fundraising for the Inner Minsk Youth Initiative. I love decorating, if that's a help."

Sasha interrupted, "You don't need to work. I will provide anything you need. You need only manage the house. I said I would take care of you, and I meant it."

"I don't doubt that for a second," Maryana said, and rubbed his elbow hanging over the back of the seat. "Fine. You bring in the money, and I will manage it and invest it. It will be our own business partnership."

Ana smiled warmly. "Only love is that foolish."

Six hours later, Maryana stood beside Sasha at the civil registration office, wearing a flattering white Pasha Matei suit, her best white shoes, and the necklace she wasn't supposed to wear in public. She carried a bouquet of pink roses bought for her by her new sister-in-law. Sasha wore new pants and a white shirt darkening with sweat in a half-dozen places, and Ana had seen to it he wore polished shoes. The waves of his thick hair had been slicked down by Ana until they wouldn't have moved in a hurricane. Never had he looked so formal. His eyes hinted tears as the clerk pronounced them married, and he kissed his new wife as Ana and Georg cheered.

Ana and Georg bought them dinner at a better restaurant. "Vodka, vodka, forget the vodka," Ana told Georg. "This is a wedding. We will have wine." She scrolled through the list of offerings on the table screen. "What do you think would be good?"

"Oh, no no," Maryana insisted. "Allow me." She rummaged through the bag that held her flowers, documents, and street clothes, and placed a bottle on the table. "A wedding celebration requires champagne. I picked through the wine cellar before I left."

Georg examined the label. "*Bozhemoi!* Tash! This is five hundred credits a bottle!" Across from him, Sasha sputtered on his drink.

Maryana waved it away as nothing. "Papa won't miss it. There were three others of the same vintage. Georg, will you do the honors?"

Darkness had long fallen when Ana and Georg left them alone. An awkward silence seized the new apartment. Three remaining roses from the bouquet stood proudly in the empty champagne bottle; Maryana rearranged them for a full five minutes. Sasha sat at the table, watching the light play off the shiny new ring on his finger.

Maryana yawned. "I'm tired. I didn't sleep last night, except for the little bit on the flight here. I guess I'll go wash up." She disappeared into the bedroom, through which lay the bath.

"Yeah. I didn't sleep much, either."

He followed, removing the fancy new shirt and sitting on the side of the bed. What did she expect him to wear to bed? Would she be offended that he didn't own night clothes? His Tash was a strange bird, hardly letting him touch her, but surely she understood what marriage entailed? Should he just sleep next to her and worry about it the next day, when they weren't as tired? Hooking up with most girls he knew was as easy as waiting for them to make a comment about the meaning of the size of his feet, to which he'd offer to satisfy their curiosity. At worst, it meant asking a drunk girl, "Want to get it on?", and they almost always said yes. Tash was nothing like those girls. Her sophisticated wardrobe added maturity to her image, but he couldn't erase the vision of her coming to bed in children's pajamas.

He would never imagine such a vision again.

The door opened. He turned his head, and his heart stopped. He slid to his knees, lips mumbling a prayer in a lightning strike of piety.

Maryana stepped forward, enrobed in a sheer white negligee. Her hair, blonde as morning sunlight, hung loose down her back. The light from the lavatory shone behind her, encircling her in a divine glow that illuminated the translucent fabric until girl and gown and light were one and the same.

The light shut off as she stepped forward, reverting her to corporeal form. Maryana caught his open-mouthed stare before dropping her head and blushing. She adjusted the fabric self-consciously. "I bought it in Paris. I wanted to wear something special for you. I hope you like it."

Words failed him, each and every one that came to his tongue inadequate and humiliating. He whispered stupidly, "You are the most beautiful thing I have ever seen."

She kissed him as he knelt, an ambitious kiss that didn't let up for several seconds. "Just remember, my husband, you're bigger than I am. Go easy on me."

He hadn't slept for more than twenty-four hours, but the turn of events left Sasha wide awake. In just hours, his life had gone from grinding drudgery to something... out of an ancient myth, was the only way to rationalize it. He, a nothing, a landless drifting *muzhlan* living on a sofa by the grace of an acquaintance, lay curled on a bed of his *own*, in his *own* apartment, watching his new *wife* sleeping softly on his arm, her long hair spread out behind her like the feathers of some rare exotic bird.

Wife.

In fifty years he would not have imagined such a thing, not like this. He'd been so terribly afraid of hurting her, with his clumsy hands and graceless motions, that she'd laugh at his lack of cultured finesse. He'd tried to be so very gentle for this angel of mercy who had never known violence. He knew he'd done something right when she reached out and asked him to love her again. Watching her sleep, he traced a timid finger up her pale thigh, the curve of her hip, the warm rounded handful of her naked backside, its skin the color and texture of fresh-poured cream. The fingers dared to brush over the teacup breast and candy-pink button of nipple. Every inch of her bore the same light perfume, and he found himself aroused just by the scent. He leaned and kissed her neck softly until she woke and kissed him back.

Their honeymoon lasted one day, walking through old Tbilisi hand in hand, eating *khinkali* and *sashlik* from a corner vendor, drinking *grappa* and learning the streets. Maryana found the city quaint, a rich blend of historic European and Middle Eastern influences combined with modern design and cosmopolitan flair wherever rebuilding had occurred. The soft folds of the Saguramo mountains gave a peaceful backdrop to the congested hustle of traffic. Their budget apartment had no complimentary comm system, no satellite reception, the three windows faced north, leaving the rooms dark and dreary most of the day, but the balcony on their landing was decorated with fancy scrollwork in purple and white, framing the view of the distant hills.

"And we're not getting one," Sasha insisted. "No comm system; we're silent for now. Anything with a bill is traceable. Maybe in a few months. We can use Ana's comm."

Sasha's single duffel required less than three minutes to unpack. He watched in awe as Maryana stuffed outfit after outfit into the closet and drawers. From the houseware bag came window scarves, bright table cloths, lacey bed covers and the softest towels, everything vacuum-packed to conserve space. From the decorator bag came photographs, a music system, text reader, small paintings, a roll-up keyboard, statuary, mementos from various travels, and two small lamps. Within an hour, the bare walls and basic furniture had a welcoming, home-like feel.

Maryana admired it with approval. "Much better."

Sasha's job paid, but he hated it. He never complained, but Maryana could tell by the hard set of his jaw and the way he softened when he saw her. He arrived home filthy each night, and she made him bathe before sitting on the furniture. She rubbed the pains from his long back herself.

"Did Ana say what day the laundry service came by?" Maryana asked him as he soaked. "This was your last clean shirt. You can't go to work in this."

Sasha laughed. "What laundry service?"

"The one that does our laundry."

His smile faded as he realized she was serious. "Tash, no one does our laundry. We have to do it ourselves, just like we have no cook, no one else to make the bed, and no one to clean the floor."

Maryana frowned. "How? Where would you do that? Isn't it easier to just find a service?"

What Sasha knew about laundry could have been written on his thumbnail, but he located a public laundry, carried the clothes there in his duffel bag, and taught her the little he knew. They sat outside as their clothes were reconditioned, a beer in Sasha's hand and Maryana on his knee.

"There's so much to know," she fretted. "This stuff wasn't taught in household management class. That's why you have staff."

"It will get easier," he promised. "We'll have that someday. Give me time."

"You've got to find a place to register for classes. Summer semester starts in a week or so. Two classes, at least."

"I can't work like this, be with you, and go to school as well. Let's get settled first, then we'll see."

"Of course you can. Time wasted is money lost," Maryana quoted Papa. "You don't want to be doing this the rest of your life?"

"Georg's done it for ten years. They own their building, with four apartments for income. Ana stays home to manage them. They took a holiday to Portugal this year."

Maryana stroked his cheek. "For the first time in five years. She works herself to death, addressing complaints. You can do better. You have *dreams!* Why not follow them? You can do anything! I will read along and help you. It will be our time together."

Summer flew by, consumed with work, school, and socializing with Ana and Georg. Sasha's final average for the two classes was 96.

"See? I told you it would be easy," Maryana said as she scrubbed him after work. "You should have no problem then with four for fall."

"Not while working," he insisted. "That would take up every free moment."

"Can you cut back your work hours?"

Sasha snorted. "Not if you want to keep money coming in."

"See if you can, and I will cover the difference from my accounts."

"No." It was a command.

Maryana leaned in to kiss the stubbly cheek. No matter how much beard inhibitor he used or how often he cleared the growth, his cheeks always seemed to bear a prickly shadow. "It's *our* money, Sash, but if you insist it's not yours, then let me spend it as I wish. Covering your education is not the same as living off my money; it's doing my share.

Let me get you your schooling, and then you can do all the rest on your own, I promise. Please, darling. It will get you along that much faster."

Sasha eyed her with a devilish gleam. "You're that sick of laundry already? Have some more of it." He seized her and pulled her into the bathwater with him, stripping her clothes as she shrieked with laughter.

Seventeen

Tomas spent the summer at home. He flew up to Moscow once or twice a week, but neither he nor his parents had much mind for work. The trip to Mars was cancelled. Papa's temper was short and his concentration poor; he cut his hours and worked from home as much as he could. Mamá canceled all social engagements, even church appearances, afraid of missing some shred of information, of not being home if Maryana somehow turned up alive. In her heart she was convinced it was an instance of rape-murder, at the hands of a known violent criminal who had been allowed to walk the streets, something she reminded the police about with a weekly check-in. Papa remained only slightly more optimistic. Tomas did his best to remain upbeat and reassure them without directly giving away promised secrets. Not that he knew much more than they did.

The police believed it to be a matter of rebellion by an adult daughter living at home, and did little to pry further. Surveillance cameras caught a very tall man boarding a flight to Kiev, accompanied by a small figure in a hooded jacket. It could have been a child, but the jacket and carry bag matched ones missing from Maryana's closet. Papa hired and fired four sets of investigators, but each time the trail died in Kiev.

From Tomas's sources, he knew the Kirushenko man had quit his job the day before Maryana went missing. He had reportedly married some girl and left for an unknown location. That confirmed both the police's theory and Maryana's hints. Helina had been his key. Evasive and ambiguous through untold police interviews, heavily chastised by her parents, harassed by tabloid media, it took a lot of patient charm to pry information from her.

She met him uneasily at a café.

"I've already told them everything I know," she said curtly. "We stopped speaking two weeks before she disappeared. Arkin Laritsky asked me on a date and she was so jealous we wound up in a fight."

"Maryana never fights with anyone, she just cries over the injustice of the situation. If she were that upset at you over a boy, I would have heard about it. I know you're involved, Helina, whether you want anyone else to know or not. I have nothing invested in this," Tomas swore. "No matter what you tell me, no matter how wild an orgy you participated in, I will not say a word. I won't tell your parents, I won't even tell my parents. I just want the truth, off the record."

Helina's eyes widened until they seemed about to fall out of her head. "He took her to an orgy?!"

"You didn't go with her?" he said with a straight face, only to laugh at her shock. "I was joking." Helina glared. She didn't know the street or remember which tram stop, but she did fill him in on the more sordid details of Sasha's living quarters, that Maryana had actually kissed him, but although Helina didn't trust him, he was polite and well-mannered, and seemed to care a great deal about Maryana. Tomas kept the secrets to himself.

* * *

Georg waited for him as Sasha's feet slammed down the outside stairs as he left for work. "Ana up?" Georg nodded, and Sasha darted into the apartment. "Ana, do you have anything for bad stomachs?" he asked. "Tash was sick yesterday. She felt better last night, but she's still bad this morning. She's in bed."

Ana rummaged through a cabinet. "Poor thing! I'll find it and bring it up to her. Change of season always brings out the germs. She's probably just tired. Newlyweds don't remember beds are for sleeping, too."

A week later, Maryana still didn't feel great. Ana brought her to a doctor. Sasha returned from work to find the table set as fancy as Maryana could manage, down to an arrangement of blooming wildflowers and grasses in an empty beer bottle tied with a ribbon, and a waiting bottle of wine. She let him sit down without changing. That was his first clue something wasn't right.

"Well? What was it? Are you all right? Is it just a virus? Did they prescribe anything?"

"It's temporary," Maryana said with a smile. "I need lots and lots of vitamins. It happens to many newlyweds. Do you prefer Dada, Papa, or Father?"

Sasha's face matched the dust coating his clothes. "What?"

"I'm pregnant."

Sasha's face clouded over. The thick dark brows pulled together until they made a bridge across his eyes, hiding them in the shadow. "Tash! What do you mean? Weren't you on something?"

Maryana shrugged. "I'd never slept with anyone before. It never crossed my mind."

Sasha's breath came in heaves. "Tash, you're seventeen! You're too young to be a mother! We don't know how to raise a baby! We have two rooms – I'm still in school – Where will we put it? How will we support it? We've been married four months. I'm not ready for that. I like having us, not we."

Maryana's cheeks glowed with hormones; her sweet smile completed the picture. She put her arms around his neck and kissed his ear. "Lots of girls my age have babies – you see them at the park all the time. And they don't have such a wonderful man as the father. A crib doesn't take up much room; by the time it needs a bed, we'll have a bigger place. You'll see. Mamá can be mad at me all she wants, but she won't be able to ignore a grandchild."

Sasha didn't return her embrace. "We're hiding from your parents, remember? I don't think we should have one right now. I've never even held a baby, Tash. The smart thing to do is terminate. We'll try again after I have my degree. I promise."

Maryana let go. "Sash, you don't mean that! It's a part of you! It's a part of me! How could you kill it, like a gopher tearing up the lawn? It's a *baby*. I've never held one before either, but no parent knows what they're doing at first. That's just fear talking. Don't you want children?"

He hesitated too long. "Yes, but when we're ready for them, when we have something to offer. We have nothing, and that's a shitty way to raise a child."

"We have love," Maryana said with finality. "We'll do fine."

* * *

The Feast of Kazan had passed and Tomas's birthday was approaching when shouts echoed in the quiet halls of the estate. He rushed to the upstairs balcony in time to see his father sprint through the foyer to his mother's office in the south wing. Outside of sports, Tomas had never seen his father run for anyone. The world turned on Fyodor Ivanov's command; he did not need to run. Tomas raced down the stairs after him.

"We've got her!" Fyodor crowed, waving a printout. "Her bank statements. There was activity on an account, from a bank kiosk in Tbilisi. Hurry! We're meeting with the *politzei* down there in three hours. They're working on it now." He pulled Andrea from her office chair.

Andrea tried to move in all directions at once. "Tbilisi? For certain? She's alive? Oh, Fyodor! You found her!"

"Of course she's alive, Mamá," Tomas reminded her. "You know exactly why she left."

"Tomas, stay here," his father ordered as Tomas dove for the exit closest the vehicle hangar.

"I'm coming with you, Papa!"

"No. I need you ready here, should I need anything. I'll call as soon as I have news."

"I'm her brother! I want to be there, too."

Fyodor turned at the door, finger pointing back down the hall. "You are in charge of everything in our absence; don't disappoint me."

* * *

On Friday, Maryana made a special dinner to cheer him up. It was hard to look at beef, let alone smell it, but it was Sasha's favorite. He'd been silent and broody at her gentle inquiries, working his way through several beers and then going over to Ana's to drink with Georg. He'd come around; no one could look at a baby and not love it. She bought him a marvelous red wine to accompany the steak, though she would not touch it herself. Every report she read said to abstain during pregnancy. Candlelight, a bowl of hardy blossoms, a pie from Ana and popular Georgian music on her wave receiver made their little kitchen area as good as any restaurant – minus the cook, the waiters, and the busboys. He perked up, just as she expected.

She picked at her baked potato. "I was going over my bank accounts today. My dividend deposit should have been made available as of the eighth, but when I went to transfer it this morning, it claimed insufficient funds. It's got to be a computer error. I'll have to contact them tomorrow and straighten it out."

Sasha stopped chewing. "I thought we agreed you wouldn't touch your accounts."

"Well, yes, but that's not my regular account. I was getting a little low on spending money, and with the holidays coming next month, I wanted to boost our savings up."

Sasha swallowed at last. "You *fool!* Your father set up that account! It's traceable! They'll know where we are."

Maryana blanched. "I'm sorry. I didn't think of that. Do not raise your voice to me, Sasha. Yell at whom you will, but I am your wife, and you will not yell at me."

The fury on his face eased somewhat. "I'm sorry. I won't yell. Like you said, it's not a regular account. Maybe it will be okay."

"I'm sure it will. I was looking at the projected reports for Parallax Space Systems – nothing to do with Papa whatsoever – and they're expected to go public in two weeks. It could be an excellent chance to jump on something that could make us a very nice profit. What do you think?"

Footsteps sounded outside, up the stairs and across the landing, preceding a knock at the door. Maryana rose to answer it. Ana and Georg were the only people they knew socially; the fewer contacts they made the better right now. Ana knew about the dinner and wouldn't have disturbed them, so it must be Georg.

The door slammed open as she released it, knocking her backward into the wall. Four law officers burst in, stun weapons drawn and ready. Maryana shrieked in fright, then shrieked again in surprise as her parents entered behind them.

Sasha jumped up. "What's going on?!"

The officers seized his arms, knocking over glassware and scorching Sasha's hair on the candles as they forced him down over the table. "Alexander Kirushenko, you are under arrest for the stalking and kidnapping of Maryana Ivanova."

"Like Hell I am!"

Mamá's mauve Gensar tunic and plum pants signaled informal approachability. She smothered Maryana in a tight embrace, crying, Fyodor holding them both. Maryana clung back, gripped by homesickness at the scent of Mamá's *Zolara* perfume, but she ripped away to claw at the officer holding an energy weapon to the back of

Sasha's head. "He didn't kidnap anybody! We're married! He's my husband! Let go of him!"

"Like fuck you are," Fyodor swore, and grabbed her arm. "You are no such thing."

Maryana had never heard such language from him. "Papa!"

"You have proof of this?" an officer asked.

"Of course we have proof!" Sasha snarled from the table.

Maryana wrenched away from her father. She pointed a finger at the room. "Don't you move! Don't anyone move!" Try as she might to look fierce, the effort seemed comical. She was too delicate and radiantly pretty to look dangerous. She dashed into the bedroom and retrieved her marriage certificate. "I left that house under my own free will, a legally declared adult. I even left them notes to that effect."

The officer read down the print. "Tenth of June. That's the day the report was filed. It looks in order. Let him up." To Maryana he asked, "You are Maryana Ivanova? You have identification?"

Her first instinct was to protect her husband, to tear the officers to pieces for touching him, but the presence of her parents stole her fire. Misbehaving in secret was one thing; in front of them was another. The pride of her new name disappeared in shame of offending her father. "Formerly. My name is now legally M. Natasha Kirushenko." She retrieved her official bio-encoded ID.

"Are you here of your own free will?"

"Yes."

"Are you being held against your will, under intimidation, threat of intimidation or blackmail, or of harm to you or other persons?"

"I most certainly am not! It's more the other way around. We've had to stay hidden to avoid exactly this kind of persecution."

To the Ivanovs, the investigator said, "I'm sorry. She does appear to be legally married. She is a liberated adult, not in any obvious physical danger, and doesn't appear to be a prisoner. We have no evidence of a crime. Release him."

Maryana hugged Sasha as he rubbed his freed wrists. "What gives you the right to break into my home and threaten me?" he rumbled. "What gives you the right to assault peaceful citizens in the middle of their dinner?"

"I'm sorry, sir. We received an outstanding interstate missing persons report and we had to follow through."

"Don't take your hands off him!" Fyodor Ivanov shouted. "Can't you see he has brainwashed her? He has deliberately lead my daughter astray to satisfy his depraved criminal lifestyle. I demand you run a chemical screen! I want a physical exam! She would not have done this on her own."

"Sir, unless Mrs. Kirushenko wishes to press charges, there is nothing we can do. If you wish to discuss the matter with her privately …."

Fyodor stamped his foot in rage. "That's not her name! Then arrest him for theft! Those candlesticks are from my house! That painting's mine as well! It's a signed Dittrick, worth more than thirty thousand credits. It's documented and fully insured."

"It's a painting, Fyodor," Andrea murmured. "Let him have it. We came for Maryana."

Fyodor's face burned magenta, right through the thinning hair on his scalp. "What about the necklace, Maryana? Where is your necklace? The one you stole from the safe."

"What necklace?" Sasha scowled.

Maryana peeked at her father from behind Sasha. "You said it was my necklace. Since as young as I can remember, from the first time you ever showed it to me, you said that was *my* necklace."

Andrea held out her hand. "It is yours. Just come over here, Maryana."

"Four point three million credits in platinum, rhenium, and diamonds," Fyodor told the officer, who used his voice recorder to capture every word. "It is insured in my name. I want it."

"What?" slipped from Sasha's lips in a gasp.

"That isn't something we can settle here," the officer said. "I can write up the charge, but you'd have to take it to claims court."

Fyodor seethed, but he kept control. "Fine. Maryana, let's go. You're coming home." He made a grab for her.

Maryana danced out of reach. "I *am* home, Papa. This is *my* home, and Sasha is my husband. We wouldn't have done this if you'd just given us a chance. I'm not going unless he comes with me."

Andrea put an arm around her and tried to walk her toward the door. "Don't be silly. You're a naïve young girl; you were easy prey to persuasion. You made your point, you had your little coming-of-age fling, and now it's done. We're willing to forget all about it. Take your necklace, he can keep the paintings, you can have a divorce within three days and we will all get our lives back in order. Now come."

"Mamá, stop." Maryana wiggled free, but her voice faltered.

Sasha stood himself up tall, thirty-five centimeters taller than Papa and oh-so-much bigger. His face stiffened colder than Siberian ice, and his voice rumbled so deep it seemed to be leaking up from under the floor. "You drove her away once. She has been free to leave any time, but she is my *wife*, and she knows her place is here with me."

"Stay out of this, you spineless bastard!" Ivanov spat with fury. "*You* are the trouble behind all this! Trash like you thinking you can get a free ride." He pulled his bank ID from its folder and waved it in the air. "How much? How much are you after to let her go? Fifty? A hundred? Two hundred thousand? That's more than your kind sees in a lifetime."

Sasha's jaw clenched until the muscles bulged below his cheekbones. The long arm swatted the card from Fyodor's grasp. It flew halfway across the room; an officer retrieved it for him. "I don't want your filthy money!"

"Papa, stop that! I won't let you say things like that about Sasha!" Maryana felt her dander rising. Anger was detrimental to negotiation strategies, but classroom practice never included irate parents in the dialogs. "I'm not going back without him. You're not being fair! Why can't you listen?"

"You don't know what you're saying, dear." Andrea's eyes took in the apartment, its items of quality grossly out of place against a backdrop of uneven turquoise paint, worn floors, and a ceiling line that appeared to dip in the middle of the wall. Her slender hand clutched her neckline, pulling the cloth tighter in an unconscious effort to keep the mediocrity from invading her person. "You were not brought up to live like this. This is how you want to spend the rest of your life? Like the common masses?"

"Everyone starts out somewhere, Mamá. When Sasha's finished with school, we will have so much more. I am willing to wait. I'm not a baby anymore; stop treating me like one!"

Fyodor raised a threatening finger. "If you don't come home right now, Maryana, I will cut you off from every credit ever meant for you! I will not waste the lowliest coin on this unholy union! I will remove your name from my accounts and I will write you out of your inheritance. You will slowly starve when this whore-spawn runs out of money. I will see that your name is struck from every social register in this quadrant of the galaxy. No one will see you, no one will call you, you will be shunned from every financial and economic opportunity I can stick my finger in! Do not think of coming to me for so much as a kind thought when you are sleeping cold in the street, because I will not let you in!"

Pregnancy was not the best condition for stress. Tears poured into the blue eyes, and a sob broke free. "Papa, stop it! You're overreacting!"

Sasha put his hands on her trembling shoulders. "This is *my* home," he rumbled with dignity. "You will not talk to *my* wife that way. I would throw you out, but this is her home too, and if she wants, you may stay. We didn't want your money. She just wanted your acceptance."

"I'm sorry, Papa," Maryana said meekly, feeling every bit the child she still was. "Like it or not, Sasha *is* my husband, and I won't come back. I'm... pregnant."

Andrea's thin face blanched as pale as her coifed hair. She grabbed her daughter and held her to her shoulder in a desperate motherly hug. "*Maryana! No! Oh no, no!* How could you *do* that to yourself! You're too young!"

Maryana's father seemed to age ten years before their eyes. Everything about him sagged at once, and he staggered as if under a great weight. The frigid look he shot Sasha screamed pure hatred. He breathed hard for a full minute, then took his wife by the elbow. "Come, Andrea. We have a loyal son at home. We will attend to him."

Andrea looked as confused as her daughter. She and Maryana clasped hands. "Don't be crazy, Fyodor. That changes everything. Maryana needs us. She can't handle this herself... "

"This whore is not our daughter!" He ripped their hands apart, grabbed Andrea and dragged her to the door. "We have no daughter. I don't think we ever did."

"What do you mean? We can't leave her! She can't raise my ..."

"I ORDERED YOU TO LEAVE!" Ivanov's roar shocked the room into silence. Maryana and Andrea froze, stunned by the unimaginable outburst from a man who hadn't lost his temper in thirty years. He flung a finger toward the door. "NOW!"

Andrea reached backward for Maryana, but Fyodor's hands seized the delicate fabric of her Gensar tunic, leaving permanent creases as he propelled her through the door. "I said NOW!"

Andrea backpedaled to stay on her feet. "Fyodor! What are you doing! I will not leave her... !" The slamming of the door rattled the nearby windows and cut off Andrea's retort. Shuffling resistance and shouts faded downward.

The *politzei* followed them out. "I strongly urge Mrs. Kirushenko to come to the precinct tomorrow and file a statement as to her situation and her desire to remain here. It will prevent any further issues on the matter. Our apologies again," the lead officer said, and closed the door softly behind him.

Silence followed. Maryana stared at the door, unsure what had transpired or even if it was real. Candle wax hardened amid the puddle of red wine on the tablecloth. One of the overturned goblets had broken. Her plate had fallen to the floor. Melted butter and flecks of potato decorated Sasha's shirt.

Sasha massaged her small shoulders. "You did the right thing. You'll see. I'll die before I go to them for money. Pthah! They can keep it. I swear to you, Tash, I will get you anything you want, even if it kills me."

Maryana sank to her knees.

"Don't. Please, don't." He sat on the floor and took her in his arms. "It will be okay. We'll make it together, I promise. Please don't cry."

Footsteps pounded up the stairs again. They glanced at the door in alarm. Sasha started to puff himself out, spine straight, shoulders wide, ready for battle. The guest chime sounded as the door opened, but only Ana and Georg entered. Georg carried a brutal-looking wrecking tool from his work bag.

Ana stared at the shambles of the room. "What's wrong! We saw the *politzei* arrive, and they left your landing. Did someone break in? Who did they take out? Tasha, are you okay?"

Sasha avoided Ana's eyes as he held Maryana. "I think I just met my inlaws."

Ana and Georg cleaned the mess, while Sasha did his best to console her. His tenderness only broke her heart further. Later, when she had exhausted herself, Maryana lay in his arms in bed.

Sasha played with her hair. "That necklace he mentioned. Is that the one you wore when we got married? Four million... ? Was he joking?"

"No," Maryana said blandly. "Do you have any idea how much Papa is worth, Sash? Millions of credits. Maybe hundreds of millions. Even I don't know how much. I gave all that up for you." She blinked her long lashes at his ashen face. "That makes you one very expensive investment."

Eighteen

The Galaxian Airblade stopped under the flythrough just before midnight. Tomas ran outside as his parents emerged on opposite sides of the vehicle and stormed into the house. He tagged behind. "Well? Where is she? Did you find her? Why didn't you answer the damned handicom? I must have called you priority at least twenty times. What happened? Is she still with him? Well?!" It wasn't until then he noticed his father was walking at least six meters in front of his mother. Mamá held a handkerchief to her nose, hiding her face. She rushed past and headed up the stairs.

Tomas dogged his father to his office, barging in without hesitation. The outdated imperial mustard walls of the office, hyper-masculine forest and gold draperies, ring of staunch and unyielding chairs never failed to grate on his sensibilities. "What happened? Where did you go? Did you find her?"

Fyodor logged in at his workstation, waiting out the retinal scan encryptions. He poured himself a drink from the cart in the corner – not the top-label vodka or the imported rare brandy, but the fifty-year old single-grain Arcturan Ujan *Yor* whiskey so strong and expensive it normally sold in shots of only ten milliliters. Perhaps sixty milliliters graced the glass before he sat at his desk; a third disappeared in his first swallow. He drew a shaking breath. "You will do me a favor, Tomas. You will carry out my orders without question, is that understood? I don't care about the hour. Get Manoog to help you, and take down that painting over the stairs. Bring it out behind the hangar and burn it until nothing is left, frame and all. Understood?"

Tomas ran through the instructions in his head. "The painting on the stairs…? That's Maryana's portrait, Papa. That cost…. It's only been up there since last Christmas. What do you mean, burn it?"

Fyodor Ivanov didn't move his head, but glared at his son from the corner of his eye. "Don't question me, Tomas. You have your orders. Now carry them out."

"Papa, you're not making sense. What happened? Did you find her? Where is she?"

"TOMAS!" Fyodor slapped his hands on the desk. "I gave you an order! I have no daughter. No such person exists. I will not display portraits of harlots in my fine home. Now do as I bid! Leave my office or my foot will escort you out implanted in your ass. Good night." He swung around to his comp screens.

"Papa!"

"Dobriye noch!"

Tomas paused in confusion. "Could someone in this house tell me what the hell's going on!" He strode out of the office and ran up the front stairs to his parents' suite.

He banged on the door. "Mamá?"

Tessia opened the door, but wouldn't let him in. "Madam is resting and does not wish to be disturbed, Master Tomas."

Tomas pushed through her into the suite and into his mother's bedroom. *"Mat*, I want answers, and I want them now! She's my sister and I deserve that courtesy. What the hell happened? Why does Papa want her portrait destroyed?"

Andrea howled into her pillow. She controlled the reins of several hundred million credits on a daily basis, shuffling them about until they produced a gain. In the process, she dodged threats and epithets, both real and figurative, without ever showing a milliliter of fear. Above all else, Mamá was strong, unshakeable and capable of intimidating even the hardest of clients with her steel-gray stare. Never, ever, did Mamá cry like this. Not for anything.

Tomas's anxiety increased, and he softened. "Mamá, what happened? Is she – dead?" Mamá cried harder, and a cold chill wound its way up his spine. He knelt by the bed and rubbed her arm. It was only then he realized other staff rushed about the room without a sound, unloading his father's possessions from the drawers and tables and removing them from the room.

"No, Tomas," Mamá gasped behind her handkerchief. "She has left the state and she has married him. By choice."

"Married? I feared as much. She'll tire of it soon enough. He's a day laborer of the lowest sort. Wait until she can't afford anything off the new spring fashion line."

"Your father ... has declared her dead to us. He wants to erase her existence."

Tomas made a face of disbelief. "That's ridiculous. You can't erase a person. I know she exists. Tell me where she is and I will speak to her myself. Mamá. Mamá! Goddamn it, Mamá! Tell me where she is! I will drag her back here by her hair, if necessary."

"Any other day, I would reprimand you for profanities, Tomas, but today is a day for cursing. I will curse your bastard father to the day I die. Castrated pigeon prick! That rat-fucking whore-bastard wouldn't let me bring her home! She's so very young. She needs us, Tomas, and he won't let me help her. Gods have mercy on me! I don't know what to do."

Tomas sat on his heels and folded his hands. In his nearly twenty one years, he had *never* heard his mother use any of the hard curse words, in any of the languages she knew. To hear her spit out not only the *yob-* word, but an entire assortment of foul expletives, only served to make the situation that much more bizarre.

"Mamá," he said quietly, "what are they doing with Papa's things?"

"I will not lie next to a man with no love and forgiveness in his heart. I cannot bear the chill that flows from such hatred of his own offspring. He can have the other bedroom, for he has no haven here."

"Mamá, he wants me to destroy the portrait on the stairs."

"Don't, Tomas! I beg you, don't. It's all we have at the moment. Send it to storage somewhere. Hide it somewhere safe. Don't do anything we'll regret later. God fucking damn him! God fucking damn him." Andrea strangled on a new wave of despair.

Tomas stood up. "Don't swear, Mamá."

"Here, Madam." Tessia offered her a glass of water and helped her hold it. "You'll make yourself ill."

The world had slipped its orbit. Both his parents were crazy, and he was left in charge. Never before had Tomas been given direct opposite orders from his parents. He had no favorite between them. He'd never needed one. Until now.

Maryana was his sister. She existed, and had for the last seventeen years. He knew this to be fact, memory unchangeable. First he would save the portrait, then he'd get to the bottom of the matter himself.

Nineteen

Tomas didn't have a home office of his own. He spent much of his time in his room, or the library, or even the conference room, keeping track of his aspects of the family business and playing with a few deals of his own design. He didn't have the heart for school, but with special arrangement made the commute twice a week to finish up the last three weeks of classes for the semester. His grades would reflect the upheaval of his life. He hung about the house in Minsk, tiptoeing around the broken glass that had become his parents' lives.

The first of December dawned cold and gray, the same inside as outside the house. He didn't expect much of the coming holidays, doubted anyone would even remember except perhaps the cook. The house was silent except for the occasional hushed footsteps of the hired help, heads hung in uncertainty, afraid of saying or implying the wrong thing and instigating an explosion.

The message light on his link screen flashed an incoming call and he hit receive without enthusiasm, until he saw the sender.

"Happy belated birthday, Tomas, if you won't turn me in," Maryana said.

"Thank you," he said with surprise. "You think I give three shits about all that nonsense? I utterly refused to sign Papa's decree. I told him if it was that important to him, I'd leave. I'd leave the house and leave the company and go work for a rival, because I guarantee they'd love to have me. I thought his head was going to blast straight into orbit, he was so furious. It's about damned time you called me! Do you how badly I needed to talk to you? You give me some half-crazed vow of silence and then disappear for six months? That was horribly unfair." His hands scrambled off screen. "Are you still in Tbilisi?"

"Forget tracing it, Tomas. It's a public link. Where I am is not important. I wanted you to know I didn't plan things this way. I tried everything I could to get them to listen. If they'd sat down and spoken with Sasha even once, then calmly explained their reasonings to me, I might have let things drop, but to convict and crucify a man without ever meeting him was hypocrisy at its finest. They preach one thing to your ear, but when it comes to putting their hearts where their words are, they can't imagine." Her hair was pulled back lifelessly in a braid, her fair skin pale and blotchy.

"My God, you're getting fat. Marriage isn't agreeing with you in the least." He grew concerned. "He's not hurting you, is he?"

"My marriage is wonderful," she insisted. "It's the pregnancy. I'm swelling like a parade balloon."

"Pregnancy!! Are you joking?"

Maryana grinned. "They didn't tell you. I think that's what pushed Papa over the edge. And no, the pregnancy came well after the ceremony."

Tomas blinked as the concept set in. Somehow the added weight made her seem older, more mature, not so much his hydrogen-brained baby sister. "Actually, they've told me very little. Are you crazy? What are you going to do with a baby? I wish you'd come home, just for an afternoon, help me calm them down." He glanced down at the flashing indicator on the task bar; the locator trace read *City of Tbilisi Public Vidcom*. No help.

Maryana considered it, then shook her head. "I think not. Papa said some truly awful things, things I'm not ready to forgive him for. He had no grounds to treat my husband like that."

"Awful things? Maryana, you have no idea what it's like here right now! At university, I've never heard such language! It's a war zone of words. If they so much as see each other, they start screaming. I honestly thought Mamá was going to hit him the other day. She threw a fork at him, but it missed. I think it was a warning; I know she can aim better. She wants you home, even with him, wanted to give you the guest house, but Papa's in the worst fit I've ever seen of anyone. He's stripped your room, removed every picture of you, tried to destroy your portrait. He threatened Mamá if she contacts you or sends you money. He made the staff sign an affidavit that if he hears your name spoken, that person will be fired immediately, even at headquarters. He screams if Mamá mentions you, so of course she sneaks up behind him and chants your name for spite." He gave a melancholy sigh. "If it wasn't so desperate, it would be quite funny. I wouldn't be surprised if Mamá leaves him. They can divide the businesses and all the apartments, but neither is willing to give up the estate. Papa sees it as embodiment of all his work, and Mamá won't give it up because he wants it. I've never seen her cry like this."

"Poor Mamá! They've never said a harsh word to each other."

"It's very bad, Maryana. I'm running between them, trying to keep things together. I need you to help me make a united front. Where can I meet you? We need to have a serious talk, form a plan of action. We've got to get them to make peace, before someone hears about the trouble and tries to force a takeover of the companies. I can't see the board of directors allowing me to act as an interim when I haven't finished my degree, and unless something gives, I'll never have time to get to graduate school. I'm caught in a temporal loop of duty. If you throw your weight behind me, together we can keep things going until they smooth out. I can get my accreditation and we'll be on solid ground again."

For a moment Maryana seemed as if she would name a place, but she shook her head. Her lips pressed together, staving off the heartbreak he saw in her eyes. "I can't, Tomas. Papa's lawyers made me sign a megabyte of documents, making me deny any relationship with him or you or Mamá at all, relinquish all claims to any property or inheritance from now through all generations to come. I cannot interact with any of his known business contacts or use my name in conjunction with his, or ever speak to any media sources at all, or I will be served with all kinds of lawsuits, including theft of property. Maryana Fedorovna Ivanova is now legally deceased. I broke my word just calling you; there's no way he would let me help. Nor will I go behind Sasha's back; I respect him too much for that. Sasha is estranged from his parents; now I am, too. A baby doesn't care about the house, or the art collection, the number of companies they own or the number of worlds they exploit. It just wants to know its grandparents. That's what hurts most. I love them, but they've broken my heart." She pretended not to wipe her eyes.

Tomas felt his own heart grow heavy. Maryana never looked so small and helpless as when she cried. "I don't doubt it, but I do wish you'd reconsider. Is there anything I can do for you? Papa didn't tell *me* not to help you. Well, not directly. And he's a fool anyway; if I inherited everything and died single and childless, I would leave it all to you as a matter of course."

Maryana shook her head wanly. "Just stay in touch. I miss you."

"I'll be here if you need me," he promised. "Use my school mail, just in case. If you need help, give a yell. At this point I may just force a hostile takeover in my own name. Mamá might even support me, if I frame it right."

"Do what you think is best. I don't want to see the house gone, either. Thank you, Tomas. It was so good to hear your voice. 'Bye."

* * *

Maryana's first six months of marriage had been a game of Let's Play Secret House. She and Sasha basked in each other's presence. Each morning he left for work brought a heartache of parting, each evening's return was an eagerly awaited gift. More often than not their nights ran late, entwined in fleshly pleasures. Ana taught Maryana how to prepare various simple meals; Maryana taught Sasha to wipe his feet before entering the apartment. Sasha worked, Maryana juggled the numbers to enlarge their fortune just like Mamá, and the idea of a soft, cuddly, cute baby completed the let's-pretend game. Living without conveniences like commlinks and wristcoms and private laundry facilities was just part of the word "secret;" it never entered Maryana's head that the situation would be long-term. The belief never actually left her that once Mamá and Papa got used to the idea and accepted it, she and Sash would return to Minsk and move on with their lives.

Papa's tantrum and subsequent legal "punishment" destroyed the game. No physical change had taken place, no word was spoken about it, but for more than a week Sasha and Maryana tiptoed around each other, as if starting their relationship all over again. Reality sank in. Sasha's job paid less than Papa paid his service staff. The rent of the apartment, the cost of food, laundry, clothing, left so very little for entertainment or investing. With the stroke of a finger on his send button, Papa had erased her access to the majority of her stocks and financial accounts and trust funds. She would need every credit the remainder produced as liquid capital to supplement Sasha's salary; there would be no increases to their portfolio for the visible future.

Maryana came up behind him while he studied at the table. She put her arms around his neck and rested her head on his shoulder. "I'm sorry Sash. I don't know what I was thinking about the baby. You're dead right. We have no idea what we're doing. We can't afford it. I should have taken your advice at the start."

His hand reached up and rubbed her back. "We'll do okay. You'll see. We're young, we're healthy, we've got Ana and Georg to help us. We don't have to hide anymore. We'll make it work."

By Maryana's second obstetrics appointment, optimism also became a thing of the past.

"Whoops. Looks like there's a complication," the doctor said while scanning her belly. She adjusted the resolution and searched for a better angle. "You have just moved up to high-risk."

Sasha turned white, and Maryana motioned for him to sit. "What kind of risk?" he demanded. "We can have a baby any time; her health is more important."

"We'll take each week as it comes," the doctor told her, "but your skeletal structure is rather small, and your husband's is larger than average. Your age also puts you at greater risk for premature delivery. We want to keep the babies small, to make delivery easier, but there's a high chance you'll need a cesarean."

"Wait a minute," Sasha interrupted. "You said babies, plural."

"Yes I did." She twisted the display around to show them a placental outline with a baby shape at each side.

"You've got twins."

Twenty

Maryana waddled out of the bedroom, two hands supporting her enormous belly. A year ago, she'd never have imagined she'd look like this, ever. The ZhiZhi silk nightdresses had been replaced by an old shirt of Sasha's; the shoulder seams hung at her elbows. It looked ridiculous, but it was the only thing comfortable enough to sleep in as summer heat invaded the apartment. "Sash, what are you still doing up? You have to be at work in three hours. You need to sleep."

Data cards covered the little kitchen table. Sasha scribbled the last of his project report into a second-hand computer notepad, the last remaining work he had to turn in for the end of semester. A half-dozen empty beer bottles kept cheerful company around the table.

He held up a hand. "Wait." A few more lines and he put down the stylus; twins meant he would have to work twice as hard to get ahead. "Done!" He pulled her onto his lap, taking the weight off her aching feet. His big arms still fit around her. "Me? What are you doing up? You're supposed to be in bed."

"I'm sick of being in bed. I'm all achy and I can't get comfortable. Lie down with me?" She rested her head against him, content. She'd made it through the winter, but spring found her increasingly disabled by her belly. Sasha waited on her hand and foot, in a panic every time she called him. He made her stay with Ana while he went to work. To take the pressure of gravity off her strained body, she was ordered to bed in her sixth month – with strict orders for no romance, nothing that might risk an early labor. Sasha'd been so good about it these last few months. His misery broke her heart.

She kissed his cheek. "Well, one whole year together. What do you want to do for our anniversary tonight?"

"I figured I'd borrow Georg's podcar. We'll get out for a little while." He nuzzled her hair before kissing her. A hint of perfume clung to her, even in the night. A kiss to her neck followed. Maryana tipped her head to the side, savoring the moment. Her breasts had swollen triple their size; he caressed one through the shirt, kneading it with increasing strength. The next kiss had only one meaning.

Maryana wrestled herself free. "Ouch. Stop, Sash. That hurts. Patience," she soothed, putting her arms around his neck. "It'll be over soon enough."

"I'm sorry. I ..."

"Shh. It's just as hard on me, too. Just hold me." She cuddled close in his arms, and they watched the coming dawn lighten the room, his hand rubbing the great rounded belly of babies.

After a while Maryana squirmed. An itch crept across her ankle. It felt wet when she scratched it with her other foot. "What the ... Sash!" She struggled to her feet. His leg was dark with wetness, a wetness that still trickled onto the floor. "I think my water broke!"

They celebrated their first anniversary in a birthing center, cradling their duplicate daughters. Except for being a month early, it had been a text-book delivery.

Maryana stroked the fingers of the newborn in her lap. The hands were large and chubby for such a small baby; she would be a daddy's girl for sure. "They still need names."

Sasha had handled priceless relics of civilizations thousands of years old. He'd handled porcelain vases buried for centuries under the sea. He'd learned to restore the most fragile documents through endless patience and a steady hand, but he held the second baby as if his breath would shatter it. "You're not giving them two names, are you?"

"I planned on it. It's a paper thing, mostly. It gives them a bit more distinction if they desire it."

Sasha studied the bundle in his hands, just over two kilos in size. An idea came to him. "Helina. We should name one Helina, for your friend who helped us." He pronounced it with a harder H than Maryana.

"Up until the end," Maryana conceded. "I can live with that. How about... Valeria, for her valiant father, and... Lin, for my Aunt Linné. Valeria-Lin."

"More like her valiant mother. And this one?"

"You named her. You pick."

"I don't care."

"Come on – a name from a story you like, something from history, the wife of a minister – something."

Sasha smiled, watching the baby squirm. "I can do history. Raisa Zdanovich was the archaeologist who unearthed the first complete paleolithic tomb in northern Siberia in 2162. Raisa."

Maryana smiled. "I like Raisa. Helina-Raisa Kirushenko. Your papa picks beautiful names, Helina."

Sasha kissed the infant with the utmost gentleness and placed her in the bassinet to fill out the forms. He handed the compad to Maryana to sign.

"You misspelled it, Sash," she said. "Helina spelled her name *Elina*, not *Galina*. In standard, you'd use an H at the start."

"If she goes to England, she can spell it with an 'H.' The form is in Russian and that's how I learned to spell it."

Maryana shrugged. "I guess it doesn't matter." She signed off on it.

* * *

Sasha breezed into the apartment two weeks later bursting with a secret, something hidden behind his back.

Ana rocked one baby while the other slept. "Tash's sleeping," she whispered.

He tiptoed into the bedroom and kissed his wife. Neither of them managed much sleep. One baby crying was a four-star alert for the other to join.

Maryana woke with a start. "Well? Did you get it?"

"I got it!" he exploded, waving the yellow printout in his hand. He scooped her off the bed and whirled her around, kissing her over and over.

She grabbed it from him when he let go. "Let me see! *'... inform you that your application for a hardship grant for the summer internship program in archaeological study has been approved in full. Please report to program ...'* Sash! The whole amount, too!" It had been her idea to pad the numbers a little, anything to get ahead. "That's incredible!"

Ana kissed him. "Congratulations! When do you leave?"

"Seven days. The whole summer spent on Regulus B II! We come back the day before classes start. If I'm careful, I'll make contacts and get a jump on next summer." Sasha grabbed three glasses from the cabinet and opened a bottle of Maryana's favorite wine. Not only his first chance to do real work at an actual archaeological site, but his first trip off-planet, a chance to see the universe first hand – and at someone else's expense.

Tears clouded Ana's eyes as she gazed at the baby on her arm. "I'll miss them."

Maryana hugged her. Childless Ana loved the girls as much as she did, and spent every free minute helping with them. "Don't be sad. It's only eight weeks. They won't have grown much."

Sash handed out the glasses. "Let's celebrate! To Tash, the greatest wife a man could dream of, and to Sasha, the man with the highest grades in the program!"

Twenty-one

S asha graduated at the head of his class, with two distinctions for his classwork. He had no idea if he was the first in his family to finish a university; Ana hadn't gone further in her studies and he doubted his mother ever had, and his father and half-sisters were lost to him. All he knew was that for the first time in three years, he didn't have to attend summer classes.

The joy was bittersweet. Graduate work would begin in Moscow in September, necessitating a move north. He'd been hired by the university as an assistant, ending his miserable years as a laborer. The news tore Ana apart.

"Please don't cry," Maryana begged, almost as upset to be losing her sister-in-law, eager babysitter, and new best friend. "We've still got all summer. We'll find a way to visit, I'm sure." Most of all, she would miss Ana's extra hands. Maryana found chasing twins more than she could handle, especially now.

"Tash, get them *out* of here!" Sasha bellowed as he peeled a golden-haired toddler off his field project photos, only to have an identical one grab his binoculars and take off. He brought his hand down on the butt of the seized one with a single sharp smack. The girl looked stunned, then cried in shock.

Maryana shrieked and grabbed the child. "Don't spank them! They're babies! They don't know any better!"

"I wasn't spanking them. It was only a tap, enough to get their attention. They'll never learn if we don't teach them right from the start."

Maryana was adamant. "You are not hitting my babies! I will not allow them to learn violence."

"It's not violence," Sasha insisted. "It's discipline. Behavior shaping. You'll see."

"Not. My. Babies."

Sasha captured the second girl, retrieved the binoculars, and put them up high. The toddler began to pull at Maryana's side.

"Up! Up! 'Ina cryin'!"

Maryana put the spanked one down, and the two of them hugged each other. "Either way, Sash," she continued, "I have got to have help. Ana can only be expected to do so much. She has a building to look after. I can't rest, watch them, and pack our things at the same time. They don't sit still for a minute. I know it's not the best time, but I *need* to hire someone. Just until this is over." She held her back as she waddled to the coldkeeper for a bottle of juice, her belly rounded out again with the imminent birth of another baby – only one big one this time.

Sasha maneuvered the controls to erase the scribbles from the notes in his compad. "Whatever. I'll find someone tomorrow."

Early the following morning Sasha pushed a girl in the door. "Tash? This is Ohanna, your new helper. She loves children. I'll see you when I get home." Maryana eyed the girl with horror, not fit to greet anyone, wearing a pair of maternity shorts and one of Sasha's oversized shirts, a breakfast-grubby toddler perched on a hip and a half-naked one clinging to her leg. She smoothed her sweaty hair back and summoned her hostess face. "Welcome, Ohanna. I'm Tasha. Please forgive my appearance, I'm running behind today."

Ohanna smiled joyously, but didn't say anything. Sasha's idea of hired help was a fourteen-year old neighbor's girl, done with classes for the summer. She spoke no French, no English, no Kartuli, and barely any Russian.

"Pomagu," Ohanna tried, reaching for a girl.

Maryana sighed. Yes, she could help. Maryana handed over the one she held. She lifted the child's hair to show a letter inked on the back of the neck. "Galina." She peeled the other off her leg and put the hand in Ohanna's. "Valeria." She went into the bedroom and lay down.

She mentioned her concerns to Sasha.

"A month of Armenian won't hurt them. They won't remember it."

"That's not the point, Sash. What if there's a problem? She can't tell me. I can't tell her."

"Ana will find someone to translate if necessary. Is she good with the girls?"

"Yes."

"Does she clean?"

Maryana frowned. "Yes."

"Does she work cheap? Then where's the problem?"

Maryana couldn't tell him. For the first time in her life, Maryana, barely twenty herself, burned with jealousy. Why this girl, who could taunt her behind her back and she'd never know? After all, she'd only been sixteen when she fell in love with Sasha – just three and a half years ago. Why shouldn't this girl feel the same? Fourteen, with a lithe tanned body and pert black hair and sultry midnight eyes, happily playing Reach for the Stars and Where'd It Go? for hours, teaching her girls to put on their shoes, making them lunch, and cleaning the apartment while they slept. Alone with the girl who could easily touch her own toes, Maryana never left her bed, the baby inside her kicking and punching as if boring its own exit. Fifteen minutes before Sasha arrived, she made sure she was up and dressed for a night on the town.

Three weeks later, the baby looming large on scan, Maryana gave birth by cesarean to a son who looked just like his father, long and dark-eyed, with a full head of black hair. The girls were fascinated, poking and pulling at him until Ana took them next door with her.

Maryana's eyes misted over. She wiggled Alexei's toes as he lay next to her on the bed. "Look at him, Sash! He's so beautiful! He's got your big feet."

Sasha burst with pride. Any worries about three children crammed into the apartment disappeared the moment he confirmed he had a son. "Of course he does. He's my son." He lifted the week-old infant and cradled him in his huge hands. No longer did he fear newborns, especially when this one was the size of both twins together.

"You know your Papa already, don't you?" he cooed. "We will be best friends, you and me. I will show you the stars."

"You're silly. He can't understand you yet."

"He's my son. Look at his eyes, Tash. You're the smartest baby ever born, aren't you."

The soft gray eyes locked onto the father's, listening with a wonder far beyond his days. "I will never run out on you," Sasha promised.

> *He worshipped the memory of his father. His father had worshipped him. He read to him, played with him, taught him to skate and play hockey and soccer and chess.*

116

His father took him to concerts, to sports, showed him museums, taught him to swim and wrestle. Anything to be out of the house.

They'd had a lovely time, that last day. The autumn landscape glowed a warm honey-gold. They'd hiked out into the country, the young boy riding his tall father's shoulders. They'd picnicked by a stream, soaking in the warm sun, his father telling him story after story.

"Remember days like this, Sasha," his father had said dreamily, sprawled in the golden grass next to him. "Remember me when you think of them. Remember that I love you."

The next day he was gone, all of his things with him. For days, the boy sat by the window, watching, waiting, until his mother beat him when she caught him near the glass. She cursed his father day and night, crying and drinking. He never passed a window again without checking.

Maryana didn't think she could love Sasha more for taking such a delightfully goofy, excessive interest in his son. He talked to the baby every spare minute, and the boy seemed to listen. Maryana's belly shrank again, her bust remained curvy, and her hair and skin regained their luster. She felt stupid for harboring jealousy of a man who so obviously loved her. She let Ohanna go a week early, to let Ana spend as much time with the girls as she could before they left.

When they got to Moscow, she hired an elderly *babushka*.

Twenty-two

Moscow!

How Maryana missed Moscow! She'd been to Paris, New York, London, even Yuwei Nel Oor on Centauri, but Moscow was a world city like no other. Her home away from Minsk, she skipped down the streets with her little family, pointing out the theaters, and her boutiques, and that restaurant with the baked custard, and Oh! the kiosk where she used to buy handbags! Three years hadn't changed it at all.

Sasha remembered Moscow, too. "I kissed you under that metro sign," he reminded her. "And this very park bench. And outside that *apteka*. I think I pinched your ass under that tree."

Maryana stopped pushing the cartabout to slap him lightly on the arm not holding his son. "You, sir, are a fiend!"

"Fiend?" Sasha stopped walking. "Do you know what happened on this very spot, in front of …" He hunted for the sign. "… Yaroslava's Fine Fruits?"

Maryana eyed him suspiciously. "No."

He bent down to kiss her. His empty hand snaked up to honk a breast. "I felt you up."

Maryana leaped back. "You have daughters! Not in public!" But her smile matched his laughter. "You're evil!"

"You'll see, Tash. We're on our way. A real job, a real apartment, actual furniture…. This is the start of something wonderful."

Wonderful, except for the glaring reminders of happiness lost. Whatever Papa said, he meant. That was the cornerstone of his empire. He did not jerk clients around, changing the wording of a contract in the fine print. He didn't substitute materials without informing the client. Everything was on the table. A client knew exactly what he was getting, that if A was to be made of 99% aluminum in the shape of a Z

118

and delivered on Tuesday, then by God, the Z-shaped A of precisely 99% aluminum would be there by noon Tuesday, if Ivanov had to deliver it himself – which he was known to do. Better in a pinch to lose a half million credits on a deal than lose a client's business, which in the long run would be worth much more. Fyodor Ivanov did not fail.

Maryana steered the cartabout up to the gates of Villovsky Academy. She still fit in her navy suit, accented with some of her better jewelry. She would show off her beautiful son and perfectly matching daughters, dressed in identical pink dresses from a sale at Zander's Fine Clothiers. As legacies, they were practically guaranteed acceptance to the school, as long as the financial obligations could be met. Maryana still had ten years to save for that part. It was never too early to show her girls the right path, or get their names known.

The receptionist greeted her in the lobby. "Welcome to Villovsky. May I help you?"

Maryana's hand reached out. "Mrs. Brovin! How nice to see you again!"

The woman started to rise, welcoming recognition on her face, then froze in horror and sat back down. "I'm sorry. Your name?"

"It's me, Maryana Ivanova. Kirushenko, now. I married an archeologist over at the university. I brought my family with me to visit." She lowered her empty hand.

The woman seemed flustered. She pretended to be absorbed in her compad screen, randomly scanning data as if searching for something. "I'm sorry, I don't have anyone by that name on today's registry. Did you have an appointment?"

Maryana pushed a girl back into her seat and straightened her dress. "I'm Maryana, Mrs. Brovin. I just graduated three years ago. My mother is a trustee."

"Let me call the headmistress." She paged her. "This is Mrs. *Maryana Ivanova* Kirushenko, but she doesn't have an appointment on today's calendar," Mrs. Brovin explained.

Maryana smiled and tried her hand again. "Mrs. Mirinova. What a pleasure! I don't understand the problem here. I'm here in Moscow and I wanted to stop in and say hello to a few of my friends and teachers."

Mrs. Mirinova looked no less shocked by her presence. Her voice faltered. "I'm sorry, have we met?"

Maryana's cheer evaporated and her smile faded into a tight line worthy of Mamá. Enough was enough. She didn't even stop the girls from kicking each other and yelling. "This isn't funny anymore. I have four entire pages in the 2239 yearbook. I have a diploma with your very signature on it. I graduated number eight in my class. My name is on the programs for senior theater, student symphony, dance troupe, and three separate senior awards. I know you know me."

Mrs. Mirinova took her hand at last. "Look, Mrs. Kirushenko, it's nothing personal, I assure you. I'm certain you'd know many of our staff and students *outside* this school. But, and I am speaking *officially*," she drew the word out, "no Maryana Ivanova has ever attended this school. I must ask you to leave."

Realization slapped Maryana in a cold wave, and it took all her grace not to sputter. "I see. Very well, then. Please give my regards to the staff."

Mirinova escorted her to the door. "Absolutely. It was a great pleasure to meet you, Mrs. Kirushenko. You have a most beautiful little family. Life seems to be agreeing with you. I'm truly sorry we were unable to help you. I wish you every happiness."

Maryana smiled graciously. "Thank you. It must feel wonderful to know your financial endowment has reached new heights."

She waited until she got home to cry.

She spared Sasha the details. "I told you, Papa knows many people, and his reach is parsecs long. That's it, you know." She stared through the window into the distance. "You can see it clear across the river. The Imperial Towers is Papa's building. That's his world headquarters. He could be there at any given time. Or Mamá. Tomas is working out of the New York office, but he could be there, too."

Sasha came up behind and hugged her. His voice turned cold and dark. "Don't look at it. Don't think about it. We do fine on our own. The towers are black because they're filled with hatred."

"It's solar sheathing."

He turned her away from the window. "Tash, promise me! Promise me you will not go in there. You will not try to contact anyone in that building. Promise me you will stay far away from it. Don't even walk in front of it. Cross the street. He would have you arrested for trespass as soon as give you a glass of water."

She nodded sadly. "I know. I promise. But it still hurts, knowing they're so close. Promise me the same thing? You won't go there and start trouble? No throwing rocks at the tiles, or making evil faces at the security cameras, or leaving dog droppings in the lobby arboretum? Whatever you do, no slander, and always deny any connection in an interview."

"No," he promised. "We are stronger than those towers, you and I. They do not exist for us. Someday, though, Tash. Someday, when we are victorious, we will rub it in their faces."

Twenty-three

S asha arrived home to find chaos. Maryana jostled screaming baby Alexei on her hip. One crying twin sat in a chair holding a coldpack to her face, the other rolled on the floor kicking her feet and crying. Maryana looked ready to join them.

He put his work bag high on a cabinet. "What happened?"

"Alexei had a toy. Galina put her face near him and he hit her in the eye with it. She started crying, Valeria got mad that he hurt Galina and hit him back. She's mad because she's in a corner and I won't let her sit with Galina. I cannot wait for spring!"

"Knock it off!" he yelled at the twins. "Stop your noise, or I'll make you stand there on your head." Tears stopped as two toddlers put their heads on the floor and tried to pick their feet up.

"Why make yourself crazy? The university has numerous preschools. I'll find out tomorrow if they have space. You're entitled to classes as a spouse; sign up for an art-history class or something. Have fun." He traded her his cued handicom for the baby, hunted for a bottle and plugged the mouth. Alexei was a big baby, and always hungry.

"What's this?"

"It's an invitation to a conference on ancient cultures of the Middle East. There's a reception for the speakers on 11 March."

Maryana knew an opportunity when she heard it. "You're going, aren't you?"

Sasha grimaced in disinterest. "It's not my favorite topic. I prefer Northern Mediterranean."

Maryana handed the 'com back. "You are going to both. The more you get your name out there, the more you get known, the better your offers will be." She ran down the event in her head. "We've got three weeks to find you something to wear. I'll find a sitter. Let's go shopping."

If Sasha were designing Hell, the social party would have been one of the deepest circles. A bunch of strangers who had no desire to be there, dressed uncomfortably in a foreign manner, forced to speak about insignificant topics and not allowed to drink as much as it might take to make the event fun. He would much rather have stayed home with Maryana and a bottle of good wine.

He lost track of her not long after arriving. Cocktail snacks. Yes, appetizers belonged in that circle of Hell, too. Funny little bites of unidentifiable food, never enough to fill the stomach, and if you ate enough to curb your hunger, it was a mortal sin. He passed the tables several times, picking at items with one hand and filling his pocket with the other to eat on the other side of the room. Hell was a perpetual *zakuski* hour, without a meal to follow.

He followed Maryana's recommendation: a single drink to loosen up, then only water unless someone else suggested it. The graduate students stood in a circle, griping yet again about the same injustices they griped about every time they gathered. Except for the location, the entire evening could have been a recording.

One of the professors tapped his arm as he passed. "That really your wife over there, Kirushenko? Galaxy's sakes, she's something else. You're a damned lucky bastard."

He heard her tinkling laugh before he saw her, hidden behind an interstellar crowd of respected researchers. She perched on the arm of a sofa next to several other patient wives, but unlike them, she was far from bored. In fact, he'd never seen her looking more beautiful. The soft dusty purple of her tailored outfit coordinated with the blue of her eyes, the ballerina neckline exactly enough to catch attention without being overexposed. Her hair swung in a sheet of sunlight to the center of her back. She'd chosen silver jewelry inspired by ancient designs, no doubt bought at a museum shop, advertising her commitment to the cause. She worked her crowd flawlessly, keeping a dozen old men and women riveted on her words, never letting their ears stray. To make it worse, she was younger than most of the students in the room, still not yet twenty-one.

She spotted him. The manicured hand lifted in his direction. "Sasha, darling! There you are! Come join us. We're discussing excavations."

"Your wife is a perfect delight," Heinrich Fischer of Bonn University told him. "She knows her Biblical history better than my supervisor."

Maryana shot Sasha a smile of encouragement. He took her hand and kissed it. "Who do you think proofs my papers?" The round of laughter told him he'd said the right thing.

Anatas Doloshenko of the Kiev Scientific Institute nodded his way. "You must make a great team."

"Now, now, let's not get our fields confused," Maryana admonished gaily. "I study *art*. Sasha studies arte*facts*." The circle laughed again.

* * *

Riding home in a taxipod, Maryana felt satisfied. "That was a wonderful evening. You should have at least two dinner engagements coming, and several offers for field work. Don't be surprised if you move up soon."

"This is my second semester here. I'm not going anywhere for a long time," Sasha said. Academics moved slower than ice jams in January.

She pulled his arm around her shoulders and leaned into him. "Don't count on it. We're making waves."

As Maryana predicted, summer brought good news; they would spend the fall in Greece, while he studied comparative cultures. Good news always put Sasha in a good mood, and a good mood usually went straight to his libido. After three years and three children, Maryana had tried various forms of birth control, but each time a severe side effect would make her stop for several months. July was one of those months, but Sash was confident he'd pulled out in time, so she didn't think about it again until October, when she couldn't tell if it was a virus or the Greek food that wasn't agreeing with her. After a week, she realized it was neither.

"What?"

"We have a stowaway. Sometime mid-spring."

"What do you mean? Tash, we can't!" His face held no panic this time, only anger. "No. Things are going too well. We have two girls and a boy – what more do we need? My salary only goes so far, Tash. This will screw everything up!" He ransacked a cupboard for a glass and opened the bottle of ouzo on the counter by the readicook.

Maryana tried to push the glass down. "Save that for company, Sash. Unless you're celebrating, there's no need."

He spun in the other direction, out of her reach. "We're in Crete, and it's what the Greeks do after dinner. I'm here to study culture, aren't I?"

"Stop pouting, Sash. We'll be fine. Once you hold it, you'll love it just as much. How could you not want a baby? You held Alexei more than I did."

"And now he's a brat and breaks and hits everything. He's a fucking year old, Tash! *A year old*! This is it! Four. *Four!* That's more than anyone else we know. Real people don't have that many children, only colonists trying to populate planets. There are plenty of people here already. My mother had four, and I know how well she handled that. We must be extra careful from here on in – no more."

She kissed his nose. It was always easier to kiss him when he was sitting down, where she could reach his face. "You're right. It's not like we planned this one."

"We didn't plan any of them, Tash. We need to limit our chances after this. That's four kids in four years of marriage. Do you know where that rate will put us in twenty years? I can't afford a hotel."

Maryana pursed her lips sourly, but she nodded. "It will be almost five years. We've had two under two before, if you'll recall. The girls will be almost four – that's more than old enough to help watch Alexei or fetch things I need. I'll ask the doctor if there's anything else we can try. I'm twenty-one years old; I'm not getting sterilized just yet."

Sasha drained the shot of ouzo and poured a second. The dark eyes glared at her from under his hair, but this time there was a playful gleam in them. "That's the only good side of it, isn't it: six months you can't get pregnant, and six months we don't have to worry about birth control."

Maryana spent the days touring cities and relics and resting by the sea; Ana flew down to spend a week with them. Lying in the Greek sunshine, eating fresh pomegranates and apricots while Moscow froze at Christmas, made life seem especially idyllic. This. This was how life was supposed to be.

Sasha threw himself deeper into his studies, as if he could increase his salary simply by studying harder. In the long run the manic days and lack of sleep paid off; his thesis passed on his first try, and the following August Alexander Kirushenko, twenty-eight years old, received his *Magistr* of Science with highest honors. Maryana beamed and clapped from the second row of the auditorium, dressed like royalty in a stunning Zenaida Ruchman floral tank ensemble, with a net of shimmering beads wrapped over her pinned-up hair. Cherubic baby Viktor slept in her lap; their identical little angels stood on their seats to clap for their papa in identical little outfits and shiny pink gloves, though the gloves were coated in Cosmic Cracker crumbs. On her other side, Ana and Georg amused bouncing Alexei, the center of attention in a miniature suit and a head full of black wavy curls.

Ana and Georg stayed for three days, days that seemed like one long party. At their celebration dinner, Maryana raised her glass of champagne. "To Sasha, the man with the plan!"

"To my baby brother, whose brilliance cannot be contained!" Ana said proudly.

"To the hardest-working fucker I've ever met," Georg added.

Sasha grinned like a little boy on his birthday. "No." His face filled with utter devotion, and his eyes never left Maryana's as he raised his glass. "To Tash, the woman who made the man."

Twenty-four

*H*eat. Maryana hated the Israeli landscape. She couldn't recognize a single plant or tree, the foods were odd, she couldn't read the street signs, but she didn't have much choice. All the handshaking and name dropping had paid off; Alexander Kirushenko, instructor, was requested by name to assist in a year-long excavation outside of Jerusalem that would count as part of his doctoral work, and she would have to live with it. Then maybe they'd get back to Russia.

In the last three years Sasha had outdone himself, gaining an excellent reputation in the field of archaeology. He knew what he talked about, knew the sources he quoted, remembered terabytes of information, and made sound interpretations. He'd published three papers, all of which were well-received. Every summer they traveled somewhere to see a site, or an exhibit, help on a dig, or perhaps so he could give a lecture. Maryana loved to travel, but she didn't necessarily want to live every place she went.

If it were merely a holiday, she'd steer Sasha elsewhere. But his digs – she would never interfere with those. They were too important to him. He returned at night filled with stories of what he'd done and seen and what each thing meant, face so alive with interest that the children caught his enthusiasm, shrieking with delight at every discarded piece of refuse they found in the dirt outside. He was truly happy, out there in the dirt. She had little time to wash him herself anymore; it shamed her to see him that unkempt. His hair had grown long, and he'd grown a thick beard to match; Goliath in the land of David. She liked it. It fit him. Sometimes, when the work had quit for the day, he'd take the older children out to see what had been done, teach them what he knew. She was proud of him, being such a good father to his children, and children seemed to be taking over their lives. Ekaterina followed Viktor almost two years to the day, and the celebration over the Israeli fellowship gave Maryana an unexpected surprise: her next would be an Israeli citizen.

A blow from a rock hammer wouldn't have stunned Sasha as hard. "What? Don't screw with me like that. They've got to be wrong. Tash, we're shoved in here with five children in a five-room rental. There is no room for a sixth. We can't do it. *We have a six-month old baby*! How can you be pregnant?"

"It's not like I planned it! How was I supposed to know I could get pregnant again that fast? I hadn't even cycled."

Sweat beaded on his face, and he began to breathe hard. "You've got to terminate. There's nothing else to do. We can't. We can't, Tash! We just cannot handle another!"

"I can't," she admitted in a small voice. "I already asked. They estimate I'm nineteen weeks or so. They won't do it. I'm so sorry, Sash. I didn't realize!"

Sasha sat down with a thud, his eyes blank, as if someone had dropped a stone on his head and it stuck there. "We'll... squeeze it in somewhere I guess." He retrieved himself a beer, topped it off with a shot of whiskey, and headed to the bedroom to sulk.

The Jerusalem project became his escape, and for many months it helped, even when he had to take children to the site with him. His boys loved to play in the piles of loose sifted dirt, and the twins, at seven, were fascinated by everything he did, from learning to run the scanners to "cleaning" stones for him with picks and brushes. When he came home at night, all he wanted was to rest his body from being bent over the hot ground, or crouched in a trench, even roped to a cliff face examining dust on some newly-mapped section. Sitting in a building doing research made him restless, and painstaking cleaning cramped his muscles even more. At their small rental in Israel, it could be hard just to find a seat for himself. Maryana felt bad he couldn't have the peace he deserved, and forgave him being short-tempered sometimes.

Sasha hauled young Viktor to his feet. The child had been sitting cross-legged in front of the entertainment screen with his brother and sisters, the wide, short legs of his pajama bottoms gaping open to reveal all he had.

"Shame!" Sasha brought his thick hand down hard on the three-year-old's bottom. "Showing your *peretz* to your sisters! Alexei, go put some real pants on him."

Five-year-old Alexei whacked his younger brother hard in the back of the head, doubling the cries. "Now I'm going to miss the best part, stupid!"

As Sasha returned to his chair, he nearly sat on sixteen-month old Katerina trying to climb into it. He gave her a boost and abandoned the recliner.

Maryana had left four-month old Dmitri in his bassinet and tried to slip back to the kitchen unnoticed. Sasha sneaked up from behind and lifted her off the ground, kissing her cheek while she laughed and swung her feet.

"Oof! Easy, Sash! What are you doing?"

He carried her that way to the relative privacy of the little kitchen and sat her on the table, arms around her.

He snuggled his face against her neck, kissing it. She leaned her head back with a sigh, enjoying the attention. It was hard being an adult in such tight quarters.

"Do you have time for *me* tonight?" He nosed her breast, then lifted an inquiring eyebrow when he realized she wore nothing under her light tank. She felt his groin stir against her leg. He nipped her breast through her shirt.

Maryana pushed him back. "Ow! Stop that, Sash. You know that hurts." She looked closely at his face – the shining eyes, the devilish little-boy grin – and she could smell his breath. She petted the sides of his beard. "You've been at the *sabra* again, haven't you."

*They started him drinking when he was thirteen. That's what his group of friends did: stand around places, wishing there was something better to do, drinking to look tough. They **did** look tough, and they **were** tough, hassling the unfortunate passerby. Sometimes they just sat around someplace, talking and drinking. In the summers, outside; in the winters, breaking into closed buildings and invariably pissing in some forgotten back corner or closet where it would take someone a good while to figure out where the stench came from. They pilfered here and there, but they weren't yet into the hard crimes the older gangs were.*

Drinking always seemed to make his mother feel lousy, crying and screaming and throwing up, but it made the young Sasha feel good. A couple of ill-gotten beers and he forgot his shyness, his embarrassment of being too tall and

*too thick and too clumsy and too poor. He belonged. He had
friends. He was fearless. He never drank as much as some,
never passed out, never made himself sick, but he did love
that feeling of happiness, of belonging, of just being one of
the guys.*

*Drinking brought him women, too. A group of equally
tough, equally hopeless young girls hung around them,
pounding back beer as fast as the boys, trading pills and
perpetually fixing the thick makeup that caked their faces in
a vain attempt to look older and less worldly. Partners
traded around the circle like playing cards: Lydia and Igor
this month, Lydia and Venya the next. The sad-eyed girls
didn't care. This was as good as it got for them, too.*

*"I think it's high time Sasha had himself a girl," Igor
said one night when the partying was exceptionally heavy.
The guys pushed him forward, the girls pushed forward one
of their own, and Sasha was forced to meet destiny head on.
Torn between burning adolescent desires and sheer terror
of what was expected of him, it was the four beers they
shared beforehand that gave him the courage to prove
himself a man. He was almost fifteen.*

A dark shadow crossed his features. He grabbed her face much
harder than she held his. "Are you saying I don't work hard enough to
come home and have a drink now and then?"

"Not in the least," she said mildly. She alone knew how hard he
overworked himself in his quest to rise to the top. She put her arms
around his neck and pecked his lips. "Just not in that quantity. There's
beer and wine. Leave the *sabra* for when we have company."

From the other end of the house came the shouts of young boys
and the squalling of a small baby. Maryana dropped her head against
him in defeat. "They woke him up, didn't they?"

Sasha kissed the top of her head. "I have an idea. Don't move. Sit
right here. I'll be back. Don't move!"

"Bed! All of you!" he bellowed at the children.

The house fell into silence. Maryana still perched on the table
when he returned. He poured two glasses of wine, held them in one
hand, and carried her easily on his other arm.

130

He set her down in the bathroom, where he already had the tub filling. Water tax be damned! He locked the door behind them.

"Alexander, are you planning something naughty?" she teased.

Sasha's nostrils flared. He grabbed her by the back of the head. "*I told you never to call me that!* You sound like my mother when you say that."

"I'll bet your mother never did this." She pulled him down by his neck and kissed him deeply.

A shudder racked the large body. "No."

As she had done so many times for him, he bathed her with the utmost care, with the perfumed soaps he loved to smell on her. He ran his hands over her slowly, deliberately, caressing the fair skin with creams to counteract the harsh sun while she melted backwards into him, completely at his mercy. Despite the cold hard tile, she let him have her there on the floor.

Twenty-five

"Mama? The baby's crying," said a girl's voice, while an identical voice finished, "Do you want us to get him for you?"

Maryana's head dropped back onto the sofa pillow. "If you could, girls. That's my helpers. Watch his head; he's heavy." At nine, the twins were quite used to handling babies, even small ones. Ofttimes the two acted as one, coordinating activities and outsmarting younger siblings with a nearly psychic plan. Baby David had been the biggest of all, four fat kilos, a failure of yet another form of birth control, and Maryana hadn't yet recovered from the cesarean. She depended rather heavily on the girls.

"Perhaps it's your turn," she said to Sasha when the subject arose. "I've done everything modern medicine can provide, short of surgery. Sterilization for you is a ten-minute procedure, in and out, and we'll never have to worry anymore."

Sasha gave an irritable sigh and jammed his finger on the switch of his compad. "Don't bother me with that shit right now! Don't I have enough to worry about? Every waking minute I'm not at school I spend building the arguments to defend my thesis; no fun, no games, no doctor appointments, just work. Raksentis in Anthropology was turned down twice; it took five years before they approved his degree. We can't wait that long. I have to be perfect, unquestionable, flawless on the first try if we are to make ends meet. Three exams and a defense are all that stand between us and the final success of ten years' blood and tears. How much difference is there between six and seven? It's the same toys, the same furniture, the same screams coming from the other room. You can't tell the difference. Besides, what if the surgeon sneezes? My parts stop working and that smile of yours is going to disappear like light. We just have to be more careful."

"Ha! Careful is how we got the last five. You may be a respectable educator, sir, but you're an animal in other aspects of your life."

Sasha swept her off her feet with a growl and attacked her neck with kisses. "You bring out the beast in me."

Maryana couldn't stop her smile. "Maybe if you let up on the beer. That's your fifth one tonight."

"So? It's over the whole course of the evening; it's not like I drank them all at once. It relaxes my mind, let's me think. A thousand years ago, even back to the Egyptians, that's all they drank. At my size and weight, I could drink six in a row before they had any bad effect."

Maryana hung her arms around his neck and rubbed noses. "It's not the alcohol, darling, it's the calories. You've gone up two sizes in two years."

Sasha glared at her in jest. "You think I'm fat? Could a fat man do this?" He swung her onto his shoulder, around his neck, then back into his arms, kissing her a dozen times as she squealed and kicked her feet. The kissing and horseplay continued far into the night.

He made an appointment but never kept it, his mind focused unwaveringly on his degree.

The following December, Sasha donned full academic regalia to be honored with a PhD in Archaeology. Maryana waved at him from the audience, three perfectly attired children lined up on each side of her, and chunky sixteen-month old David squirming and jumping on her lap hard enough to bruise her thighs. All that was missing was Ana, caught in the midst of an ugly divorce from Georg and difficult to get in touch with.

In his mailbox the next day was an offer to interview for a position at the Kiev Science Institute, later in January.

Life was good.

By the new year, his mind was rolling again. If one PhD was good, surely two would be better?

"What do you think," he asked. "Think I could do it?"

Pride radiated upward from her smile. "You can do anything you put your mind to, my love. You are brilliant, you always have been, and now the world is starting to admit it."

"It probably means more travel. I can't promise we won't be off world again."

Maryana kissed him. "I would gladly follow you anywhere. My bags are waiting under the bed; just tell me where we're going so I know how to pack. I can have everything ready in three days."

Sasha gave a playful growl and attacked her with kisses. "I love you!"

Kiev! Bright, bold, the first capital of the Russias, a city with a history even older than Moscow's. A first-class metropolitan city with the best Moscow had to offer, and less of the worst. And best of all, Papa had no holdings in Kiev. Maryana loved the city. After two call-back interviews, Alexander Kirushenko, PhD, would begin his professorship at the Science Institute, but the May trip was to scout out living arrangements. For the first time, they were prepared to purchase a home of their own.

They left the children to explore the city in peace. There were few properties in their price range with four bedrooms or more to hold their brood – excitement over the granting of his degree had left Maryana eight months pregnant with number eight. Four hours of cruising the *raions* and neighborhoods left them deeply disillusioned over the quality of the choices.

Near the end of their patience, Sasha took a wrong turn down a side street. As they rounded the corner, it appeared like a starburst, a corona of soft yellow trimmed with white above the curve of the Earth. And it had an availability sign before it.

Maryana grabbed his arm. "Look, Sash! That one! It's even got a yard, with trees!"

Sasha gave a soft snort. "It's the size of a school. I won't go into debt, even for a house."

"No! Sash! Stop. I want to see it. A mortgage isn't regular debt. It establishes credit, it provides collateral, it's a steppingstone to capital wealth. It's not a bad thing."

"I can't afford to carry large debt."

They returned with the sale coordinator. Maryana saw only sparkling visions of glory. "Oh, *Sasha*! Look! It's like being back in Minsk. Six bedrooms! A conservatory – we can get a real piano, not just a keyboard for them to play. Two lavatories and four baths – no more lines! With ten of us in twelve rooms, we can actually spread out. There will be privacy." Her inflection suggested the privacy already had a use.

Sasha played along with her fantasy. He turned to the coordinator. "And they are asking…?"

"Do remember property prices are much higher in this *raion*, and the plot is larger than average. It is fully up to date on power systems, technology, and global environmental regulations," the coordinator said. "The asking price is one million."

Sasha kept a straight face. "Rubles, or credits?"

"That would be interstellar credits."

Sasha nodded and turned away to examine a molding before he could burst out laughing.

Maryana wasn't laughing. She concentrated on the numbers in her head. "Would they take 800,000?"

The coordinator tapped his palmcom. "I'll put in a query."

Sasha pulled her into the empty pantry, where there was no echo. "Tash, what are you doing? We can't afford one floor here, let alone the whole house. I told you."

Maryana met the dark eyes. "Sash, I want this house. I want this house like I haven't wanted anything before. We *need* this house. I think I can do it. You have to trust me. Put down as much as you can. Let me get the rest."

"I can't afford a light fixture here! You are not going to your parents."

Maryana gave him the coldest, darkest look she'd ever given anyone. For an instant, a flash of her mother's features came over her, a fearsome steely look of power that dared not be questioned. She even seemed taller. "How could you even insinuate that! No, but I want it bad enough to liquidate some assets. I'll explain when we get home. Let's get them to the bottom price."

Back in Moscow, Maryana dug into the deepest recesses of the topmost cabinet in their rented home. She withdrew a bio-lock safe-box, opened it, and withdrew a jeweler's box.

She found Raikov's Fine Jewelers from memory. "I would like to see Mr. Raikov himself, please. I would like him to appraise a special piece."

The clerk paged the owner. "May I help you, Miss…?"

"Natasha Kirushenko." She opened the box. "You originally made this for Fyodor Ivanov, about twenty-five years ago. I am updating an insurance policy on it, and need a current statement of value. It's a rhenium-platinum alloy, with thirty-eight point three carats of natural diamond."

The delicate strands of necklace sparkled in a waterfall of shimmer as Raikov lifted it from the box. "I do remember this. It was quite the undertaking. It took me several months to find stones so closely matched."

"Undertaking? It's a registered work of art."

Her next stop was to set up anonymity. That done, she stopped at a public com kiosk and sent a message.

Dear Tomas,

If you are receiving mail, please reply.

She used his priority code, and moments later a live feed responded. She draped her jacket around her shoulders and tucked her belly under the table of the booth to hide it.

"Hello, Tomas."

He seemed genuinely shocked to see her. "M! What a surprise, and it's not my birthday. Where are you?"

She gave him a coy look. "Your tracer's on; you know precisely where I am."

"City of Moscow Communications Outlet 218 isn't exactly precise."

"More than you need. I have a deal for you, Tomas. Under the table and in secret only. I am in town liquidating a specific asset to invest elsewhere. It's a sound move for me. If you or Mamá are interested, I will offer it to you first as a private sale for a fraction of its value. Otherwise, I will put it on the open market for significantly more, but it would attract some rather unwanted attention for both parties involved, if you get my meaning."

"Papa's Dittrick that he still whines about. Or have you sold that already?"

Maryana grew cold. "Tread carefully, Tomas. My financial situation is not yours to speculate on. And no, I still have the Dittrick. I grew up in the same house, Tomas. I know how to play hard and I don't play for kopeks. This is strictly a personal business capital venture. I'm liquidating a specific piece of jewelry. Mamá will know which one. It has appreciated in value and is certified by Raikov at 5.5 million Interstellar. I am willing to offer it at 2.1."

Tomas wagged a finger at the monitor. "You should have stayed in school, baby sister. You've got it all backwards. You're supposed to start high and then accept when they meet your price."

Maryana sighed. She'd sat through every economics class offered in Moscow; she'd just never bothered rounding out her general ed classes to get the degree. Same school, same classes, same background – Tomas was no more than her equal in the game; she had every confidence of that. "It's not about the money, Tomas. Believe it or not, there's more to life than money. It's about not causing trouble and keeping it in the family, no matter what they think of me. Unless you want the publicity. I'm sure I could invest the extra elsewhere. In a rival company, of course. I'm forbidden from making money off the Ivanov Corp and all its subsidiaries, if you'll recall."

He shifted disinterestedly in his chair. "I'll tell Mamá. I'd doubt I can do anything for you. I don't think Lora would like me buying expensive jewelry I have to keep locked away. If it's worth that much Papa will remember it, and if he sees her wearing it he'll know we've been in contact. If he doesn't make me eat it stone by stone, he might choke Mamá with it."

"I'm sure your wife has plenty to choose from. I'm transmitting the name of the broker handling the sale. You have three days to give your intent. Good day, Mr. Ivanov."

Maryana ended the call, pleased enough. Tomas's wife was All-American legs and teeth; the piece wasn't trendy enough for a New York lifestyle, and she wouldn't keep it long. But Mamá had both the capital and the desire to recover the piece without the need to flash it about. Mamá would come through, if for no other reason than it would make Fyodor furious.

Twenty-six

If a house could be a blessing, the yellow house was. Of the older children, only the twins, and Viktor and Dmitri had to share rooms, and the pairings were friendly. Noise levels disappeared, and Maryana found herself relying on the house's intercom to find her children. Outside of needing to keep David off the stairs – he fell three times on the first day – Maryana didn't mind children in a house like this.

As she had gambled, Mamá met her price. The house purchase went through at nine hundred, minus Sasha's contribution of two hundred thousand, meant a million interstellar credits left over to furnish it and invest elsewhere. Sasha couldn't speak.

"That's the way it works, Sash," she explained. "We have taken our investment of gemstones and sold it for profit, which we turned around and invested in real estate. When the market is right, we sell this for another hefty profit, and reap the benefits to invest in another good deal. It's no different than archaeology. If I buy a three-ruble bottle of wine – if you can call that wine – and bury it in a cave for five hundred years, how much will it be worth then? A whole lot more than three rubles. Now, if I could live that long, and sell it myself, for, say, three million rubles, see how much I made on that three-ruble investment? We're doing the same thing, only on a shorter term. Short-term archaeology. You can do that with almost anything, if you know what you're doing and invest wisely. I think I've done quite well for us."

He sat sulky and dark at the long dining table, now sequestered in its own room. "It's not *our* investment, it's *your* investment. I had nothing to do with it. I couldn't have bought it for you in fifty years if I paid one stone at a time."

She turned his face to her. "That necklace became yours the day you married me; it was one half yours, just like everything you owned became one half mine. It was nothing to me. I wore it perhaps three times in my life, a white elephant that was too expensive and too

138

grandiose to wear without attracting the wrong kind of attention. Think of it as my dowry. There is only one piece of jewelry I care about." She flashed her left hand under his nose. "This one, Sash. The best gift I was ever given, and you are attached to that. You paid a full quarter of a house this wonderful from your own pocket, on a teacher's salary with seven children to care for. That is nothing to be ashamed of. You should be very proud."

He made the hike to the kitchen, no longer five paces from the table, and retrieved himself a beer, Maryana consoling her belly as she followed. He drained a few centimeters, opened another cabinet, removed a bottle of whiskey, and topped the beer with it. "Maybe in time. I can't – You don't – I started out with *nothing*, Tash. You know that. You can tell me I own this free and clear, you can tell me I banked a half million credits – interstellar credits, not even rubles – but you can't make it seem real. I'm not ready to patronize arts as financial speculation. I dig up pieces of junk from the ground and ship them to museums, where they are uncrated and set up by shuffling slobs just like me. I can't be both. It's like a dream, and I keep waiting for the moment when I'll wake up."

"It only took twelve years, Sash. Imagine where we'll be twelve years from now. You always had the ability, you just didn't know how to start. You had your education, I had mine, and mine was all about knowing how to start. You did your part, I did mine. That's teamwork. I told you we would get here. If you don't believe in your dreams, they won't come true. Wait. This is just a stepping stone."

She hugged him as best she could. He embraced her with one arm, but his mood didn't change.

Summer arrived, and Maryana hired a *babushka* to help with the children. Her 1 July due-date came and went, much to her surprise. None of her babies had actually made it to date – the twins a month early, three within two weeks of the date, and both cesareans were done in advance to spare the need to rush during labor. By the fifth day, she went for a check. It was a tough situation, changing cities and states and doctors with just three weeks to go. The clinic doctor scanned her, showing a reasonably sized baby of perhaps three kilos, happy and content. All signs said go. Give it another few days.

Maryana felt the first pang at breakfast. "Ooh! I think he may have made up his mind." She tried to finish eating, but a harder pain made her sweat. She pushed her chair back and stood up. "Girls, keep order until Vima gets here."

Sasha had already found his shoes. He practically carried her to the skimmer.

"Ow! I think it's going to be another fast one," she panted.

Maryana's longest labor had been the twins, at nine hours. Her shortest had been Viktor, at just over two. Forty-five minutes into labor, in the lift to the birthing room, Sasha holding her hand, Maryana gave a shriek.

"It's coming!"

The nurse wasn't concerned. "Not yet. Just breathe. We'll be in delivery in just a second."

"This is her eighth baby, I think she knows what she's doing," Sasha growled. "Do something!"

"Now!" Maryana howled. "Ow!"

The nurse took a peek and saw wispy white hair crowning. "Mother Mary of Space! Don't push!" The doors to the lift opened, and the nurse hurled the gurney through the hall, shouting orders. Staff flew to assist. The baby's head emerged as the gurney locked into place in the delivery room.

The birthing team swarmed. A nurse sterilized Sasha's hands. Another saw to Maryana, a third rattled off information from a compad, while the doctor cleared the baby's mouth and awaited the last hurdle.

"Push," the doctor instructed.

"What do you think I'm doing?" Maryana grunted, her fair face dark and shiny with sweat. Sasha, out of place in any medical situation, stood by uselessly, fidgety, sweating, and not a little green above his beard.

The doctor shook his head. "No change. Get me a scan, let's rotate a little. One good push should do it."

The nurse ran a wand over the baby, inside and out. The doctor watched the screen. *"Fuck,"* he said, just above his breath. "Run the measurements again. Get the attending in here."

Maryana gave a shriek, and Sasha panicked. "What's wrong? Why isn't it out?"

The doctor tried to work a finger in around the baby's neck. "He's just a little stuck. Her pelvis let his head through, then snapped back before the shoulder made it out."

Maryana let out a scream, but the baby didn't budge. A nurse administered an anesthetic.

"Do something!" Sasha bellowed. "Push it back and cut it out!"

The doctor watched the progress of his finger on the scanner screen, but the tiny hand on the image remained out of reach. "I wish it were that simple. If I can work an arm out, he should slip right through."

The obstetrics chief arrived on the run. He glanced at the scanner. "Too much time. Cord's not pinched, that's the only thing saving him. Get me an emergency kit. Stay with us, Mama."

"Fundal pressure?"

"Not with two previous C's – she'll rupture." He removed tools from a kit that hadn't been used on his shift in more than ten years.

"Stop playing with those!" Sasha demanded. "Help her! Just pull it out!"

"Papa, your job is turn around and mind her," the chief said. "Keep her calm, keep her focused, let us deal with the baby. Everybody, do your job."

"Do it, Sash," Maryana panted. "It's okay. Look at me. Look here at me. I'm scared. Hold my hands."

"I'm sorry," he mumbled. "I'm sorry my babies are too big."

Maryana smiled weakly, trying to ignore the frantic pulls and tugs on her numbed lower half. "Better too big than not at all. I'm sorry I'm not strong enough."

He chased a bead of sweat from her nose. "You're stronger than I am."

"Here we go," the chief said, and Sasha turned to see a long baby with big feet slide into the world, already screaming. A nurse whisked him away before Sasha had a chance to confirm the sex. Blood coated the end of the bed.

"Mrs. Kirushenko?" the chief said. "We're going to check him over, but I think he'll be fine. I had to break his collarbone to make him fit, but it should heal without any problems. They should have caught that before you went into labor."

"We just moved here," Maryana said. "I've only had two visits."

"That's unfortunate. We're going to take a good look, see what kind of damage he did trying to crawl out. Papa can wait for you in recovery, or stay with the baby."

Maryana patted Sasha's arm. "I'll be fine, Sash. Don't worry. Stay with the baby."

Sasha kissed her in return. "I'll check on him, but I'll be there when you're done."

Maryana stayed in the birth center for four days, recovering. For two days she couldn't walk, her hips strained to their limits from a baby weighing 3.7 kilos and stretching 59 centimeters. Her belly and her underside ached with repairs. She slept most of the time, and let Sasha feed the baby.

Sasha made a face in disgust. "*Anton?* A name like that will get him beat up. Something with a bite. Dragos."

Maryana gave him a playful shove. "I'm not naming a baby Dragos. I prayed to St. Anton to get me through delivery, so Sergei Anton it is."

The doctor conferred with them before she left. "Mrs. Kirushenko, it's my place to discuss these issues with you. You underwent two hours of surgery to repair the damage done by this baby, and two units of hemolyte to replace the blood you hemorrhaged. With your degree of grand multiparity – seven pregnancies, eight babies, six deliveries and two cesarean births, including the trauma of this one, the risk of serious complication in a subsequent pregnancy is rather high, including the possibility of uterine rupture, which will not only kill your baby, but most likely yourself as well. I would strongly urge you to consider family planning measures."

Maryana cooed at the baby sleeping in her arm, jiggled him, then kissed him with an adoring smile. She gave a lighthearted giggle. "We've tried that with the last six. Number three was a ruptured prophylactic. Number four was slow withdrawal. Number five was an IUD. Number six was natural planning. Number seven was my husband's attempt on Freedom, but his sperm count never hit zero. I had insomnia with Norval Estrate, blood clots on Lestren, severe headaches with Novex, and lost too much hair on Metronex. They tried a low dose of Impreban, and I'm holding the result. Everything has failed at some point. My husband has some very determined swimmers."

The doctor failed to see the humor. "Perhaps you should both consider sterilization, then. It's possible you may not be able to carry another pregnancy to term. From here on, any pregnancy should be considered extremely risky."

The words frightened Maryana — just twenty-nine years old — and she was properly contrite. She gazed sadly into Sergei's precious little face, a face framed with white fuzz, not the dark shock of hair the other boys all had. "I will give it serious consideration."

Twenty-seven

Maryana settled into life in Kiev. This was exactly what they'd both worked so blessedly hard to achieve. Sasha had a secure, prestigious job, they had a house to die for, a place for the expensive art, fancy carpets, a full-sized concert piano, a well-rounded investment portfolio, good schools for the children, and hired help for the cleaning and cooking. She stuck rambunctious David in a toddler class for the fall. Sergei was a quiet baby, as content in her arms as in the cartabout while she roamed the parks and streets and shoppes of the city. She took a class in galactic literature. She met with the other professors' wives and volunteered for committees. Sasha was the happiest she'd seen him.

So why wasn't she?

Blues, the doctor told her. It's just a hormone shift from the baby. Sometimes they can last a while.

She'd never had them before; why now? Maryana knew better. She knew why, every time she looked at Sergei. She loved babies. Until they became stubborn and independent, they were the most precious jewels to be had. The innocent stares, the gentle slobbering kisses, the soft breath and floppy bodies as they slept every bit as hard as they played. The cuddle times, the miniature clothes, the soft smell of lotions and the velvety feel of powder on a tiny bum, the strangers that stopped to admire them. Every milestone Sergei passed was another reminder of No More Babies. The last to sit up. The last to crawl. The last to pick up a cracker and gum it into slush. The last little joy as he took his first steps. Soon he, too, would pass off into the crowd, and her arms would be empty. She was turning thirty years old, and her youth and her reproductive years were over.

"You must be thrilled," a wife said at afternoon tea. "Another year or two and no more diapers. What will you do when they're all in school?"

"The same things I do now," Maryana replied with an ungracious touch of irritation. "My children have never interfered with my life."

By his first birthday, Sergei's head had sprouted into a cloud of tow-headed curls. The other boys all had dark brown or black hair; the oldest children had swirly waves, but nothing like his ghostly springs.

"Where did you ever get such curly hair?" she asked him. She stretched several out and let them snap back.

Sasha watched them play, his face flat as stone. "My mother," he grunted, and left the room.

Life was never easier. Six children were in school, one in preschool, and one easy toddler at home. Maryana still could not shake her unrest. Whether she realized the cause, or simply turned her worry onto a cause that didn't exist she didn't know, but after the idea came to her, she became obsessed by it. After a week of hard observation, she shared the concern with Sasha one night.

"Think about it. He's fourteen months old, Sash, and he's never said a word. Not one. Not even mama. They all say mama. They said the twins might be slower to talk, but they were talking by a year. Katya could say Mama by nine months. Viktor was the slow one, and he was eleven months. Serzha's fourteen months and hasn't said a thing. Eight children and I've never looked up anything from experts, but I did today and you know what it said? He's at the upper limits for speech. Sash, what if he's got a problem? What if he had brain damage from his delivery? What if he's deaf?"

Sasha stared as if she'd suddenly grown a second head. "Since when do you worry like this? He's fine! They aren't born knowing some artificial schedule someone wants them to keep. They do everything when they're ready. He can't be deaf; he comes when you call him. Maybe we just don't hear him over everyone else. Swear a lot. That's what they love to say the most." He rolled over and went to sleep without a worry.

Maryana tried her best to stay positive. He *did* come if you called him. He'd wave bye-bye and hand her things on command. That ruled out hearing issues. He understood her fine, some words in Russian and some in English. She talked to him until her voice was scratchy, read him stories until he cried to run, sang songs until he fell asleep.

Nothing.

He cooed happily for the twins, laughed when Sash swung him, babbled to himself while he played, David taught him to stick his tongue out and blow raspberries until the spit dripped off his chin. But no words.

"You're making yourself sick over nothing," Sasha said with annoyance. "If it bothers you that much, take him to a specialist. Take him to the Academy – they run entire departments for child evaluation."

Maryana looked so upset he sat her in his lap for a long hug. "I might. But it's not going to help the 'what if's'."

The holidays passed before Maryana got up the nerve to bring the baby in for evaluation. Several impatient messages from Sasha flashed insistently on her handicom queue before she was able to return the call.

"Well? What did they say?"

"I don't know," she said with a helpless sigh. "Three hours! They put him through every kind of test for three hours. He is eighteen months old, has the motor skills of a twenty-six month old, and if you ask him to point to a picture or hand you an object, he has the vocabulary of a thirty-two-month old. He can draw circles and can even draw a face like a two-year old. All in all, he's one to two years ahead in everything. Except speech."

"So they told you he's fine."

Maryana's sweet forehead pinched in helplessness. "They say it can happen with the youngest in a large family. He has no need to speak, because there's always someone to hand him what he wants. If he's not speaking by his birthday, come back. Otherwise, he's great. I don't know if that's a help or just prolonging my agony."

Sasha regarded her with a raised eyebrow. "Want the advice of a Doctor of Philosophy? Spring registration is open. Take another class. Something you'll have to think hard about. Find a new company to invest in. Then you'll stop worrying. You're going to scare him from ever speaking."

"It's a Science Institute, Sash. Everything's technical."

"There are core classes outside of science. Take a sport, if nothing else. You dance, you play tennis, you swim."

"I'll think about it," she promised. *Urban Planning for the Galactic City* wasn't her first choice, but it did keep her mind focused on other things through the winter and into the spring, until bigger worries took over.

For her thirty-first birthday, Sasha brought her an armload of roses and a bracelet set with pink diamonds and glittering Denebolan lava pearls. The thought – and expense – of the gift floored her. Maryana added up the projected cost in her head and tried to figure out where she could pull five weeks' salary out of their budget; decimal places fell off the numbers in her reserve account. They left the children in charge of themselves – the twins were nearing thirteen and quite capable – and he took her to dinner at an exclusive restaurant he'd booked two months in advance.

Maryana looked radiant in fuchsia and white, with gleaming new Fujio Kasaki slings, the bracelet sending shimmers of artificial candlelight rocketing onto the ceiling as she sipped from her water glass.

"And a bottle of your finest red with that," Sasha ordered.

"None for me," Maryana said.

Sasha waved the waiter on. "I'll finish it. What's the matter? You always like red with dinner."

"I do, I just…" Maryana turned her head, but not before he caught sight of the tears.

Nothing could upset Sasha faster than seeing her cry. He grabbed her hand. "What? You don't like this restaurant? The children acting up? Alexei and his mouth? Or did David break something else?"

She sniffed and dabbed her face with her napkin. "I'm sorry. I'm so sorry, Sash. Everything here is splendid. You are incredibly thoughtful. I'm just scared."

"Of what? What's happened?"

"I've felt lousy the last few weeks, and just on the chance, I took a pregnancy test today. I failed it."

Sasha sighed in defeat. "I thought they said you couldn't?"

"They weren't sure, remember? They said it would be dangerous. I never got around to getting sterilized, so it's my fault. I don't want to die." She dabbed her eyes again.

"It's half my fault," Sasha grumbled. "Perhaps this time we should terminate. For your sake."

"I've been over that idea already. It may have been back in February, when I gave you the tickets to the Valentine's basketball game. Their win was our loss, I guess. I'm figuring early December."

Sasha shrugged. "Two and a half years. I think that's our record. We'll make do. Everyone will have to help. You rest, make sure they know you're not having another natural birth, and they can take the parts then. You'll be fine. Where's your smile?"

Maryana brightened for him. "I mean it Sash. This is the last one."

If the discovery of her situation sent her into despair, the following day gave Maryana a birthday present she desperately needed, one that sent her spirits soaring for weeks to come.

Answer, answer, answer, flashed through her head as she waited for Sasha to answer the 'com in his office. "Guess what!" she gushed as soon as he connected. "Guess what! He spoke! Sergei spoke! Twenty-two months old and he finally spoke his first word!"

"About fucking time. What was it?"

"I took him to Victory Park, because the weather was so nice and they have that little playground by the pond? And I gave him one of those oat cookies he likes, and then I started talking with one of the other mothers there. He kept saying 'oooh, oooh,' just babbling to himself like he does, you know? And suddenly he just shrieks out, 'Mama, oo'ka! Oo'ka!' and I looked, and a duck had come up and was eating the cookie in his hand! How strange is that? His first word was *ootka*! Almost two years old, never said a word, and suddenly he spits out an entire sentence."

"Well, now we know he likes ducks. He was just waiting until he had something worth saying. Maybe he didn't want to look stupid in front of the others. Now you can relax and stop trying to overcompensate."

Maryana gave a soft laugh. "It's such a relief."

"You worry too much. Throw him in the pack and let him run. He'll catch up soon enough."

"Must you always be right?"

"For you? Always."

Maryana's laughter bubbled over. "I love you, Sash."

Fourteen years of marriage, and he still blushed like a shy schoolboy. "I love you, too, Tash."

Maryana weighed forty-four kilos when she met Sasha. Bloated with the twins, she weighed a massive fifty-eight. With sticking Sergei, she'd weighed fifty-two and a half. Now, at forty-eight kilos, she knew this one had to stay small. Nature seemed to be her ally, for never had morning sickness hit so hard and stayed so long. Too many nights Sasha found himself the only adult at the dinner table; he learned fast to feed the youngest ones early, and sat down to eat peacefully with the oldest. Sergei was content with a child's scribble board, or listening to a story while Maryana lounged on the oversized sofa. If she felt better, she'd settle him in the cartabout and they'd walk several kilometers, burning up any calories she did consume. Dreading the lecture she'd suffer, she waited until late summer to see a doctor. It wasn't as if she didn't know what to do.

"Mrs. Kirushenko, you've gained exactly one kilo in two months," the doctor told her in October. "That's a little low for thirty-two weeks. Try to fit in a few extra snacks – fruit, yogurt, protein if you can. The baby is still rather small."

"I've had small ones before, too," she reminded her. "Half were less than three kilos. Perhaps the dates are off."

"Perhaps," the doctor said, but she didn't sound convinced.

By her 2 December due date, Maryana had gained less than four kilos. But, like Sergei, her date came and went. A week, and no baby.

"No, you don't understand," Maryana said in a sweat. "I want it out *now*. Today. No more emergencies."

"Every indicator is the baby's fine," the doctor said. "I assure you, he's still quite small, so I'm betting our dates are off. We'll set you up with a home monitor; turn it on four times a day and send us a feed. That way we can all rest easy. If you can manage, try sex. Sometimes that shakes them loose."

Doctor's orders were doctor's orders. She and Sash made up for lost time.

Two weeks, and no baby.

"He's turned," the doctor said. "He's thinking about it. He's just afraid to do it. Shouldn't be much longer."

With Christmas just two days away, Maryana felt a pain. Not a big one, but after a while she felt another. She made sure the presents were where Sasha could find them, made sure the *babushka* had a checklist of names and faces to avoid trouble, and waited, nerves on edge. No two deliveries were ever alike, and as the hours wore on, her nerves faded with them. After eight boring hours, the baby slid out as easy as a fish through water, not even two kilos in size.

"Put that back, it's not finished," Sasha kidded her happily. "Are you sure that's mine?" He took off his shoe and held it up; the baby almost fit in it.

Maryana hugged the baby close. Baby Vladimir was tiny, her smallest, with miniscule fingers and miniature feet and a nose the size of his mother's fingerprint. "Not all of them are going to look like you. This one is a throwback to my side, that's all. He reminds me of Dmitri when he was born. The doctor said he's perfect. I promise, Sash. Six weeks from now, I'm getting sterilized."

"Absolutely," Sasha agreed.

Maryana's brood ranged in age from birth to thirteen; after eight successful babies, she knew right from wrong. And this baby was not right.

"Nothing. Whatever goes down comes right back up. He doesn't sleep more than an hour or two. He's all jumpy; I spoke to him the other day and he nearly startled right off the bed."

The pediatrician checked him over. "His nervous system's still developing, that's all. You have a busy house with lots of noise. Give him time. Babies always seem to spit up more than they take in. He's gained a hundred grams, so he's getting some of it. He's a little guy, he's got a little belly. Feed him small amounts and burp him well, even before a feeding, if it helps. As he gets bigger, things will get better. Try swaddling him at night; get one of those heartbeat toys so he'll think he's not alone. It will help him sleep, and sleep is when they grow."

Maryana wasn't convinced. The baby was ravenous; stopping to burp him made him cry until he spit up. Longer feedings settled him, but half came back on the first burp. Overcome with worry and exhaustion, scheduling a surgery was the last thing on her mind.

"He's not gaining enough. Perhaps he has an allergy to the formula," the doctor said. "Let's try something different."

After three months, Maryana, Sasha, and the twins were exhausted, passing the baby and bottle around in shifts. Hourly feedings had managed to produce a growth of barely a kilo since birth. Maryana's stomach twisted into knots until she felt as sick as the baby. The pediatrician changed tactics. "How are you holding up at home, Mrs. Kirushenko? Do you have enough help? Perhaps another baby is too much right now. Our social worker can have someone come in to give you a break, perhaps get you some help around the house so you have more time to spend with the baby. I'm concerned with his failure to thrive."

Maryana struggled to pull air into her lungs. She straightened herself up as tall and imposing as possible. Her words came out clipped and icy, all authority without a trace of charm. Mamá would have been proud. "I beg your pardon. I believe I misunderstood. I thought I heard you say you were ordering a complete scan and workup to make sure he's okay, as I've been asking now for two months, because that's the first thing my lawyer will ask when he serves you with papers."

Irritation crept over the pediatrician's face, and he scribbled the order into his compad with a vengeance. "Fine. If it will make you happy you may go over to the imaging room and they can run a full scan on him. When he's done, you will then speak with social services voluntarily, or I will file a concern and it will become involuntary."

Maryana clutched tiny Vladimir to her chest and stood up. "Do not threaten me, sir. I'm not the one who isn't concerned. And when something is found, be assured, I will file a concern over your lack of competence." She stormed off to the imaging room.

Sasha cancelled his afternoon class and flew home at Maryana's hysterical call, to find her holding the baby and crying her heart out while Sergei played with a scribble tablet on the bed next to her. He held it up to show his father three spidery lines.

"K for K'enko!" he said proudly.

"Good," Sasha said, but his attention was on Maryana. "What did they say?"

She related the threats. "I was right! I was right all along. His stomach is kinked at the bottom. I bring him back tomorrow for tests, and in two days he has to have surgery so the food can drain out better. He's so weak and tiny, and they're going to cut him open!"

Sasha pulled her onto his lap, baby and all, rocking them. "He'll be all better afterward. You'll see. He'll probably become the fattest one."

"What if he's not? It's all my fault," she confessed. "I deliberately starved him when I was pregnant. I didn't want another big baby."

Sasha paused. "That's stupid, Tash. He grew that way on his own; you can't cause it by not eating. No more than if you didn't use your arm, he'd be born without one. I'm not a biologist, but I know that much."

Maryana didn't leave the baby's side while he was in the hospital. At home she held him constantly, afraid to put him down or even let the girls handle him. His little stomach was so used to rejecting food it had become almost reflex, but more food stayed down now than came up, and he gained five hundred grams before leaving the hospital. Five months old, he finally had the strength to roll himself over, and could sleep long enough for her to catch a nap. She found a different pediatrician. Life settled back down. After Sergei's tough birth and Vladimir's tough start, Maryana was done. Her heart couldn't handle another crisis like this. Enough was enough. It was time to fix her reproductive problem.

Twenty-eight

She walked into the clinic with confidence. Maryana'd come to terms with not needing any more babies. No more spit, no more cries, no more nightmares, no more interruptions during dinner parties. No more milestones, no more runny diapers, no more fencing across the staircase ruining the ambience of her lovely foyer. Nine was more than fine. An appointment to meet with the surgeon and take care of the preliminaries, a date set, and she would be free. She was thirty-two years old, and it was time.

"I certainly won't counsel you against it," the surgeon joked. "I think you've done your part for motherhood. In the old days, they'd have awarded you a medal. Hop up here, I'll see how everything looks. You've had some sections and a significant reconstruction. I want to make sure there are no adhesions where I'm headed."

Maryana chattered away as the doctor pressed around her belly and watched her scanner. It took her a moment to realize the doctor had stopped answering.

"How many pregnancies have you had?"

"Eight pregnancies, nine children."

"When was your last cycle?"

Maryana laughed. "I couldn't tell you. Everything's been so hectic, I haven't paid attention. They've never been that regular anyway. Why? Is something wrong?"

The doctor frowned. "I'm not sure. Hold on." She fiddled with the scanner, then turned the display. "I can see if they still award medals, but I can't do the surgery."

"What do you mean?"

"See this? It's a heartbeat. By the size, I'd estimate you're about fourteen weeks, give or take."

Maryana stared in shock. "That can't be! My youngest is twenty-seven weeks old."

"A scan is proof positive. It's in there, and it looks like it's pretty happy."

Maryana left the clinic numb.

"Madam Kirushenko is in the bedroom," the housekeeper informed Sasha when he arrived home. "She's dreadfully upset about something."

Sasha paled. "The baby? Is the baby okay?"

"Miss Valeria and Miss Galina have him in the playroom. Madam didn't discuss it with me."

Sasha tore into the bedroom and seized her in his arms.

It took a moment of gasping before Maryana could sputter, "They won't operate. I'm pregnant!"

"How the hell did that happen? It's not like we've had energy to do much of anything."

"It only takes once," Maryana reminded him. "Oh Sash! What will we do! Vladya's so tiny and weak; he needs me so much, and he'll hardly be a year old when this one's born! What if he's still having problems? How will I manage?"

Sash gave her a knowing look from under the wave of hair that covered his eyes. He bent until they touched foreheads. "We have twins – two the same age; how did we manage those? We've had two less than a year apart before, Katya and … D'Misha," he remembered. "How did we manage then? We had four sick all at once with Vegasian flu *and* a small baby. David will be in kindergarten by then; put Sergei in a nursery class. You have a woman three days a week to clean. How much easier can it be? Like we'd ever notice."

Maryana took a deep breath and gave him a kiss. "That's my Sash. Always right."

One of the wives pulled her aside at the archaeology department exhibition. "Tasha, that's not another bump under your blouse? Don't you still have a tiny one? When are you going to tell him to knock it off and leave you alone? Is he trying to populate his own country? Let me give you the name of my doctor. She knows all about family planning. He doesn't even need to know."

Maryana blinked, unable to respond fast enough. Long ago at Villovsky, the final exam in etiquette seemed impossible, given a series of difficult social situations and being graded on performance.

In reality, the exam wasn't nearly harsh enough. Never did it touch on situations such as this.

"I appreciate your concern, but I would thank you to not speculate on my health or marital situation," she said stiffly. "I don't recall asking you to assist me in raising my family, nor have you ever volunteered to help. Such matters are between me and my husband." She found Sasha, and left as soon as possible.

Vladimir would be a year old on 23 December; the baby was due 5 January. If it held off a little, it could even share Sasha's 10 January birthday. Maryana entered her sixth month with confidence. Vlad had finally doubled his weight and now slept as much as three hours at a clip. Her last scan showed the new baby growing steadily, with all organs on target. Over the years, various doctors had preferred she and Sasha refrain from marital relations until eight and a half months, due to the size disparity between them. With her tendency to have her babies early, and some of them very fast, the doctors wanted to get the babies to maturity with as little stress as possible. Overall, Maryana had been cooperative with the decree, but Sasha would get cranky after a few weeks and distract himself with shots of vodka. Now and then they'd sneak a little fun, as cautiously as possible. True, Katerina had been born within two days of such a time, but that was past the waiting point, so it didn't count, and it apparently had no effect on Vladimir – not for lack of effort. Thus, Maryana wasn't overly concerned when Sasha got frisky.

He kissed her bare knee, then an inch above it, then an inch above that. He blew air up her thigh, puffing out the hem of her nightshirt. "Come on. It's been three weeks. I know you want to."

Maryana could barely breathe amidst her laughter. "Stop it!" she gasped, squirming under the beard tickling her knee. She tried to push the big paw off her hip. "Six more weeks. Come on, Sash! You know what the doctors said. Stop! You're too big. It could hurt the baby. You know better. Stop!"

"I've never heard you complain about my size."

She hit him over the head with a pillow. "You know what I mean. You outweigh me by more than a hundred kilos, you Betelgeusian bull! You're taller, and wider, and heavier, and stronger. They've never asked about the other."

He slid up the bed next to her, rubbing his body the length of hers. "Just this once? I'm *dying* for you, Tash! I don't want to wait. I want the *whole thing*," he whispered, and left a trail of burning kisses down the side of her neck. He pulled aside the neckline of her nightwear and continued his trail. "You know it's better when you're pregnant. We've been careful before. It's not like we don't know what we're doing."

Maryana closed her eyes, body responding to his deliberate caresses. "*No*, Sash!" she groaned. "Six weeks. Just six more weeks." Her resolve slipped as his tongue burned a path down her aching breasts. "Stop?"

He found her hungry mouth with his. "Have I ever hurt you?"

"*No*," she admitted breathlessly. He knew just how to make her crazy with desire. *"No, Sash!"*, not only not resisting, but guiding him. Pregnancy hormones surged, throbbing with a fire he could quench, but she couldn't let him. She wasn't supposed to do that... He could hurt her without meaning to... but she was being consumed by fire!... Six more weeks... but if she didn't she would scream!

"*Okay!*" she panted. "Okay! But I mean it, Sash! We have to ... be careful. You ... You have to ... control yourself."

They *were* slow, and they *were* careful, so honestly determined to keep control, a release so long overdue. Lying together afterward, Maryana grasped his beard and shook his chin.

"You! You always do this to me!"

Sasha replied with his impish half-smile. "What? That wasn't enough for you?"

"Once is never enough for me," she teased. "I want you over and over and over." And the game began again.

Not as desperate the second time around, they were slower, more passionate, more tender, but in the end Sasha grabbed her helplessly for one solitary deep thrust. Still entwined, Maryana felt something that didn't feel quite *right*, a trickling wetness of a quantity too great for what they'd just done.

She squirmed underneath him. "Sash? Sash, get up! Something's wrong – " His face clouded with concern and he rolled back. Maryana pushed herself upwards. The trickle became a gush. Her husband's face was as white as her own.

"My water broke!" She glanced up in fear, one hand on her belly as the first familiar cramp began.

Maryana didn't dare sit up, let alone stand. She was twenty-four weeks pregnant, give or take. Sasha threw his clothes on so fast he tore a sleeve. Down the hall, Vladimir began to wail. Sasha sprinted to the nursery and grabbed him. He bounded into the twins' room.

"Here!" he ordered, dropping Vlad on Galina as she sat up. "Something's happening to your mother; I'm taking her to the hospital. You're in charge until we get back."

The twins trailed him to his room with the baby. "Mother?" Val asked in a frightened voice, and Galina finished, "Are you okay?"

Sasha ran around in a frenzy, stuffing random clothes into a travelbag. "I'm fine. The baby's trying to come now," Maryana explained. "Don't forget, feed Vladya slowly or he'll spit up." Sasha carried her down the stairs to his speeder.

An hour. The drugs they gave her to stop the labor held for an hour, and the pains started again. More drugs. More waiting. Maryana lay motionless on the biobed, tilted head down, resting. Sasha sat in a chair next to her, but neither could bear to look at the other, too ashamed to speak. It was bad enough to admit to the physician what had probably caused it; they couldn't hide the evidence.

Sasha rested his head in his oversized hands. "It's my fault. I never should have suggested it. I'm sorry, Tash. I can't control myself around you. I never could."

Maryana reached out to rub his arm. "No, no! It's my fault. I'm such a pushover. I can never say no to you. I love you, Sash."

He buried his face next to her in the biobed, causing the monitors to squawk at the double inputs; she stroked his head, smoothing the black waves. "I love you, Tash."

Three hours had passed when a sharp pain tore up her middle. A monitor gave a warning chirp. "I killed it!" she cried. "I killed my baby for my own pleasure."

Sasha held her hand. "Why can't you stop it?" he begged the doctor. "There has to be something. This is a top-rated maternity center; do something!"

"We're trying everything we can," the doctor insisted.

More drugs, again it stopped, but the medical team stepped outside the room and whispered among themselves.

Maryana, filled with a half-dozen medications, had managed to doze around sunup, Sasha asleep in a chair next to her, when a piercing alarm jolted them awake. Medical personnel flew in, crowding a fearful Sasha out of her reach. Incomprehensible displays were watched, scans lit up the portable monitors, more drugs were tried, but the level of urgency didn't diminish. Equipment rolled into the room. The baby was in distress; ready or not, it had to come out. Maryana wept, heartbroken, as she was prepped for an emergency cæsarean, while two large orderlies escorted a dumbfounded Sasha out of the room.

Sasha sat on the hospital bed, Maryana's head resting in his lap. Once in a while they'd speak, hopeful one moment, realistic the next, but mostly they were silent. Vladimir had been the smallest of all their brood, able to nap in just one of his father's huge hands. This baby, though – this baby made Vlad look like a monster. Six hundred seventy grams and thirty-two microscopic centimeters long. Half the size of tiny Vlad. Less than a quarter the size of bruiser David. Smaller than the piece of meat Sasha'd had for dinner the night before.

"We should go see it," Maryana said softly. "While it's still alive."

"It's better you don't." Sasha'd been to the critical care floor at the urging of a nurse. The sight of a hand smaller than his thumbnail sent him running to vomit. "You'll get attached, and it will only hurt more."

"It would have been nice, a little girl, after four boys in a row. I would have finished the family in ribbons and lace. Take me there, Sash."

They cried together. The dates must have been wrong, for the baby seemed younger than expected. Veins the size of hairs pulsed through transparent skin glistening in the prenatal tank, a liquid environment that protected it. The bulging eyes were closed but covered by gel pads anyway. When ready, the eyes could open but little light would reach them, just as if in the womb. Thread-like tubes sprouted from the stump of umbilical cord, and sensors seemed to be connected to every exposed area. Every five minutes a blue light fanned through the liquid incubation chamber and the resulting body scan would appear on a screen to the side. Blue lights flashed, red and yellow lights blinked, green lines crawled in waves across screens, orange level indicators bobbed up and down to the beeps and hums and chirps and sighs of the monitors. The worst thing, the very worst, was the respirator threaded through the tiny mouth, circulating the oxygen-rich suspension fluid through lungs that were too immature to breathe dry air. In fact, the baby had never taken a single breath on its own. If it weren't for the respirator, it would be dead.

* * *

Galina shook her sister awake. "Val! Someone's downstairs!" Cabinets banged and glassware clinked.

"Probably Alexei sneaking beer out of the cooler. He's such a toad." Val grabbed a tennis racquet, just in case. Galina found a pair of scissors. Together they tiptoed out of the room. All the lights had been out when they'd last fed Vladimir three hours ago, but it was now two in the morning and a faint glow came up the stairs.

"You go first."

"No, you."

"You're older!"

Val gave her twin a sour look. "Four minutes doesn't count." They circled around the long way to get a better view. They didn't expect what they found in the kitchen.

Father sat at the table, face down on his crossed arms, a bottle of Tauran whiskey in front of him. He made strange little barking noises. The twins glanced at each other, uncertain what to do. They hadn't heard a word from their parents in two days.

Valeria stepped into the room. "Father?"

He sat up quickly, sniffing. "Why are you up?" he demanded. He tried to wipe his face without looking obvious. "Go to bed. It's late."

"We thought one of the boys was up," Galina explained. "Is Mother okay?"

Sasha gulped from the glass before him, then nodded as the twins took seats on either side. "Well enough. She might be home tomorrow. If not, the next day."

Valeria hesitated. "Does she still have the baby?"

Sasha moved his head slowly side to side and drained his glass. He poured another. "It was a girl," he said at last. "But it's too small. It can't breathe on its own. It won't live long." He covered a sob with a cough.

"Oh, Father!" They were three girls against six brothers; a baby girl would have been nice. "I'm so sorry!" They leaned in together, hugging him from both sides. "Take care of Mother. We can hold things together a little longer. Maybe we could ask the ladies at the church to pray for her."

159

He put an arm around each of them in return. "It couldn't hurt."

* * *

For the first time, Maryana left a birthing center empty-handed. No baby, no blankets, no bottles or diapers or the sweet smell of expensive lotion, no congratulations; nothing. The evicted fetus didn't even look like a baby, with no hair, no chubby cheeks, no fingernails yet. She carried Vladimir around everywhere, curled against her belly. He was nine months old, and had just learned to sit up. She returned to the hospital the following day, as she would every day, hovering over a fish tank baby that hadn't died yet. She focused only on her vigil, praying guilty novenas that the baby would live. After a week, Maryana felt a name was the least they could give it for its short life.

"She's got to have a name, Sash," she said mournfully. "Even if it's just for a memorial, there has to be a name. The church won't recognize her without a name." Sash would never agree to Andrea-Marie, even if there was a chance it would make Mamá angry. Come to think of it, in fifteen years of marriage Maryana wasn't sure she'd ever heard Sasha mention his mother by name.

"What was your mother's name?"

Sasha flashed her a murderous glare. "I would never name a child after my mother, even a dead one."

"I didn't suggest it. I was just curious."

The petulant scowl didn't fade, as if fighting the request. The voice softened, but it couldn't disguise the shame that clung to the words as they formed in the air. "Kiranta. She went by Kiki."

Nothing with K. Nothing with K. "Sarah," Maryana said at last, the same moment as Sasha said, "Irina."

Maryana played with it. "Sar'ina. I like that. Sar'ina. The serene one, who never gave a cry."

Sasha agreed with a nod, as somber as if they'd just agreed on a tombstone.

Baby Sarah was a fighter. One week, two weeks, and still she kicked inside the Liquigen tank, Maryana at her side eight or more hours a day. Four other babies in the special care nursery died, but at three weeks, Sarah had gained more than seven hundred grams – what Vlad had gained in twice that. Sasha could not bear to visit the baby or even click onto the private camera that offered around-the-clock

160

monitoring, haunted by guilt and memories, but he listened to Maryana's daily report.

Some days were good, others she cried inconsolably. "The little boy next to her, Tosya, is going home next week. Oh, Sash! He looks awful! He's thirteen weeks and he's like a dying old man, with a huge head and droopy eyes and see-through skin, and he's fed through a tube, he can't even nurse. Sash! I don't want a baby that ugly! It's not a baby, it's a monster!"

Sasha held her tightly, his imagination filled with ever-worsening images. "Shh. Our baby won't look that way, I promise. That baby didn't have you for its mother. You said his brain bled when he was born, right? Well, ours hasn't. Okay? Just remember that. One day at a time, just like you said. She's made it four weeks longer than we ever expected, no? Give her time." But when Maryana went upstairs to check on Vladimir, he chased the images from his head with a shot of spine-strengthening vodka.

Sarah's brain didn't bleed and her kidneys stayed strong. Her eyes began to open. At eight weeks, she was removed from the Liquigen incubator and took her first breaths of real air. Five days later, she was back on a respirator, her fragile lungs assaulted by bacteria from the air. Maryana prayed by her side, prayed in her church, paid for prayers to be prayed when she couldn't be there, sent the older children in to light candles and say prayers, and millimeter by millimeter, the baby pulled through. She dragged Sasha in at last; his daughter looked like a bald baby, not an old man, and the funeral in his head was replaced by a miniature but living baby.

Maryana had been able to hold and feed Sarah for a week when the baby made a face and turned blue. Monitors beeped shrilly and Maryana screamed, upsetting several infants in the nursery. The nurses took over. Unable to coordinate swallowing and breathing, the baby had inhaled formula. A second wave of pneumonia followed. Maryana held her breath, sometimes hour to hour, but again the baby pulled through.

Sasha wrote it off as modern scientific medical care; Maryana took it as Christmas miracle in answer to her prayers: Sarah came home the day before Vlad's first birthday, two kilos strong, with pinchable cheeks and perfect little fingers, a baby with so many instructions a nurse made a visit the same day to go over everything again.

Maryana stuck printouts of the more basic instructions on the wall above the bassinette. She watched the baby sleep, unable to tear herself a room away, even with a sound monitor strapped to her wrist. She moved the baby to the cartabout and wheeled her room to room with her. "We can't do this, Sash. Something will happen. She's too fragile. Someone will hurt her. I'll never sleep."

Sasha didn't look any more confident. "We've managed to keep nine of them healthy. She's made it this far. One day at a time."

Vitamins. Supplements. Immune boosters. Don't take her out in the cold. Keep her warm. Keep her from germy siblings. The instructions ran on and on. Despite her experience, Maryana called the care nurse almost daily. The baby wore a harness that monitored her breathing, and would for an entire year. Maryana watched the blinking lights obsessively: peaceful green, a yellow lengthy pause, or the red that indicated not enough oxygen and triggered an alarm that could wake the dead. In February her fears were realized when the alarm went off in the night, shaking the house. Vladimir screeched down the hall, Maryana shrieked, the baby startled and took a breath before crying, and six children came running from bed to check their sibling. Sarah struggled for a week in the hospital, pneumonia clogging her lungs, before coming home again. Maryana added respiratory therapy treatments to her knowledge of infants.

Babies took over Maryana's life. She wouldn't let anyone handle Sarah but Sasha or herself, yet runty little Vladimir, now creeping, needed her just as much. She fell into bed each night exhausted, her sleep disrupted by incubator nightmares and the strain of listening for alarms or Vlad's cries. Neither she nor Sasha looked at each other when they slid into bed at night. On Valentine's Day his hand crept to explore her breast, but it slid down a moment later merely to hold her close.

Guilt was the strongest form of birth control.

Twenty-nine

2255

It was quite by accident they made the discovery. Maryana went to check on baby Sarah, sleeping in the living room bassinette, when she found Vladimir, also tiny but double the size, sleeping next her.

"Who did this!" she shrieked, snatching the smaller infant from potential danger. "Why is he here?"

Ten-year old Viktor confessed. "I did it."

"Are you trying to kill her? What if he rolled over and suffocated her?"

Viktor shrugged. "The monitor would have gone off. I didn't think it would matter if they were both asleep."

Maryana's tongue loaded with a bitter punishment, then stopped. The babies had been asleep more than three hours, the longest nap Vlad had ever taken. He still woke up at least twice a night. Viktor was right about the monitor.

Her anger fell. "Next time, tell me." She plucked up her nerve, and after Vlad was in bed for the night, she tucked baby Sarah next to him and tiptoed out, ears straining for the sound of an alarm that never came. Sarah woke up once to be fed; Vladimir slept nine straight hours, the first time in fifteen months. From that day on, Maryana treated them as twins.

* * *

Twins for size, twins for age, but not twins in abilities. Maryana reheated the dinner the housekeeper had prepared earlier, while the girls ran back and forth to the dining room. Sasha sat in the kitchen with his after-work beer, watching the news headlines on the wallscreen. From the cuddleseat in the corner, the baby began to fuss.

Sasha turned an eye to the room, but everyone remained busy. He gave an annoyed sigh. "If you get me a bottle, I'll feed her."

Maryana retrieved a bowl from the heater, spun fast, and knocked one of Vladimir's toys across the floor. "She can't be hungry; I just fed her a half hour ago."

Sasha retrieved baby Sarah anyway. He swooped her up over his head, blew on her belly, and swooped her up again, dodging drool as she coughed and giggled. The breathing monitor on her harness turned yellow with the sudden motion, then back to green. "What are you whining about? No whining."

He crossed his legs as he sat and settled the baby in the crook of his knee. "You want a bottle? You want this one?" He tipped his beer toward the baby; Sarah grimaced and turned her head. "You can't have this one. Girls shouldn't drink beer. Listen to your Papa."

"Ba. Ba pa ba ba." Sarah waved her arms at him as if pleading her case.

"So you say."

"Pa pa ba, pa ba pa pa."

Eight-year old Katya ran over. "She talked! She said Papa! Did you hear her?" She clapped the baby's hands and rubbed her cheek, cooing.

"Babies make lots of sounds. It won't mean anything for a long while yet."

The fuzzy white-blonde head turned back to the kitchen, kicking and fussing.

"Now what?"

"She can't see Vlad," Katya said. "She likes him. Don't you, sweetie."

"She can't see that far," Sasha said. "She's seven months, minus four months early, means we have to think of her as three or four months old. Four month old babies can't see that far."

"Yes she can. Watch." Katya hefted the baby and placed her gently on the floor.

"Get a cloth under her!" Galina screeched, a fourteen-year old expert in babies. "You want her to get dirt in her mouth and get sick?" Valeria whisked a cloth under the baby almost without breaking stride.

Katya retrieved Vlad from where he stood holding onto a chair, and sat him in front of the baby. Tiny Vlad – no bigger than an eight-month old himself – poked a finger into the baby's cheek; Sarah wedged herself onto her elbows and gave a happy coo. "That's it, Vladya. Play nice with Sar'ina."

"Bay-by," Vlad agreed.

"That doesn't mean she can see him from back here," Sasha insisted.

Vlad turned and crawled across the room. Sarah's face grew dark and she let out an angry wail. Katya pulled him back; Sarah gave a squeal of delight.

"See? She likes him."

Sasha watched with amusement. "She's a baby. Any face will do. It doesn't matter."

Vlad pulled himself up with the table leg, caught his balance, and toddled stiffly across the room to the cabinets.

Baby Sarah arched her back, fists flailing, feet kicking air as if conducting it. The cry became a shriek.

"She's trying to crawl after him," Valeria said with a grin.

"Too cute!" Galina said.

"Ba pa, va!" Sarah complained. "Va. Va? Va.

"Va?" Then, in an angry shriek, "VAT!"

Valeria's grin became a frown. "I don't care what you say. She's calling him." "She's calling him," Galina said at the same time.

Katya turned to Sasha for confirmation.

"VAT!"

Maryana picked up the baby. "Bring him here." Galina brought Vlad over. "Sarah, who is this? Is this Vladimir? Is this your brother? Can you say 'Vladya'?"

The harness flashed a momentary yellow as Sarah gave a gooey cough. She stretched out an arm and whapped her brother down his face, ending up with a fistful of his shirt. "Vat!" How dare he crawl away without her.

"Bah! Nonsense." Sasha's eyes returned to the wallscreen. He took a swallow of beer and belched. "Random noises, that's all. Ask me again in six months."

Maryana eyed the baby warily. "In six months, she might tell you herself."

Indeed, Sarah seemed to live for catching up to Vladimir, and he was willing to wait. When she managed to creep at nine months, Vlad reverted to crawling alongside her. By ten months, she had a fifteen-word vocabulary to his twenty. When the experts said they shouldn't expect her to walk until at least fifteen months, Sarah tore down the milestone one day before her first birthday. In the process of potty-training Vladimir, Maryana found him hopeless but Sarah completely trained by eighteen months. The pediatrician praised Maryana for Sarah's rapid gains, assuming it was from intensive care, but Maryana knew her only role was putting her two babies together. Her little girl burned with a determination all her own. How much so would leave Maryana stunned.

The big house was silent, no blasts of repetitive rhyming songs, no crashing of block towers, no screech of racing pods, not even the cough Sarah got when she ran around too much. When not crying, Vlad wasn't a noisy child, and without the older children to wind her up, Sarah could keep herself busy for hours, but instinct whispered *check*. Maryana tiptoed to the playroom and peeked in the door, expecting to see them napping. Instead, she found a scene to warm any mother's heart. Her inseparable pair sat on the child-sized play sofa, Vlad, two weeks shy of his third birthday, clutching a stuffed dog and sucking his thumb, and twenty-six-month old Sarah – now three centimeters taller than her brother – holding a book tablet and reading to him. She noticed her mother.

"Vladya wanted a story, so I readed him one," Sarah told her.

Maryana smiled. "Oh really? Which one?"

"The Sleepy Little Puppy."

"May I listen, too? I like to hear stories." Maryana settled on the floor, expecting a fantastic tale that would have very little to do with the actual story. Sergei had been great for that, staring hard at the pictures and inventing long rambling explanations until he mastered decoding.

"The sleepy little puppy didn't like the hard shelf," Sarah read off the screen. Her finger skimmed along under each word. "He wanted a soft place for his nap. He poked his nose in the old lady's basket. The clothes were soft. He put his foot in the basket. 'You dirty little puppy! Stay out of my basket!' said the old lady, and she chased him with a stick."

"My, what a good memory you have, Sar'ina!" Maryana said with surprise. "You know the whole book."

"That's what I readed."

"You can't read, Sar'ina," Maryana insisted. "Not yet. You do write your letters very pretty. When you know them better, then you'll be able to read. You must always speak the truth."

"I know my letters. I can read them all." Sarah gave a hard gooey cough and cleared her throat. She pointed to the various easy reader

166

cards littering the floor. "I can read that one, and that one, and that one, and that one…"

Maryana chose one at random, placed it in the reader, turned off the voice option, and thumbed it to the middle. No child could memorize that many books and know a random page. Recite them from the beginning, maybe, but not randomly. "Go ahead. Read me that."

Sarah studied the textreader for a minute, coughed, then read in a stumbling voice, "Ivan picked up the box. The box was heavy. 'What is in the box?' he asked. 'It is too small to be a racer. It is too big to be a music box. What did Papa send me?'"

"Stop," Maryana commanded. "You can't be reading that."

"S'rina reads to me," Vlad said around his thumb. "I like… I like… I like the books about puppies."

Maryana rummaged in the card box until she found a more difficult book. "Here, Sar'ina. Read me this one. I like this story."

Sarah frowned. "I don't know that one." Her stumblings became pauses as she decoded the longer words. "One time in the forests of Li-va-ni-a lived a bear. He was a big bear, with fur as dark as … as… What's this word, Mama? *Ch-e-r-n-i-l-a?*"

"Ink," Maryana said with a sinking feeling. "Sarah, will you play a game with me? If I write you some words, will you tell me what they say?"

Sarah perked up. "I like games! I can play. Will they be easy words or hard words?"

"I want to play," Vlad echoed around his thumb.

"We'll do all kinds of words," Maryana promised. "First, everybody use the sanitary."

Maryana fed her duo lunch, changed Vlad's diaper, gave Sarah a breathing treatment, and set them down together for a nap. She called Sasha at work. "Hurry home as soon as you can."

"It's exam week," Sasha said. "I can't leave early. I have papers to read and questions to answer."

"As soon as you can get away," she insisted. "I've got a surprise that will knock you on your educated butt."

Children swarmed Sasha as he walked in the door. Maryana skipped and jumped as hard as any of them, grabbing him by the hand and pulling as if she were seventeen again.

She dragged him into the kitchen. "Come! Come! Have I got a surprise for you! Everyone quiet! Don't tell! Let your Papa see for himself." She sat Sarah on the kitchen table and pointed to a waiting compad and stylus.

"Write something you want Sarah to say."

Sasha wasn't in the mood for nonsense. "What?"

"Write something. Anything."

"This is quantum, Papa!" Valeria gushed. "Watch!"

Sasha scrawled something across the compad.

Maryana sighed. "Something legible." She rewrote his sentence in neat block print and held up the pad. "Tell Papa what he wrote, Sarah."

Whispers erupted around the crush. "You can do it." "Sound it out." "Shhh!" "Don't tell her!"

Sarah licked her lips. *"Ya hachu vorsinu."* A cheer went up.

Sarah clapped her hands. "I did it! I readed! But I already taked a nap."

Sasha eyed Maryana strangely. "How did she do that?"

"She can read!" Maryana squealed. "I caught her reading to Vladimir. She can read all the easy stories in the nursery. It's amazing! Try it! Write something for her!"

Sasha sat, intrigued. He covered the screen, then held it up so no one else could coach her.

Sarah concentrated. "'The dog ran after the cat.' That's easy words!"

"I'll be damned," Sasha said vacantly. "Our baby can read."

"Sergei's smart, and he read at four," Maryana reminded him, "but she's twenty-six months and nobody taught her, she just did it herself. What do we do?"

Sasha shrugged. "Buy more stories. What else do you do? They won't let her into kindergarten at two. I guess all those dire predictions she would be slow can be shoved back up the doctor's ass. Maybe that incubator grew too many brain cells." He lifted the toddler and flipped her upside down in front of his face. Sarah's giggles turned to hard coughing. It looked cruel, but it helped keep her troublesome lungs clear.

"You! You think you're so smart, little *kapusta*? You think you're ready for Papa's school?" He lowered her to blow on her belly, sending her into gales of laughter and coughing. He flipped her rightside up and sat her in front of him with an amused grin. "Are you going to make your Papa proud? You work hard reading to your Mama and I will take you to school with me so you can show all those old professors how smart my little girl is."

Sarah launched herself to hang from his neck. "I want to go to school."

Papa hugged her back.

As Vladimir and Sarah began to sleep through the night, so did their parents. An increase in energy meant an increase in libido, but neither of them were taking chances. Two forms of birth control had to be better than one. And they were. The gap between Sarah and *Surprise Again!* would be the longest yet. If Vlad's pregnancy frightened Maryana, this one filled her with dread. She had two small toddlers with lingering health issues; how would she ever manage another? Three days passed before she could break the news.

"There is no question about it," Sasha insisted. "We don't need it, we can't handle it, ten is crazy enough. Termination is the only answer."

Maryana cried harder. "I know! I know that, Sash. I absolutely agree; I just can't bring myself to do it. I'm so sorry. Please don't hate me! After almost losing Sarah, after praying so hard to let a dying baby live and God answering my prayers, how can I ever rationalize willfully killing this one? That would be like breaking a promise; the Universe or God or Fate or whatever you want to call it would demand payment in return. Laugh at me for being superstitious, but I can't risk that. Can you understand that at all?"

Guilt fell over Sasha like a pall. He stroked her hair, then kissed her head. He sighed heavily. "*Da*. I'm not happy, but I understand. But we will do absolutely everything the doctor says, like a textbook! No more nightmares."

Maryana snuggled against him, wrapped in the arms that never failed to chase away her demons, but she didn't smile. "No. No more nightmares."

With the baby due in May, January was a good time to start Vladimir in preschool, but Maryana had forgotten just how difficult it was to separate twins.

She pulled Vlad's shirt over his head and waited for him to push his arms in. On the floor, Sarah struggled stubbornly with her own shirt. "Guess where you're going next week, Vladya! You're going to your very own school."

"Like Sergei?"

"The school Sergei went to last year. Remember? It has games, and toys, and lots of other boys to play with. You'll have such fun there. Sergei loved his school."

Sarah's hands found the end of her sleeves; one less child to dress. "Me?" she demanded. "Me too? I can go to school now?"

"Next year, Sarah," Maryana promised. "You have to be three to go to that school. We'll make our own school, just you and me."

Sarah's face fell. "I want to go to school. I don't have diapers. I read like Sergei."

"You have to be three. That's the rule."

"Why?"

"Because it is."

Vlad's mouth caught up to his worries. "The boys will hit me?"

"No! No one will hit you. Only nice boys can go there. You'll have lots of friends to play with, all your size."

"I can go with Vladdy," Sarah insisted. "I know my ABV's, and my colors, and …"

"No, Sarah. No more. You will see on Monday."

Vlad didn't cry, but he did vomit on the couch a half-hour later.

On Monday, Maryana wore her pink pantsuit and her Seruki winter boots. It was a rather exclusive preschool, and first impressions were most important. Family feuds notwithstanding, her children bore a distinctive lineage that separated them from the common bourgeois mass, and they would be educated to uphold that pedigree. Parallel to her family, perhaps, but no less elite. It was a flight of fantasy, yes, but she could just imagine the joy on Sasha's face if someday one of their children rose up the ranks and bought out Ivanov Industries in some great corporate takeover. A long shot, but not impossible. Not with the secrets she kept.

She scrubbed Vlad and dressed him for success in new high-end children's wear, then packed extra padded underpants in his carry bag. A dose of his stomach medicine, just in case, and they set off for the school, Sarah bundled extra tight against the cold.

The bright blue school looked cheery against the winter, the play area full of sleds and toys. Inside the foyer, a lady greeted them.

170

"This is Vladimir," Maryana beamed. "He's starting in Mrs. Vouchenko's class today. He is most excited to be here."

"Don't you look nice today!" the receptionist said. "All ready for school? Take my hand, Vladimir, and I'll bring you to your class."

Vlad's dark eyes seemed to take up half his pallid face. He buried himself in Maryana's leg and wouldn't let go.

"I can come, too?" Sarah asked the lady.

"Next year, Sarah," Maryana said in a tone that said the subject wasn't to be discussed any more. "Perhaps if I walk him to the room."

"In our experience, that makes things worse." The receptionist tried to pry Vlad off, but he began to wail.

"Just today." Maryana picked him up. Vlad crying upset Sarah, upset Sarah could stop breathing, and she didn't need a bigger scene. "Show me the way, please?"

Inside the class, children were painting, or building, or being read to. Some played with an interactive wallboard. Everything was bright, calm, and inviting. Maryana let go of Sarah to speak to the teacher.

Sarah wandered off, intrigued. She caught sight of an oversized calendar and stopped to read the words. Another child drew circles on a wallboard; Sarah found a stylus and wrote her name alongside him. Vlad followed her, wearing his worry-face, and slipped his hand into hers. Sarah put the stylus in his hand and made him "write" his name.

Maryana picked her up. "Come, Sarah. We'll be back later to get Vlad."

"No!" Sarah ordered. "I wanna stay! I writed my name."

Vlad burst into tears and ran after them.

Sarah kicked her feet. "Vladdy's cryin! Mama! Vladdy's cryin! We have to help him!"

The teacher caught Vlad and held him back. The cry became a high-pitched scream. Sarah made a final lunge for the room as the door closed. A new scream sounded in the hall.

"Stop that!" Maryana admonished on the ride home. "You're a big girl! When you cry like that, you make Vladya sad." But Sarah wouldn't stop.

As soon as Maryana set her in the house, Sarah opened the door and ran out, calling her brother. She ran down the walk and into the street, coatless, shouting for Vlad between coughs. Maryana carried her back and locked the door. Sarah climbed on a table by the window and pressed against the glass, crying until she choked, and Maryana made her inhale medicine to ease her breathing.

171

"Come on, we'll read a story. I'll read a page, then you can read one to me," Maryana suggested, but Sarah slid from her lap to lie disconsolate on the floor.

"How about watching Starshine Express?" Maryana offered, naming a preschool program on the vidstream. "Today is a trip through the planets. You can tell Vlad all about it."

Sarah howled.

"Come eat some lunch," Maryana said at last. Sarah sat at the table, rubbing Vlad's pajama shirt over her teary face. She drank some juice, but wouldn't eat. Maryana left her on the sofa in the playroom, where she lay sobbing on and off until it was time to retrieve Vlad.

Maryana mustered her cheer in the classroom. "How did it go? Did he settle down?"

The assistant handed her a limp Vlad, so exhausted by tears he couldn't stand. Sarah jumped up and down for Maryana to pick her up, too, but settled for holding onto Vlad's foot.

The teacher shook her head. "He wet three times, vomited twice, and wouldn't eat a thing. We sat him in the circle for group time, but he didn't want to participate yet."

"I'm so sorry…"

"Some children take time," Mrs. Vouchenko said. "Stick with it. He'll settle in by Friday. You'll see."

Vlad was asleep on her shoulder by the time they left the building, Sarah hardly five minutes after they reached her speeder. Maryana woke them for dinner. Sarah ate, but Vlad still looked ready to cry and wouldn't open his mouth.

Surely day two would be easier, now that everyone knew what to expect. Separating was not the end of the world, Vlad would be home mid-afternoon, and they would have so much to tell each other. All of the children had loved preschool.

Vlad began to weep the minute she dressed him. He dragged her backwards as they approached the school, Sarah dragged her forward until Maryana felt about to tear in half. Inside, the receptionist tried to take Vlad just as he vomited, hitting her, Maryana, and the floor. Vlad screamed and lunged for Maryana. Sarah grabbed the receptionist's leg and bit her.

Maryana took one, the receptionist took the other, and the count to three o'clock began.

At home, she tried to hold Sarah on her lap. "Sit still! You were a very bad girl, Sarah! You never, never bite anyone! That poor lady was trying to be nice to your brother, and you hurt her! Think how sad you must have made her feel."

Sarah cried and squirmed until she broke free from Maryana's grasp. She ran to the forbidden living room and stood on the chair by the window, mournful tears rolling down her face.

"Sarah, you don't belong in this room. Off the chair." She carried Sarah to the kitchen and tried to distract her with a cookie. Sarah ran to the window in a flash.

Maryana's mouth pressed into an unhappy line. She pulled Sarah back down – four times.

"Sarah, I'm losing patience! Stay out of the window or I will lock you in your room!" Sarah wound up in the crib, but Maryana couldn't bring herself to lock the door. The issue of breathing difficulties was far too real, and she kept a trained ear on the room monitor.

"Any better?" Maryana said at the end of the day. The aide shook her head and passed Vlad over, so weary he seemed comatose except for relentless hiccups that shook his little body like earthquakes. Another aide pulled Sarah out of the crawling tunnel so they could leave.

"This isn't going to work," Maryana told Sasha with defeat. "He hasn't eaten a thing in two days and he looks like death. Maybe we should start him out slower."

"Keeping him home isn't going to help his separation issues," Sasha reasoned.

"No, but maybe it's too much, too soon. He's always been slower than the rest. Maybe he still needs to grow a bit."

"You've been saying that for three years. If you wait that long, he'll be thirty. You can't keep babying him."

"Seriously, Sash. I'll keep him home tomorrow, let him recover. That's probably all he needs."

On Wednesday Vlad was still a bit tired, but he and Sarah played and ate and napped as if nothing had changed. Maryana kept them apart, giving Vlad a new toy and working with Sarah in the dining room, then setting Sarah up with a computer program and teaching

Vlad his numbers clear across the house. Neither of them had the least difficulty with that.

"I don't know," she said to Sash. "They really aren't a problem, home. Maybe I'll wait until fall. Then they can go together."

"Bullshit!" he grumbled. "You made the arrangements; he'll go. I'll take them, tomorrow."

"Sarah, you will come to work with me," Sasha said as he strapped them into his copper-colored Cosmic Apogee runabout on Thursday. "Your mama will come get you at lunch."

"Me too?" Vlad said hopefully.

"You will go to school, like a man. I go to my school every day, your brothers go to their school every day, you will go to your school every day."

"Vladdy doesn't like school," Sarah said. "He's a-scared the boys will hurt him, like David."

"No one will hurt him."

"The teacher yelled at him, in a BIG LOUD VOICE!"

"The teacher wouldn't yell unless he did something wrong," Sasha said. "No one makes him piss his pants. Only babies do that. Babies don't go to school because teachers don't get paid to change diapers. The teacher has every right to yell."

Vlad never gave a peep as Sasha walked him to his classroom. "Do you need to use the lavatory?" the assistant asked, seeing Vlad clutch the front of his pants. Vlad nodded and ran. Sasha gave the teacher a wave and left; no tears, no hassle.

"I can play too, Papa?" Sarah tried, hoping the answer would be different.

Sasha carried her on his arm. He rubbed noses with her until she giggled. "Today you will go to school with me. You can read to the teachers, and they will know you are the smartest girl in the school."

"Will they clap for me?"

"They will clap."

"Can I show them how I write my name?"

"You can write your name."

"Can I spell?"

"*Da.*"

"Can I do my numbers? I can count to fiveteen, and sixteen, and seventeens and eighteens and nineteens."

"You can do everything for them. Enough, now."

Sasha didn't have classes until one. Instead of planning time, he charmed the administration with his baby girl. Sarah started out shy, then became a chatterbox as a horde of candies and cakes and fruit appeared from drawers and cabinets. As word spread, the academic lounge filled with professors come to see the child, picture-perfect with her rosy-red cheeks, white-blonde hair up in two tiny bows, eyes so bright and blue they seemed purple. When he had an audience, Sasha set Sarah on the table and turned her loose. He didn't smile, but a sparkle lit his eyes.

"Sarah, what does Papa do for work?"

"You teach big kids."

"What do I teach?"

"Arch-e-ol-o-gy."

"Very good. What is archaeology?"

"Things people forgot in the dirt." A few of the professors chuckled and Sarah broke into a grin, happy to please.

"And where do I teach?"

"At the In'stute school."

"Close enough. Are you ready to study at the institute?"

Sarah grew excited. "*Da*! I can read, and I can write my name, and I can work Katya's textreader, so I can go to school with Sergei. Can I go there tomorrow?"

"You've got her reading sight words?" Elena Rishkin, Professor of Russian History, asked. "Aren't you pushing her a little fast?"

"No, no," Sasha insisted. "She teaches herself. It's all her. Test her. Write it; she'll read it for you. Ask her, she will spell it."

"And counting," Sarah reminded him. "I can count this many," and she flashed all her fingers to her audience, twice.

"Can you spell, 'cat'?" Bronas Groshenko of the Anthropology department asked.

"*K-o-t,*" Sarah spelled with annoyance. "I can spell Kiev – *K-i-yi-v.*" The words got harder; so did the reading, but Sarah held up through a second-form level. The crowd around her cheered and clapped. Sarah clapped with them, increasingly energized.

"Ah, but can you read this." Yuri Kucia, language studies, held up his compad with one word on it.

"That's not fair," Sasha said.

"Let her try. Memory is one skill, but decoding is something different."

Sarah stuck a finger in her mouth, thinking. "I don't know that word."

"Sound it out."

"Nat?"

"Very close. Sound it like *x-a-t*."

Sarah tipped her head. "Hat? But that's 'n'."

"In Russian, yes. This is English Standard. You just read an English word. Some of the letters are the same. Some look the same but sound different," Kucia said. "In English, the 'N' is called '*aich*', and says 'ha.'"

"You'll confuse her," Sasha said. "Tash speaks it most of the time, so she's used to hearing it, but let her get good at Russian first."

"Anglish. Can I learn to read Anglish, too, Papa? *P'zhalsta?*" Sarah asked. "I know 'H.' It looks like 'N'."

"When you are three."

"Can I be three now?"

Kucia stood and patted Sasha on the back. "If she's like this now, you won't stop her. She's a time bomb, Sash. Take her over to the Psych building, have them test her. They live for things like this. She'll break their charts."

Sasha picked Sarah up and shielded her possessively with his arms. "No. She's a baby, not a guinea pig. Let her be a baby first. Good starts can go wrong at any time. Maybe when she starts school."

Maryana retrieved Sarah at noon, fed her lunch, and woke her from her nap to get Vlad.

Sarah ran across the room to hug him. "I went to school with Papa! I read an Anglish word! And they clapped for me!"

"Any better?" Maryana asked the teacher.

The teacher made a semi-hopeful face. "I think so. He just sat and watched today. He stayed dry, so that's a step forward. He'll be fine by Monday."

Sarah led him over. Vlad looked like a zombie, devoid of life. He leaned his head against his sister and put his thumb in his mouth. He didn't even lift his arms when Maryana bent to pick him up.

She gave a hard sigh. "I thank you for your gracious efforts, but I don't think it's right to torment him like this. I'll keep him home."

"You can't give up," the teacher insisted. "It's not even a week yet. Patience is the key. I've never graduated a crier yet."

"Thank you, no. Perhaps we'll try again in the fall. Sarah can come, too, and you'll see a big difference, I think. Thank you again." And Maryana took them home.

Thirty

2257

From February to April, Maryana and Sasha didn't even kiss.

"Eliza*vyeta*," Sasha corrected. "With a 'v'."

Maryana held the new baby, red-faced and small but text-book healthy. After three and a half years of vigilance over fragile infants, it was hard to remember what normal was like. "No. Eliza*byeta*. In all the other languages it's a 'b'. It makes it more global, a fusion of cultures, at home both in Russia and the rest of the world. And Viktoria, for such a victorious, healthy birth."

* * *

Sasha's giant dress shoes thumped down the stairs. His gray outfit was the most expensive article of clothing he'd ever owned in his life, chosen by Maryana, custom tailored for his size and worn only on the most important occasions. He checked the reservations on his palmcom one last time. As he passed the entry to the living room – off limits to children under ten – he did a double-take. Somehow a toddler had managed to pull the new baby from the bassinette and was lying on top of it on the floor.

He charged in, bellowing. A smaller child dove under the sofa. "Get off her, you son of a bitch! Are you trying to kill her?" He cuffed the two-year old away and snatched the gasping infant, holding it close in his big hands.

"She was cryin', so I gave her a kiss," Sarah explained.

"Tash! Get in here!" he yelled before Elizabyeta caught a breath and let loose with a scream so high and loud it could be heard outside.

Maryana appeared quickly, hopping as she slid her foot into a Foré Reál heel. She looked stunning in a royal blue beaded Kiri Zuba gown, her hair professionally styled to fall in a layered fountain of long curls dotted with tiny crystals to catch the light when she moved. "What's wrong? Is she okay?" She took the red-faced infant with alarm.

178

"Somehow she got her out of the bed. I don't know if she dropped her." He tipped his head toward Sarah.

"She waked up, so I was gonna bring her to you," Sarah said from the floor.

Maryana rocked the baby. "Shh. Find me the nurser. Sash, how can we go out? She's too young. What if something happens? The girls can't be everywhere at once. Maybe we should take her with us."

"We're going, Tash," he said with finality. "It is our eighteenth anniversary and I am taking my wife out, alone. Three are old enough to mind themselves; the girls only have to watch the other six. That's three each; I think they can handle it. If not, give one to two of the middle ones, and that only leaves two. Even Katya can watch two." Maryana nodded at the truth, and went to pass the newborn to one of the twins.

Sasha waited until she left, then seized the toddler by the elbow and brought a huge hand down across her backside, three times. He flipped her around, shook her near his face, and bellowed, "Leave the baby alone! Touch her again and I will spank you until you can't sit!" He slammed the little girl down in a chair. "Don't move!"

Sarah's face grew red and her eyes filled with unshed tears. She took a deep breath and held it, turning dark before coughing hard. She kicked her feet defiantly against the chair.

Sasha glowered. "You need more?" He turned the child over and delivered three additional blows before reseating her. This time the tears fell. "I told you not to move! Now do it!"

"If we're going, let's go," Maryana called from the foyer. A final threatening stare, and Sasha left to join her.

* * *

Vladimir peeped like a mouse from the tight space under the sofa. Coast clear, he climbed next to his sister and slipped his small hand into hers. "See?" he said. "When you cry, he stops."

Sarah leaned over and bit a hole in the arm of the chair.

Galina quieted baby Elizabyeta with a fresh bottle. She, too, was dressed for celebrating, but in nothing close to her mother's style. Her dressed-up twin slouched across the table. Valeria looked as angry as Galina felt.

"Happy seventeenth birthday," Gal muttered. She leaned Elizabyeta against her hand and patted the tiny back until a bubble rolled its way up.

"Ha!" Val laughed to keep from crying. "It's not fair! We had our plans *first!* Mother *knew* that! Everyone will be expecting us at Nina's party, and now we can't be there. Seventeen years old, graduating next week, papers for Declaration of Adulthood signed, filed, and awaiting their final stamp. How more important of a birthday can we have? This rots like a dirty diaper. So much for being an *independent* adult. Why couldn't we have been born the day *after* their anniversary?"

"They'd still pick that day for their celebration."

" 'Leria?" called a coughing, weepy little voice from the other room. " 'Leria? Vladdy peed his pants ..."

"Tell him to go change," she called back.

"He was under the couch, and now he's on the green chair."

Valeria grimaced. She poked her head in the living room. "Why didn't you make him go the lavatory?"

Sarah sobbed and gave a cough that should have torn a lung. "Papa said I couldn't get up."

Val pushed Vlad toward the stairs. "Go, Vladya. Sarah, come get your mask, you're wheezing. I'll get the chair in a minute."

She carried Sarah to the kitchen and spoke to the intercom. "Vitya? Vlad's on his way up. New pants."

"Thanks a lot," came Viktor's reply.

"Want to clean the chair instead?" She sat Sarah on the counter and clamped an inhalant mask over her face. Vlad had his issues; Sarah's lungs still had theirs.

"How fast do you think we could get them all to bed?" Valeria asked her twin. "Katya's old enough to handle the baby, and Viktor can handle the boys, especially if they're asleep. All he has to do is keep taking Vlad to the sanitary."

A herd of footsteps pounded down the stairs, accompanied by screaming. Dmitri and David raced through the kitchen, chased by Alexei.

"Hey!" Val grabbed David; Dmitri stopped by the opposite door. "No running!"

David dove behind her. "He's got a booger!"

"Knock it off or I'll make you eat it," Galina threatened Alexei.

"You and what space fleet? I haven't even got anything." He held up his hands.

180

Galina shoved him hard with her free hand. "Twin fleets! Leave them the hell alone, or we'll hold you down and tickle Vlad on you without a diaper."

"I'd kill the little pissbag."

"Go!"

Alexei lunged around her and flicked his finger at David. "Yah!" The younger boys ran screaming through the dining room. Alexei chased them upstairs.

"All done, Sarah," Valeria said. She relieved her of the mask and set her on the floor. "Go play." Sarah gave a clearer cough and ran to find Vlad.

Galina sighed. "Bed? At 19:00? We still have to get them dinner! The boys'll never go to bed this early. We'd just get caught sneaking back in." She placed the baby in the carry seat on the table.

"I don't care!" Valeria declared angrily. "We're going to that party, one way or another. They have anniversaries every year. We only turn seventeen once. Everyone will split up this summer. When will we ever have another chance to party with our friends?"

Galina's face brightened. "They said *we* have to watch everyone, right? Meaning you and me. He never said we have to do it *together*, did he? Vik will help if we ask him right. What if you go for two hours, then come back and I'll go for a couple hours? We'd both get to go, and they couldn't say anything about it."

Valeria broke into a smile. "'Lina, that's the most perfect idea I've ever heard! Must be because you're now an adult." She gave her twin a hard hug. "Your idea; you want to go first?"

"You're older, you can go."

"I promise, I won't be late, and I'll make sure everyone waits for you!"

* * *

Maryana looked at the sender ID on the commlink and hit the receive switch with a smile. "Hello, darling. What's news?"

Sasha gave half an amused smile. "The news is you're beautiful, even on camera."

She sucked up the compliment, then tossed it away with a sassy flip of her head. "To hear you speak, that's old news. Tell me new news."

A full smile brightened his face. "You're more beautiful now than when you answered."

Maryana laughed. "You are nothing but a horny schoolboy, half full of poop."

"Which is why I'm calling you from school, isn't it? And I just finished lunch, so my belly is very full of shit at the moment."

"You're also a pig. What's new?"

"We're having a guest speaker the end of the month, a lecturer on ancient Viking cultures. He's speaking one day, there's a big reception that night, then he's doing two other local lectures. On the day between, they wanted someone to entertain the speaker and his wife. I know I should have asked you first, but I offered ..."

Maryana started as if she'd won a contest. "Oh Sash! You invited him here, didn't you? Tell me you offered to have them to dinner here? How many? What date? Sash, they took your offer, didn't they?"

He watched her spring alive with a spark in his eye. "I thought that would make you happy."

"Happy?!" Her thoughts raced across her face at lightspeed. "You know I live for that! We haven't had a big party in ages! I'll have a menu by tonight. Let me know how many. I'll need a new dress – you need at least a new shirt – we'll need a sitter – make it two – the older children should attend as well; they don't get enough exposure to real social functions. They'll need something better to wear. Oh Sash! We're going to shine all the way to Centauri!"

"Spare no details," he said, as if she ever would.

Maryana bounced on the desk chair. "I can't wait! I love you, Sash!"

Adoration crept over his face as he watched her squirm in delight. "I love you, too."

The upcoming event became a family affair. Maryana clamped down hard on manners. Sasha clamped down on education.

"James Winters is the leading researcher on Viking cultures. By tomorrow, I want every one of you to tell me five things you've learned about Vikings," he instructed at dinner.

"Vi kings, and vi queens," Vlad said knowledgeably. A round of laughter circled the table.

"Durak!" Alexei swore. "No such thing as vi queens."

"And you know better?" Sasha challenged. "Give me a fact, smartass."

Almost fifteen, Alexei wasn't as stupid as he often acted. "They buried their dead warriors in boats, with their horses, wives, and everything, like the Egyptians."

"You just saved yourself a whack."

"They called their Heaven Valhalla," Valeria offered.

"Another with brains. Two points."

"They helped settle Ukraine," Viktor said.

"Point."

"They lived in Norway and Sweden?" Galina guessed.

"And Denmark. Point scored."

"I want a *huy*."

All eyes turned to Sarah, perched on her booster seat next to Maryana.

Maryana blushed. "What did you say, Sar'ina?"

Sarah gnawed a piece of bread. "Vladdy gets to pee with a pecker, and I want to pee with a pecker like Vlad."

Screaming laughter erupted around the table, right down to Sergei.

Sasha's good humor turned dark as summer borscht. He thundered over the noise. "Who taught you that word?"

"David."

"Liar!" David shrieked.

Vladimir shook his head seriously. "Boys have peckers, but girls don't."

"LEAVE!" Sasha ordered, and David ran for his room so fast he never let go of his fork. The laughter died.

Maryana cleared her throat and regained her composure. "I can't do anything about it during dinner, Sar'ina. Tell me again later, okay?"

"Okay."

The snicker built until Alexei couldn't hold it back, and several soft giggles echoed him. He coughed into his hand. *"Pckr!"*

"Pckr! Pckr!" came a chorus of coughs. Sarah grinned with delight at the spectacle. Not to be left out, Vlad faked a cough into his palm, and Sarah followed swiftly with a crowing hack.

Sasha's fist slammed the table, rattling dishes and making everyone jump. Sergei's hands clamped over his ears, and Vlad startled so hard he nearly fell off his booster seat.

183

"No more! The next person to laugh will write me three pages of research. Is that clear?"

Subdued yessirs sounded around the table, and dinner resumed.

"Why?" Sarah asked.

Maryana sat her toddlers down to explain very basic gender differences, and the fact that *'huy'* was never a nice word. Even after so many children, explanations were Maryana's weakness; as a child, she'd never questioned Mamá about strange things, she'd just accepted them intuitively as fact and therefore had no experience to draw from. Explaining why someone should sink money into an investment fund was easy; it was factual. Explaining why a Hermitage 2241 was the best white wine to serve with a baked fish dinner was also rather simple. Explaining cultural norms – especially to a hyper-inquisitive toddler with argument capabilities, like Sarah, or slow comprehension, like Vlad seemed to have – was especially frustrating.

"I don't care. Nice people don't say that word, and I will not hear it again. If you must discuss it, you will use the word 'penis,' and nice people do not discuss penises. They are private things, meant only for their owner. No one else's business." Maryana tried her best to look stern and threatening. It rarely worked on a child over four, and Sarah was far too cagey for two and a half, but she had to try anyway.

"Penis," Vlad repeated obediently. "David's not nice, that's why he says the bad word."

"Why?" Sarah said.

Maryana bristled with impatience. "Because it just isn't! Just like it's okay to run around the bath naked, but not to run down the hall and get your pajamas. Same rule."

Sarah thought hard. "Like blow your nose, don't pick it like this," and she shoved a finger far up a nostril.

Maryana nodded in relief. "Yes, Sar'ina. Please remember. Now, bed, both of you."

"Maybe it's time to get them separate beds," Sasha said as they crashed into bed themselves. "Once they discover the differences, they're not babies anymore."

Maryana cuddled close. "Of course they're still babies. That was just David telling them things they don't understand yet."

"I fixed his ass good. Maybe he'll think twice next time."

"He's seven, Sash. Don't be too harsh on him. He doesn't think yet."

"Seven is the age of reason. He'll remember now."

"Anyway, we'd have to buy more beds, move the rooms around to make space. I don't think we can fit three beds in the nursery without making it look crowded. No one will want to sleep with Vlad when he can't go three hours without wetting. He's not ready for a full-sized bed, and the last thing you want is Sarah wandering around in the middle of the night exploring where she shouldn't be. Wait a few more months, when Byeta's ready for the crib. We'll break them up then."

Maryana had the dining room chairs reupholstered and bought an expensive new oriental-weave carpet for under the table. New pillows and accents freshened the off-limits living room, and a retro-fitted antique chandelier now hung in the conservatory, changing the atmosphere to one of reverence and respect. The table had been set as for a state reception: the guests of honor, ten staff and students from the Science Institute, six Kirushenko children dressed like royalty and threatened with pain for misbehavior, and their parents.

Maryana seemed straight from a fashion ad in a pink and white Henri-Claire cocktail dress that favored every curve, with matching pink Wu Tau heels. Jewelry shimmered from her neck, ears and hands, her hair and cosmetics as perfect as a model in an advertisement. Like a classic, she seemed ageless; possibly twenty-one, probably twenty-eight, but certainly not the thirty-five she was.

Sasha tried very hard not to touch his hair after Maryana lacquered it in place. The unruly waves had a mind of their own, but the lacquer made his head itch. He paced the house in his grey suit, the sweat-battling fibers of the new shirt already nearing their limits trying to hide his nerves. He spoke no Norse, and he knew James Winters spoke little Russian, so English was the language of the evening. Faculty wouldn't have trouble, it was good practice for the children, but how good were the students? The door monitor chimed, and he ran to hide in the living room while the caterers brought out appetizers.

Viktor and Dmitri had door duty; Viktor pushed his brother toward the door first. Dmitri glared at him before smoothing his hair one last time and opening the door.

He gave a small bow and used his best English. "Good evening, Sir. Good evening, Madame. Welcome to the Kirushenko home. May we take your coats?"

Mrs. Winters melted. "I wish I'd brought one. You are the most charming doorman I have ever seen. What a perfect little gentleman! Can I take you home with me?"

It didn't hurt that Dmitri was short and slender, looking no more than eight when he was already ten. He glanced across the hall at his mother, cuing from the shadows. "You could ask."

Maryana swooped in to save him. "Delia! James! How kind of you to come to dinner. Welcome! Come in!"

"It was kind of you to invite us. What delightful boys you have!" Delia Winters exclaimed. She and Maryana pressed cheeks in greeting.

"Viktor Kirushenko, Ma'am; Sir." He stepped forward to shake hands with the guests.

"I'm Dmitri," and he followed suit.

"I have many delightful children," Maryana said. "The older ones will be joining us tonight, but the younger ones are upstairs readying for bed."

"What a shame. I would love to have met this little army you claim. Ohhh! Is this little one yours as well?" Mrs. Winters caught sight of Byeta sleeping in the bassinette in the corner of the living room.

Jim Winters peeked over his wife's shoulder. "A perfect little angel."

"When she's asleep," Sasha agreed.

"Elizabyeta's the tail end," Maryana said with pride. "She's seven weeks old. I hope you don't mind; I didn't have the heart to send her upstairs until everyone is quiet up there."

"Not at all, not at all. She's absolutely precious, Maryana! I don't know how you do it."

Maryana smiled demurely. "Everyone helps. I could never do it all myself. These are my biggest helpers, our eldest daughters, Valeria and Galina."

The twins towered over their mother, over Mrs. Winters, in their dress heels edging taller than even Mr. Winters, who stood a meter eighty two. Dressed alike, hair combed deliberately to exact sameness, they could have passed as clones, a long-standing habit so that if something went wrong, no one would know which was to blame. They each shook hands with a guest, then crossed hands and shook the opposite guest in synchronized rhythm before turning on cue and shaking with each other.

Mr. Winters grinned at the display. "My goodness. Can your parents even tell you apart?"

The girls glanced at each other with identical timing. "Not always," they said in unison.

"What can I get you to drink?" Sasha offered.

The caterers lived up to their recommendations, and dinner proved exquisite. Alexei flaunted company manners no one would ever have guessed he had, and the twins displayed conversational talents almost as adept as their mother's. Viktor, Katya, and Dmitri behaved as if crowned with halos, silent unless spoken to. Maryana and Delia Winters had discovered numerous common interests by the time the party retired to the living room.

"Two colleagues and I even gave a concert to benefit a local program," Delia admitted.

"How exciting!" Maryana gushed. "Sasha never told me. I studied dance for eight years and piano for ten, but I haven't had a recital in twenty years; I would never have the nerve to give a concert. Usually I just do the organizing for events like that."

"Oh, you get used to it. Concerts are my last resort. No one likes dragging a cello through galactic customs. I spearheaded the membership drive for the San Francisco Philharmonic when we were teaching out there, and I helped campaign to bring Niamen Gigrin to give a benefit for the Greater Oslo Orchestral Society as well."

"That must have been wonderful. We've always been great patrons of the arts ourselves. All the children started piano lessons by five. Some of them have become quite accomplished. The girls have all had some dance training, and one of my youngest is showing some early promise with drawing."

"Really! If it's not an imposition, perhaps we could hear them play," Mrs. Winters suggested.

"Oh, I wouldn't want to bore you…"

"Not at all! That's why I teach music. James, their children study classical music. Wouldn't you love to hear them play?"

Mr. Winters glanced over from his conversation with the professors. "Of course, dear. That would be lovely."

Sasha looked embarrassed. "You didn't come all this way to listen to a children's recital."

Jim Winters waved the idea away. "Delia gets bored listening to me talk about research all the time, so I humor her when I can. We do our best to encourage the humanities whenever possible. It's the humanities that define us as a culture."

"Perhaps just one or two," Sasha relented.

Boris Venerek, the Dean of Ancient Studies, patted him on the back. "You heard the guest, Sash. Show them off."

The group adjourned one room over to the conservatory to listen to Valeria and Galina play a four-handed piece on the shining concert grand. Alexei claimed a mysteriously sore wrist, leaving Viktor to play a well-rehearsed tune. Katerina's piece was short, but she played with more flourish. Maryana pulled Dmitri forward.

"Dmitri is our virtuoso. He's only in his fourth year, but he won a second-place ribbon at the school exhibition last year. We have great hopes for him." Dmitri scanned through the list of sheet music on the display screen and chose one of his more practiced pieces, a jazzy, modern selection. He had to perch on the edge of the bench to reach the pedals.

"Not that one, D'Misha," Maryana said after he began. "Where's that Brahms you were working on?"

"Don't worry about it," Mr. Winters said. "Let him play what he likes." Dmitri played his piece heartfully, to a roar of applause.

Delia Winters clapped with gusto. "Fabulous! You're right, Maryana. He's got great potential. Don't let him quit."

Mr. Winters shook his hand. "Excellent job, son. Keep it up, you'll make it into the school of fine arts."

Sasha ruffled his son's hair, a rare glow crossing his face. Maybe it was the glass of brandy in his hand, or maybe it was pride. "They don't accept students until seventh form. He must study hard first. Grades are just as important as skill."

A movement at the corner of his eye caught his attention. Two escapees sat noiselessly in the doorway in their pajamas.

"I see two children far past their bedtime." He motioned to them to come in. Sarah ran to him, and he swung her up on his arm. Tiny Vlad climbed into Maryana's lap and curled up sleepily, thumb in his mouth.

Delia's heart overloaded. Vlad was three and a half, but could have passed for half that. "Oh, Maryana! He's a doll! Would he sit with me? Would you mind? My babies are twenty-six and twenty-eight, and no grandchildren in sight. I miss cuddling the little ones."

Maryana placed Vlad in her lap. "Certainly! I must give you full disclosure, though. He's diapered. If he falls asleep, he could wet."

"Oh, it's all organic. Nothing that won't come out in the wash." Vlad rolled a wary eye to her, but dozed off in the midst of hugging and kissing and rocking.

"This one's our little prodigy in the making," Sasha gloated. "She's smarter than all the others combined."

"She's not yet three, so she hasn't started formal music yet, but she's started ballet, so she's learning rhythm," Maryana boasted. "Sarah can already read Russian and she's starting to pick out English. She knows several poems from memory."

"Ya znayu archeologia!" Sarah announced from her father's arms.

"Po-angliski, Sar'ina," Maryana explained. "Talk like Mama. We are all speaking English tonight."

Sarah slowed; she paused as she hunted for the right words, but it didn't dampen her enthusiasm. "I know arc'yology! I help Papa – things." Missing a word, she moved her hands in a brushing motion. "In museum they have pirate monies, but Vladdy's ascared of pirate stories."

"I can't believe she's already bilingual!" Mrs. Winters sputtered.

"Not fluently yet," Maryana said, "but we do our best to raise them bilingually. She heard me sing a French lullaby the other day and now she's obsessing on French."

"Pirates are very frightening men," Mr. Winters agreed solemnly, "but you are as charming as they come." He gave Sarah's cheek a soft pinch. "What's your favorite story?"

Sasha stood Sarah on the piano, and she launched into surprising detail about the legends of the Sky-City palace on Alpha Centauri, Sasha prompting her with the correct words when needed.

"And when they digged it up, there was city all over 'gain." Sarah finished with a wave of her arms.

Delia Winters cheered. "Oh, she's too much for words! You must be the most blessed woman in the universe. I'd never stop hugging her." She squeezed and kissed sleeping Vlad instead.

"There's a future collaborator for you, Sasha," laughed Ingvar Venerek, Boris's partner. "Whatever happened to fairy tales?"

Jim Winters shook a finger in the air. "Ah, ah! There's wisdom in those stories. Today's fairy tales are tomorrow's excavations." Sasha put Sarah back on the floor, and she wandered about as the conversations picked up again.

She stopped next to Bronas Groshenko, Anthropology chair, and his wife; he handed her a cookie from a nearby platter. Leaving a trail of crumbs, she wandered over to Jim Winters. "You know the Trojan horse?" she asked.

Mr. Winters smiled down at her with delight. He bent over to her level. "I do believe I've heard of it, yes. One story says it was a huge, empty horse the Trojans built on wheels, that ..."

Sarah leaned on the arm of his chair until her feet dangled, and she swung them. "I know that," she interrupted. "Was it boy horse, or girl horse?"

Mr. Winters raised an eyebrow. "I don't know. I don't think anyone has ever asked that question. The city burned up, and the horse burned with it, so nobody..."

"If it was the boy horse, it would have a *huy*," Sarah informed the room knowledgeably. "Girl horses don't have them. Except *huy* isn't a nice word. We have to say penis. You're a boy, so you pee with a penis like Vlad."

Ingvar covered his mouth with his hand. Alexei's whispered *"Fuck!"* was audible before he buried his face behind Galina. The remaining children looked to their parents for protocol, horrified. Sasha sat immobile as the children.

Maryana's face burned crimson. *"Sar'ina!"*

Mr. Winters' face turned white, then red. "Um, well, ..."

"Way past bedtime!" Valeria said. She snatched Sarah and ran upstairs. Galina took the sleeping Vlad from Mrs. Winters and followed.

Boris Venerek sniggered and downed his drink. "Can't fault her logic there, can we Jim? That's no small matter."

"I'm *terribly* sorry, Mr. Winters!" Maryana said. "Please forgive her. She's just recently learned ..."

Jim Winters leaned back and gave a hearty guffaw. A full minute passed before he was able to speak. "Oh my word! Out of the mouths of babes...! She's priceless, Kirushenko!"

Sasha clenched his glass, the evening's success and his career sinking along with his stomach. "An absolute treasure. I won't tell you where I dug her up."

After the hired help left, Maryana found him in the kitchen, nursing a waterglass of vodka and ice. "It's late. Time for bed. I'm keeping the caterers, but the sitting service is off my list. I didn't even tip them." She tugged the glass from his hand and squirmed onto his lap.

Sasha pulled the glass back for another swallow. "They're lucky you saw them out. I wouldn't have paid them at all."

"They managed to keep David quiet, walked a screaming baby for almost two hours, changed Vlad twice, and kept Sarah in one place until 21:30. I can't fault them too much. They were dealing with Elizabyeta when the escape happened." She shook his cheeks with her hands. "Lighten up. Delia said it was the best laugh they've had in years. They get all kinds of invitations, and most are insufferably boring. She said this was the most enjoyable event they've ever attended, and she wanted to know if we would stay in touch. She wanted to visit again before they left."

He leaned around her head to drink. "She was just being polite. I'm going to be roasted on Monday. My office will be decorated with horses and giant pricks."

"Will you stop that! Give me." Maryana pulled the glass away again. "What do I have to do, drink it on you?" She took a swallow, made a face, and took another.

Sasha took the glass and put it on the table. "You shouldn't do that. You don't know what I might do to you if you pass out."

Maryana batted her eyes. "I hope the same things you do when I don't. Now enough. It was a very successful evening, and outside of one child who is still a forgivable baby, everyone had impeccable manners. You should be proud. We're moving up, Sash." She slid off his lap and pulled his hand until he stood up. "Now sleep, my love."

Thirty-one

As Maryana expected, two dinner invitations, invites to three conferences, and an invite from the Winters to give a lecture in Norway followed their party; she made Sasha accept each offer. He endured a week of friendly harassment at work, accepting his fate with good humor, but Maryana sensed the change. She'd seen it before over the years. His playfulness disappeared, and he withdrew first from the family, then from her. He went from a casual beer after work to silent hard liquor after dinner. His temper flared over matters that used to be fixed with a glare and a pointed finger. She'd planned on getting sterilized, but he was in no condition to be in charge of everyone, not even for a day. Not right now. The success of the entire family rode on his back. He was her prime focus.

She found him slouched in front of the workscreen in his study, staring at a document; she could see he wasn't reading it. Her hands slid over his shoulders, fingers kneading the tension coiled within. "You feeling okay? You aren't usually that short with Viktor. He's a huge help around here; I think you hurt his feelings."

Sasha gave an irritable sigh. "Maybe. I just… This research is pissing me off. My advisor doesn't like the material I'm covering; he says it's overcited. He wants to see something new, something original from someone who already has one PhD. He says I should be striving for a *deeper understanding*. What the hell is that supposed to mean? What the hell are they looking for? I'm not a mind reader, Tash! I thought I was coming up with original interpretations. I swear, they're stalling me on purpose so I will do research for them. I do the work, then they turn around, interpret my work, and make money off of their monkey. My first PhD took five and a half years. Seven years I've been busting my balls with this, and for what? They can string me along forever this way."

"Is it worth driving yourself into the ground over? You have a PhD. You're the only one insisting on a second."

"It makes me more valuable, and the more valuable, the higher the salary. I've never heard you say no to money."

The comment could have been innocent enough, or it could have been a nasty barb meant to start an argument. Maryana decided to treat it as the former; Sash was never rude to her, and no doubt the bottle of vodka next to him had some play in it.

"Money does get us places, doesn't it. Perhaps if you laid off this," she reached across him and seized the bottle, "you might be able to think better."

The dark, dark eyes swiveled toward her, and the thick brows curled over them in an unpleasant scowl. "No, it relaxes me so my mind clears and I can think about something besides the noise in the house."

"Perhaps one glass, but not the whole bottle." Maryana put it back on the desk and squirmed her way onto his lap. Her fingers marched slowly up his chest. "Maybe you're just thinking too hard. Why don't you take the night off, and I'll take your thoughts off the whole annoying debacle, hmm? I can relax your mind, free your thoughts, and give you something to interpret in a very primitive and highly uncivilized way." She pulled his face down until they were nose to nose and he had only one visible eye, then kissed him. "I'll bet I can put a smile back on that face."

He didn't warm to the idea as he should have. "You think so?" His voice carried doubt, let alone lack of enthusiasm.

He left the bottle to follow her, but fell asleep while she massaged his back.

By September, the twins were gone, ensconced in Moscow as university students themselves. The loss of four very capable hands was going to take some adjusting to. Vlad was edging toward four, not much taller but more outgoing, and Sarah would be three in another month. Vlad now stayed dry one day out of two, and Sarah, who hadn't had a toileting accident in eight months, was consistently reading and computing at a second-form level. Screams or no screams, Maryana was determined to start them in a preschool. It wasn't a law that children begin school at three, but it was a very rare child indeed that didn't attend some sort of program. It would help wear them out during the day, make them sleep better at night, and give Sasha more quiet time in the evenings to work on his research. Prestige or not, Maryana wasn't sure about trying the same preschool as before, and found another of similar reputation. She held Vlad back until 15 October, after Sarah's birthday, so they could start together. Perhaps this time Vlad would share some of her excitement.

What a difference ten months made! Maryana walked them into the school, two shining-perfect children with a story-book mother, an angelic-looking baby on her arm. Vlad and Sarah held hands, *skipping* to the door. Vlad was dressed like a miniature businessman in a sweater and a new red bag to hold his spare clothes, crisp white bows adorned Sarah's blonde braids and a blue pack hung over her shoulders; their scrubbed cheeks shone like ripe autumn apples. Maryana introduced them to their teacher, Mrs. Akmatova, kissed each goodbye and was kissed back, and watched her pseudo-twins wander off to explore the class without so much as a look back, let alone a single whine. Her heart swelled, knowing she'd done the right thing in waiting, and she went home content.

How strange to be home with only one small infant! Maryana hadn't had such freedom since Sergei was little. She treated herself to a manicure and lunch at a small café. Life was on the right track again.

Until she went to retrieve her pair.

Maryana arrived five minutes early, eager to hear how the day went. The teacher pulled her aside to another room.

"Mrs. Kirushenko, in fifteen years of teaching I have never had two children have a more difficult adjustment to preschool. If they are to stay here, you and I must come up with a program to help them transition. Vladimir did well enough, but he became so upset over Sarah's misbehavior, he vomited his lunch. He needs to be separated from Sarah. Sarah... had a most difficult day. She cannot follow the simplest directions, disrupted the class, insisted on writing during rest time, left program areas, and ruined an untold amount of school materials by throwing them outside in the sand. If her behavior continues, I would like to call in a specialist."

Maryana stared in shock. "I'm having great difficulty believing what you're saying. Of all my children, they are the best behaved... Sarah's always the first to follow a direction. She can't wait to help. What happened?"

Akmatova went into more detail, some of which Maryana suspected was skewed, but she held her tongue. She returned to the class to retrieve her terrors.

Both children leaped for her. The hope of the morning's success evaporated into faint memory. Vlad cried against her leg. Sarah pulled her hand, pleading.

"I want to go home! I hate this baby school! Don't make me come here!"

"Stop, Sarah. Let's go. You can tell me all about it," Maryana promised.

On the way home, and once there, she heard two more sides to the tale. Vlad, it seemed, enjoyed the class until things went awry. Apparently Sarah's lines of questioning and play were a little more involved than what the teacher was used to. Outside of Vlad, Sarah wasn't used to being around children her own age; Sergei was her other playmate, and he was so advanced for six he'd been jumped ahead to second form instead of first. Sarah'd outgrown 'touch-your-nose' two years ago.

Maryana related the details to Sasha in the privacy of his study, one child on each of his knees.

Sasha stared as if she'd said that Sarah had taken the skimmer and piloted the both of them to school herself. "She did *what*?"

Maryana sighed, trying to look stern when she wanted to laugh at the whole thing. "She questioned everything the teacher did, corrected her a few times, and then got mad when she was told to sit down and shut up. I guess she was quite the little sour puss, repeatedly asking when they were going to learn something. I think what sent the teacher over the edge was when she marked off squares in the sand pit during outdoor play, buried a number of toys in the sand, and then showed the other children how to dig them up, clean them with paintbrushes she stole from the classroom, and claimed she was running an archeology dig. The teacher has no idea what's missing."

Sasha brightened for the first time in weeks. He gave a deep rolling chuckle that seemed to come from his feet. "No shit! Really? She did that?"

Maryana waved her hands. "Apparently. The real problems seemed to begin when the teacher thwarted her dig. That's when she yelled at Sarah and sent her inside, which made Vlad cry, which made Sarah mad, which made Vlad so upset he didn't want to eat lunch but they pushed him, so it came back up, which made the teacher mad, Sarah mad, Vlad more upset, and basically started a two-child sit-down strike that lasted most of the afternoon. So they are questioning if *Sarah* is ready for school."

"I'll be damned. An archaeologist in the making at three." He stared down at Sarah with the false sternness Maryana couldn't muster. "Tell me about outdoor time." Sarah went into detail, marking out the squares with a stick and everyone working together and having fun until the teacher ruined everything.

"Do I have to go to that school?" she asked softly. "It's not fun. They don't learn anything. Can I go to a fun school?"

"Do I have to go?" Vlad echoed.

"Not everything is fun," Sasha said. "You cannot ruin the teacher's materials just to play a game. You should have asked her first. But she should have told you the rules first, too. No, you do not have to go back, Sarah. I think you can wait for big school, where the teachers are smart enough to answer your questions. But Vlad will go back, and I won't have one bit of bullshit about it. No crying. No wetting. He won't have the same teacher, though. I won't have a teacher yell at my children."

Sarah's chin quivered. "I can't go to school?"

"I'll make you a deal." Sasha glanced at Maryana with an apologetic look. Maryana had been fighting Sarah's wish for three months, but it would distract her from the other issue. "You wanted to take karate lessons, no? To learn to kick?"

"*Da.*" Sarah punched her hands forward, one after the other. "Yah! Yah!"

"You wait until next year for school, and I will tell your Mama to let you have karate lessons now, okay? But you have to behave. Your mother has enough bother with the baby. Understood?"

Vlad and Sarah nodded. "Yes, Papa."

He set Vlad down, but hugged Sarah and kissed the side of her head before her feet touched the ground. "Too smart, Sar'ina! That's my girl."

Maybe it was the fading of autumn, the darkening of the days as winter encroached. Even in Kiev, December daylight lasted a mere eight hours. Maybe it was the chaos of the holidays, with numerous demands for appearances at parties that Sasha didn't want to attend but felt obligated by his job. Perhaps the fact the Academy was on hiatus, as were the schools, and all the children were home and in each other's hair. Maybe it was because his birthday rolled around and he realized two of his children were already in university themselves; at forty-two he was no longer considered a young man. Or maybe it was the weather, the fact it was Wednesday, or the color of the winter bedsheets. Maryana was at her wits' end. Sasha stopped working on his project entirely, and his elbow seemed to have a permanent bend in it, along with his temper. She tried favorite foods, sent children off to entertainments to make the house quiet, bought racy lingerie, but nothing would break his mood.

She climbed next to him as he lay morosely on their over-sized bed, custom-made to accommodate his height. A half-empty bottle of vodka and a sticky glass sat on the side table.

Maryana ran her fingers through his shaggy hair and fluffed it off his neck. She kissed him behind his ear. "What's the matter, Sash? You've been in here all night. We missed you at dinner. What's wrong?"

He stared ahead, vacant as a broken statue. "Nothing."

"Something's bothering you," she insisted sweetly. He'd been so successful for so long; someone breaking his backside was bound to happen sooner or later. He just needed his confidence back and he'd be on his feet and clearing hurdles in no time. If she could only figure out how.

She made him sit forward and squeezed in behind him, rubbing the massive shoulders. He held his hand out; she handed him his glass.

Steps sounded down the hall. David stuck his head in the door. "Mother? 'Mitri's eating all the banana chips and he won't share and when he did gimme some, Alexei punched me in the back and took them from …"

"Get out!" Sasha screamed, moving so fast he nearly knocked her off the bed. The glass in his hand flew across the room. David shut the door just before it hit and shattered. "Goddamned son of a bitch whining *brat*!" sounded through the door.

"Easy, easy, Sasha!" Maryana soothed. She pushed him down on the bed and stroked his cheek. "Please tell me what's bothering you."

The big lip curled in a little-boy pout. "I got passed over. They gave the tenure spot to Schneider. They said it was because I didn't publish again this year. My degree is stalled, I missed out on the grant, now this…"

"So Schneider got lucky this year. Next year will be your turn." She flicked her long hair behind her and kissed the back of his neck.

He jerked away from her touch. "It's not that simple, Tash. To move forward again, I have to publish; I've got to be out doing fieldwork or at least doing research. I can't do that kind of work without the grants. We can't afford to just up and relocate for a year on our own. We can't afford to drag everyone around with us, and I can't go off and leave you alone that long by yourself. All Schneider has is that graduate student he's banging. He can go anywhere at any time. We're buried under children."

Maryana threw her arm over him and cuddled close. "I can't believe I am listening to the star pupil of the class of '42. Where is my biggest pride? Where is the Sasha who was so determined to be the Best of the Best?"

"Failing miserably."

Maryana kissed his nose, the large pores covered in a mist of alcohol sweat. "Nonsense! Figure it out, my dreamer. Figure out what you want to do, where you want to be. We'll write out the proposal together, just like always. Grant or no grant, we'll make it work. We always have. Next year you'll have the grants and the tenure. I'm sure the children will be happy to travel again. Let me clean up the glass and get some of them off to bed. Once it's quiet, we'll sit and work everything out." She kissed the blank stare once more and got up.

* * *

Maryana set the older children to getting the younger ones off to bed. Having a chain of command worked well, each child responsible for the one below, and Maryana in charge of babies. It fostered cooperation, caring, and freed up her time.

Maryana out of sight upstairs, Sasha wandered down to the playroom, the bottle of vodka in his hand since he'd lost the glass. Three boys and a girl watched a program on the large wallscreen. He stopped in front of Dmitri. "You!" He slapped the boy's face with a powerful hand. Dmitri cowered silently, arm raised to block a second possible blow. "Stop eating like a goddamned pig!"

"And you!" He slapped David with the back of the same hand before he could get away. "Stop being such a goddamned snitch! *Bastard!* Get to bed! Now! I have work to do and I'm not listening to any more whining." The children fled.

He walked down the hall to the study. "Move it!" he barked at Viktor, using the main interface. "Go! I've got work to do." He took a long drink from the bottle and sat down at the desk.

Maryana dragged him through the application process, one painful step at a time. Sasha searched through untold postings, looking for something to catch his interest. He narrowed his choices down, did a few interviews over the commlink, and Maryana prayed for a miracle.

Not long after Byeta's first birthday, he called her at lunch. There was a brightness in his eyes, a lightness in his voice that she hadn't heard in months. "Gamma Europa IV," he said in greeting.

"Gamma what?" Realization hit. "You got it?!"

The broad grin lit his entire face. "Start your packing list. Come August, we spend the next year on Gamma Europa IV. It's a temperate zone on a class-M, level-2 world, just a little behind in technology. Good money, a promising site, and I should get at least one, maybe even three papers out of it. This could be exactly what I need."

Maryana's heart soared upward until she thought it would hug that wonderful, unseen planet. "Oh, Sash! I'm so happy for you! I can't wait to see it!"

* * *

Sasha found her hiding in his study, far from the chaos of the rest of the house. Somewhere a diaper smelled bad, there was a three-way fight screaming in the upstairs hall, one child was reading peacefully under the kitchen table while finishing off a box of *kozinaki,* another fighting a spacebattle with a simulator game in the playroom while two others watched, another practicing piano, and no hint of what might be for dinner. In three weeks they were leaving the planet for his year-long sabbatical; this wasn't the time for Tash to be off on one of her social-organizing functions. There was far too much to organize at home.

She sat at his desk, face glued to the viewscreen interface, a different news program running in each corner and a fifth in the center. She didn't even look up when he entered.

"Something happen to the stock market?"

Maryana turned; her eyes were large with grief. "I'm sure it will. Oh Sash! It's all over the news." She played back a clip she'd saved.

In United States news, a transcontinental commuter flight on route from San Francisco to New York went down today east of Des Moines, Iowa. Lora Denning Ivanov, wife of New York investment titan Tomas Ivanov, a partner of the galactic giant Ivanov Industries Corporations, was believed to have been on board. There were no survivors. The Moscow-centered Ivanov Corporation has not yet released a statement.

Sasha hung his head. "Your brother's wife? I'm sorry, Tash. That's terrible." She wrapped her trembling arms around his thighs; he pulled her tight against him in as best a hug he could do without kneeling.

"Oh Sash! I feel so awful! I should be there, comforting him. I've tried getting through on his private line all afternoon, but it goes straight to messages."

He pulled back a little. "You're not calling him direct, are you?"

She dabbed her face with a disposable tissue. "It's fine, Sash. It's the line I set up to route through South Africa, untraceable. It hurts, Sash! It hurts so bad! Most of the time I don't think about them, but then something like this comes along and I know I should be there. I belong there."

Sasha lost his sympathetic edge. Maryana was brilliant at managing money, but she wasn't always smart in concerns of the heart. "You can't go to the funeral, Tash. The media will be crawling all over something like that. They feed off people's pain, especially successful people. You can't be seen even in the background under a false name. They took that right from you. If your father sees you, you can be arrested. You can't even sign the virtual guestbook."

Pain twisted Maryana's face, a heartache no medication could ever erase. "I know that. I just want to talk to him. Maybe I could meet him somewhere privately, give him our sympathies in person. Surely Mamá... "

"If she cared, she would have been in touch before now. She would have prevented all that legal shit, but she didn't. Don't you risk it. They've held their truce this long; don't go stirring up something we don't need."

"No," she said faintly.

The twins had returned home for the summer break, helping with children, packing, and locking up the house for the year-long trip. Perhaps they could make dinner, and give Tash some quiet time to herself. "The twins home?"

"They went shopping."

"Oh." *Damn.* He paused, sighed, then finally said it. "Stay. Find out what you can. I'll get everyone dinner."

"Thank you, Sash. I love you."

He gave a her a wan smile. As much as he hated her family, he felt a small shred of sympathy for her brother. Only her brother had the balls to go against The Tyrant's wishes, to speak to Tash in secret, at his own risk. If something happened to Tash like that … His brain blanked and his chest hurt and he couldn't breathe, just imagining. "I love you, too."

* * *

Nothing. Nothing would go through. She tried his business line, his private line, even a public mail link, but each responded with *unavailable, leave a message.* Maryana could see it playing out in her head, the grief, the seclusion, Mamá hovering close, the attempt to make private funeral arrangements yet announce it to those who might want to attend. Such a delicate balance at such a time of agonizing crisis. She couldn't, she just couldn't let it go by without telling him she felt his pain.

Do I dare?

It was two days before she found the courage. She waited until Byeta was napping and the other children occupied, double-checked the configuration to assure anonymity, and pressed outgoing message. She kept it to voice message only; videofeed was out of the question. She hadn't placed a call to that address in… nineteen years.

Please, Tomas!

"Allo. Eta Andrea."

The words turned Maryana's nerves to ice, trapping frozen breath inside her lungs. The voice seized her heart, squeezed it so fast and so hard it exploded in shards of dust. *Mamá.* Oh, how she wanted to say something, anything, to tell her how much she missed her!

On the other hand – how could she say *anything* now? Surely Mamá would know her voice, and the contact would violate the agreement she had signed. She was dead and buried to the world, and she must remain dead.

She tried anyway, dropping her voice and trying her best to imitate an accent, any accent. Mamá would know her French and her

201

English; Maryana had never picked up much Israeli, so she tried Georgian Kartuli.

"Allo!" Andrea repeated.

"Allo. Too sheheedzlebah, Tomas Ivanov. Please."

"I'm sorry, Mr. Ivanov is not taking calls at this time. Who is this? How did you get this number?"

"Please give him a message. Tell him … South Africa sends its deepest condolences. Thank you."

She ended the call quickly while she still had her wits about her. Mamá would be confused, which made it more likely she'd tell Tomas, hoping for an explanation. He would understand, but would he give away the sender? That was the wild card. Or would Mamá hear the Kartuli, ask for translation, remember Tbilisi, and connect the dots? Surely, Mamá wouldn't say a word if she did.

Please, Mamá!

She was still crying long after Byeta was begging to get up from her nap, but she managed to stop before Sasha got home.

Thirty-two

Gamma Europa IV settled them at the end of a dirt road in a cool, damp coastal village, with salty ocean breezes and the calming sounds of endlessly rolling surf hissing into the distance behind them. The rocky treeless hills of the Hantovalli region were a far cry from the dry flatness of their part of Kiev. Contracts and a twelve-month sabbatical in hand, Sasha wedged the family into a bright blue four-bedroom house ten minutes out of the town. Maryana would have preferred somewhere warmer and drier – it hadn't taken long for half the children to become sick with the climate change, and little Sarah, dangerously ill, had actually had to be hospitalized at the mercy of second-world medicine. Now, five months later, the preschooler was sick again, and they still had four months to go. There was no governing university to socialize at, just the Ministry of Culture that hired Sasha, leaving Maryana without much peer interaction. Translators had to be hired for most trips to the city, the children traveled an hour to a disorganized Alliance diplomatic school, and there were no preschools, trapping her home full-time with three children. Still, the worst part of the move was leaving the twins behind on Earth; no visits, no semester breaks to return home on. Never had home seemed so far away – or communication charges so expensive. Viktor and Katerina were a huge help, but not yet as adept as their oldest sisters.

She shouted into the handicom she held. "What? Easy, Sash! I can't make out what you're saying. Your finger's blocking the solarcell again. Be careful, okay? Slow down. I love you, too." Maryana slid the handicom into a pocket.

She stood in the room, thinking. Sasha was terribly excited about something. He'd been working almost around the clock for seven months, desperate to do everything right, to make the work count, to find the miracle he needed to push his second PhD to completion, to prove to himself he was as good as his heart wanted him to be, as good

203

as his self-esteem needed him to be. The ministry was thrilled by his work, thrilled at the training he was giving their own scholars. Half an ancient fortification located and uncovered, eight thousand documented artifacts recovered and cataloged for study, ancient paintings, architecture, tablets of ancient script, and still some morbid self-doubt tormented him.

Until now.

She would go out there, she decided. If it was that big, she should be there helping him. She ran down the list of *should's* in her head, and realized it would take her a while to get ready.

First she checked on Sarah. The four-year-old lay motionless in bed, wheezing and choking breathlessly on tears, her brother rubbing her arm for comfort.

"Was she up here again?" Maryana asked as she pulled Vladimir out of the way. She flipped up Sarah's pajama shirt. Sure enough, a number of small red bite marks ringed her chest. She snapped a vial of inhalant into the medication mask and pressed it over the girl's mouth and nose. "You're not a baby. Stop crying. You only make it worse. Breathe!"

"Katerina! Viktor!" she called, and the two appeared in the doorway. "Katya, it's your responsibility to keep Elizabyeta out of here. You're going to have to switch beds with her. Sarah can't keep getting bitten like this." With so many children squeezed into the temporary house, they'd had to settle for doubling the younger ones up at night. Unfortunately, some of the arrangements just weren't working. Little Elizabyeta had the face of a Renaissance angel, and the temper of the Devil himself.

"Your father's found something at the dig. He's working straight through the night. I'm going out there with him. You'll have to keep things together here."

The timer beeped, and Maryana removed the mask. The girl gave a gurgle, a long, strangling wet cough and hacked up a large amount of thick goo into a towel she kept in her hands. "Better?"

The child nodded, breathing normally for the moment. Despite Maryana's wary eye and the prevention efforts of several doctors, it was the fourteenth time the child had contracted pneumonia.

"Viktor, keep an eye on her. If she's having trouble, throw the mask on her. There's still a couple of doses left in the can."

"Yes, Mother."

Maryana stood before the girls' mirror and brushed out her hair. She braided it, wrapped the two braids around her head and fastened them in place. At thirty-six, she still looked like a Russian princess. Her hair still blazed of its own accord, her skin was firm and good; she could see changes, but they weren't that obvious yet. After eleven children and three cesareans, she was only four and half kilos heavier than she'd been at seventeen. She chose tan slacks that clung tighter than skin in just the right places, and a soft blue Borealan-silk sweater against the damp air. The mirror met with her approval.

"I'm going out to the dig," she informed her group. "Dmitri, David, mind your brother and sister and stay away from Alexei. Lights out by ten. Sergei, books away at eight. Vladimir, sleep in your own bed! Let Sarah rest. You don't want her back in the hospital, do you? Katya, keep him out of there, and make sure you take him to the sanitary at least twice during the night. Alexei, carry those boxes out to the speedster for me."

His sneer begged otherwise. "Can't Viktor do it? He's not doing anything. I was about to call my *friends*. You know, back *home*? Where we're supposed to live? Where I have my own damned room and I don't have to share it with a bunch of piss-assed losers? If you won't activate my handicom here, why can't I have a private line to myself? I'm the oldest, I should be getting something out of this fucking mess."

Maryana stared fearlessly up at her eldest son, sixteen and towering over her like Sasha. "You will speak politely or I will take you with me and you may haul rocks for your father all night. Viktor has his tasks, you were given yours. Do it now."

Cursing, Alexei hefted the stack of boxes and brought them outside.

At the dig site, Maryana parked the vehicle near the equipment hauler and struggled to carry the heavy boxes to the work tent, one by one. She'd brought Sasha only one case of local grog. He could be hospitable and celebrate with his crew, but she didn't want him screwing up something important with too much vodka. He could drink that when he got home.

It was just after sunset, and the flood lights blazed down brighter than noon under the weather canopy that waved and shook with the ocean breezes whipping up the mountainside. Sasha folded low on his knees, working with four students deep in a pit, all armed with laser cutters and brushes, picking away at something large emerging from the soil.

"Three millimeters, no closer!" he barked at the closest student. "Don't nick it!" He seized the tool in his massive hand and demonstrated.

Maryana paused, hidden by the blinding glare of a lamp. She loved watching him at work, so in charge, so knowledgeable, so fearlessly in command, confidence and passion and competence unstoppable. Here was her hero, tearing time itself from the heart of the planet, history sifting through his fingers like sand through a screen, master of eternity. Here was her towering Zeus, her Odin, her Perun wielding his rock-hammer with a thunderous bellow, immortal, and her love overwhelmed all other thoughts.

She bounded lightly down the ladder to the current floor of the site and laid a gentle hand on his back.

He smelled her perfume before she touched him. "Tash! What are you doing here?" Backlit by the floodlights, white light shining like a halo through the stray hairs on her head, Maryana beamed at him like a heavenly spirit, and he smiled.

"You sounded so excited, I figured I'd better see for myself, in case you needed help. I brought dinner for everyone. You'll need your strength if you're going to work all night."

Sasha shut off the laser. He put a damp arm around her and gave her a kiss, leaving a trail of dirt down her sweater. "You're too good for me. Break time!" he announced to the crew. "Dinner, on me!" The translator repeated his words for the locals. A cheer went up from around the dig.

Maryana studied the ground. She'd helped Sasha through enough work to know what the various markings meant. "What did you find? Is this still the agora?"

"Underneath. We're pretty certain this is a temple." Sasha pointed out the boundaries. "The early datings are putting it about four thousand years old. We've found what appears to be a collapsed altar, three partially intact pieces of pottery, and a huge pile of small bones, perhaps sacrifices. We've got the edges marked, and there are partial walls in the back there. The scanners show they may go down more than two meters. The way it's all tilted and the consistency of the soil, my guess is a mud flow for some reason."

"Fantastic! Maybe that's the break you've been looking for."

"That's *nothing*. Look!" He took her by the hand and moved to the side of the rectangle marked off in front of them. Bits of bone showed above the ochre soil.

"Look, Tash!" he said with reverence. "It's the find of a lifetime, and I wasn't even looking for it! It's only supposed to be legend. There are a number of petroglyphs, some clay representations, but no one's ever found a remnant of such a creature, not a claw. And I may have found a *whole* one. See?" His finger traced gently in the dirt. "Wave scan showed probable wings bent backward this way. I'm no paleontologist, but I'm not wrong on this. It's *here*, it's *real*, and *I found it*!"

"That's wonderful!" she gasped. "What is it?"

"It has to be the legendary dragon of the Maridionias Cult. By our measurement, it's three hundred centimeters long, with a wingspan almost twice that. No one's understood how such an influential animal-based religion could spring up over something that didn't have some basis in fact. The dragon was just thought to be symbolic of power, but here is proof to the contrary, and *I* found it! See! See these discolorations in the soil? We took samples but we haven't run them yet. It's most likely some sort of cage that decayed. Caged, right here in the temple! Tash, this is bigger than I ever could have hoped for! The kind of discovery fewer than one in ten *thousand* archaeologists ever comes across!" He gazed down at her, coated with dust and damp soil, excitement pouring off him like so much sweat. "It's the stuff *dreams* are made of! This will turn everything upside down."

Maryana threw her arms around him. "Oh Sasha! I'm so happy for you! I told you this would be a good thing!"

They ate with the crew, watching the native members dance and sing. Gamma Europa IV had left Maryana with a bit of social isolation. With no cook or housekeeper, no local playgrounds or preschool activities, no licensed sitters and no tag-team twins for help, the youngest three drained her with demands. With no wives' club, no fundraisers to direct, and the diplomatic sector inconveniently far, she spent as much time as she could with Sasha and his crew, filling in whenever needed. The last thing she wanted in the middle of their celebration party was needless interruption. She ignored the chirping of her handicom for eight or nine squawks, playing with the notion of flinging it off into the dirt. A growl rattled her throat as she activated it.

Viktor sounded worried. "Mother? Sarah's awful purply… "

"Find the aerosol with the yellow label. Take the red one off the mask, put the yellow one on and have her breathe that. It will expand her lungs. Use one of the aerosols to crush up two of the big blue pills and give them to her in some pudding. Wait five minutes, then pound on her back. That should loosen it. If not, there's that suction thing in the closet, but she hates it." Even Vladimir knew that by now.

Viktor sighed half-heartedly. "We'll try."

* * *

Sarah sat up in the bed, head back, pulling the skin away from her throat in a vain attempt to gain more air as she struggled to breathe, her large violet-blue eyes looking even bigger and more purple in her peaked face. Her lips and fingertips were a dark dusky color.

Katerina held her up with shaking hands, more panicked than Sarah. "Hurry! She's making the bird noise again! What do we do if it doesn't work?"

"Then we'll call Mother back!" fourteen-year old Viktor snapped. "It'll work. It's got to. She knew this would happen; why the hell'd she have to go out?" He wrestled the medication canister onto the mask, slapped it over Sarah's face and pulled the straps tight. She forced it tighter with both hands.

"Breathe," Vladimir coached next to her. "Deep and slow."

Alexei watched from the doorway. "You're a bunch of fucking pussies. Why don't you just call for medevac and stick her in a hospital where she belongs? Do you know what kind of germs she's probably spraying everywhere? She could die in the middle of the night and you'd be sleeping next to her and never know it until she was cold and stiff in the morning."

Katya's face darkened. "You are so evil, Alexei! Why don't you go choke yourself? It should be *you* lying here instead of her, except I wouldn't take care of you."

"Hmph. You children are so cute when you're mad. It's not me, and I wouldn't let you, anyway. You're as likely to kill her as cure her. She's probably choking from Vlad puking on her."

Vladimir hung his head. Stomach difficulties continued to plague him.

208

"If I were you, I'd check my pillow when I went to bed," Katya shot back, "because that's where I'd puke if I were him." Alexei laughed again, knowing it would never happen, and walked off.

"Save it," Viktor said dismally. "It's not worth arguing with him. Okay, Shining Star. Let's try it." He took the inhaler from Sarah and lay her upside down over his knees. He pounded short little bangs on her back, trying to shake the thick goo loose from her lungs, bottom to top.

After a minute the child began to cough. And cough. And cough. Deep hacking coughs that shook her body and strangled her with the force. When she tried to breathe, they could *hear* the sucking noises of the fluids shifting in her chest. She coughed up a torrent of thick, frothy slime.

Katya wiped the spit with a towel. "My God, Viktor! She's so sick! What do we *do*?"

"Same thing we are doing," he shrugged. "What else can we do?"

* * *

Around dawn, Sasha caught a nap on a folded canopy in the supply tent. Dust and hardened foam from the immobilizing compound caked him head to toe. Maryana found him sleeping an hour later. She brushed his lips with hers.

"I have to go home, Sash." She pushed the thick black hair from his eyes with a loving hand. "I'll expect you home for dinner. You'll need your rest to see this through."

"You could give me some energy." He pulled her down on top of him. The big hands squeezed her rump and his lips locked on hers.

Maryana fought him off, laughing. "Stop it, Sash. I will not fool with you here at the dig. There's probably a half-dozen students with their ears glued to the tent."

"About time they learned something. You won't let me sacrifice your chastity on the altar?" Sasha said with his endearing half-smile. "We can recreate a living legend."

She giggled, lying across his broad chest. It felt so *good* to see him this happy again! It had been far too long. Everything would straighten out now. "I probably should have told you before this, but, I'm not a virgin."

"I'll be the judge of that." A hand fumbled at her clothing. "Come on, just a quick ..."

"No." Maryana kissed him longingly, pulling away with a promise of things to be. "This way you'll be thinking about me all day, and then I know you'll be home on time."

Thirty-three

2259

Maryana tipped her head, afraid of his words. "Are you serious? All of them? But it's his moment. The spotlight should be on him."

"No, no," the minister insisted. "It is true, his genius must be honored foremost, but this is an important inspirational moment for our people. You brought your family to our world at great hardship, all to benefit us. It is a moment for your entire family. It is only correct all should share the honor. It reminds our people how important family is. It reminds us that we are not alone in the galaxy, and that we are no different and no less important than the people of other worlds."

A thousand disasters flashed through her head, most of which would be invisible even in the front row of an audience, but on stage, before a thousand live people and cameras that would catch every second of every action of every person for the posterity of trillions of people across the galaxy? But how could she decline without upsetting an entire country, if not an entire planet? An asteroid seemed to strike her insides, shaking them until she wanted to cry. There was no declining such tribute.

Maryana's hostess smile lit up her face, and she pressed her hand against the minister's, as was Hantovallan custom. "We are most honored by your graciousness."

In the hallway outside the auditorium, she circled her brood together. Thank the stars she had decided to pack at least one top-quality outfit for everyone, and at the last minute made everyone wear them. A few of the boys' were a little tight, but no one would know. Everyone looked more or less well-cultured.

Maryana stretched herself up even higher on her heels, taller than all but her oldest boys, and from somewhere deep in her DNA drew up a look so steely and venomous even Mamá would have been taken aback. Sparks seemed to hit the air with her words.

"You will all listen, and listen well. I have learned we will all be sitting on that stage behind your father, where everyone in the galaxy will see us. Your father has worked his entire life for this moment. In all the Institute, in all the universities, there is no honor as high as this. You will not ruin it with a laugh, or a pinch, or a single frown. You. Will. Be. Perfect. No pocket coms, no message answering, no palm-com games; hands folded only. You will look ahead. You will smile on cue. You will look proud of your father. If I must get up and leave because of the baby, you will sit there as if I had never left. One incident, just one, and no matter how big or small you are, I will tell your father to spank you until you cannot sit, and I swear by all the Saints, the Gods of all the Heavens and the Grand Maker of the Universe, I mean every word. Not only the perpetrator, but the child on either side as well, so make extra sure you mind your own business. Vladimir, there will be no wetting, no vomiting, and no trips to the sanitary once you sit, so make sure you squeeze out every last drop. Sarah, there will be no questions until after the ceremony. Understood? The seating order will be Dmitri, Sergei, Viktor, David, myself with the baby, Vladimir, Sarah, Katya, and Alexei, no exceptions. Am. I. Being. Received?"

Subdued agreements and nods worked their way around the group. To her relief, even overgrown Alexei squirmed. The thought of telling Sasha to spank one, let alone two or three of her children, made her dangerously queasy.

"Good. Dmitri, take Vladya to the sanitary one last time. The rest of you, line up."

The ceremony lasted a little over an hour, filled with pomp and ceremony, national choirs singing anthems and folk songs, a short documentary on the history of the Maridionias dragon, a speech by the Greater Secretary of the Emri Sal Bureau of Historical Affairs (whose title took up half a door in script), and then Sasha rose to give a brief speech which was translated in subtitles on a screen above his head. Bolstered by a tranquilizer – Maryana made sure there wasn't a drop of alcohol available – her Herodotus stood tall and proud, clothed in a new brown and green outfit that was considered extremely high-end among the Hantovallan elite. Her esteemed professor didn't shed a drop of sweat as he read from his prompter, thanking the people of the country of Emri Sal, the people of the Hantovalli region-state, the people of the city of Yamir for allowing him such a privilege. When he was done, Naan Atle Bo-Jun, Grand President of Emri Sal, Gamma Europa IV, hung a Medal of Honor around his neck.

Her darlings clapped on cue.

Maryana sent each of her children a personal note, thanking them for their behavior, and by the time they boarded their long flight back to Earth, each child possessed a new expensive item or toy previously denied.

Success never felt so sweet.

* * *

As much as Sasha loved being out in the field, loved working with the Hantovallan people, it felt good to be back in Kiev. With everything involved in a major discovery – the files, the reports, the infinitesimal documentation, the formal papers, the questions, the press conferences – let alone the agony of turning the whole project over to the Hantovallans to continue on their own as his contract specified – he found the return to Earth and home and work and all its routines a mixed blessing. Some archaeologists spent their entire lives working the same excavation; he missed the excitement. On the other hand, he was enjoying the quiet, too. The children had space to themselves again, picked up their lessons in dance, music, karate, sports, and etiquette, were re-enrolled in the proper schools and preschools, and peace – as well as nine children could manage it – reigned once more.

He needed that peace. The last few months following his sabbatical had become a whirlwind of awards and interviews, lectures and papers, a year of his face plastered on every archeology journal in the known galaxy, the incredibly fast granting of his second PhD in Ancient Civ – a year beyond any dream he could ever imagine. Him, another fatherless bastard from the rubble of the Sochi slums, being voted one of the top ten names in science for 2259! It was priceless luxury to have an entire week with no special appointments scheduled.

He parked himself in front of the communications screen in the study and checked the mail feed for household messages. The first twenty were for one child or another. Another twelve were advertisements from Tash's favorite stores. Not until the thirty-fourth was one addressed to him, a reply to a job offer. Job opportunities –

213

some applied for, some not – were rolling in almost faster than he could read them.

His thick finger paused over the button. It was a document feed, not a videomessage. The Interstellar Space Fleet Academy of the United Planetary Alliance. The finger trembled, and his stomach contracted until he felt a burn of acid crawling upward.

The United Planetary Alliance Space Fleet Academy was an unthinkable dream, a galactic facility where members of all planets, all species, could come together as one and share the most up-to-date and groundbreaking information available. It was for the most brilliant minds in the galaxy, where studies of quantum mechanics and physics were warping the very fabric of time and space itself. A place where the needs of the military forged bonds with the latest advances in physics and engineering and non-human biology, training the greatest spaceship crews ever known. A place where the future of mankind met the present on a daily basis. He was a nobody, a bumbling fool who had merely been in the right place at the right time to stumble on something extraordinary. All he'd done was uncover it. Eight years' work, and he didn't even have tenure.

A deep breath, and Sasha reminded himself that a letter of regret, especially a printed one, was not necessarily a personal affront. Reaching for the stars and only attaining a moon did not constitute failure, only a better place to launch from. He had a respectable job that paid more than he'd ever thought possible, and he was grateful for that each and every day. What more did he really need? He pushed the message button and read the words on the screen with resigned irritation.

We are happy to inform you that your application for employment has been reviewed ...

Sasha blinked at the word *happy*. He was fluent in Interstellar English; he knew what *happy* meant. Adrenaline pounded in his veins with faint but growing hope, and he read faster

... Andwearepleasedtobeabletoofferyouaninterviewforapositionon ourteachingfacultyPleasecontactFarfalleMizettiassoonaspossibleatthef ollowingcommlinkaddress...

Sasha sat back in the chair, too stunned to speak. He read the letter several times, then printed out a hard copy. He carried it to the kitchen as if it were made of thin glass, terrified that if he tipped it, the words would slide off the page and it would become null and void before anyone could verify its reality.

"Can you imagine! *The Allied Fleet Academy!* An offer from the Space Fleet itself! To *teach* there!"

A dozen people stared at the magical printout. Most of them didn't understand what it was, but their father wasn't often excited like this, so it must be something very good.

"Imagine, Tash! *The Space Academy!*" he beamed, trailing her around the kitchen like a small boy promised a big surprise. "It's enough just to be accepted as a student there! Imagine what it must be like to be a professor – to *teach* the best of the very best! You know what they must think of me, to send me an invitation to apply? The *honor*! The *prestige*!"

Maryana placed a massive bowl of Casseiopeian cheese twists on the table; six children dove for it all at once. "They finally realized you're one of the best of the very best. You earned every word they said."

"It means we can write our own ticket! There are branches everywhere! Want to spend a semester on Altair? We can! Centauri? We can! The travel opportunities! The education opportunities! As long as I teach there, the children can take classes, no admissions exam necessary! You can study the art history of a dozen worlds! Cultures, languages, histories – the entire universe, right there at our fingertips!"

"I'm sure it wouldn't hurt Sarah, or Sergei for that matter," she reflected. "I take it this is the offer you're going to follow?"

"Like a dream!" Sasha hugged her tightly, despite her advancing state of pregnancy. One too many intoxicated celebrations, a burning indiscretion on the seat of the flyer, and here came number twelve.

* * *

Grooming and deportment were never Sasha's strong suits. Left to himself, he wore whatever clothing he grabbed, whether it was dirty, didn't fit, or in poor repair. His fingers combed his hair more often than any brush, and his beard carried crumbs of his previous meal. Maryana scolded him repeatedly for eating sausage and garlic before meetings. His trick of a quick drink to calm his nerves before an event sometimes turned to two or three, fogging him. For every other interview he'd had, Maryana had accompanied him, inspecting his clothes, his shoes, cleaning his nails and combing his hair, making absolutely certain he looked his best. This time, the interview was far off in western America, too far for a single day's journey.

"Even if I could fly that far, I can't leave them all alone for three days," Maryana said as she packed his clothes in pre-matched, bagged sets. "Not that far away. It's not fair to ask the girls to come home. I want them to concentrate on their studies. Valeria's trying to squeeze two degrees into five years; she can't waste time to nanny for us."

He sat on the bed with an anxious face. "No, but you're my good luck charm. In twenty years, we've never been apart that long. What if I forget something important?"

She held up his palmcom. "I made you a detailed list of things to check, every step of the way. If you lose it, or the power fails, I have a printed copy already folded in the pocket of the pants you will wear to the interview. I will fix your nails just before you leave, so that's one less thing you'll have to worry about. I included reminders of etiquette as well. You've defended two theses and given umpteen lectures and interviews to news sources. This will be a breeze."

Her hands cradled his chin, forcing him to look at her. "Promise me, Sash. No alcohol before the interview. No beer, no wine, no vodka, no liqueur candies, nothing. You will be fine. Have a ginger fizz; it will soothe your stomach. You have my permission to drink an entire bottle of Chateau Rivard or its American equivalent after you return to the hotel, but not until you are finished. Promise?"

The dark, dark eyes broke from hers, but he nodded. "For you, I promise." He didn't look any happier when she kissed him on the forehead. She spent the next three days glued to one communication device or another, answering his million nervous questions with unfailing patience.

The interview was a mere formality, the open position his for the taking. Sasha returned home triumphant, full of stories and small gifts for the children.

"Tell me, Sash," she said as they got ready for bed. What he'd bragged to the family and what his face said now were two different things. "What did they *really* say? What was it *really* like?" She didn't add, *Is it really worth it?* He was set where he was; a career move now wasn't necessary. No academic institution denied tenure to a highly-decorated professor.

He sighed heavily, a sound that rumbled forever like distant thunder. "I was hoping it would be at Seattle. It's a beautiful campus in a beautiful city. The weather's livable. The children speak English. But it's not."

Maryana didn't like the disappointment in his voice. He'd turned down several other highly prestigious - and profitable - offers while waiting on this dream. "Where is it?"

His shirt dropped on the floor. "It's only an assistant professorship. A demotion, when you think about it. And it's at a sub-branch. On Navara."

"Navara!" Maryana's nostrils flared as she climbed onto the bed. An entire planet of hot desert sands... and a race of people who never so much as smiled. "We'd have to relocate to another planet? We'd be so far away from the girls."

"Three days, minimum, and that's in a Davies' drive ship."

"What did you tell them?"

He slid into the bed next to her. "I said I needed to confirm it with you, that I needed three days."

"Did you decide?" She held her breath. *Say no. Say no.* He'd lost his enthusiasm. Not good.

"No," Sasha admitted. "Yes, it's the Allied Space Fleet. Not the center of the glory, but still the Allied Fleet. Navara's a tough sell, so the salary incentives are beyond excellent. It's a new language to learn, a tough one, and the laws for foreigners are strict."

Maryana tried to be optimistic. "If we start Sarah now, she'll probably be able to translate for us by the time we get there. She catches on quick."

Quick? The child scared the hell out of Sasha.

It was a new family record, called into a school on only the second day of class. Sasha and Maryana sat with the teacher in an administrative office. Two days was the longest Sarah'd lasted in a school yet; they braced for another round of argument.

Instead, the teacher showed them test results, bewildered. "We've never had a student like this before. To be honest, we don't know what to do with her. She passed a second-form mastery test with a score of 100%. She passed third form with a 79%. Eighty would pass her, but it amounts to misspelling a word, that's all. She managed a 71 on the fourth form exam. She claims she's fluent in other languages as well?"

Maryana was quick to nod. "She's fairly fluent in English, and she enjoys speaking French with me."

The teacher heaved a heavy sigh. "We would like permission for a full work up, evaluate all skill areas, get a firm assessment of her abilities. Right now we estimate her IQ as somewhere between 190 and 230."

It wasn't what they expected to hear. Sasha's defensiveness eased. "So what form will you put her in?"

"We can't put her in **any** form!" the teacher replied. "She'd have to start halfway through fourth, and we cannot skip students five years. She's six weeks short of turning five! We would place her in a self-guided classroom with other students who don't quite fit the system. She'd work at her own pace for academics and join the kindergarten for all non-academic programs, such as arts and recreation and lunch."

Bad school memories bounded back. He shook his head. "I don't like that. Isn't the self-guided program for those who can't keep up with regular classes?"

Disappointment weighed on Maryana's face. "It doesn't matter, Sash. They have nowhere else to put her. It's that or she sits home until she's older, but she'll just be smarter by then and we'll still have the same problem. It's not like there's no one at home for her to play with."

Sarah was sent into the office. They turned toward her.

Sarah stayed by the door. "I'm sorry I pushed that boy. I can't go to this school, either?"

"No, you can stay." Maryana beamed the soft little smile that lit up her face like spring sunshine. "Come sit. The teacher has been talking to us about what class you'd like."

Sarah approached with caution, nose out, sniffing. Father didn't smell of the Nasty Stuff in the big bottles, he just smelled work-nice. He lifted her up effortlessly and balanced her on his knee.

Sasha tugged on one of her blonde braids. He gave only a shy half-smile, but his eyes glittered with pride. "You're too smart for kindergarten, too, Sar'ina. That's my girl!"

"How long is the contract?" Maryana asked, hoping it was short.

"Three years, minimum. You get a bonus after three years, and every two after that." He lay back on the bed; Maryana slid closer and put her head on his shoulder.

"When do they want you to start?"

"As soon as possible."

Maryana struggled to sit up with her expanded belly. "I can't do that, Sash. I can't go until the baby comes. I won't risk giving birth on some dirty transport ship, and I'm not changing doctors just before delivery again. No, no, no! Promise me you won't make me go through that."

He rubbed her arm absently. "Of course I wouldn't. I told them that might be a complication."

"What do you think? Are you going to take it?" *Say no. No deserts.*

Sasha played with her hair. "It's not what I envisioned, but it's double the money, for no more effort. Do you think we could stick it out for three years?"

Maryana kissed him lightly. "If that's what you want, then I want it too. Where ever you go, I will be there beside you. Did you ask about housing? Did you tell them we need a minimum of five bedrooms?"

"There's a house available, I was told. It's a hundred and twenty kilometers out of Shir P'an, out in the desert. No neighbors, no anything for almost thirteen kilometers. Only three bedrooms, but they're supposed to be big. Two baths, at least."

"Oh Sasha! How could we ever fit? We worked so hard to get to this point. How can we just throw it all away?"

"I know, but I hate to miss what might be a good opportunity. If I can get a foothold in with the Allied Fleet, maybe I can transfer someplace better three years from now. Think of it, Tash! With that on a résumé, we can pick and choose anything we want. It's a modern university city – the children can keep up with all their activities. There is a strong foundation for performing arts. The city has great galactic diversity; there are all sorts of influences."

"If it makes you happy, then do it," Maryana said with resignation. "The children will learn to live with it. I'm sure we can make it sound adventurous to them."

Sasha ran a hand down her side and over the rising belly. "I missed you, these last three days," he said, a real smile starting at last. "What do you say we convince him to come out early?"

Maryana chased the hand away. "Not this time, Sash. I fell for that once. Two more weeks, and you can do what you will."

Thirty-four

Maryana paced the house restlessly. She knew it was a sign the baby was imminent, but the rest was helplessness at a dream ending. Her house, her beautiful big house, a symbol of everything she'd once lost and fought so hard to regain, was going. Movers had boxed up most of their possessions, crated and awaiting expensive shipment to Navara. The children squabbled, both excited for the move and furious at the sudden upheaval less than a year after returning from Gamma Europa. Sasha's introverted silence didn't bode well, either. He worked his way through several bottles in the liquor cabinet before it was packed.

"You don't look happy," he noticed.

She brightened. Nothing good would ever come from a pessimistic outlook. "It's just a big change. There are so many unknowns. We've never been away from Earth so long. We've never sold a house before. We have no idea what to expect."

He hugged her from behind, holding on. "It will work. It's a Class-One world, fully modern – probably better than we have here. Medical facilities are cutting-edge. Education. Innovation. Students who are highly motivated. A world with no major crime. What better place can there be?"

She smiled briefly, locked in the comfort of his arms. "You can make anything sound like paradise. You forget the fact humans can roast in their skins in the day-time heat. We'll have to drill that into the children, they can only play outside at night. If the baby gets out…."

"We'll get safeguards if necessary," he assured her. "You'll see, Tash. It's the last stepping stone we've been looking for. After this, we're good as gold."

Nikolai arrived the following morning, quick, easy, and perfectly healthy. Maryana took it as a sign of good fortune, but when they flew to the Moscow Interstellar Spaceport four days later, she blamed her tears on the baby and bidding goodbye to the twins.

It was no mean feat, moving ten children and two adults several star systems away, in the middle of birthing a baby. The brunt of the trip fell on Sasha, from last-minute packing to counting heads to counting luggage and claim checks and locating lavatories to assigning overseers for the younger ones. Maryana was proud of him, handling everything so well with not so much as a beer in his hand to give him strength.

The passenger ship's lifts couldn't accommodate everyone at once, and each time they moved as a group there had to be a pause for the other half or even thirds to catch up. Three cabins were needed to hold everyone; two adjoined, but the older boys were two doors away; Sasha trusted them about as much as he trusted a dog in a butcher shop. Maryana set up their room, saw to the boys' room, and praised Katya for setting up the younger children as nicely as she herself would have done, then crashed onto the bed, exhausted. Ship's gravity never felt the same as planetary gravity, and nausea from the difference only added to her woes.

Maryana was used to childbirth, but she'd always had time to recover. When she brought the twins home, her sister-in-law was by her side so much Ana all but lived with them for the first few weeks. There'd been hired help after her cesarians; extra days in hospital with Sergei and Sarah, and she'd relied perhaps too much on the twins to keep the house running smoothly. She was also younger. Lying on a bed on a space cruiser a few days after giving birth, her life upended, eight of the children relegated to other cabins unsupervised, post-partum hormones twisting her emotions in every direction, Maryana wanted nothing more than to cry and go home.

Mamá had been thirty-seven when Maryana was six, Tomas ten and not yet at boarding school. Mamá worked the Minsk office, with forays up to Moscow, but they'd had a nanny to cover for the times when she wasn't there. Mamá had worked hard, seven days a week at all hours of the day, to forge an alliance with a top Altairan technology firm at the same time as she was courting a galactic communications company looking for a backer for an Earth-based expansion. Mamá managed to close one deal in October, the other in November. With stock options, Mamá had increased their net worth nearly 300 million credits, all by herself, multiplying their fortune by a factor of six. She was named the 2238 Person to Watch by three different leading business syndicates, her circulating portrait one of mature yet youthful strength, a face of supreme confidence that planned to be around for many decades to come. Papa signed Tomas into Northern Academy for the following year, bought Maryana the platinum and diamond necklace as an investment for her future, and they all spent four entire weeks in France with Mamá's family, celebrating, vacationing, and recuperating in the lush countryside. Mamá's smile never dimmed, not once, no matter what Tomas did wrong or how dirty Maryana became playing in the vineyards. Lying exhausted in her overheated cabin, all her worldly treasures crammed into shipping containers like so many refugee goods, her five-day old son asleep beside her and her two-year-old standing on a chair to sing to the wall mirror, Maryana never thought thirty-seven would feel so *old*.

Sasha caught her weeping. He brushed the hair from her face, bent down to kiss her cheek. "You okay? You need something?"

She sniffed delicately and gave him a faint smile. "Fine. It's just the hormones crashing. You think I'd be used to it by now. I probably just need a nap."

He reached over and took the baby. "You sleep. Katya can watch him. I'll send Byeta next door. Rest while you can. You'll need your strength once we arrive." He put the baby in the cartabout, lifted Byeta off the chair, and headed to the next cabin.

* * *

Sarah and Vlad, five and six, sat on a bunk silent and out of the way, watching card game at the table and half-heartedly playing Spacewalker on the gamepad before them. Alexei had banned them from speaking, but Mother and Byeta were napping, Katya took the baby for a walk, and Viktor was supposed to be watching them. Sarah wasn't supposed to run around, lest her breathing worsen in the stuffy ship's air, and too much movement made Vlad space sick, so all they could do was sit and watch.

Ten-year old David played a card. "No! Wait." He consulted his hand and tried to take the card back.

Alexei punched him hard on the arm. "You cheat, you prick! You fucked up my play. You can't play for shit, fucking baby." As his brother twisted away, Alexei punched him twice more, hard enough to leave bruises. "That's for crying."

David flung his cards on the floor. "Fucking bastard! I hate you!"

"Dickless loser! Come back when you learn to play."

David locked himself in the lavatory. The door shook and rattled as he kicked it.

Viktor tossed the hand on the table with a sigh. "Great. Now what? You need four for decent poker. Seryozha, you know how to play? Want to learn?" Sergei was eight, but he was better at maths than David.

Sergei looked up from his text reader. "Not right now. I'm reading this art story about this Norse God, and he comes back to Earth but in modern times, and at the end of the chapter, if you push the button, it has this animation of …."

Alexei flung an empty snack wrapper at him. "Ah, shut up, Braniac. Nobody cares about that shit."

"Think Katya's back yet?" Viktor said.

"I could play," Sarah said.

"Yeah, right!" Dmitri hooted. "Except you don't know how. It would be different if we were playing for money."

"Look who's talking!" Alexei said. "You can barely read the numbers."

Sarah hopped off the bed and knelt on David's seat. "I can learn. Show me how."

"What, so you can piss your pants and cry when you lose a hand? Get lost."

"I don't pee my pants. I haven't since before I was two. And I don't cry over stupid games. Teach me. Or are you afraid I'll win? Maybe you're the crybaby."

"You wish, Diaper-ass."

Viktor thought it over. "You know, she just might. She's practically the same form as David; she can't play any worse. Give her a chance."

Alexei shuffled the cards. "If she can, I'm kicking the shit out of that asshole. All right. Listen close."

It took five hands for Sarah to grasp the basics of five-card stud. After ten hands, they switched to five-card draw. After an hour and a half, Sarah had won seven hands all by herself.

Dmitri folded. "I'll be damned. She really can play."

"I'm gonna kill that little prick," Alexei muttered. "He plays worse than a preschooler."

Sarah took offense. "I'm not in preschool! I'd be in fourth form if they'd let me. That's the same as Sergei. I could do fifth if I tried, maybe even sixth."

David had been watching a program on the room's vidscreen. He stormed out of the cabin. "I fucking hate all of you! And I'm telling Father about the naked U-view videos you watch on your Unilink!" He ran for his life.

* * *

Katya shared her stateroom with Sarah, Vlad, and Sergei; it adjoined her parents' room. She tiptoed in so as not to wake Maryana and Byeta and parked the cartabout near the bed. Sasha looked up from the table where he read over his paperwork for the new job. She sniffed and hurried into her room.

"What's wrong?"

"Huh? Nothing, Father. He's so sweet! He drank quite a bit and I burped him, and now he's sleeping fine."

"Come here," Sasha ordered.

Katya walked slowly until she stood before him.

"You took the baby for a walk and you come back crying. You will tell me what happened."

Katya hesitated, but there was no escaping a command from Father. "I was walking the promenade deck, looking in the shops, minding my own business, when some woman came up and started yelling at me that I ought to be ashamed to have a baby, not out parading it around, that girls like me should be locked up, and how awful my parents must feel. I tried to tell her he wasn't mine, but she practically spat in my face and walked away." Katya rubbed her tears on her hand.

"Did you get her name, or cabin number?"

"No. She ran away too fast. I didn't do anything to her! Why would she say things like that?"

Sasha hugged her with an inescapable crush. "Don't cry, my 'pupka. The universe is full of evil people; you just ran into one of them. You're a good girl. I know you are. You are much like your mother, in so many ways. If you see that evil woman again, you will tell me, and I will set her straight. No one speaks to my girl like that. She owes you an apology." He wiped her tears with his thumbs; the touch was gentle, but his skin was scratchy and rough.

225

Katya hugged him back. "Yes, Father. Thank you."

The door opened and David slid into the room.

* * *

Father strode into the boys' room at full speed. David followed a few meters behind.

Each step seemed to make Father's face redder. "Can't you behave for one goddamned hour so your mother can rest?" he demanded of the room.

Viktor was the only one brave enough to answer. "We didn't do anything. Alexei started calling David names and punching him. David got mad and it broke up our game."

"Is what he claims true? You've been watching adult content?"

"No," Alexei drawled with annoyance.

Viktor eyed Alexei, glanced at David with a bruise already visible below the hem of his sleeve, and made his choice. He turned to his father. "Yes. He had it on before. I won't tell you what he slapped me with."

"I slapped you with soap," Alexei insisted. "That's all it was. The rest was your perverted imagination."

Father was a man of bold words and fast action; when he held still, silent, something was truly wrong. The stiletto gaze never left his captives. "Dmitri, bring me his Unilink." Dmitri rushed to comply.

"It was a bare ass in a drama," Alexei said. "David's just trying to get me in trouble because I told him he couldn't play for crap. That's *my* Unilink!" He made a futile grab for it.

Sasha hit menu on the Unilink, then the first item on recently accessed. He viewed several seconds before the massive arm flashed out and skewered Alexei around the throat. Alexei backed up until he hit the door, but the wide hand remained clamped. "How dare you bring that filth with us! You think this is funny? Are you proud of this?"

Alexei squirmed against the door. "Not *proud* ..."

"Perhaps you should show it to your mother. Explain to her why you felt it was something you needed to bring with you."

Alexei gave a gasp of panic. "Papa!"

Sasha glanced back to Viktor. "Who saw this?"

"I only caught a glimpse of it. I made everyone get out; we went to the ship's arcade for a while."

226

Sasha nodded. "Smart." He towed towering Alexei by the ear. "You can sit with me while I erase this and make sure there isn't more."

"Ow! That's my private... Ow! Papa!" He had just enough time to mouth, *You die!* at David before being dragged out the door.

* * *

Getting everyone ready for dinner was a project on its own. To prepare the passengers for the harsh reality of Navaran heat, the ship's temperature was set to twenty-three Celsius for the first day, increasing four degrees each 'day.' It helped, but it often left passengers and crew cranky, with recycled air and no refreshing breezes. In the cartabout, baby Nikolai began to fuss, the back of his tiny shirt soaked with sweat.

"You poor thing." Maryana stuck a nurser in his mouth and lay him on the center of her bed to wipe him down with cool water.

Shrieking sounded in the adjoining room. Katya poked her head in. "Mother? Byeta won't get dressed. She keeps hitting me."

Maryana wiped the sweat from her own face. "Sash, watch the baby. Don't sit on him."

Next door, Byeta lay on the floor clad only in padded underpants, kicking her feet and shaking her head. "Don't wanna shirt! I'm hot! I want juice!"

"Kat, find me that little pink top of hers, the sleeveless one with the ruffles, and we'll leave her in the coverups on the bottom. Up, Byeta," Maryana urged. "This shirt won't make you feel hot. Put it on, and Mama will comb your hair out pretty. Everyone in the dining room will say, 'Oh, what a pretty little girl in that ruffly shirt! I wonder what her name is.'"

Byeta stopped kicking. "I can have sparkly hair?"

"Of course you can have sparkly hair! Come on." She pulled Byeta from the floor as Katya brought the shirt.

On the other bed, Sarah and Vlad sat crosslegged, prodding each other and giggling.

"Poke!" *giggle*

"Poke!" *giggle*

"Poke!" Sarah gave a hard, gooey cough, then another.

Maryana looked up sharply. "Sarah? Do you feel okay?"

"Yeah. It's hot in here."

"Vlad, get her medicine, the blue one."

Vlad fetched the blue canister from Sarah's daypack, attached it to the face mask and handed it to her. Sarah reassembled it correctly and clamped it to her face. She pushed the auto timer and breathed deep. The medicine would clear the congestion in her chest and prevent another round of pneumonia.

An older couple stopped the parade in a lobby of the Green deck. "My goodness! Aren't they precious," the woman cooed, bending down to pinch Elizabyeta's cheek. Byeta smiled until her eyes squeezed shut. She toddled a clunky spin, twirling a curly braid shining with hair glitter. The older crew stood straighter, putting on the practiced public glow they'd perfected from Father's many photo opportunities during his lecture tour.

"Are they all yours?" the woman marveled.

Maryana smiled sweetly. "Every last one."

"My condolences," the man said to Sasha.

"Nonsense!" the woman said. "They're beautiful. I'll bet they bring you much joy."

Maryana started to speak, but Sarah cut her off. "My Papa's an archaeologist and he discovered a dragon and now we're going to Navara so he can teach about it. Navarans aren't human, they're humanoids, and we'll get to see some of them."

"Is that so!"

"On Navara you can't say lavatory, you have to say 'Where is the *garakat*'," Vlad added.

"*Garakad*," Sarah corrected.

"It's the only word he'll ever know," Alexei muttered from the back of the crowd.

"It's the only one he needs," Dmitri grumbled back.

"Is that so! You must know all about dragons, then."

In the middle of the group, David jumped and gave a silent scowl as Alexei pinched him. He bumped into Dmitri, who shoved him back.

"Uh-huh! I got to skip kindergarten!" Sarah said eagerly. "I…"

"Enough, Sarah," Sasha warned. "The nice people want to keep their ears. Let's not keep them from their business."

"Gods Bless," the woman said to Maryana.

"Thank you," Maryana replied. "And you as well."

Dinner seating had to be prearranged for such a large group, when the worst of the crowds wouldn't be there. Long gone were the days when Maryana traveled highest class; the dining room for their level was clean and bright, but bland and uninspiring in décor. Maryana looked impeccable despite her condition. The baby slept next to her in his carryseat, wearing only a diaper and shirt and a light blanket. Sasha stared blankly at the menu selections on the table's holoscreen as if choosing one would take too much effort.

"Fifty-two hours," Maryana informed the group cheerfully. "Then we'll be in our new home. Anyone want to guess what color it will be?"

"I don't want a new house. I want our old house," Byeta said. "It's hot and yukky here."

Sergei was the only one who answered. "It's a desert world. I'd guess brown or turquoise."

Sarah sat next to Vlad, as she had since they both were able to sit at the table. Vlad drove a finger into her middle.

"Poke."

"Poke," Sarah returned with a giggle.

"Poke."

"What are you doing?" Katya said. "They've been doing that for hours."

"Playing poker!" Vlad crowed.

David stretched across the table. "I want to poke 'er!"

Sasha pushed him down. "Sit!"

Alexei sniggered. "Dumbass. It's illegal with your sisters."

Dmitri stuck a finger into Katya's arm. "Poked 'er."

"Poked 'im," Katya returned. Poking engulfed the table.

"Enough!" Sasha commanded. "Stop, or leave."

"I played poker today," Sarah informed him. "It was fun. Ow!" she cried as Byeta reached over and yanked her hair.

"Byeta, no," Maryana said, pulling the hand away.

Sasha glared. "Who taught you to play poker?"

"The boys."

Sasha's cold eye turned to Viktor. "You taught a baby to play poker?"

"After Alexei kicked David out we needed a fourth player, so Sarah filled in."

"She's better than David," Dmitri added.

"Prick," David grumbled.

229

"I was against it," Alexei said, "but they insisted. It was kind of cute, actually. I made sure they didn't cheat her."

"Byeta, no!" Maryana said, but her grab missed. Tines first, the fork dropped onto the baby. It scratched his arm and he began to fuss. Maryana had to pick him up.

Byeta slid down on the chair until she lay flat and her feet rested on the table. "Can we go home now?"

A deep space ship was usually large, but passenger space was often limited to a few decks or a certain section, to protect passengers and crew alike. It also increased the likelihood of running into the other passengers. Katya spotted her aggressor entering the dining room. She slid from her chair and waited next to Sasha until he spoke to her.

"Forgive me, Father, but you wanted to know the woman who yelled at me earlier. That's her over there in the green shirt, four tables over."

Sasha's head shot up. His jaw clenched and the thick eyebrows lowered in a glare so vicious Katya took a step backward. "You're absolutely sure?"

"Yes, sir. She's still wearing the same shirt."

"Sasha, no! You can't make a scene here," Maryana pleaded. "Think first! You have a public reputation to uphold now." When he didn't pause, she added, "For Gods' sakes, at least be polite! You don't want to make a wrong headline!"

He took Katya by the hand and dragged her to the other table. He didn't wait for the woman to finish speaking to her party, but spoke as if she were nothing more than a video recording.

"This is the woman who yelled at you?"

Katya stared at the decking but nodded. "Yes, sir. She told me I should be ashamed of myself."

The woman didn't seem the least put off. "And she should! It's written in the Holy Scripts of Altucar, 'Thou shalt banish the unchaste maiden, give her not refuge nor charitable offerings, lest you encourage abomination in the eyes of the Gods.'"

Katya took a step behind her father as his face darkened. His voice dropped to a register so deep it seemed to echo in the tabletop itself. It carried throughout the dining room like a minor earthquake; all conversations came to a stop.

"You have the nerve to call my daughter a whore? My daughter, who did nothing more than walk her baby brother so her mother could nap? My daughter, who is thirteen years old and does the work of a woman twice her age without a word of complaint? Look at my table. Look!" He pointed to where Maryana fussed over baby Nikky, at the long table where Byeta stood on her chair, waving, where Sarah and Vlad had turned around to watch.

Alexei stood up, puffing himself up to look as huge as his father. He flexed his arms threateningly and cracked his knuckles. Viktor gave a short nod. "Strength in numbers," he said softly, and five boys seemed to move as a single entity to join their father. Sarah tailed them before Maryana could object, Vlad followed Sarah like a magnet, and after a brief struggle with her mother, Byeta ran after the crowd. Maryana closed her eyes, bent her head, and pretended to be absorbed in the baby.

The children surrounded their sister and father. Sarah and Vlad each seized one of Katya's hands. Byeta squirmed between the forest of legs; Sasha lifted her onto his arm. They had no idea what the situation was, but Katya was upset and Father was angry enough to pick a fight, therefore they glared as a single unit, intimidating through sheer numbers.

"If you'll take your head out of your ass long enough to notice, they are all mine, right down to that baby over there. You insulted a caring, obedient daughter and made her cry. You owe her, her mother, and me an apology."

"Well, I ..."

"Apologize to her!" Sasha bellowed. Katya wiped away a tear, and an army of hands reached out to touch her in support. The dining room fell silent except for the soft hush of the air circulation vents.

"I think you'd better," said one of the woman's companions.

The woman frowned and gave a pompous flounce of her shoulders. "Hmph. Very well. I'm sorry. She was so involved with him, I thought she must be the mother. I didn't know."

"And you were so caught up in your self-righteousness you didn't even ask. If you speak to any of my children again, I will file a grievance with the captain, and I will roll up that Script of Altucar and shove it up your bloody ass. If I remember, there's something in there about bearing false witness. Maybe you should reread it. Very often, the loudest accuser is the one most guilty of the same crime."

231

He waved the children back. "Go. Eat. Don't let this space trash ruin your appetite."

Katya hugged him before she sat. "I love you, Father!"

Hot. Oppressive heat. Drop-in-your-tracks-and-wish-you-were-dead heat. Worse than running a fever in a burning house in the middle of summer. It had been mid-February in Russia; stepping off the orbital shuttle hit them with a fifty-one-degree temperature difference and a sunburned-red sky to adjust to. Sasha led the parade off the shuttle.

"Thank you for flying Navstar Spaceways, the smart choice for all your interstellar flying needs," the attendant said with a smile. She handed Sasha a bottle of water. Maryana carried Nikky behind him; the attendant gave her two bottles. "Good luck with your family, sir."

"Thank you," he grumbled.

A fiery blast of air sucked their breath away as they stepped into the access ramp. "This is worse than the damned ship," David said.

"David!" Maryana reprimanded. In her arms, Nikky began to wail.

"Just walk slowly until we get used to it," Sasha said, his breath heaving in the thinner atmosphere. "We'll rest when we get to the luggage claim. Don't lose your water. Put it in your bag for now."

"David already drank his," Alexei said.

"Then he will have none later."

"Booger face," David hissed at his brother.

"Looking in a mirror again?" Alexei taunted back.

They made their way through the connecting access tunnel, the slight upward grade just another obstacle to be overcome. Benches lined the walls; a good number of newcomers were stopped to rest, unable to bear the heat and gravity and feeling of high altitude. As they neared the end, the spaceport proper sprawling before them, Maryana stumbled, almost dropping the baby.

Sasha grabbed her. "Are you okay?" He took Nikolai and handed him to Katya.

"I'm fine," Maryana panted. "It's just because of the baby."

"Sit. Rest."

"Sarah's walking like a turkey," Dmitri called out.

Maryana's head whipped around, discomfort overridden. Vlad and Sarah brought up the rear of the line. Sarah's head tipped back as far as it would go, mouth open to the sky, fingers pulling the skin away from her throat in a parody of turkey wattle. She made an odd crowing noise.

"Turkey turkey, turkey turkey," Byeta sang. She shook her head, letting her braids bounce against her scalp.

Sasha plowed through the children. He knelt on one knee and sat the girl on the other. Maryana grabbed Sarah's carry bag, tearing through the puzzles and text reader chips until she found the face mask and a canister. She put the mask over the girl's nose and mouth and hit the timer button.

"Breathe!" Sasha commanded. Sarah nodded, releasing her skin. "Everybody just sit where you are." Eight children dropped gladly against the wall.

"Really, Sarah!" Maryana said. "You're smart enough to tell someone when you can't breathe."

"Out of my seat," Alexei ordered David.

"I was here first. You got the whole wall. Ow!" David cried when Alexei's powerful fist slammed into his side.

"I said, I'm sitting here." As David got up with a growl, Alexei tripped him, and he sprawled into the tunnel with a thud.

"David!" Sasha warned.

Katya dug through the baby's bag and found his bottle, hushing his shivery newborn cries. Sergei pulled out a notepad to record the moment.

Some welcome to Navara! Two minutes off the ship, Sarah's stopped breathing, Alexei's picking fights, and I've got sweat pouring off me so bad you can see it right here. He outlined the blotchy drops. *You can't catch your breath, the air's too thin, and it takes all your strength just to walk. This stinks worse than David's butt.*

David yelled out, "Vlad's playing with himself!"

"Vladimir!" Sasha barked without looking.

"I'm not! I have to..."

"Viktor!" Maryana realized in a flash. "Run! Find him a restroom!" Viktor grabbed Vlad, but it was too hard to run. After five steps, all he could manage was a fading walk.

Byeta rolled on the ground and kicked the wall of the tunnel. "I'm hot! I wanna go home!"

"Is that better now?" Sarah nodded, and Maryana took away the mask. She exchanged the mask can for a different one. "Here. Keep the oxygen with you, just in case. Sash, what are we going to do? We can't stay here if she can't breathe the air."

"Give it a week," Sasha promised. "Let's see what happens. We'll find a doctor if we have to."

A spaceport attendant approached. "Is everything okay? Can I help you with anything?"

Despite the sweat wilting her hair, Maryana's charm bubbled up. "I think she's okay now. We gave her some medicine."

"Let me call you a courtesy cart," the man said. "How many of you are there?"

"Twelve."

The man spoke into a handicom, and within minutes two passenger cars had arrived for them.

Viktor returned, Vlad on his shoulders. "We made it by a second and a half, but we made it."

Sarah's hand shot out, mask forgotten. Two tall people in caramel-colored desert robes walked past them. Their hoods were down, showing heads of dark feathery hair and wrinkled, puckered ears clinging to their heads. "Are those Navarans?"

"Don't point!" Maryana said sharply. "Yes, those are Navarans. Now be good ambassadors and behave."

The children leaned to watch them walk away. "Quantum!" Sergei breathed.

The courtesy cars remained with them to retrieve the immediate luggage and see them through customs. A small bus was located, since no taxi could hold them all. While the glass and stone city seemed bright and promising, the longer the ride, the more dismal the landscape became.

Ahead, concrete walls loomed high, topped with curved scaffold towers that bore radiating arms like metallic snowflakes on stalks. Safety lights blinked to warn flying ships of their presence. Sarah leaned over Sasha's seat and pointed. "What are those, Papa?"

"Dune walls," he explained to his audience. "The land is like a sea of sand; waves and sand storms would bury the city, so they build the walls to help keep it out. During storms, the towers will form an energy shield over the city, sheltering it from blowing sand. Every so often, diggers will clear back the built-up sand from the walls and make way for the next one. If you look carefully, you'll see gates, so craft can still get in and out even in the storms. We live outside the walls."

"Won't we get buried by sand?" Katya asked.

"I don't know."

Red sky, coral pink sand, red-brown stone wavy in the heat, as far as the eye could see. No trees. No houses. No people.

Nothing.

A high rock ridge loomed ahead, a mesa sticking up thirty meters as if it were punched up from the other side of the world. For a minute it seemed as if the vehicle would fly right into it.

"Maybe we're gonna live underground, like in the city," Vlad said to Sarah.

"Here you go," the driver said as he stopped, but they had to blink several times before they realized they were looking at a house.

The rusty-brown ridge rose high above them, creating a shrinking shadow. Before them, the same color as the rock, squatted a long, rambling, shapeless mass of... something. The flat, high roof sprouted an array of antennae, dishes, collectors, tanks, and other equipment. Only three windows were visible in the front. It looked more like a sand castle than a house.

The driver noticed their dismay. "That's the Navaran style. They like things to blend in. The back side is probably built right into the cliff. Good thing, too. That's the direction most storms come from. It should keep you nice and sheltered."

Maryana glanced at Sasha with alarm. "And how often do storms come?"

"Couple times a year. The sky will give you plenty of warning. Keep the little ones in until the dust settles, though. It's bad for the lungs."

Sasha scanned the group for Sarah. She was still breathing.

"Well, at least it's cooler in here, and it's clean."

Maryana sat on a suitcase in her new home as they waited for the cargo containers with their furniture to arrive, trying her best to keep an open mind and be optimistic. The heat outside radiated from every direction, made skin shrivel, eyes squint and water, made noses dry until they bled. Never had twenty-one degrees felt so blessed cold. *Only one computer link.* They'd left four; she'd hoped for at least two. It was hard to split one commwave among so many inquisitive minds.

Each added peripheral unit slowed the access wave, and to add a second channel would mean paying to upgrade the entire satellite system, too expensive an undertaking for a rented house. Perhaps Sasha could get the Academy to set him up with a portasat for his personal use. That would ease some of the strain.

The living areas were quite large but open; any noise would echo throughout all the rooms. The bedrooms were large enough, but there were only three of them. Without the twins, the three remaining girls would fit well enough in the smallest bedroom. But seven boys – where to stack them? It would be a few years yet before Nikky would be out of the crib, but meantime…

"Like fuck!" Alexei protested. He stumbled as Sasha cuffed him in the back of his head for his vocabulary choices, but it didn't stop him from rolling his eyes and waving his arms and pouting over the injustice, a hundred and ninety-eight centimeters of persecuted teen. "Why should I be squished into a room with five little brats! Vlad will get puke all over my stuff! Why should the baby get a room to himself? It's not like he gives a damn. I'm the oldest; why can't I have it? Bad enough we're in the middle of the mother of all fucking deserts! This place is so fucking tenth-century!"

"Mouth!" Sasha barked.

Maryana sighed. Sandwiched between the other two bedrooms, the room termed 'office/storage' on the rental sheet was little more than a dead-end corridor, not even two and a half meters wide and four and a half long, the last meter carved directly into the mountainside behind them. It had no windows, but two skylights let in light without much heat. It would have made a perfect nursery for a single baby, quiet and cooler at its subterranean end. "I supposed he could have it," she said. "If we get two sets of bunks, the other five will fit well enough in the bigger bedroom. There's plenty of room for the baby to stay with us for now."

"We can try it," Sasha agreed.

* * *

Vladimir lay on the cool stone floor of the new living room with his brothers and sister, wishing with all his heart he was back home. He was whiney on a good day, and discomfort only made him worse. "There's nothing to play on outside. There aren't even any trees. I hate this place."

236

"You couldn't play out there anyway, stupid. The gravity would throw you to the ground and you'd burn your hands on anything you touched," David reminded him. He sprawled out, cheek to the floor. It was too hot to sit up. It made you feel dizzy and thirsty and sick in your stomach. "This whole planet's going to burst into flames and we'll all burn up."

"Sand doesn't burn, it melts," Sergei corrected. "It will turn to glass and shatter."

"Maybe we could sleep during the day and play at night," Vlad said.

"*Tuvalos*," Sarah recited next to him, already hard at work on her latest challenge. "Irregular verb. To recreate, to perform an activity for purposes of personal satisfaction. To play. *Turis, turol, tuvoka, tur...*"

David punched her in the head. "Shut up! It's bad enough I gotta learn that crap in school now. I don't need to hear it from you."

Thirty-five

S asha stepped through the airlock into the humanities building and removed his hood. The desert robes were bulky large-hooded things, but survival depended on them. They insulated against the blistering days, keeping out heat and burning ultraviolet rays and the chill of the desert night, where, without cloud cover to trap the heat, temperatures could freefall into the single digits. Buildings were not air-conditioned; chilling a room and then stepping outside made the heat worse. Circulation of air and geothermics kept the buildings around twenty-three degrees, comfortable enough by Human standards.

The foyer was tall and spacious; white plastic and stone, the typical large statuary of a Historical Arts and Philosophies building – the word Humanities lost its meaning when applied to multiple planetary cultures, the requisite dedication plaques, and a two-story scrollboard of upcoming academy events. Casual seating areas with colorful cushions and a flood of natural light from the glass front wall kept it bright and inviting. A three-sided interactive directory column stood in the foyer. "Anseña," he told it.

"Level 2, room 206. Mr. Anseña is in," replied the board, and proceeded to show him a three-dimensional holographic map of the shortest route. He found the lift, then the room. His feet stopped outside the office door. In the hall, he was nothing, nobody, invisible, with no expectations or confrontations or demands upon him. He could leave and no one would be the wiser, say 'No, thank you,' by mail and retreat. On the other side of the door lay expectations based on his record of accidental success, dozens of people he would have to impress through manners and speech and deportment and education. There might be Navaran natives, whose rigidity in social customs was legendary and expectations of educators profound. He was nothing more than a welfare brat from the streets of Sochi who failed a year of school, product of a broken home and a mother who did her best work on her back. Who was he to instruct Navarans?

The sweat running down his back had nothing to do with the heat.

Tash would laugh at him. She'd sacrificed her dreams for his career. Picturing her loving face made him smile inside, and he opened the door before the feeling faded.

A man stood up from a desk. He was thin, of average height and perhaps fifty years, hair halfway to gray, dressed like a native in loose, light clothing. He left the desk, hand out. "Ah! You must be Kirushenko. Alexander, isn't it?"

Sasha shook the hand. "Only to intimidate students. Sasha."

"Paolo Anseña. Welcome to the Space Fleet Academy at Kar Ku'umi City. I'm the Chair of the Arch program here; it's me, you, and Gissa Reynolds. She doesn't come in today until afternoon. Have a seat! Would you like some water? A good portion of the customs, you'll find, revolve around water. Very important to the desert cultures, both on Earth and here. To have water is to be rich; to share is generosity. Navarans, especially the nomadic ones, still accept payment of some debts in water. There are even a few water banks."

Sasha chose the larger of the chairs before the desk; it creaked when he sat in it, dried out by the arid atmosphere. He accepted the offered water. It was blissfully cold.

"So, are you out here alone, or did you bring a family?"

Idle conversation had always eluded Sasha. "I brought my family."

"Children?"

"Twelve."

Anseña did a double-take. "Did you say twelve?"

"Yes. Only ten came with us. We were delayed by the birth of the last one. He's ten days today."

Anseña whistled. "Well, that's impressive, I guess. You must have one very patient wife."

"There is none finer."

Anseña settled into his chair. "Your resume is rather extraordinary. How did you manage two doctoral degrees with so many children running about?"

"Determination. After the first, I knew the process, and it wasn't difficult. We spent every summer and holiday somewhere I could do research."

"And your wife didn't mind?"

"No. She enjoys travel."

"Hmm. Well, as I said, I am the Chair of the program. All programs and curricula go through me for approval first. You'll be starting at the bottom of the seniority ladder, but it doesn't take long to gain tenure here. The climate results in a fairly high staff turnover; most people can't wait to finish their contracts and leave. You'll be teaching three classes this semester, four next. That shouldn't be too much for someone as decorated as you, should it?"

Sasha didn't like the man's tone, but considering he'd just met him, he didn't want to start off poorly. "Not at all."

"How many awards did you win for your great discovery?"

His feeling of discomfort increased. "Five so far, plus four papers and nine lectures on it."

A greasy smile slid across Anseña's face. He gave a faint laugh that over the thin air sounded more like a grunt of pain. "My, my. You must be very proud. I'm afraid things here aren't as exciting. I hope that won't bore you too much. Just remember, we work as a team here. There are no superstars."

Enough. His welcome at Kiev was warm and inclusive. The only thing warm here was the room. Sasha remained calm and business-like. "Then I'll feel right at home. Perhaps you could show me where I can leave my robe. I assume I have a desk?"

Anseña chuckled to himself. He rose to his feet. "You have a whole office. Come."

Sasha parked the craft outside the house and rested his head on the control panels in front of him. His hand went to push his hair out of his face, but found nothing there. Tash had cut the thick locks just yesterday, hoping he would stay cooler. He didn't feel any cooler, but it kept the sweat from plastering the hair to his forehead.

Ten minutes passed before he escaped the vehicle and entered the chaos.

"Papa! Papa's home!" Elizabyeta ran up and hugged his legs. Tiny like Vladimir, her blonde curls came hardly past his knee. He picked her up and hugged her mechanically before releasing her.

Alexei was the second one to assault him. "Father? Father, if you're not going anywhere, can I take the skimmer? Some of the guys invited me to a game at the school, and it would really help me break in with the crowd if I showed up, you know what I mean? Mother said she wasn't going to need it. Please, Father? You're the one that made me change planets five months before graduation."

Sasha held out the coded ignition tag and tipped his head toward the door.

"Nova!" Alexei gushed as he grabbed the tag.

Katya sat on one of the two sofas in the main room feeding Nikolai, but half of it ran down his cheek, and he coughed.

"Pick his head up higher. Slow down."

"Yes, Father." She adjusted the baby and wiped his face with a cloth. "Mother said dinner will be ready an hour from now."

"Where is she?"

"Lying down."

Sasha started down the hall when he caught two children exiting the bathroom together. "What were you doing in there?" he demanded.

The pair jumped at the sight of him. "Vlad had to go," Sarah answered. She was now a full head taller than her tiny brother.

"It takes two of you to take a piss? You're too old for that bullshit." He lifted the undersized boy by an arm and swatted his rump with a hand that was bigger than the bottom. The girl didn't move, though she knew she was about to receive the same. "Let me hear of that again and next time it will be ten! Understood?"

"Yes, Father," and the mice disappeared in a blink.

Sasha entered his bedroom, shutting the door on the rest of the universe. Seeing her, his rugged features seemed to soften. "You all right? Is the heat too much for you?"

Maryana sat up. Her hair was braided but hung down long. Piling it on top made her feel hotter. "No. It's not bad in here. I'm still recovering, that's all. It takes a while to get my strength back, especially at my age. I just needed a nap."

"Thirty seven isn't old. Try forty-three."

"It's not the age, it's the twelve children. How about you? How was work? Did you finish meeting the faculty? Is anyone there of your caliber? Anyone we might connect with socially?"

He stripped off his sweat-soaked shirt, loosened his pants and dropped on the bed next to her, making her bounce with the force. "I'm still feeling everything out. I met some people who seemed okay. Time will tell. I think I'm going to rest a bit before dinner," he decided. "Keep them quiet."

Maryana kissed him on the nose. "Okay. Why don't you start with a cool shower," she suggested tactfully. "You'll feel better, anyway."

* * *

"Sasha, I thought we talked about this."

Maryana climbed onto the bed next to him and ran a hand across the hairy chest. They'd brought the custom-length bed with them, one of the few pieces of furniture that made the trip. They bought the rest locally, at exorbitant prices. Almost everything was imported; little could be grown or manufactured in a desert. "We agreed the import charge on vodka was too high to drink it by the bottle. It's hardly been a week … "

Sasha slouched against the pillows, chin on his chest, hand balancing his glass on the convex curve of his bare belly. His jaw clenched and he stared blankly at the stone-colored wall. The bottle on the side table had a considerable dent in it. He didn't answer right away, but sipped slowly at his glass. Like everything else on the planet, even the vodka was disgustingly warm. The ice maker wasn't working, and he hadn't had time to look into it.

He stirred himself at last. "Tash? Did you ever have the feeling that you made a mistake? A very – big – mistake?"

She put her head on his shoulder. "No. I don't think I ever did."

Sasha took another swallow. "This week I signed away the next three years of our lives, and I don't think I can do this."

"Of course you can." Maryana smiled knowingly. It was just another wave of self-doubt talking. He'd be afraid of failure in the unfamiliar setting, she'd point out his supreme talents and accomplishments, talk him through the fears, and after a week or two he'd settle into the new routine, make new friends, and get his confidence back. He always did. "What is it? The heat getting to you?"

"Bah. We'll get used to the heat." He gestured with his drinking hand; the liquid sloshed but didn't quite spill over. "I mean the position. At the Institute – at Kiev – I had more control over the program. There were four of us in the department – six if you counted anthropology, too. Everyone knew where they stood. Everyone's opinion counted, and we worked as a team. Respect came with merit, not title. This place is so – *regimented*. I'm at the bottom of the deck again, and I can see where the problems are going to be already. That snotty shit Anseña…." He sucked his glass dry in a long gulp.

"You've been there five days, Sash. Give it time. You'll make friends," Maryana insisted. "If worse comes to worst, you break the contract and we go home."

"To what!" His voice raised, brows banging together in an angry scowl like two black thunderclouds. "I *quit* my job, Tash! We *sold* our house! No one's going to hire a professor who breaks his contracts."

"Then we'll take it one day at a time," she promised.

Thirty-six

The screams pierced ears at the other end of the house, hair-raising shrieks of rage that stopped only long enough for the screamer to gulp more air. Sasha gave Elizabyeta a final spank and sat her on the chair, but she flung herself to the ground, screeching and kicking in fury. Across the dining room, Sarah glared murderously on an aching bottom, eyes brimming but too stubborn to let the tears fall.

"This will stop now!" he thundered. "No more fighting or else!"

Byeta waited until his back was turned, then launched herself at Sarah, yanking the white-blonde braids and trying to bite. Sarah grabbed Byeta's thick honey curls and pulled her head away. She slammed a backfist into Byeta's ribs several times.

"Goddamn you, you little shit!" Sasha picked one up in each arm. "Do I need to use a stick? Tash, take her!" He handed Byeta over.

Maryana struggled to hold the twisting, kicking toddler. "I swear, Sash, if they stay in the same room, one will kill the other. I don't know what else to do. They can't play outside, so they're always in each other's way."

Sasha put Sarah down. "Separate them. Sarah's always with the boys; let the boys watch her. Keep Byeta with you. She can sit in a corner until she learns. I have enough to deal with. I need a drink."

Vladimir was a leaky child, runty and tearful and anxious, and therefore unwelcome by his siblings. At six, his fragile digestive tract continued to torment him. If his food sat high and he became the least distressed, his stomach could turn inside out with little warning. If his food sat low, his bowels would turn to water. He did not gain reliable control over his excretory functions until the age of five. Nighttime was still risky, even with reminders. He longed for the glory of an upper bunk bed, but withered at the ridicule heaped on him by his brothers, who refused to sleep underneath him. Sarah, who had shared a crib with him until he was three, had no qualms, and protected him from the brotherly beatings. She reminded him to pee, when he needed his stomach medicine, and when to wipe his nose. More often than not, if he woke during the night, he crawled into her bed to sleep next to her, or she could be found asleep next to him in his, hands clasped. She held his hand to guide him through any fearful situation – which was almost everything. Maryana was grateful for the partnership; they kept each other out of trouble. Therefore, finding Vlad alone meant there was a problem.

He moped around her silently in the kitchen for fifteen minutes before speaking.

"*Mat*? Where's Sarah? Did she get sick and go to a hospital again?"

Maryana changed Nikky's diaper, slathering cream on the tiny buttocks. "No. Why?"

"Because she wasn't on the transport, so she must be sick."

"She's not sick. You must have missed her."

"But we *always* sit together!"

"*Shah*, Vladya. Don't whine. Go hunt for her."

Maryana didn't think twice about it, until she found Vlad weeping alone in a corner.

"Sergei?" she called. "Where's Sarah?"

"Haven't seen her," he replied. "Not since this morning. Isn't she with Vlad?"

Maryana gave the problem her full attention. Sarah was always with the boys, and never more than a breath from Vladimir. *Never.* If she'd wandered outside… Sarah was smart, but she was still only five.

Two more inquiries among the brood, a search of her own, and Maryana hit the commlink switch.

"This is Maryana Kirushenko, out beyond the walls? I was wondering if my daughter Sarah somehow missed the transport shuttle home. She didn't get off with the boys, and they say she wasn't on it at all. She's in the independent class, with Mrs. Iwata."

The secretary consulted her computer screen, tapping her way through several menus. "My records show she was absent again today. Has she been ill?"

Maryana felt chilled despite the oppressive heat. The polite cheer dissolved into confusion. She leaned closer to the picture on the receiver. "What do you mean, absent again? Sarah got on the transport this morning; I put her there myself. She hasn't missed a day in eight weeks."

The secretary shrugged. "Mrs. Iwata has left for the day, but if you'll hold, I will try to contact her at home."

Two minutes passed before the secretary reappeared on the screen. "Mrs. Iwata confirms that Sarah's been absent the last three days. She did not come to school today."

"That's impossible." Fear gripped Maryana. She cut the connection and turned on her son. "Vladimir! Tell me the truth! *Did Sarah go to school with you this morning?*"

The undersized boy nodded. "She walked me to class, just like always."

Maryana hit the commlink switch again, this time to Sasha there in Ku'umi.

City Security arrived fifteen seconds after Alexander Kirushenko began pounding on the outer doors of Kar Ku'umi Public School Number 4. The director of the school arrived thirty seconds after that, with the security access number for the building.

"Sarah!" her father bellowed into the echoing hallways.

"She isn't here," the director insisted. "She hasn't been in school for the last three days."

Kirushenko turned his towering bulk toward the woman. "My daughter arrived at this building this morning," he growled. "Whatever has happened to her since is on your head!"

Down two hallways, to the doors the students were dismissed from, and a bright yellow lump sat on the floor between the glass doors of the airlock. It jumped up at the sound of the crowd. Sasha shoved the door open so hard his hand cracked the glass. The brave little face in the yellow hood of the heat robe wasn't crying yet, but it shed brief tears as Sarah leapt for her father's shoulder when he bent down.

"The transport went without me! I'm sorry, Papa!" Sarah wailed.

"I came for you. Shh." Sasha kissed her cheek and held her close.

"I didn't go outside. I didn't want to burn up with the sun."

"Shh. You did the right thing, Sar'ina. That was very smart. You were a very smart girl not to do that." Sasha stood up and returned to the hallway, temper blazing to match the weather.

"No, she's not here," he began to rumble. "She wasn't in school today! *How can you lose a five-year-old child!*"

246

The director's mouth moved several times before any sound came out. "I - I'm sorry! I'm so sorry, Mr. Kirushenko! I don't understand. There must be a problem with the attendance computers..."

Maryana ran down the hall. She'd had to wait for a public taxi to fly her into the city. "Oh Sasha! You've got her! My goodness! Oh, Sarah!" Sarah was big and sturdy for five, but with her help Maryana managed to hold her on a slender hip. "What happened?"

"If you don't mind, Ma'am, we'd like to ask your daughter a few questions," one of the security officers asked. "Is there a classroom we can use?"

"There's a conference room in the office," the director said, unlocking the office doors. "I will call Mrs. Iwata and we will investigate this matter right now."

An officer stopped the Kirushenkos at the door. "We'd like to interview her alone. Just for a few minutes."

Maryana was about to give permission, but Sasha spoke first. "No," he said with authority. "She is my child and I will know what you are saying to her. She is a little girl who was left abandoned in an empty building for the night. We will stay."

"That is your right. If you could sit to the back, though." The officer set two chairs at the side of the conference table. He sat in one and motioned Sarah to the other.

Maryana kissed her daughter and pushed her toward the chair. "Tell the truth, Sar'ina. Tell the man what happened." The director pulled a seat near the Kirushenkos.

"I'm glad we were able to find you, Sarah," the officer said kindly. "That was very good not to run out after the transports. That could have made you very, very sick. I just want to know what happened, okay? To make sure it doesn't happen again, to you or any other student in this school. Do you understand that?" The white-blonde head with its two tight braids and bright blue bows nodded.

"How did you get to school today?"

The little girl shrank in the chair, but she answered clearly. "On the transport, with my brothers."

"And you came in through the front doors?" *Nod.*

"And then you went to your classroom?"

"No. I walked my brother Vladimir to his classroom. I do that every day. He's only in kindergarten. He's scared he'll get lost."

The officer smiled. "You're a very nice big sister to do that. So, after you brought your brother to his class, you went to yours?"

She slouched a little lower in the chair. "No."

"What do you mean, no?" Sasha demanded from the back. "Where did you go? Why weren't you in class?"

Sarah knelt on the chair to peer over the back. "I had to use the lavatory!" she said in a stage whisper. Maryana smiled sweetly, and the officer chuckled.

"And after you went to the lavatory, you went to class?"

The little girl's shoulders seemed to creep up to her ears. She slouched in the chair again and sucked on her lip.

"Sarah? Did you go to your classroom today?"

The purple-blue eyes looked about to cry.

"Answer him!" Sasha demanded from the back.

Slowly, slowly, the girl shook her head.

"Did you go to class yesterday? Where did you go?"

"Sarah, come here," Sasha ordered, his voice deep and deliberately slow. It was not harsh, it was not threatening on its own, but the little girl obeyed quickly. She slid off the chair to stand before him, glancing up through her bangs.

"When was the last time you went to class?"

"Friday, sir."

Maryana stared in disbelief. "Sarah, I sent you to school every day! Where did you go? The truth!"

"I hid in the lavatory, then, depending on the day, at second bell I followed the first- or second-formers to the manipulatives library and then I went behind the curtains on the performance stage and sat there to read. I found the ladder to access the catwalk!" she said with delight. "I went to lunch with kindergarten like always, then followed the fourth-form toward the gym on Monday, because they go past the door to the stage, and today I followed sixth-form to the computer lab because I have my honor pass that says I can go there any time, and they're working on a project about invertebrates. Invertebrate means animals that don't have backbones, like worms. There are more than twenty-four kinds of worms in Gantankar province, and six of them will suck your blood. I downloaded the work onto my homework pad and went back to the catwalk and read about them. I was going to meet the transport at last bell, but I fell asleep after lunch and I missed it."

Sasha's eyes bored into the child, but he said nothing.

Maryana drooped in her seat. "Why, Sarah? Why would you do that? That's dishonest."

The tears threatened to return. "I hate that class! I asked you if I could stay home! I hate it! They're all stupid there! I'm not stupid! I don't belong in the Stupid Room! I don't want to be here! Please let me stay home? I'll study hard! I won't make noise! I'll help with the baby! *S'il vous plait, Mamán?*"

Maryana's heart melted. She held her arms out, and Sarah jumped into them.

"How did you know all those schedules?" the director asked.

"They're posted on the school's AXS network. I downloaded them all into my homework pad with my AXS number, and then I could pick where I wanted to go. I finished all the work on this week's syllabus already, and I did the fifth-form grammar homework for practice so I can do David's when he asks me."

Silence fell upon the room once more before Sasha gave a deep sigh. "Five years old, and she can run the entire school from a catwalk with her homework pad. I don't know if that makes her very smart or the system very, very stupid. At the very least, there are severe problems with security and accountability. How much more do we have to fight to get her into an appropriate learning environment?"

"Mr. Kirushenko, we're doing our best," the director pleaded. "Sarah presents with learning needs every bit as special as our more challenged students. She follows an independent curriculum allowing her to work at her own pace. Her classroom has enhanced staffing to allow her individual attention when necessary. She attends supplemental programs in the upper grades. She has virtually unlimited access to school services. For social and safety purposes, we *cannot* place her in a regular classroom at her appropriate academic level."

Kirushenko's voice raised just a little, less than a bellow but louder than a bark. "*Obviously* your best isn't good enough, when a preschooler can beat you at your own game! For a child who feeds on learning to hate school says a great deal about how she is treated here. We will discuss Sarah's behavior tonight, and you will meet with us and our lawyer tomorrow, at which time you will present an alternative educational program for her that meets her needs both academically and emotionally. I do not condone her behavior in this matter and she will be punished accordingly, but I understand it is only a symptom of the deepness of her unhappiness. I will not allow you to destroy her love of learning. She will remain home until I am satisfied you can ensure her safety."

249

"I have a meeting with the Council on Educational Affairs tomorrow afternoon," the director tried, "but perhaps we could meet Friday morning…"

"We will be here at four tomorrow, with our lawyer," Kirushenko repeated. "You lose my child, deny her arrival, forget her in a building, and you think you will tell *me* when I may have restitution for your oversight? Kiss my fat …!"

"*Sasha!*" Maryana hissed.

He stood up, stretching his spine, breathing deep, pushing his shoulders down until he seemed the size of a small fortress. He lifted his daughter on one arm as easily as if she were an infant, picked up her school bag with a finger. "You will be here at four tomorrow."

Maryana leaped to follow, but she couldn't possibly be as rude. "I'm sorry we had to have a conference under such circumstances, but I know it will work out for the best. Thank you for your prompt attention to the matter. I look forward to our meeting tomorrow." She smiled as she shut the door.

Memories flashed through Sasha's mind, another child who skipped classes, so bored with school he almost didn't graduate, showing up only because the building was warm and he received a free meal. The shame still burned; it couldn't be allowed to repeat. "This is ridiculous," he growled on the ride home. "First they hold Sergei back, then they can't handle David, now this. Do we have to teach them how to run a school? Prickless bastards! I have enough shit at work. I don't have time for this."

"How are we going to get a lawyer by tomorrow?"

"I have an idea."

Sarah listened from the seat behind them. "I'm sorry, Father. I'm sorry, Mother. I'm sorry I missed the transport."

"Lying is very bad, Sarah," Maryana admonished. "You frightened a good many people, including yourself, I think. You will never do that again."

"No, Ma'am."

The crowd flocked around them when they returned. Vlad grabbed Sarah's hand and didn't let go.

"I missed the transport."

Her answer brought a round of laughter from her siblings.

"Hah!" David hooted. "Little Miss Smarty Pants can't catch a shuttle on time! Nyah, nyah! Who's smarter now? They didn't teach you to tell time?"

Sasha and Maryana retreated to the bedroom, the only bastion of privacy for discussion. Neither said a public word about the incident, until after dinner. Maryana's lips pinched into a tight line, and she stared anxiously at the floor.

Sasha called them all to the dining room. The wide canvas strap to the equipment bag he used at digs sat alone on the table.

"Sit," he ordered, pointing to the floor, and eight children – Alexei had a night class, and Nikky didn't count – sat.

"Your sister was caught skipping classes at school," Sasha explained, face as devoid of emotion as the empty desert outside. "Not just today, but three days. Every day she came home, she lied to her mother and me as to where she'd been. No matter what you may think of school here, I will not hear of a Kirushenko skipping class again." His dark eyes pierced into David's until the boy shrank with future guilt.

"As for lying, that is even more unforgivable. I expect truth, and nothing less. Less than honesty demands discipline. Sarah, come here."

"*Sar*ah's in *tro*uble," Byeta sang. "Sarah's getting a spanking."

Sarah's eyes grew wide, but she stood. Vlad hung on her arm, holding her back, until Viktor pulled him onto his lap.

Sasha took the strap and doubled it. "I will not have a liar in my house. Drop your shorts."

"Sasha! She's a girl!" Maryana protested.

"She's a baby. It doesn't matter."

"All the more reason this is too harsh! She's still a girl. You will not ask that of her."

"Very well. You may leave your undershorts." Sarah pushed her shorts slowly to her ankles and stood before her gang of brothers in sleek red underpants with gold stars on them.

The room held its collective breath as he placed his foot on a chair and lifted her over the big knee. The bulky arm rose high and brought the strap down with perfect accuracy.

Whack!

A strangled shriek shot from Sarah's throat. She tried to cover her bottom with her hands, but he held them out of the way with two thick fingers.

Whack!
Whack!
"Sasha, enough! She's too young!"

Byeta clapped her hands. "More, Papa! Do more!" Sergei's hand sneaked out and yanked a lock of her hair.

Whack!
Whack!

The arm lowered a final time. He slid her to the floor. "Five years, five times. Fix yourself! Are you going to lie to me or your mother again?"

Sarah didn't cry, but squawking sobs burst from her lips. She hiked her shorts over the gold stars and shook her head hard.

"Are you going to skip class again?" Another shake.

"Go to your room."

Sarah ran.

Alexander Kirushenko was no liar. At the dot of four he and Maryana appeared at the administrative office with a lawyer in tow. At least, he had law credentials. Moving across the galaxy was not a cheap undertaking; it was not the best time financially for a drawn-out legal battle. The man was a colleague of Sasha's, a PhD in Law and able to spout educational legal precedents like a fountain. The director had cancelled her other meetings and sat on the opposite side of the table with Sarah's teacher Mrs. Iwata, the Director of Specialized Education, the school's social worker, the school psychologist, and the Superintendent of Education.

"First off, I wish to extend my deepest apologies for yesterday's incident," the superintendent said. "It was a gross oversight on our part, and we are thankful that no harm was done. We don't like being made fools of, especially by our kindergarteners. Mrs. Iwata has been reprimanded for not taking the initiative to find out why Sarah was not in class on the first day. I can assure you, this will not happen again."

Sasha started off slow and calm. He was still dressed for work, and with Maryana's last-minute adjustments made a formidable, polished presentation. "My daughter was sent to school in good faith that she would be supervised. For three days she was left unattended. Teachers saw her come and go in the halls. She attended classes with other forms. She went to lunch and play time every day, but no one ever questioned why she was there when she was marked absent. She has five siblings in this school, and no one thought to ask them.

Anyone could have walked off with her and no one would ever have known she was missing. She could have fallen off a catwalk and been hurt, and no one would ever have looked for her. Then you leave her locked in an empty building for the night all alone and tell me she's not there?" The building anger rose to a thunderous yell. "You expect me to forgive this? You bet your goddamned ass it will not happen again!"

Maryana laid a gentle hand on his arm. "Easy, Sasha. *For God's sake, know your tongue!*" she muttered in Russian.

"In our defense, any system can be broken by someone determined to undermine it," the superintendent said coolly. "We are a public educational facility. One thousand children in nine grades come through the doors of this building every day. We can handle discipline problems, but we have to know they exist before we can act."

Maryana's eyes burned at the accusation. She wore a cream-colored business suit – no one wore navy or black on Navara – and with her long hair wrapped tightly in a bun, she looked as imposing as her mother once did. Her words were clipped, almost hissy. "Sarah is not a discipline problem. She's a smart little girl who has cried to be allowed in school years before she could attend. She cannot learn fast enough to suit herself. She is the type of child who belongs in a promotional ad for education."

"Sarah is an anomaly," the director said. "A fluke. One in a billion. A bright twelve-year old trapped in a preschool body with the ambition and ability to manipulate her environment to suit her purposes. Our greatest mistake was underestimating her abilities and trusting her to travel alone from class to class. We do not expect deceit from our students, at least until sixth or seventh form, when we try to give them the benefit of the doubt."

"You let a five-year-old child have free run of the school, with no accountability. That's an error you cannot dig yourself out of," Holland Evers, the law professor, said. "If a parent let a five year old run through a shopping center unattended, the authorities would want to know why. She is far too young to tell wrong from right, no matter what her mental abilities."

The superintendent looked annoyed.

"The alternative is to put her in a kindergarten room and send her out to academic classes in the higher grades with an assistant. You refused that option at the beginning, Mr. Kirushenko," the director said.

"They tried that at her old school and it didn't work," Sasha said firmly. "Sarah cannot relate to children who are just learning to count. They don't understand the words she uses, play the games she plays. She becomes frustrated and refuses to interact. Take the aide and put her in a higher class."

"We *can't do that*!" Mrs. Iwata insisted. "Besides being socially inappropriate, she would be trampled in fifth grade. We have some very large fifth-graders this year, including a new one with some discipline problems who's as large as the eighth graders! What are we supposed to do if he bullies her? Tell his parents we have to move him to another room because we want to put a five-year-old in his place? You know who I mean," she said to the school panel. "Darrin, Devon …"

The director remained silent and looked grossly uncomfortable. The school psychologist took the heat.

"Uh, the tallest student in fifth form is Mr. Kirushenko's son David, who is perfectly placed where he is. I think that fear is utterly ungrounded, seeing that Sarah and her brother appear to live in the same house without damage. Indeed, I think the stronger argument for not placing Sarah in fifth grade is not concern for her, but for her brother. If I may say so, David is a capable boy who currently feels very insecure in his own academic situation. He's still trying to find his niche in a new school. To place his little sister in his class would be a gross disservice to him and would only increase his feelings of alienation. I strongly recommend against such a move to protect *David's* interests."

The independent classroom teacher turned a rich shade of magenta, and didn't speak again.

"She has a brother in advanced third-form as well," Maryana said stiffly, the closest she could come to being rude, "but she has already tested out of third. You would have to place her in sixth."

"Impossible," the director said. "You can't place a preschooler in a room with pre-teens. Some of them are starting puberty. That's hardly the appropriate peer group."

"Sarah has no peers!" Sasha barked again. "Even your advanced class is three years behind her! She is with adults or older children all the time. At this rate, she'll be ready for university by the time you want her in fifth form. What will you teach her then? Or shall we just put her in a box for the next five years and take her out when she suits your needs?"

"There may be one possibility we haven't considered," the social worker said. She tapped her computer stylus against her lip. "We're sitting on a planet of academicians, some of the galaxy's greatest minds. They have to start somewhere. How good is Sarah's grasp of Navaran?"

Maryana hesitated as if sensing a trap. "Fairly good. Languages are her strength. She speaks three others, and she does most of the translating for us when necessary."

"It might take some doing, but how do you feel about trying her in a Navaran school?"

The director snorted. "Honestly, I can't see that ever happening. They don't mingle outside their kind. She would be shunned as inferior. Not appropriate at all."

The psychologist looked indecisive. "It's not exactly a normal peer group, but it might work. The Navarans are more academically advanced; she'd be placed with younger children than she would here. They don't play around, though. It's by the rules or not at all. They're very high on discipline."

"Sarah *is* a highly disciplined child – when the rules are clear," Maryana said. "Sash?"

He let out a thoughtful sigh that seemed to last for a full minute. "I don't know. It's a possibility I am willing to investigate. The few Navarans in my classes are serious students, by far the best I have. I could ask them how the schools are structured, the subjects taught. I suppose the person with the final say should be Sarah."

"If I can get through the red tape, write up a proposal for the placement of a visiting student, arrange a meeting with the master of a district school, are you willing to consider placing her there?" the psychologist said.

Alexander Kirushenko looked as if he'd leaned on a wall and revealed a hidden passage he'd never seen before. He exchanged inquiring looks with Maryana. "I will consider it."

"That is not possible," the tall and normally serene Navaran master said.

"You have the ability to *make* it possible," the taller but unusually serene Alexander Kirushenko insisted.

"The lack of self-discipline in human offspring is known throughout the galaxy," Master Jinariam said. His Standard English was flawless, as was the disdain coating the words. "Such a child would disturb classes, disrupt the learning process our students are taught to respect. A Human child that young cannot keep pace with Navaran peers and would find herself outcast when she continued to act in an emotional manner that her classmates would find abhorrent. The confusion created between the encouragement for such behavior at home and the intolerance for such behavior in the educational setting would be profound, and lead to further outbursts in a child who is, by nature, unable to adjust. We cannot allow the education of our students to suffer for the purposes of a social experiment. I do not believe your intention is to have your daughter serve as an object of our students' disapproval."

"If you would just meet her!" Maryana remembered not to smile a fraction of a second after she did. Human manners didn't work, here in the land of stone-faced people. It was a lawyer's paradise, where facts and only facts counted. She did adapt by wearing a flowing blue gown, covering her chin to toe. Made for and by Navarans, it kept a body remarkably comfortable. "She's a very exceptional child, very obedient, very self-driven to learn. Please, sir, if you would speak to her before making your final decision, you'll see for yourself."

The master gave reluctant permission. His expression didn't change, but his assumptions soon did.

Sarah entered the office with trepidation. If she wanted out of the Kar Ku'umi school, she had to be perfect. With the guidance of his students, Father had coached her on how to stand, how to speak, how to show profound respect. She'd studied the language programs until she could barely remember how to speak anything else. David took it upon himself to be her personal trainer in Navaran customs, inventing his own lessons in torment, shoving, hitting, taunting, and pulling her hair when she least expected it, only to yell, "Nyah, nyah! You lose! Gotta keep a straight face!" when she turned to retaliate. She had to admit, his efforts helped, but in her heart she still wanted to beat him over the head with a rock every time.

It was a performance, that was all, her mother insisted. Impress her father, that was all. That was what counted, not the funny, feather-headed wrinkled old man behind the desk. He was just part of the game. Sarah never glanced back at her parents. She greeted the man properly in his own language. She answered his questions fearlessly. She was impassive. She was impeccable. She was impressive. She was five years, six months, twenty-three days, and seventeen and a half hours old, and in two days she would be commuting alone an hour and a half a day, to an alien school she'd never seen, in an alien city, on a blistering alien planet, a hundred and twenty kilometers from her home.

Thirty-seven

May 2260

With nine children settled at last in four different schools, Maryana turned her attention back to Sasha. His new-job sours hadn't improved; if anything, they'd grown worse. His relaxation ritual had grown expensive; all liquor had to be imported, making the price of frequent consumption uncomfortable, and at times dangerous.

It was difficult to say which came first, the awful boom in the empty darkness outside, the horrific crunch of metal and plastics, or the shudder of the stone ridge and thus the house itself. Maryana burst out of the kitchen, terrified the ridge was collapsing on them. Children, formerly in bed or asleep, flew out to the main room with screams and shouts.

"A meteor! It hit the wall! We saw it outside! It crashed all over! It just missed us!" the boys chorused. Sarah was the first one to the door. Maryana hit the exterior floodlights before following the crowd.

Outside, no more than two flyer-lengths from the side of the house, Sasha emerged from their wrecked hovercraft, outcursing the Devil himself.

"Goddamn piece of mother fucking shit no good cocksucking worthless cheap-ass whore 'lectronics!"

"Sasha! Are you all right?!"

"Wou'n't turn! Cheap-ass bassards an' their piss-poor 'lectronics! Try to park like always an' it woudn' turn, ran me right into th' fucking wall! Fucking shithole! Pro'ly imported the shit from the goddamn Burin-jai fucking Empire! Out to kill us, fucking prickless bassards!" He swung a foot at the wreck but stumbled backwards to keep his balance.

Maryana observed with a pained heart. The fifteen-passenger commercial skimmer was top of the line and had drained her reserves of more than 100,000 credits. Just a few months old, the entire right front quarter was now crushed into the ridge, including the structural stabilizers. That much damage couldn't be repaired.

"As long as you're not hurt."

"What the fuck you staring at, little shits! Get the fuck inside!"

She turned the children to the house. "All right everyone, back to bed. No meteor, no crashed satellites, no alien invasions. Sand got into the electronics and jammed the controls, that's all. It's a hazard out here. Thank goodness your Papa's such a good pilot he was able to avoid a head-on crash. Go, before you get sandy again. Wipe your feet before you go in." A wave of protests erupted, but the crowd headed inside.

"Did you see that?" "It's crunched up like a candy wrapper!" "Did it make a hole in the rock?" "Now how will we get anywheres?" "Imagine if it exploded? That would have been awesome! KaBOOM!"

"He's not walking very well," David observed. "I'll bet he's drunk."

"He's shaking from the crash," Maryana corrected. "A scare like that will make anyone shaky for a while."

Viktor stared at the scene with a look of disbelief. "Is she kidding?"

Katya shrugged. "I'm still shaking from the boom."

Alexei gave a snort as he headed into the house. "Hmph. Sure as fuck glad it was him and not me."

Sasha resumed kicking the wreck. "No good dog-fucking moldy-whore shit waste of money…"

"Viktor, help your father to the kitchen," Maryana said.

"What th'fuck do I need help for?" Sasha shouted, stumbling in the sand. "Do I look like I need help? I tol' you, I'm not hurt. Don't need no fucking help. S'goddamn fucking navigation fault. Get our money back!"

"Fine. Viktor, go see that everyone's back in bed; make Vlad pee first. Sash, come with me." She took him by the hands and turned him toward the house. "Come on. We can't see how bad it is until daylight, anyway. Come tell me all about it." He followed, grumbling, but the damage was done.

Nor did Sasha say much about his supervisor that didn't involve profanity. What she didn't know was whether the problem was warranted, or a fault of his self-doubt. The cure depended on the cause. It was time to find out.

His Thursday schedule gave him three hours free at lunch. With Byeta in preschool, she left baby Nikky with a sitter and got ready.

She chose his favorite dress, a clingy silver thing that showed off her legs, youthful and quite trendy. Her makeup enlarged her eyes and made them seem bluer. Although it wasn't coolest for the heat, she combed her hair down long and braided several narrow strands near the front as accent. She looked ten years younger than her age on a bad day; her efforts took away years more.

A taxi dropped her off at the building, a long squat boomerang of glass and castcrete four stories high, shaped to diffuse the breezes that battered the landscape. She took in the aesthetics of the foyer, appreciated the Navaran influence, the ethnic varieties of students gathered to socialize, then hunted for his office on the second floor.

"May I help you?"

A man stepped from another office. He was average in height, perhaps fifty, hair thin and receding but not yet balding. He wore a pale yellow desert suit that would have made a fancier pair of pajamas.

"I'm looking for Professor Kirushenko's office."

"He's not in at the moment. If it's a question, perhaps I can help you. Which class are you in?"

Maryana laughed. "Oh, I'm not in any of them. I already know the material. I'm his wife, Tasha."

The man's jaw dropped. "You're... *the* Mrs. Kirushenko? Married to that big .... tall man? With a dozen children?"

She smiled proudly. "The very same."

He pushed a hand through his hair. "Whoo. Oh, my. I can't believe... "

She extended a hand. "Pleased to meet you, Mister ...."

He acted as if she'd just materialized. "Oh! Of course. I'm sorry. Paolo Anseña. I'm the director of the Arch program. Your husband is one of my staff." He took her hand, cradling it until she pulled away.

"Mr. Anseña! How very nice to meet you. Sasha has told me so much about you." Etiquette was about making the other person feel welcome and at ease. Thus, she was under no compulsion whatsoever to tell him not one word of it was pleasant.

"Really? How nice of him. Please! Won't you come into my office to wait? We can talk."

"Of course." She followed him. The room wasn't particularly exciting; a few exotic travel posters on the walls, cabinets and stacks of computer data tags, a handful of museum-quality replicas, and a potted palm with wide leaves, a welcome sight among the endless spiky browns of Navara.

"This is lovely."

Anseña cleared his throat. "Thank you. Here! Let me take your robe for you." She relinquished her rose-colored robe, inwardly amused to watch him trip and stumble in his haste to be polite. His eyes drank in her outfit, caressed her legs to at least her hemline, lingered on her hair. "What a lovely dress you're wearing. Did you purchase it here on Navara?"

"This? Goodness, no. This is Pasha Matei, from her limited edition celebration line. It came from her signature store in Moscow."

He gave a strange little shiver. "It's quite flattering. May I offer you water? Or perhaps you'd like something stronger? I have an assortment of wines, or an exquisite Portuguese almond liqueur."

"Water would be delightful, thank you." She accepted the glass with grace and examined his wall of diplomas while he stood too close. His three university degrees were prominently displayed, along with several certificates for high grades. A single award for research hung among them, and it was only a university award.

"Ah! You studied in London. They have such excellent programs there. What was your research on?"

"Hmm?" He'd been staring at her, lost in thought. "Oh. I did some comparative work between Vikings, Celts, and Inuit peoples and their adaptations to climate changes, cross-referencing with the ancient Kudiru Jen of Antlia VI and the Fi of Go Tev."

Maryana brightened. "Then you must know James Winters' research!"

Anseña frowned. "No, I don't believe so."

"He's the foremost mind in Viking cultures, at the University of Oslo. He and his wife are incredibly nice. We had them to dinner when they stopped in Kiev for a lecture series. We stay in touch to this day. Perhaps I could arrange a teleconference for you."

Anseña didn't seem the least bit interested. "I'm sure I ran into his work along the way. Tell me… Tasha? How long have you been married?" He picked up her left hand and examined her rings.

Maryana's first instinct was to pull away from his unsolicited familiarity, but she held still, observing. Her face retained charm, but lost its warmth. "Twenty-one years, next month."

He continued to fondle her hand, blushing. "You must have been a baby. How did you ever meet someone like that?"

Maryana blinked. "Like what?"

"So – big, and... and... rough." He chuckled to hide his transgression. "You're such a charming little sprite hovering in his shadow. Are you happy with that arrangement?"

She pulled her hand back. "I've never been in Sasha's shadow, Mr. Anseña; I've always been at his side, through his education, his research, his papers, his discoveries. In fact, I myself helped him cast up the *Eo Draconis kirushensis* at Gamma Europa. It was such an incredible honor, them naming it after him. Excavations continue on the site to this day."

A tic quivered under his right eye, but she didn't have time to contemplate it. A shadow walked past the open door, then doubled back.

The bearded face registered nothing. "Tash?"

Her glow returned. "Sasha! Surprise!" She pulled him down and kissed his mouth, holding him to it a bit longer than polite.

"There you are, Kirushenko." Anseña coughed. He shifted nervously, scratching his ear. "I ... We were talking while she waited for you. She's ... quite a knowledgeable lady."

Maryana hung on, picking robe lint from his shirt. "Your schedule said you're free, so I came to take you to lunch. I can't make it a steak dinner, but I'm sure you'll find something." With sparse flora and few sizable animals for consumption, Navaran people as a whole were strictly vegetarian, and would not allow carnivorous habits even in Kar Ku'umi. Importing live or butchered meat of any kind was illegal, as was the eating of it. For Sasha, it added to the hell.

"Then let's go." Sasha held out his elbow; she retrieved her robe and took his arm without hesitation. He gave Anseña a nod, but didn't ask him to join them.

Maryana didn't correct his manners, but she did give his boss a carefree wave.

She picked at a fruit bowl while Sasha shoveled in a large casserole with rice at an underground restaurant on the edge of campus. As much of the city lay below ground as above, prompting its nickname, "the Mole City."

"I'm so sorry, Sash. I understand your frustration completely. He's mediocre at best. He did Norse research, but doesn't remember consulting any of Jim Winters's material? That's utterly negligent. I would never have granted him a degree."

262

Sasha gave a grunt. "He's where he is because of tenure. Eleven years he's suffered, because almost no one stays more than three. He can drop his pants and wave his *huy* around without ever leaving the safety of his office, simply because he's been here longer than anyone else. Of course, you can't tell all that from his signature, so he looks good. Prickless walrus-fucking shit! He's never even assembled a team for an expedition – he poked around sites with his brother and father as assistants, neither of whom had any training whatsoever. I did more as an undergrad than he's done with his entire life, but I have to answer to him. For half a credit, I'd slug him so hard his eyes would fly from his head."

"Easy, Sash. It's quite obvious he's jealous of you, that's all," she assured him. "Your kind of brilliance is a threat to those who struggle just to participate. Do you want his job?"

He paused. Maryana reached across to wipe sauce from his mustache. "No. I hate administrative bullshit. If I had my way, I'd do nothing but teach lab on site."

"All right, then. Ignore his posturing. People aren't stupid; they'll know where the talent is. You're here to teach students, not impress him. Shine bright, my love, but do it humbly. I'll work the wives, find out what I can. You know, I like this. I think we should dine out every Thursday. What do you think?"

His face lightened, and a smile pulled at the corner of his mouth. "I wish you could be here every day."

* * *

Sasha entered the house, whistling a happy tune. He put his work bag and a flat box on the table by the door, hung up his robe, but held onto a second package.

"Good afternoon, Father," came a chorus of voices.

"Good afternoon!" he said lightly. Three-year old Byeta ran to greet him; he swung her up to give her a kiss before setting her free. He handed her the package. "Careful! Give that to your Mama."

She did as bid, but turned around. "Where's my present? Did you get me a present? I want a present, Papa. I want a Steffi Starmaker doll like on the vidlink. I want that as a present."

"Today is your Mama's turn."

Her bottom lip stuck out in vicious scowl. "I want a present *today*!"

263

Maryana cut her off before the scream could start. "Your present is a piece of candy, in the kitchen. If you ask Katya nicely, she will get it for you."

"That's not a present. That's to eat."

"Well, if you don't want your present," Katya baited, "I guess it goes to me." She headed for the kitchen.

"NO! My present!" Byeta ran at full speed.

Maryana smiled at him. "You shouldn't have. It's too much." She pulled the glass container out of the insulated box and sniffed under the lid. Inside stood a single perfect red rose. Roses – any legal non-native flower – couldn't survive the heat for more than a few brief minutes, and thus were sold only in refrigerated containers, at the hefty price of fifty credits a stem. She placed the container on the grand piano.

"Nothing's too good for my Tash." He waltzed her around the room, humming.

She batted her eyes at him. "You're in an awfully good mood."

"Exams are done, grades turned in, semester over, two whole weeks without that sonofabitch calling me names. What isn't there to be happy about?"

"What's in the other box?"

He glanced back at it. "That? It was a gift from one of my seniors in Advanced Lab Techniques." He retrieved the box and removed a thin black rope, as long as Maryana.

Maryana stepped back. "What is that? That's not a creature of some sort?"

Sasha held the handle and swung it through the air with a crack. "A whip. He said I was a slave driver when it came to learning, so I should have the proper tools to motivate the less dedicated students."

"That's an awful thing to say. Is that leather? Sash, leather's illegal here. You can't keep it."

"I don't know. It could be a good imitation. Akh! I know what this would be good for." He slapped it loudly on the floor. "David! Come here."

David leaped from the sofa. "I didn't do it! I had nothing to do with it! Dmitri spilled your cologne, I saw him! It wasn't me! Smell him if you don't believe me!" He took off at light speed, followed a second later by Sergei, Vladimir, and Sarah, clawing each other to be first down the hall.

Sasha let loose a laugh that boomed in the open rooms. "I like this kind of motivation!"

Maryana grasped the bearded chin and shook it with affection. "You would! Take it back to work, before the children get hold of it." Then she remembered his difficulties with his boss. "On second thought, maybe you better leave it here."

Thirty-eight

Maryana used the hand control to shut off the holovision, dropping the room into a dimness lit by the faint light from the bedroom, around the corner and down the hall. The holovision was huge, a platform two meters square, along with a separate integration unit the size of a credenza. It cost more than the second-hand twelve-passenger flyer parked outside, the replacement for Sasha's misjudgment. The double hit had been hard on their savings, harder on his mood. The holovision had been an anniversary present for him, a chance to seem ringside at sports events or travel documentaries of places greener, give him something else to look forward to than numbing the misery. And it did. Sometimes.

Thursdays were good days. He left in good spirits, knowing she'd be there, and came home in a good one, boosted by her visit. Several weeks into the pattern, they were saying goodbye when he held her close, running his hands over her back.

His lips lingered over hers. "If we weren't here, you know what I'd do?" His hand lifted the back of her skirt and crept past her underthings.

A thrill shot through her middle. Her tongue slid over his lips. "Are there cameras in your office?"

"No."

"Then put a poster over the window in your door and lock it. Let's do it."

The dark eyes widened, and his breath caught. "You mean, here? In the office? Tash!"

She hiked herself onto the edge of his desk, legs folded in a suggestive pose. She had his attention, every last molecule. "Here and now. It's your office, isn't it? Are you game?"

On his desk, dress around her waist, feet on his shoulders, or bent over his file cabinet, her slacks barely off her cheeks, lunch became a secondary matter, but his mood improved.

266

Today was Tuesday. Tuesdays were for staff meetings, a time when he swallowed his tongue and allowed criticisms to bounce off without retort. He'd learned the hard way not to make useful suggestions when multiple disciplines were present: Anseña would corner him later and accuse him of flouting his authority and making him look bad. Tuesdays left Sasha short in temper. The children learned to tiptoe on Tuesdays, or face their father's wrath.

She stroked his cheek, then resorted to shaking his shoulder. "Sash? Sasha. Come on, wake up. It's late. Come to bed. You fell asleep in the chair again."

He picked his head up and tried to focus. An empty liquor bottle rolled from his lap onto the floor, clattering sharply against the stone.

"Come on, darling." She retrieved the bottle and left it on the chairside table. "Time for bed. Stand up, Sash. I can't carry you."

He dragged himself up with her prodding. He wobbled a bit; she did her best to steady him.

The sheet was pulled down on their bed. She got him to sit and proceeded to undress him.

Once in bed, he wasn't as sleepy. Maryana felt the familiar hand snaking up her thin nightshirt as she bent over him. She twisted out of reach. "Not tonight, Sash. You need to sleep. You've had too much to drink. Tomorrow, when you know what you're doing."

He belched loudly, a boiling vapor of hot peppers, beans and *titob,* a local fermented sauce. "I know what I'm doing. I t'ink I know what to do when I'm in bed with a beau – beau'ful woman." He kissed her lips clumsily, sloppy and wet. He wrapped his arms around her and rolled on the bed, pulling her with him.

He got in position, then stopped.

"Sash, you're crushing me. Up a little. Sasha, I can't breathe!" Maryana almost laughed as she realized he had fallen asleep. *My big baby!* She couldn't get out from under him. He was too heavy, the bed too soft. She couldn't call for the boys to help, to see their father so undignified as this – let alone their mother! Holding onto the headboard she wrestled herself out, centimeter by centimeter. She pulled the sheet up as he snored naked in the center of the bed. Curling up in the space next to him, she kissed him gently and went to sleep.

* * *

October 2260

The Fearsome Four were unsupervised again.

Sarah and her brothers studied Father's chair from the safety of the hall. A promotional program played on the holovision, trying its best to convince Father that the redesigned anti-grav lifters on the new 2261 Windslayer six-passenger sandskimmer were so superior to other vehicles that he just couldn't live without it. Father's reply was a steady rumbling snore, deep asleep. Sarah knew that for a fact. Father didn't drool when awake.

"Chicken!" David goaded in a whisper.

"Am not!"

"Then prove it." He held Vladimir tight against him, a hand clamped over his brother's mouth to prevent any noise that might put everyone in danger. Vlad squirmed and pulled to no avail.

"I think you're both crazy," Sergei hushed. "You're going to get *all* of us killed. He'll wake up the minute you get within a meter of him. Then what are you going to do?"

"I learned a new archaeology fact. He'll think I've been standing there the whole time waiting for him to wake up so I could tell him. Relax," Sarah reassured Vladimir. "I can do it, no sand about it."

She patted his leg, took a deep breath, and moved out of the safety of the shadows. It wasn't her first Dangerous Mission. She was six now, and now that she attended the Shir Tal Nin school, David couldn't pretend he was smarter than she was. She had a plan.

Mother relaxed in her bedroom; that was a fact. Alexei had a class until 2200 hours. That was a fact. Viktor, Dmitri, and Katya would be studying in the boys' room. Byeta and baby Nikky were asleep. Everyone had to stay where they were just a few minutes more. She wouldn't need long.

On her hands and bare toes, Sarah crept across the cool stone floor until she crouched behind Father's chair.

She looked back. Vladimir sat still, too frightened to move. Nine-year-old Sergei looked scared, but gave her a weak three-fingers-up. She flashed back a half-hearted set of fingers herself. Scaredy, bah!

Sarah peered around the chair, sighted her prey, and reached up to the table. As gingerly as if picking up a single snowflake, she closed her fingers around Father's glass of vodka and eased back until she clutched it to her chest. Five or six centimeters of liquid remained, the ice long but a memory. She checked with the safety crew.

David nodded. He let go of Vladimir long enough to curl a hand around an imaginary glass and tip it toward his face.

Sarah raised the glass to her lips.

Only the fear of being caught made her swallow. The liquid burned her insides like fire, blistered her tongue and the back of her nose and deep into her stomach, like the smell of the chemicals in the school lab. Instinct said *Poison! Reject!* but the deal said she had to dispose of the evidence. The fumes made her need to cough; not coughing made her feel as if she were drowning.

All of it! David mouthed at her. *Dare's a dare!*

Holding her breath, Sarah downed the rest of the vodka in three tries. She held the glass up, upside-down. David grinned his approval, and Sergei gave her a victory sign.

She reached up to return the glass. The chair gave an unexpected rustle as Father shifted. Her hand whipped back, dropping the glass on the table.

Father's snoring resumed, soft and steady.

The glass lay on its side, but she didn't have the courage to straighten it. She raised herself up on her toes and sprinted for the hallway.

David released Vladimir to clap her on the back. "Way to go, Brainiac! Nerves of tritanium, man! Nerves of *tritanium!*"

Sarah gave a deep raspy cough at last. "Pay up," she insisted. "Three credits."

"I'll get them," David promised, hands crossed behind him.

Sergei curled his lip. "What'd it taste like?"

"Ghastly! Like when David made us lick the floor cleaner. Next time it's his turn."

David's 'turn' came four days later. Father didn't have classes on Tuesday afternoons, and it made him mad. A bad day meant Father needed to relax, and relaxing meant everyone had to be quiet and let him sleep in the chair, or else.

Sergei squinted from the shadows. "It's not empty. I think it'll be safe."

Sarah agreed. "Dare, double-dare! I want my three credits! If you don't pay me, I'm telling Viktor."

"Then let him pay you!" David studied the chair with trepidation. "How can you be sure he's really asleep?"

Sergei shrugged. "Same as always. Look and listen. He hasn't moved in more than ten minutes."

"I don't know… "

"He won't do it," Vladimir whispered. "He's as scaredy as an Altairan Ice-jumper."

David shoved Vlad so hard the boy fell over. "You should talk, babyshit! Not like you could ever do it! Better check his pants, Seryozh… "

Sarah locked eyes with David. "Chicken! I did it, so that means I'm better than you!"

"And you fell down drunk, and Vik and Kat and Dimi had to sit with you all night to make sure you didn't die," Sergei reminded her.

"David's bigger. I think he's going sandy on us. *I'm* braver than *you* are…."

"Shut the hell up before I pound you! I'm going." David took a step, listening. Like Alexei, David, too, would take after his father, already taller than his mother, with the build and grace of a galloping bull, far too large to crawl inconspicuously. He tiptoed around the back of the room and stole forward directly behind the chair. He took up position and waited for the go-ahead.

Sergei studied the sleeping figure with a critical eye, then gave the okay.

David peered around the chair, planning in his head. His job would be tougher – today's bottle stood between him and the glass. He'd have to reach around it. Millimeter by millimeter he moved, until his hand grasped success. He sat back and sniffed the contents. Peppermint, not vodka. Raising the half-filled glass in a toast to his siblings, he tossed the liquid back like his father did. His eyes watered, but pride was pride. It didn't matter he was five years older and twice her size; he did it in one gulp and Sarah'd needed three. David crossed his eyes at the witnesses and pretended to wobble, then smiled and held up the empty glass.

He began the process of returning it. Around the back of the chair, forward over the table, left around the bottle, release on mark, and from nowhere a giant hand clamped down, pinning his wrist to the table.

David shrieked. The rabbits in the hall scattered.

Thick fingers encircled his hand and the long arm reeled him in. Father stood up, up and up to his monstrous height.

"What the Hell do you think you're doing?" Sasha rumbled in a voice that chilled the room. "What were you doing with my glass?"

David cringed at the glazed eyes. "Nothing, Father!" In the darkest shadows of the hall the rabbits reappeared, quivering.

"You were in my schnapps, weren't you? That shit's too goddamned expensive to waste on a rotten little shit like you! That's a man's drink! You think yourself a man?"

"No, sir!"

"I did not give you permission to speak!" The wide hand let go of the wrist and clobbered the boy on the side of his head, knocking him into the sofa. David slid to his knees, holding his face.

"Get up! You think you can drink a man's drink and then cry about it?"

"No, sir!"

"You know what it feels like to be a man?" Sasha shouted. "Like *that*!" The huge foot shot out and kicked the boy in his side. David gasped.

"You like that? You think it's fun to get up every morning and have people do that to you all day?" The foot smashed home again. "You think it's funny to come home and have some little shit punk think he can make a fool out of you in the refuge of your own home?" *kick* "I don't hear you laughing now!"

"Shit!" Sergei whispered in the hall.

"Get Viktor!" Sarah pushed Vladimir toward the bedroom. Vlad froze in terror, unable to move. Sarah made a gamble and ran down the hall to Mother's room.

She knocked fast and entered. "Mother?"

A program chattered on the wallscreen. Maryana lounged on the bed, rubbing scented cream on her pretty feet. Her unbraided hair tumbled down her back in soft blonde waves, all the way to the bed, Lady Godiva in loungewear. She looked up.

"Mother? You need to come. I think David's in trouble. He got Father sort of angry." The screams from the other room grew eerily silent.

Maryana returned her gaze to the wallscreen as she polished a heel. "David has to learn to leave Father alone. He brings it on himself."

Sarah tried the academic approach. *"S'il vous plait, Mamán?"* Mother had taught her French as a game, and loved to hear Sarah speak it. *"C'est moi qui te le demande. Papa –il m'effraie …"*

271

Maryana clenched her teeth. "If you are making me get up for nothing, Sarah, I will tell your father you are to be next," but she did pause her program and slide off the bed.

Sarah bounced on her toes. *"Tres vite, Mamán! Merci beaucoup!"*

Three older children had come running at the shouts. Maryana pushed through the spectators. The holovision blared its spectral programming, oblivious to the competition. David lay curled against the wall, arms protecting his head. Father launched a final kick.

"Sasha! That's enough!" Maryana said. "For goodness' sake, your foot is bigger than his head! That's not very fair."

"Lousy bastard thinks he can steal my glass," Sasha mumbled woundedly, like a little boy caught bullying by his mother. "He's not the one getting fucked by the import charges."

Maryana pulled his arm around her tiny shoulders. "And you've taken care of it now, haven't you. They're just rambunctious tonight. You know they can't play outside. Why don't you keep me company in the other room? No one will disturb you there. Which program were you watching?"

Sasha looked down at her, her hair and dress damp with perspiration from the awful desert heat. He smiled with pride. "You. You are the biggest distraction of all."

She blew a kiss up at him. "Because I like you with me. It's very lonely when you sleep out here like this." She guided him to the bedroom. The older children stepped to the side; the younger ones vanished the minute they turned toward the hall. "'D'Misha, bring your father his drink. Vitya, see to your brother."

Maryana returned a minute or two after the littlest rabbits reappeared. "Viktor, I thought I told you to get him out of here," she said, seeing David still gasping on the floor, his head cradled in Katya's lap.

Vik hesitated. "Mother? I think he might really be hurt. He can't breathe, and he says it hurts too much to sit up. Is it possible... Could he have broken something?"

David panted, trying to cry without moving his chest. Katya petted his dark hair, her own cheeks wet with tears. Maryana knelt and pushed David's arms out of the way. Under his shirt, huge marks were swelling red-purple. She felt along his side with her small sharp fingers. David flailed and howled.

"Stop your noise! You're too big to carry on like that." Maryana stood up, indecisive. Bruises caused questions.

"I can't bring him to town. Someone has to stay here and take care of your father. If you think he's that hurt, you may take a taxi and bring him to the medical center," she relented. "I'll call ahead and give permission to have him treated."

Viktor looked frightened. "I'll need help getting him in and out. Can Dmitri come with me?"

"If you're gone, Dmitri is needed here. Let me know when you're back. I'll wait up."

Maryana touched the call buttons on the commlink. She smiled so sweetly at the face on the vidscreen. "Yes! Hello! This is Tasha Kirushenko, out beyond the dune walls? I'm sending in one of my boys for a check. He was wrestling his big brother, and I think he might have hurt himself…"

* * *

Maryana trapped him in their bathroom while he dressed for work. She kept her voice low and calm, caring but not saccharine. He would sense saccharine in an instant. "Sash… We need to talk."

He froze, one hand holding a comb to his head as he spoke to her reflection in the mirror. "Don't. Just don't go there, Tash. There is nothing you can say to me that I don't already know."

"So you are aware of what you did."

He slammed the comb on the countertop and turned to her. "You want to hear me say it? I had a bad day, got drunk off my ass, woke up half-cocked to an eleven year old polishing off a glass of schnapps and lost my temper. I'm sorry I hurt him. I was still half asleep. I'm sorry. I hope to the stars I never do anything like that again. Is that what you want to hear? There, I said it."

She rubbed his arm in a forgiving manner. "Did you tell that to him?"

Shame crossed the big face, and he wouldn't look at her. "What good does it do? I've been there, Tash. You can cry rivers in front of your child, promise them the world, but they won't believe it. You break someone's ribs, any apology sounds false. I think apologies hurt worse than injuries. An injury is real; an apology is a lie."

Maryana gave a conceding nod. "You have more experience in that area than I do. But he deserves some sort of explanation, false-sounding or not. Please make some attempt. You owe him that much. And I'll hold you to that promise to never do anything like that again.

273

Discipline is one thing, hurting children is another. Do you know what happens if the doctor questions last night? You better keep your elbow straight for the next week, in case some Family Safety Coordinator makes a sudden appearance. I don't think either one of us wants that kind of attention."

There was a warning tone to his voice she'd never heard before. "Don't lecture me, Tash. I'm well aware of when I fuck up."

"You're the professor. Lecture yourself." She left him alone to compose it.

Thirty-nine

S asha backed down. He was trying, but he wasn't happy; Maryana knew that. She could see it in the way he carried himself, hunched over, head down, staring into the holovision simply because it was there. It made her feel guilty, as if his unhappiness was her fault, though she knew it wasn't. He'd spent the last twenty-one years cramming information into his head every spare minute he could, sacrificing for that day when he would be successful. With four degrees, accolades still drifting in over his triumph on Gamma Europa IV, he was left with a hostile work environment that was suffocating him and unfamiliar empty time to dwell on it.

As well as the cost.

Maryana rested her head on the desk in the dining room, trying to piece things out. She'd always been able to rely on Sasha when she felt unsure of life. He was older, more experienced, more able to cut to the core of a matter without worrying about societal expectations. Now, with him teetering once again on a bad round of self-doubt and ten children each with demands of their own, the weight of the household fell squarely on her slight shoulders, and she wasn't sure she was strong enough to hold it up anymore. *How had Mamá ever managed to juggle children and households and full-time employment?*

With Papa's help, and house managers, and a staff, and presidents of departments.... All those people Maryana didn't have.

There was a reason why Ku'umi salaries were twice the norm: everything cost three times as much as on Earth. There were so few natural resources on Navara – other than minerals, silicates, ores, and sunlight – that almost everything save glass and grinding powders had to be imported from other star systems, or grown in huge facilities at great expense. It was actually cheaper for her to have the twins purchase some items for her in Moscow and ship them privately than it was to buy locally. Not that she had purchased a single designer outfit in six months. At twice the salary, they were less wealthy than before, and the accounts were hemorrhaging money to keep up. Maryana studied their statements, studied their projected expenses, and saw a downward spiral that frightened her.

Any sensible accountant would look at the numbers and counsel against it. The smart thing would be to return home while they still could, but Sasha would never break a contract. Katya was pleading to spend a week of school break back on Earth with her sisters; the twins were pleading even harder for her to visit. Katya was a sweet girl with excellent grades who rarely ever complained about helping with her siblings. She deserved the trip, despite the 10,000 credit student fare. Maryana looked over her investment portfolios, chose a few that weren't particularly strong performers, and sold off her interests.

* * *

April

He came home in a testy mood. Maryana held dinner until seven, waiting for him. His last class ended at three; he'd had the courtesy to message her that he was heading out to a happy hour with a few of his colleagues. Happy hours were creeping into his weekly activities, but so far he'd been coming home functional. She could live with functional. Sometimes it cheered him up, other times it added fuel to his smoldering issues. She knew today was the latter when the first words from his mouth were a bellow for someone to get their feet off the edge of the holovision. The noise made her jump.

She had dinner on the table within ten minutes; Maryana had let the housekeeper/cook go a month before. It cut a huge expense, and it saved the trouble of having to gloss over Sasha's less pleasant moments. She didn't serve wine with dinner, just water.

"Not mushrooms!" Alexei flicked the brown bits out of his food and into a pile. "I hate mushrooms in my kasha. Rehydrated things taste like shit anyway."

Sasha ripped the plate away, scraped the offending food onto his own and slammed the plate back down. "There. Now you have nothing to whine about." Alexei huffed and grumbled something unintelligible.

Byeta mashed a chunk of beef-flavored vegetable protein into paste with her fork. "I don't like *these*."

"Eat," Maryana prodded. "They'll make you big and smart."

"I like sprouts," Sarah said. "Bean sprouts, and broccoli sprouts, and the *talik* sprouts they serve at school."

"I like sprouts, too," Katya said. "Alfalfa sprouts with peanut dressing."

"I like broc'li sprouts," Vlad said. "With vinegar dressing."

"I miss meatballs. *Real* meatballs," Dmitri said, and several voices agreed.

Fourteen-month-old Nikky wiped kasha through his brown curls, then flung his cup onto the floor. Maryana picked it up and handed it back. Nikky took a sip and banged the lidded cup repeatedly on the edge of the table. The noise reverberated through the open, high-ceilinged rooms.

A tremendous bang made everyone jump and all conversation cease as Sasha slammed his fists on the table. "Stop that fucking noise, Tash!" he roared. "I want a quiet fucking dinner! Is that too much to ask? I listen to students moaning all day because they're too lazy to study; can't I have a quiet fucking meal? I don't want to hear another goddamned sound!"

Maryana took a deep breath. "He's a baby, Sash. There's only so much I can do." She took the cup away and stuffed a spoonful of food into Nikky's mouth to keep him quiet. He spit some out and fingerpainted with it. The children bent their heads and ate in silence.

It was a bad pairing; Maryana should have realized that and corrected the issue before they sat. Someone had overfilled Vlad's glass; she should have checked that, too. She blamed herself for the oversights. Left-handed Vlad sat to the right of right-handed Sergei. Sergei put his fork down as Vlad moved to put down his waterglass. They bumped elbows in the process; Sergei's fork gave a loud clink against his plate. High-strung Vlad gave a startle at the noise, and his glass caught the edge of his plate as his hand released. It tipped over, sending water in a wave across the table. Vlad shrank small in his seat. Sasha noticed when the water trickled into his lap.

Sasha's voice was deep and slow, dark as a thick fogbank rolling into the room. "What the fuck did you do that for? You think that's funny? Do you know how much a tank of water costs, that you can just go pouring it over a table into my lap? You think it's funny my pants are now wet?"

Vlad's little face turned a sickly white, and he shook his head rapidly.

"It was an accident," Sarah said. "He didn't mean to."

"Mind your own fucking business." He addressed Vlad again. "Seven years old, and you can't drink without a baby cup? Of course not! You still need a goddamn diaper at night!"

"It's not his fault," Sarah said. "He's still little."

"Sar'ina," Maryana cautioned.

"Get up!" Sasha rose and seized Vlad by the ear, dragging him to the lamp table whose drawer held his whip.

"Great," Alexei muttered loud enough for Maryana to hear at the other end of the table. "Dinner *and* a show. Lucky me." He reached back to his father's plate and retrieved his kasha.

"Please, Father!" Vlad begged. "I didn't mean it! It was an accident! Please! I'll clean it up! Please no! It was an accident!" The silence at the table became deeper. Nikky stopped swinging his feet.

"Sasha, it can wait until after dinner," Maryana said. "Come finish eating."

He shoved Vlad toward the empty wall by the hallway. Tiny Vlad, barely the size of a four-year-old, crashed into it, scraping his cheek. "You dare to question me?" Sasha shouted, a wild sound bordering on hysteria. He cracked the whip close to Vlad's ear. Vlad twisted away with a shriek and cowered against the wall.

"Stand still, baby! Babies cry. Men have to stand still and take whatever shit is thrown at them and smile the whole time they're getting fucked." He cracked the whip near the boy once more, toying with him.

Vlad danced in place, trying to run in every direction at once, shrieking. The front of his shorts began to darken, as well as the stone floor beneath him.

Sasha stared, unsure what he was seeing. "Did you just…? You – you pissed on my floor! You goddamned little baby! You pissed your pants right here on my floor!" He grabbed the boy by his shirt, shaking him. Vladimir's cries became screams of terror.

A chair scraped on the floor and a streak shot across the room. Viktor leaned back but couldn't grab it in time.

Anxiety rose, chipping at Maryana's nerves, stealing her appetite. This couldn't be allowed to escalate further, but what could she do? How did one intervene in something like this? She'd learned how to avoid arguments in school, but not how to break up violence. That was for security teams. "Sar'ina! It's not your business. Sit down."

Sarah plowed into her father like an energy bolt, pounding him with her fists and feet, trained to an orange-belt in karate and half-way through a first-level badge in Navaran so-tau-kam. "Stop it! Stop scaring him, you big monster!"

Sasha stared, speechless.

"Run, Vlad!" Sarah whispered. She waved him toward the hall. Vlad ran blindly, sobbing.

"What the hell do you think you're doing? How dare you strike me!"

Sarah parked her hands on her hips. "You're nothing but a mean old bully, scaring him like that! He's little!"

"You goddamned little shit! You think you can save your piss-assed brother from his punishment?"

Sarah craned her neck to stare up, up and up into the bloodshot dark eyes. "I'm not afraid of you!"

"Oh, you think so? You don't want your brother to take his punishment? You can take it for him! And when I finish, I will punish you for your insolence!"

Sarah dared to turn her back to him. "I'm not afraid of you! Bully!" she called over her shoulder.

Maryana placed a bite of food in her mouth but it sat like lead on her tongue. It took all her will to force it down. She closed her eyes, head down, hearing the repeated slap of the whip but unable to watch. Sarah was as stubborn as her father; she whimpered a bit, but she wouldn't yell.

"Mama? Sari's bleeding," Byeta's voice said next to her. Maryana felt the little hands reach around her for comfort.

Byeta was always the first to rejoice in anyone's misbehavior; the quiet fear in her voice snapped Maryana's eyes open. Sarah lay on the floor, her shirt shredded, her back... From across the room her back looked like one giant wound, and still Sasha hit her. Maryana's stomach tried to rise, but it couldn't get past the horror squeezing her chest.

She flew to her feet. "Sasha! That's enough! She's only a child! What she says doesn't matter one bit. Come into the kitchen and finish your dinner. Right now! Come."

Maryana steered him into the kitchen, out of the shocked eyes of the other children, and sat him at the table. He breathed heavily, shaking. He crossed his arms on the tabletop and rested his big head on them, face down. She stepped back out to the living area, projecting control and making executive power decisions without second thought. Vladimir knelt next to his sister, screaming incoherently in an eerie, keening animal wail.

"Vladimir, stop that noise! Viktor, put her in her bed. There should be a healing cream in the cabinet in the bathroom. Dmitri, clean the floor. Katya, watch the babies. I don't want to hear a sound! Not! One!"

She returned to the kitchen and punched code on the food replicator. It beeped within thirty seconds. Maryana put a double-sized cup of strong coffee in front of him. This wasn't something sex would fix. This was catastrophic. Her eyes drifted toward the door.

Focus, Maryana! I must focus. Don't think about the other right now. Focus on what's at hand.

She sat next to him and rubbed a hand across his back. "Sash, that's not like you at all. What's wrong?"

Her towering husband, the invincible intimidator with arms the size of tree trunks and a voice that shook earth, *whimpered.*

"Two more years, Tash. I'm not going to make it."

"Shh, my love. What happened?"

His lip curled as if he wanted to cry. His voice agreed. "That shit Anseña shot down my second rewrite of the proposal as well. A *technicality*, he said. For a hundred credits, I'd beat the bastard's head in and enjoy every minute of it. If he just wasn't such a *smug* son of a bitch! He has no fucking right to call himself an archaeologist." The coffee in his hand trembled miniature waves across the cup.

"Shhh, Sash. You have to calm yourself. I know. You've got more experience than he's ever dreamed of. He has nothing, and you have everything. It's all jealousy. You have to remember that." She rubbed the mighty shoulders that had grown round and soft. Desks and alcohol were taking a toll. "It's their game, you have to play it their way, even if you know it's wrong. You must be strong. Keep your dignity. Don't let them see it bothering you. You'll win this, too."

"I know. I know," he said, melancholia replacing his spent anger. He glanced guiltily at the closed kitchen door. "I'm sorry, Tash. Is she... okay?"

"She'll be fine." Maryana kept up the calming tones as she massaged away his fears. "It was just the whip. You didn't use your hands. She'll heal."

He was scared of his hands. He never told her why. It was one of those nightmares of his youth he didn't want her carefree mind to know.

He'd come home to find one of his mother's male 'friends' beating her and trying to take her bank ID. There wasn't much in the account – he stole from it himself – but it was all they had. The man had dragged her half in, half out of their dark third-floor apartment. Mother wore a sliver of underwear and a sheer blouse open to her navel. She lay in the doorway, bruised, drunk and crying, a heavy breast flopping out of her shirt, her thick makeup smeared across her face as he kicked her.

Sasha didn't care too much about his mother; as far as he was concerned, she'd gotten a little of what she deserved. He hated his mother for what she was, but he hated the men who took advantage of her even more. Something inside him snapped, and he attacked the man with ten years' worth of buried rage. He knocked him clear across the hall, punching and pummeling and pounding the man with fists powered by eighteen months' of boxing practice. The man staggered and came back. In the ensuing scuffle, the man pushed Sasha down the long third-floor staircase, falling with him. Sasha slid the length of the seventeen steps head first on his back. The man cartwheeled up and over him, hitting the wall at the turn and landing wrong. The hall filled with witnesses.

"Mama? Mama?" Young Sasha raced up the stairs, dragging his mother inside their apartment. "Pull yourself together... Cover yourself!... The politzei are coming, Mama! Something... something happened... "

The man was dead. Sasha was the last one to touch him alive. It was the first time he knew the humiliation of being frisked and bound and marched before people he knew to a detention center; interrogated, processed, degraded, and left alone in a cell, his long body aching from his fall. Alone, he cried like a baby. He was seventeen, and would be tried as an adult.

His mother surprised him. She visited him, dressed in loud clothes and no underwear and her heavy makeup, her wild natural curls tied back in restraint. She went to court, *presenting herself as a victim being defended by her baby, her only son. If the situation hadn't been so grave, Sasha would have laughed. Enough neighbors came forward to swear the man had pushed the boy and the man was at fault, but the fact remained the man's liver had been injured by a hard blow before his fall. If the fall hadn't killed him, he would have bled to death.*

The final ruling held that the man was alive at the time of the fall. The injury itself had no bearing on the actual cause of death, no more than an unknown aneurysm would have. It was officially an accident, and Sasha walked away free, forever frightened of his own strength.

"*Fuck!* It's bad this time, isn't it? What the fuck was I thinking? I'm sorry. I'm so sorry, Tash. I really am. I can't do anything right. I know she's young… She just… pissed me off at the wrong time. And Vladimir… pissing …" He rubbed his face irritably.

"Shh. It's just the stress you're under. I know. She sounds older than she is. It's easy to forget." Maryana kissed him on the ear. "Viktor can handle it. I'll check on her later. I'd rather not drag a doctor in if we don't have to."

Sasha nodded. Doctors asked questions. The coffee mixed poorly with the alcohol and his emotions, and he vomited his troubles into the kitchen sink.

* * *

Maryana peered around the corner to make sure the coast was clear before walking as quietly as she could down the Arch hall. She lifted herself onto ballerina toes and flitted past the ever-open door. There were few people for whom she'd developed a profound dislike. Emil Graffia was one.

Paolo Anseña was the other.

"Natasha!"

Damn! Her face scrunched up in painful displeasure. She turned to face the source.

Anseña slipped over, so close his jacket brushed her outfit. He lifted her hand and kissed it, gazing into her eyes. "Such a pleasure to see you. Bringing him lunch this week? You are absolutely the most dedicated woman I have ever met. Can you spare a moment? I have a new piece I'd love to show you."

She smiled and pulled away, soiled at his touch. "Perhaps later. I really should be …."

"I will just take a minute." He pulled on her arm, and she followed.

He shut the door.

She waited before his desk, curt but always courteous. "Please be brief, Mr. Anseña. My lunch is growing warm."

"Of course." He pulled a cloth from his pocket and unfolded it. In his palm lay a primitive gold ring with a blue stone.

"That's very pretty. Roman?"

He breathed in short staccato exhalations, reminding her faintly of something caught in a food grinder. "From Centauri, actually. It dates back three thousand years."

"It's lovely. Thank you for showing it to me." She moved to leave, but he sidestepped in front of her.

He removed it from the cloth and held it out. "It's for you."

"I couldn't accept something like that! It's priceless."

His breathing worsened. "Maryana, I've known you for over a year now. There's … something I have to tell you, something tearing me apart and I have to get it off my chest. You … are every bit as priceless as this ring. You deserve far better than that ill-tempered, boorish yeti. I just … I just want you to know there are other options available to you."

"I beg your pardon?" This couldn't be happening. Not today. Not now. She would never stop Sasha from killing him. Not in the mood he was in. Not with the hostility he felt toward the man.

Anseña seemed to shiver. He grabbed her by the arms and held her, his breath hot on her face. "Tasha, I love you! I have from the first time I saw you. You are my Frigga, my Druantia, my Parthenope… I would never treat you the way he does, never…"

"Mr. Anseña!"

"Paolo." His lips stretched for hers.

She twisted violently away. "MISTER Anseña! Let go of me this instant!"

He complied, eyes to the floor. "I'm sorry… I don't know what came over me. Please forgive me."

Maryana was a naturally optimistic person, always looking at the best of any situation and forgiving the bad. She could count on her fingers the times she'd felt truly angry. This was another, and a line had to be drawn, here and now. She wiped her lips as if checking for injury.

"Mr. Anseña! How dare you! How dare you, sir! You're … You're almost old enough to be my father! How dare you presume I have any empathy for you at all, sir, when you have done nothing to support my husband in his teaching here, but instead blocked him at every turn. I see nothing in your heart but bitterness and envy, neither of which I wish to participate in. If you have any desire to live, you will never mention your indiscretion. If you wish me to remain silent and not press charges, you will never, never speak to me again. Is that understood? I chose my husband because I loved him, and I love him no less today. I have followed him to the ends of the galaxy; I have followed him here, and I will follow him to the next location. There is nothing he could do that would cause me to leave him. Is that clear?"

He nodded, watching the tiles beneath his feet. "I'm sorry." He opened the door, and she fled.

Maryana stopped in a restroom to cry off the strain. She patted her face with a cooling cloth and made sure she was able to present a carefree appearance before progressing to Sasha's office.

"You're late," he said softly. "I thought maybe you weren't coming."

She placed the refrigeration bag on his desk. "Traffic was slow. They were clearing sand near the eastern gate and it took time to get through." She took off her robe. "I wore the blue dress for you."

"I'm not in the mood, this week." He wasn't even digging into the lunchbag.

She unpacked it for him. "That's fine. Absence makes the heart grow fonder."

He clutched the arms of his chair as if he'd fly away if he didn't. "I'm sober."

"I didn't doubt that for a second. I never doubt you."

He sat for several minutes, staring through the food laid out before him. The question grew heavier and heavier, until it squeezed out of his mouth to land hard on the desk next to his salad. "How is she?"

Maryana couldn't lie, but she couldn't gild it, either. Not something that bad. Even here, with other worries taking precedence, she couldn't erase the image of the mass of open, angry whip wounds.

"We might be okay. There's not a lot of untouched skin left, but I bought a high-quality healing cream with growth accelerators, and some pain pills that should make her sleep most of the time. They should help. Give it three days, and we'll see how they're working. "

He moved restlessly in his chair, as if fighting his stomach. "I'm sorry, Tash. I'm so sorry. I could have killed her, my little prodigy. I should turn myself in. Perhaps there's a counselor here in the city."

Counselors could be trouble, as much as doctors. "Let's wait and see how things go first, Sash. We'll cross that galaxy if we need to. We don't want the Navarans getting word of it." She came over and sat in his lap.

"I promise, Tash. No more alcohol."

Her head curled against his chest. "Fourteen months down, Sash; twenty-six more to go. We'll make it. We always do."

The commlink beeped the following morning. Sasha's face appeared on the screen. He seemed relaxed, almost pleasant. "You'll never guess what was in my inbox. The original grant proposal, approved in full. We'll spend the fall semester at a dig on Alhena III, with a crew of twenty. Four entire months off this oven."

"Sash! That's terrific! Sar'ina will have healed by then. I'm so excited for you! For us."

He frowned, thinking. "I don't know what made him change his mind. He's been such a prick about it since the start."

"Maybe it was pressure from above," she suggested smoothly. "Perhaps the students complained about the missed opportunity. Either way, it's a godsend."

Sasha smiled at last. "That it is."

Forty

June 2261

The shrieking and growling came from the hallway. "Girlfight!" yelled David, and in a flash he and Vladimir were cheering on the combatants. The battle worked its way out to the living room, four-year-old Byeta slapping and clawing and pulling Sarah's hair, and six-year old Sarah kicking and punching in return. Sarah's aim never failed, but she knew she wasn't allowed to use full force; Byeta made up for skill with speed and viciousness. Byeta kept up a howl to wake the dead, but Sarah couldn't give more than a yell or two without having to cough. Katya was on them seconds later, but Byeta scratched her and Katya let go with a shout.

"Girls! Stop, right now!" Maryana commanded, but no one so much as paused.

"Goddammit, you little shits!" Sasha rolled himself out of his chair before the holovision. "I said no more fighting! What the fuck do I have to do? Bury you in the sand?"

"She broke my textreader!" Sarah protested. Her head pitched to the side as Byeta yanked her hair, and she pushed Byeta away with a foot to her middle.

Sasha hauled Byeta back by her braid. He lifted her easily, tucked her under his arm, and smacked the four-year old's bottom more than a half dozen times. Byeta screamed in rage. He slammed her down on the sofa. "Sit there and don't move!" Byeta arched her back and threw herself on the floor to writhe and thrash in a venomous fit.

Sasha caught her, whacked her several more times, and replaced her on the sofa. "I said stay!"

"MAMA!" Byeta screeched at such a pitch both Sergei and Vlad covered their ears. "MAMA!" She buried her face in the cushion and kicked her feet violently, but she did stay on the sofa.

Sasha reached for Sarah next, but he stopped. The anger plummeted with each passing second. He panted with the exertion of Byeta, but the sweat on his back now ran cold. Sarah locked her eyes on his.

"She broke my textreader," Sarah said softly, apologetically. "She threw it across the room."

Sasha's breathing worsened. After a terrible pause, the great arm thrust to the side, pointing. "GO!" he bellowed. "Or you'll be next!" Sarah ran.

He strode for the table inside the door. Sasha opened the drawer, grabbed the ignition tag for the flyer, seized his robe from its hook, and opened the door. "I'll be back."

Maryana flew after him. "Sash! Wait! Where are you going?" She followed him, shutting the door.

* * *

David stared at the door. "What the fuck? He didn't even crack her. What gives? He never pounds just one of us."

Sarah crept back to the living room.

"All clear," Sergei told her, but he peered out the window anyway.

Dmitri peeked over his shoulder. "What are they doing?"

"Don't know. They haven't left yet."

Sarah moved to join them when Byeta ran from the sofa and slapped her hard on the back.

Sarah froze. All color drained from her face. She was home, not at school, it was okay to yell, but it was hard to break her Navaran training. "Ow," slipped from her lips. "Ow. Ow. Ow. Ow."

She slid to her knees, then bent stiffly over onto all fours. "Ow. Ow. Don't cry. Don't cry. You can't cry. OW! OW!" Vlad ran to her side.

"Kill the little bitch!" David growled. He lunged for Byeta, but she shrieked and ran laughing to the dining room, safe behind the table.

"Can't touch me! I'll tell Papa. He'll hit you with his whip," she taunted. "You have to be nice to me, or I'll tell!"

"What's the screaming?" Viktor said from the hallway.

"She punched Sarah in the back, and I'm going to kill her!" David shouted. He tried to move around the table, but Byeta kept her distance, jeering.

Katya knelt next to Sarah. "Want me to rub it?"

"No! Don't touch it! Don't touch it!" Sarah pleaded. She held her breath against the pain.

287

"She bleeding?" Viktor said with concern.

Katya steeled herself for a glance under the shirt. "Not that I see. Vlad, run and get a cold pack."

"Here," Dmitri said. He held out a can of anesthetic spray from the bathroom cabinet. Sarah lay face down on the floor while Katya doused the tortured skin on her back. The whipmarks had healed without medical intervention but the scars were fearsome; wide, swollen, rippled, and weeks later still agonizing to the lightest touch. Byeta knew it. Katya lowered the shirt and lay the coldpack over it.

"Better?"

Sarah let her breath out with a shiver. "Yeah." Vlad and Sergei sat next to her, guards against further attack.

"Get over here," Viktor commanded Byeta. "You tell her you're sorry!"

Byeta shook her head until her braid slapped her cheek. "Nuh uh! She hit me first! Nobody spanked her yet. Not fair."

David advanced. "You haven't begun to get spanked. We're each taking a turn."

Byeta made a giggling dash around the table, dodging Viktor and slipping past Dmitri, but Sergei leaned and straightened out a leg. Byeta went sprawling. Her chin hit the stone floor, and a shrieking cry started up again.

"Sorry," Sergei said. "I was stretching."

Viktor stood her up, ignoring the cries. He turned her toward Sarah. "Now apologize!"

Byeta kicked Sarah in the leg. Vlad lunged over Sarah with a raised fist, but never connected.

Viktor shook her. "Knock it off!" He dared give her a light slap to her cheek.

Byeta spit at him and made a grab for his hair.

Viktor seized her fist and twisted. " 'Lexei!"

Alexei appeared on the third yell. "What makes you think I should come when you fucking call?"

"Your turn to watch one." He tried to hand Byeta over.

"That one's gonna cost you."

"Just put the fear of space into it."

Alexei shrugged. "Can do." He threw Byeta over his shoulder where her fists and feet did little damage, and returned to his room. A minute later, a scream of terror began.

Sarah sat up, coughing. "What's he doing?"

David snorted. "If it's anything like he does to me, he turned off the lights so it's pitch dark, spun her around til she doesn't know where she is, and he's poking her with needle grass. You okay?"

"Yeah. Can't he do better than that?"

Katya looked worriedly at the hall. "He's not going to hurt her, is he?"

David turned back to the holovision. "He's just warming up."

* * *

Maryana slid into the flyer before the great door shut, robe on her arm.

"What's wrong?" she asked.

The tense line of Sasha's jaw revealed his aggravation at the intrusion. He put the vehicle in park, but left it running for the enviro control. "Tash, go back inside. I'm going out. I'll be back later."

She kept her voice calm and soothing. "I know where you're going."

The anger bubbled over anyway. "What? I'm not allowed to socialize with friends without your permission? Don't I work hard enough? Do I not provide you with anything you want?"

Maryana ran a loving hand over his cheek. "I never said you couldn't go, my sweet. I only wanted to know why. What's spooked you? Tell me."

The anger withered under her caress, morphing into a miserable melancholic pinch across his face. Several moments passed before he could speak. His hand waved about, as if pleading for him.

"I can't do it."

"Do what?"

He glanced at the house. "Discipline her. Byeta's a brat, but Sarah's smart enough to know better than to hit a smaller child. She shouldn't get away free, but... I can't do it," he said with shame. "She looks at me and I can see it in her eyes. She knows. She knows I went too far."

"She's your daughter. She still loves you. Children have the ultimate gift for forgiveness."

Sasha shook his head tensely. "No. Look in her eyes, Tash. Look deep. I know that feeling. I've been there. I know exactly what she's thinking. She can't understand how I hurt her like that. I crossed the line. A child forgives a parent for spanking them. They know when they did something wrong; they expect to be punished. But... What I did..."

"Everyone loses their temper at some point, Sash, even me. I think we've done remarkably well, all things considered. This place has broken stronger people than us."

He shook his head again. "Not like that. Every time I look at her I see myself, and I hate her; and I hate my mother, and I hate me and everything I am, all over again. It all comes back, and all I can think of are the bad times. It's all I can do to look at her when I'm *not* pissed off. I almost killed her, Tash. How can I spank her after that? 'No, trust me, I'll do it right this time?' What do you say to a child you almost killed with your bare hands?"

Maryana eyed him with sympathy. "I think you're making it out to be more than it is. You mean well, you just forget your strength now and then. Sarah's fine now. She healed. Just don't use the whip. And you shouldn't need to spank her; she's the easiest to reason with. Byeta's the bigger problem. One more month, Sash. One month, and we'll be on Alhena for fourteen whole weeks. It will be the best vacation ever."

She knelt on the floor between the front seats and snuggled against him. "I'll tell you what. Why don't we both get out for a little while. We'll have a glass of wine – just one!, get a platter of fried mushrooms, relax a bit, talk like adults, and we'll come home better for it. They'll be fine until we get back."

The dark eyes glanced at the house once more before a hint of smile nudged his cheek. He raised the craft into hover mode and spun it slowly toward the city. "I can live with that."

Forty-one

Alhena III was a struggling planet. Six countries were considered first-world, one hundred thirty-nine major cities in the developing countries were considered modern, but the remainder of the planet was still desperately undeveloped, full of dire poverty and occasional unrest. The countryside was beautiful: rolling hills, lush flora, and fresh rainy days made Navara seem like a bad dream. Sasha's mood lifted immediately, his mind focused on his students and their project. The sodden nights dried up, replaced once again by the award-winning professor striving to share his passion. Twenty students were housed in an empty dormitory for the semester; Sasha and family were given the third floor, ten rooms all to themselves. Nikky, full of toddler energy, found delight in slamming doors and listening to the noise they created. The concept of outdoors and sun and play were foreign to him; Maryana spent every possible minute outside with him among the bright-leaved vegetation.

Leaving Navara, even briefly, disrupted the homeostasis of germs and allergies, and within two weeks the children came down with bland viruses, sneezing and coughing in an orchestrated medley. Maryana started Sarah on preventatives immediately, and her cold remained just a cold. Maryana was the last one to catch it, chilled to the bone by the extreme climate change, her head pounding as her immune system objected to the strange assault.

Sasha kissed her as she lay sipping tea while waiting for the anti-viral medications to kick in. "Stay in bed. Sleep. Katya can handle Byeta and Nikky. I'll take the rest out to the site for the day, show them why we're here. They can picnic in the grass. It's been a while since I could do that."

"Danks, Sach. I dove you."

He winked at her. "I 'dove' you, too."

In a four-month field class there were no days off, just half-days twice a week where students could catch up on readings, sneak a nap, or check out the local town. As much had to be learned in as short a time as could be done, not just the students, but the professor trying to stay one step ahead on questions, on planning, on what the dig was showing them, and where to proceed. It was not an in-depth long-term project, just an anomaly dug up in some farmer's field that the local board of antiquities was willing to have investigated by a team of students. There was some evidence of prior civilization, not a lot, but enough to make an excellent work-study for the students.

Sasha would have taken only four children, but Sarah craved every learning experience she could get, and if he didn't take Vladimir, Sarah would whine about it the entire time and Vlad would cry, upset his stomach, and not let Maryana rest for a second, so he piled the six of them into the open track-wagon for the twenty-minute drive out to the site. On a civilized world he would have been detained; the open vehicle had three bench seats, no safety restraints, and no sides at all, just a wide step over the track, caked with dirt. By the third bounce, the children screamed with laughter. Without Maryana to suggest otherwise, he made the vehicle rock, spun tight circles, looped around obstacles – including a large grazing animal, and climbed hills so as to throw up showers of dirt. There could not be a better day; just him, his children, pleasant skies, a pile of dirt to play in, and no university administrators.

He parked the track-wagon on top of a rise. The excavation started on a hillside and was slowly consuming the hill. A fifteen-meter swath of land had been shaved down, four meters deep at the inside edge. From here it was a short hike to the dig, down a little hill and over the next rise.

"Take a leak," he ordered Vlad.

"I don't have to."

David scowled at him. "You always have to. You're like a water bottle with a pinhole in it."

"I said go," Sasha repeated, so Vlad peed against the track of the vehicle. Once it was safe, Sasha swung him up onto his shoulders to ride the distance. Vlad grinned ear to ear.

He glanced down at Sarah. Six months ago Sasha would have held her hand to keep her from running ahead, but since… *the incident*, she'd been very reserved near him. It broke his heart each time, but he understood. From the depths of his memory, he understood completely. He held his hand out to her, just a little, and gave an encouraging nod. She gazed up at him with a face as devoid of emotion as any Navaran, and slid her hand into Viktor's.

His junior crew followed, around the cut and down the grassy hill toward the bottom. Sasha explained the lay of the land, pointed to the towns on the distant horizons, and the rise where the owner of the land lived. He gave them a history lesson on the area, quizzed them on what they knew about the development of cities.

"Are there any dead bodies?" David asked.

"Just yours, when we get done burying you," Dmitri said.

"Shithead! You first!" They each got off one punch before Viktor broke them up.

Sasha ignored the scuffle. Boys were boys. "Nothing yet. It doesn't appear to be a burial mound, more likely a horde stashed for later use, either for wealth or to conceal it from an enemy. Where on Earth do we see burial mounds?"

"The Americas," Viktor said.

"England?" Dmitri guessed.

"Norse countries," Sarah added.

Pride caused him to smile. "Correct, times three. And famous treasure hoards?"

"King Tut," Dmitri said.

"Ag Jin-jo on Porrima," Viktor said.

"Troy," Sergei said, and Sarah added, "In Greek it was called Illium, and there were nine layers."

"Greek has volcanoes," Vlad said from above.

"So does my ass," said David, and paused to blast a fart.

"How did I wind up with such smart children?" Sasha said with a smile. "You know more history than my academy students."

"Because that's all you teach us," Sarah replied without a trace of humor.

They crested the last rise to the excavation itself. "Stay away from the edge," Sasha warned. "With the rain yesterday, it's bound to be a soft edge. You'll collapse the rim and we'll have to clear it out all over again. See the markings?" He pointed below. "Everything is marked out in square meters, and if we have to, we'll divide those down further."

"Can we dig some, too?" Sergei asked.

"I'll bet I can find a corner for us to work on."

Sarah's thirst for knowledge overtook her distrust. "Can I tap stakes and mark lines? I know how to measure it out. I've seen the pictures from your big dig. Can I? Did you bring your toolbag? Is that a tool pod over there? Look! There's the sifters!" She slipped away from Viktor and began to run ahead, around the edge and down the path.

"There are some here," he assured them. "Everyone will have a turn."

"David!" Viktor shouted from the back of the group. "Father!" They all turned; Sarah stopped her sprint. David wasn't in sight.

Viktor dove for the edge of the dig, fell to his knees, and looked down.

Fear knifed through Sasha. He twisted out from under Vlad; Dmitri caught him almost in midair and put him on the ground. Sasha reached the spot in five running steps. A gap marked the edge of the cut, as if a monster had taken a bite out.

"Back up!" he barked at the crowd that formed around him. "Get away from the edge!" Viktor chased them back. Three or four meters down, David floundered amid a mound of collapsed dirt. Stakes and marking tape lay uprooted and trashed.

"Don't move!" Sasha glanced to the sides, but to run around would take too long. Without hesitating, he knelt, grabbed what edge he could, and launched himself down the nearly vertical side. He slid to a stop, filling his shoes with dirt.

"Are you all right? What about your head?"

"I think so." David stood up. He was scratched and dirty, but the soil had fallen in front of him, making a soft landing.

Sasha's temper flared. "Did I not tell you – Did I not just get through saying, stay away from the edge, it could collapse? You're damned lucky it wasn't any deeper! You could have been impaled on the markers! Get the fuck over there! Watch where the hell you step!" He slapped David several times as he headed away from the wall. "Come around," he barked to the faces peering down from above.

Sasha could not remember having such a pleasant afternoon with his children in ages, despite David's carelessness. Everyone marked, poked, sifted, and played with the scanners to his or her delight. Sasha walked about like a learned sage, asking questions, giving answers, imparting wisdom. Viktor found a coin in David's collapsed dirt, only fifty years old but still a find. Sergei found a small glass bottle with a rusty cap; a more modern manufacture but worthy of excitement.

Dmitri yelled when he found a button, but Sarah pointed out it had fallen off his own shirt.

Lunch was eaten sitting on the tracks of the wagon, another activity everyone was sure Maryana wouldn't approve of. Sasha worked his way through three bottles of *haam*, a weak local brew. After lunch he sat in the grass talking with Dmitri and Viktor, while Sarah and Vlad played tag with Sergei. David dug rocks out of the bank, tossed them in the air, and hit them with a marking stake. Soon it became sport, Sasha pitching the stones for the children to hit, until sizable rocks became scarce.

Vlad poked his fingers into the excavation wall, searching for potential stones. As dirt fell away, something underneath glimmered. "I found a shiny one."

Sarah frowned and tore at the dirt with both hands. "Father? Vladdy found something shiny. I can't get it out."

The crowd circled close. Sasha squatted down, expecting to find a piece of granite, maybe even a flat face of silicate, but a hard black material shown out of the dusty brown soil, a streak of shining silver running across it where the dirt had been scraped away. He squinted, ran his fingers over it, flicked off a bit of dust.

"I looks like hard ash. It could be part of an old fire, maybe an ash dump. Something's definitely hiding in it, though. Maybe the handle to a cooking pot, or a lost tool. Bring me a hammer and pick. Let's see what we can find."

The children carried the equipment and lunch boxes up to the third floor of the dorm, then disappeared into the rooms, quiet as mice. Maryana held Vlad on her hip, his snuffling face buried in her neck. Sarah hugged her other side. An immobilizing splint covered Vlad's hand and arm, half-way to his elbow. The bright green lattice brace looked sinister on such a skinny little limb.

Sasha felt smaller than Vlad, standing before her. His eyes wouldn't lift to meet hers. "Two bones. It's a clean break. The splint can come off next week."

She didn't say anything but crossed the hallway into their bedroom, clinging children and all. He followed. From a drawer she took a box of candy and handed it to Vlad. "You can share this with everyone. Sarah, make sure he counts it out right. Go." She put Vlad down and the two ran off, worries forgotten. Maryana shut the door.

Her face held a look of sadness, a disappointment that ate at him. He didn't need her disapproval to know he'd fucked up. He knew it the second it happened. Anger rose up, a petulant twist at his innards that made him want to escape, somewhere, anywhere, far away from where he was.

"Truth, Sash. What happened?"

"I told you the truth! You don't believe me?"

The pain on her face only increased his desire to run. Her voice never strayed from soft and calm, even if her words seemed brusque. "We both shade things for the children to ease their fears. I wanted to know if there was more to it than that. The eight-pack of *haam* is gone from the coldkeeper. I just want to know if that had something to do with it."

The anger won, but he kept it to a low growl. "You think I was drunk to my soles driving my children around in an open tracker? Go! Go right out to the lunch box in the kitchen! There are still three in there. Five in six hours! At my size, three of them at once wouldn't put me over the legal limit for intoxication! It was a fucking accident, Tash! Ask any of them! Ask all of them!"

"My heart believes you, Sash, but after this spring, my head needs to be sure, so I know what to expect from outside sources. What did the clinic say?"

It took a moment before he mustered the courage to answer. The words didn't want to break air. "I told them I knocked a rock loose and it fell and hit his hand. They asked him, but he all he did was cry. Sar'ina's the one who agreed, went into a long speech about the type of soil and the kind of rock until they told her to shut up. Of all the ones to defend me... I thought she was going to tear my eyes out with the hammer when it happened – Viktor had to hold her back – and she defended me when it mattered. All she had to do was show them her back and we wouldn't be here right now."

His jaw clenched, his lip trembled, and his control evaporated. He pushed his hands over his face as if he could wipe the day from it. "Fuck, Tash! What the hell difference does it make? Drunk, sober – I hurt them just the same! It was such a nice day! We were having such a *nice day*. He was so excited to find something important. A broken knife handle, I don't know how old, but it's still treasure to them. He went to grab and all I meant to do was slap his hand away. I swear to you! I forgot the hammer was still in my hand. I never, ever meant to hurt him! A fucking waste. I can't do anything right. How the hell did

I get this far? All that work and education … and I still can't remember not to break a child. How the hell can I be a professor when I don't deserve respect? Maybe it's time to throw it all in and go back home." He sat on the side of the bed and let grief swallow him.

She petted the sides of his beard. "Stop, Sash. You're just upset. Accidents happen. I'm not mad at you. I just wanted to know what happened. You're here because you are a galactically-reknowned educator. Your students are thrilled to have you as their teacher and they appreciate your efforts. And you will go back there tomorrow and you will dazzle them, because you are dazzling at what you do. You want to hide in here and nurse your regret for the evening, that's fine, but it would be better for everyone if you didn't. Everyone makes mistakes, and you can set the example by owning up to it and moving on. Your choice." She kissed his forehead and left him to stew.

* * *

Maryana did ask the children, privately. It was hard to get Vlad alone, and she was unable to pry a single word from him that didn't sound like a rehearsed script. Sergei was usually reliable, and sided with his father. Dmitri wasn't sure, but thought it unintentional. David always spoke the first thought that came to his head and was often at odds with his father, but when pressed, he didn't think Sasha meant harm.

"Viktor, I depend on you too much, I know, but I want the truth," she said when she cornered him. "What happened out there? How much of an accident was it?"

"We were all standing right there," he insisted. "He was picking away, trying to get the thing clear, and Vlad was just really eager, sticking his hands in there trying to help. I know what you're worried about, but I swear, this time it was an honest accident."

Her heart relaxed, but her head wouldn't let it rest. One opinion remained before she would trust herself, and she'd saved it for last. "Sarah, when we're on Navara you go to school with Navarans. What do they say about lying?"

"It is forbidden under all circumstances," Sarah said gravely. "It is one of the unforgivable disgraces."

"Yes, it is. I will ask you a question, and I want the dead truth, down to the very last molecule of Navaran sensibility. Do you understand? If you can't, then I don't see the point of sending you to a

Navaran school, and when we return you can go back to the Ku'umi school."

Sarah bristled as expected. "I'm not a baby. I know what truth is."

"Then tell me what happened yesterday out at the site, every minute, from the start."

Viktor would lie to keep the peace; David would lie just to get even. Sarah, who had every reason in the world to see her father burn, who would give – and nearly had – her life for Vlad, supported her father. The press of her lip was the giveaway, torn between her promise to tell the truth and the knowledge that the truth would set him free. Maryana's heart soared, and that night she made sure he fell asleep with a smile on his face.

Forty-two

Maryana waited until everyone else left for the day. She locked Nikky in her bedroom with a few toys, put a preschool program with lots of songs on the wallscreen for him to watch, left the connecting bathroom door open just in case, stood in the vapor shower, and cried. Never had she so wanted to flee a place with every ounce of her being. If adjusting to Navara was difficult the first time, leaving and returning was far worse. The relentless heat, the suffocating air, the pervasive fine grit that invaded every crevice of furniture, floor, and body. The sunburns, the heat rashes, the nosebleeds, the lack of space and privacy and the boring repetition of computer-processed protein chains. And the dire condition of their finances.

And Sasha.

Accident aside, he'd been so good for four months. Happy, outgoing, clear-headed, not once did she smell alcohol on him or see him the least bit pickled. She'd spent four months on Alhena with the professor she'd helped make, the passionate educator who could quote textbooks, give an hour's lecture off the top of his head, felt history – the flow of time throughout the galaxy – pulling at his heart, and was only too glad to share that feeling with anyone willing to listen. On Alhena he was her Zeus, the mighty giant standing on a hillside, pointing a finger and ordering mortals to do his bidding, his muse whispering intuition from his shoulder. Twenty-two years, and her heart still skipped beats to see him like that. Everything he did in the field was like a gold star on his checklist, and he smiled at everyone.

Now, just three months after returning, his jaw was clenched, face sullen, mood volatile, withdrawn tight inside himself. Within a month the happy hours began creeping back, and his weight to creep again with it. He'd weighed an underfed 81 kilos when they married; he now tipped the scales at a hundred kilos more. Between the thin air and the added weight, he couldn't manage the stairs to his second-floor office, and always used the lift. He almost never stopped sweating.

299

There was no Russian Orthodox church in Kar Ku'umi; the closest Maryana could come was a Chinese New Reformed Catholic service. She'd tried it early on, but the music and liturgy were too strange for comfort. She ended up lighting candles and praying for strength at Galactic Reach Episcopal. God would understand.

He lay on the bed, watching an Altairan wrestling competition on the wallscreen, finishing off a liter of artificial frozen yogurt with fresh yellow Navaran *jin-sa* berries. A refrigerated Koolmate cloth sat between his neck and the pillow, keeping him comfortable. His eyes never left the screen when she entered the room.

Maryana lay next to him and rested her head against his arm. "Sash? We need to talk. Seriously. I know how you don't want to break the contract, but I think it's time we did. I don't care anymore. We need to go home. This much stress isn't good for you. It's not good for me, it's not good for the children. It's time to admit to ourselves that it's ruining us financially, the schools are awful, and we've lost almost everything we gained in Kiev. We have few friends, the children have lost their arts and sports and spiritual outlets, and we're falling apart. The hardest part of running a company is admitting it's not going to be a success, getting out while you can, and starting up somewhere else. As your financial advisor, I'm telling you we've reached that point. Please, Sash? Please, say we can leave at the end of the semester?"

The big head turned toward her, and there was no anger in the face. If anything, there was a glimmer of hope. "You think so?"

"I really do."

His arm encircled her, holding her to his side. "Tomorrow I will see about transferring."

* * *

In the second semester, Sasha taught three classes plus a hands-on laboratory class. At least one class a semester was in the evening; last year there were two. This semester it was Archaeology and Mythology, so it was not unusual for him to come home late. Half the children were asleep when the commlink chirped.

Maryana slid the privacy button into her ear. "Yes? This is his wife. Yes. Where is this? Yes, I see. No, there's no need. I'll send someone out to get him right away, should be about fifteen minutes. Yes. Thank you."

She put the receiver down. She was too small to be of help, and there was the social aspect. Sasha worked in the city; he could not lose face by needing his wife to rescue him. This was a man's territory.

She turned to the older boys sitting before the holovision. "Viktor, you're father's in the city and doesn't feel well. Please take the flyer and retrieve him for me."

Eighteen-year old Viktor was brawny like his father, but only average for height. "Can't he take the taxi?"

"No. He's not fit."

"I can't fly that thing – I don't have a permit. Can't Alexei?"

"His class doesn't end for another half-hour. Your father needs you now." She tossed him the starter tag. "Take Dmitri with you to help."

The boys glanced at each other in wonderment. Dmitri was small, freshly fifteen and hardly taller than his mother.

"Now! Here's the address. Program it into the nav unit and it will guide you. Keep everything on automatic, just watch your pitch going over any dunes. Hurry." She hustled them out the door.

The boys stared at the flyer, ghostly bright against the dark night. It swelled before them until it seemed the size of a starship. Viktor pressed the switch; the interior lights popped on and the gull-wing door opened with a sand-crunching groan.

"What are we doing, again?" Dmitri asked as he climbed into the passenger seat. "Is this a trap? Are we gonna get the shit beat out of us when we get there for taking the flyer?"

Viktor lowered the door. He set the tag in its slot. The control panels across the front lit up in a colorful array of soft lights. He studied the displays, found the nav guide, and programmed the destination. "*Mat* wouldn't do that. I'm not worried about Father. It's city security. I've never flown anything before. I know it in theory, but I've barely ever rode shotgun. I don't want to get nabbed or I'll never get a legal permit. You gotta watch the controls for me."

"Watch what?!"

"I don't know! Watch the periphery scanner, make sure nothing's coming at us."

The craft lifted fifty centimeters above the sand and paused for the parking gear to retract. The autonav spun it slowly in the right direction. Viktor eased it forward then backed off fast, jerking the craft. Little by little he trusted the speed, smoothing the ride until the sand dropped unexpectedly into the hidden trough of a dune. Following the surface, the craft pitched forward violently, a warning buzzer screeched, and the momentary lapse of gravity sent their stomachs careening upwards. Viktor yanked the control bar, lifting the nose just before it hit sand.

Dmitri let go of the seat. "If I'd known that was coming, it might have been fun."

"Yeah. I guess that's what she meant by watch the pitch."

They caught two smaller drops before coming to the gate in the dune wall. Here in the city, flying was easier. The vehicle wasn't actually a flyer, it was a hover-craft, maintaining a set cushion of air above a surface but incapable of true flying. In the city, the coordination of automated road signals, enforced speed limits and navcom units made the vehicle nearly independent, and they settled it outside the building.

The doorman stopped them. "Where do you think you're going? There's no kids allowed in here."

"We're supposed to pick up our father," Viktor explained. "They said he was sick."

The doorman accompanied them inside. The room looked like a nice restaurant, save a huge man sprawled with his head on a table. The manager came over.

"Came in with a couple of other fellows, but they ditched him after he passed out." He handed over Sasha's ID case.

Viktor accepted it. "He works really hard. He gets very tired. He can't get used to the heat."

The manager gave him a funny look. "Yeah. Well, maybe he should see a doctor to find out what makes him so tired. Maybe he won't fall asleep in public. Grace of the Sun, he's heavy!"

The manager and doorman, along with two waiters and the boys, managed to drag Sasha out the back door, pulling and pushing until he lay on the first row of seats in the vehicle.

The manager paused. "You boys all right flying this thing? You need help getting him out?"

"No, sir," Viktor insisted. "We'll be fine once we get him home. Thank you, sir."

The ride back was easier. Viktor let the throttle out a little more, but didn't yet have the coordination to manage the manual pitch control. Small waves of sand that would have been merely annoying on foot created a bobbing wallow in the craft. Viktor fought to keep it level.

Halfway home, a choking noise made them turn around. "He all right?" Viktor said.

Dmitri turned on a panel light. "He's – Fuck sand! He's puking!" He pulled the front of his shirt over his nose as the smell hit.

Viktor stopped the craft and they staggered in the open air, gagging. "Shit! What the hell did he eat?"

Dmitri didn't answer until he finished vomiting himself. "Christ on the Moon! How can he puke in his sleep? That's disgusting!"

Vik snorted. "You want disgusting? We gotta finish getting home."

Dmitri eyed the vehicle. The dim interior lights only seemed to make the darkness of the empty landscape even more impenetrable. "Can't we leave him here and walk back? Maybe he'll think it happened when he was flying."

"In the open desert? When did you grow a homing beacon?"

"Can we leave the door open?"

Vik shook his head. "Thrusters won't engage unless the door's shut. I'll max the air intake. See if there's anything in the back we can use to get rid of some of it."

A search of the vehicle turned up little of use, and Viktor used the cuff of his father's robe to wipe the worst from the beard and face. Dmitri tossed sand onto the floor to bury the rest, but, combined with Vik's seasick piloting, they had to stop once more on the short ride to walk around in fresh air.

Maryana waited on the front step. "What took so long?"

"He got sick and we had to stop," Vik said.

She surveyed the situation without comment. "Dmitri, go get Alexei." She brushed the sweaty hair from her husband's forehead. "Sash? Come on, Sash, wake up. Get yourself to bed."

Dmitri returned with Alexei.

"Alexei, help get your father in the house," Maryana ordered.

Alexei caught a whiff. "Fuck no! He's covered in puke! They can smell that in the fucking city."

Maryana took a deep breath. She didn't like anger; it served no useful purpose and ate at one's self-confidence, but her patience had evaporated. She summoned the most intimidating look she could imagine, trying to threaten someone more than thirty centimeters taller than herself. "Alexei, you may be my child, but you are as useful as buttons to a caterpillar. Your father is sick and needs our help. Now help get him to his room or I will get your father's whip."

Viktor and Dmitri stared once more in disbelief. Maryana had never so much as slapped one of them, let alone swung a whip.

With her prodding, Sasha roused enough to shuffle his feet with the four of them holding him up. They dropped him onto his bed.

"Thank you, boys. I will clean your father; please go clean the flyer." She shut the bedroom door.

"Have fun, suckers," Alexei said as he flipped them a *fig* and walked away.

Dmitri's hands thumped onto his hips. "What the hell! It'll take all night! Should we get David to help?"

"What, and have him flick chunks at us?" Viktor said glumly. "Would you rather do the sponge bath?"

Dmitri gagged. "Meet you out front."

* * *

"Professor Kirushenko?"

Sasha looked up from his notes. A student stood in the doorway, holding a notepad and several text folders. He hated this hour; an entire hour wasted by policy, forced to remain in his office in the event a student had questions about a class. Outside of the occasional serious archaeology student looking more for romanticized stories of the glory of archaeology than meaningful questions, or the hapless student he'd been assigned to as an academic advisor, no one ever showed up. First and second year students were too afraid of him, of his height, of his size, of the gruffness of his manner. He took a sinister form of pleasure out of it, laughing inwardly at the two or three students in the back row who would jump awake when he'd shout out an important concept and disturb their slumber. At the same time, he loved this hour, because he could hide in his office and read up on studies undisturbed. Except for the rare interruptions.

"Yes?"

304

"I'm in your Intro class. I was wondering if I could talk to you about upcoming grades." She was slender and shapely, brown tresses held off her neck by filigreed gold clips. She wore a gauzy blue cloak against the desert sun.

Sasha put his text reader aside and pointed to the chair before his desk. The girl closed the door behind her. She smoothed her hair and shrugged off the blue cloak. Beneath it she wore a thin dress, as red as the Navaran sky above. The wide neckline revealed sleek shoulders, and dropped in loose folds so low that if she had reason to jump up, she ran a high risk of having her breasts fly out of it altogether. The length was far too short, the mere ten centimeters of skirt hardly enough to cover her bottom as she sat.

Sasha looked her over. "Intro class? Last row, fifth seat in. You spend most of your time talking with the girl on your right. Stillson?"

The girl looked a bit astonished. "Yes, sir. Erénika Stillson."

He thumbed a switch on the desk near his computer screen. Three more taps on the pad and his grade records appeared. The girl had third-year standing, but a mediocre grade for his class. "What can I help you with, Miss Stillson?" he asked in his 'professional' voice.

"I was a bit concerned about my grade for your class. You didn't grade my study presentation very well, and I only got a 79 on the last exam. I was wondering if there was something I could do to raise my grade before final marks."

"Your project was on volcanoes, wasn't it?"

"Yes, sir." She smiled, blinking her brown eyes at him. "The Ruins of Morpheus Hale on Boötes IV."

The professor nodded, remembering. He never forgot a topic. "Your paper was two pages short, and you had only four references listed in your bibliography. As I said in my comments, you should have drawn comparisons with at least two, preferably three other similar sites. Pompeii on Earth and Trabulim on Centauri were covered not only in your text, but I mentioned them somewhat extensively in class as well. You failed to answer two of the six parts of the essay on your exam, and confused your terms in another part. I had no choice but to mark it down. I take it archaeology is not your chosen field."

"No, sir." She lifted a knee and crossed it over her other leg. The dress slid back to reveal a beautifully bare hip. "I'm a galactic governments major. I hadn't fulfilled my history requirement yet, and this seemed like the easiest class to take. I really have no use for all that ancient stuff."

"A basic exposure to history can open your eyes to many things, but not all career choices depend on the social sciences," he acknowledged. "I'm not in the habit of giving extra assignments, but perhaps if you rewrote your presentation, corrected your errors, and expanded on the ideas you only touched on, I might be able to replace your old grade with the new one."

The girl wrinkled her nose. "That would involve more research. I have a very busy schedule. I was looking for a somewhat *shorter* assignment." She uncrossed her legs and leaned forward to fold her arms on the edge of his desk. The loose neckline of the dress dropped forward to frame two firm young breasts pointing freely toward the floor. "A one-time thing, perhaps. Something that could be accomplished, perhaps, after dinner?"

Sasha gave a brief glance at the flesh almost lying on his desk, and made his eyes rest on his text reader. The girl's nipples were large and dark brown, not the blushing rose-pink of his fair Tash. The girl didn't seem to mind that she was barely covered, but it made him uncomfortable.

"You see," the girl continued in a softer voice, "I've never received a grade lower than 90 in any class I've ever taken. Even if I get a perfect score on the final exam, I can't break higher than 88 for this class. I can't get less than a 90 for a final grade or it will ruin my cumulative, and my chances of perfection on the final are pretty close to zero. I can't allow that to happen. I want you to know I'm willing to do anything." She caught his eye. "*An-y-thing*, to bring that grade… *up*?"

She lay herself over the desk to trace a finger around the neckline of his shirt, the dark tips of her breasts just shy of being officially out in the open. "Absolutely – *anything*. I'm free for private tutorial any night but Wednesdays, but, if necessary, I'm willing to skip that class."

Sasha held his breath, both flattered and disgusted. He was no longer a young man, and he'd never been considered good-looking to start with. He had children older than this girl! Such behavior was bad enough in an experienced woman, let alone someone so young. If she was his daughter, he'd… It didn't matter. Two of his beautiful daughters were lightyears away at universities themselves; he trusted they would never stoop this low over a mark on a grade sheet. His daughters had been raised as ladies, not whores.

He pushed his chair back. For her to touch him now, she'd have to crawl across the desk. He took a deep breath to steady himself. For once he was thankful that he was a naturally sweaty person, for it hid just how nervous he was. "I'm glad to hear that. With all those free evenings, you should have no trouble finding time for your research. I look forward to reading your edited paper. Good day, Miss Stillson."

She lifted a hip and parked it on the edge of his desk. "Perhaps I didn't make myself clear. I was looking for a *one-time* project that would make up any discrepancy in my grade average. Something so simple, I could complete it *from my bed*?"

Kirushenko raised a thick eyebrow, but his face stayed as emotionless as granite. "I suppose you might be able to complete it in one day, but it's very difficult to write a paper in your sleep. If you want the grade changed, I'll need that paper the day before finals." He thumbed a page on his textreader. "I will see you in class, Miss Stillson."

The girl's slimy charm slid into a scowl. She turned around and bent low over the chair. Leaning a hand on the seat, she took off one shoe, tapped the sand from it slowly and replaced it, wiggling for several seconds to get her heel in. She shifted from one foot to the other, and repeated the actions with her other shoe.

She is younger than your daughters, Sasha reminded himself. He flicked his eyes upward for only a second. As he'd guessed, the dress had bent with her, and he had an unobstructed view of a sculpted pair of naked buttocks and a well-tended dark streak arching at him, a backside worthy of an ancient statue. It had been a long, long time since he'd had anything but blonde. The eyes dared upwards again, peering out from under his hair, taking a longer look. *Displays were meant to be looked at.* He could feel his breath quicken, and he swore he could detect her scent across the mere meter that separated them across the desk.

Young and willing and experienced and motivated, wondering if the giant build extended to parts unseen... The thrill of dipping into something different and unfamiliar for a change... To be young and free and irresponsible again, involved in a mere business deal of frivolous fornication for ten lousy points on a grade sheet...

She picked up her things and turned around, checking; he made damned sure his eyes were glued to the reader, even if he couldn't focus on the words.

She spoke, spiteful and angry. "You know, all I have to do is scream and you'll be out on your big ass before you even know you've hit sand. They'll never believe your innocence over mine. I know some people pretty high up in administration."

In his gut, Sasha knew she was right. Fear replaced testosterone, and he raised a face so devoid of emotion the oppressive warmth of the room seemed to chill. "On the contrary, Miss Stillson. I believe they will, when they hear the audio recording of our conversation." He watched her expression change from triumphant to stunned. "I always record my help sessions, so I know where students are experiencing difficulty and can adjust my lectures accordingly." It was a lie, but it was fast and it was good. Seething with hatred, she flung her cloak over a shoulder and headed for the door.

"Ugly Russian bastard!" she spat as she slammed the it behind her.

His big head fell into his trembling palms. He lifted it to rest his chin on his knuckles, and caught sight of the picture of Tash he kept in the office. Heavens help him, she was a beautiful woman! Her hair swirled about her shoulders in a golden cloud, and she smiled. The ocean-blue eyes looked out at him proud, trustful, adoring. If he concentrated, he could smell her distinctive sweet perfume, the same one she'd worn every day for over twenty years, even in childbirth.

Whatever possessed me even to consider cheating on a woman like that? A crushing wave of guilt seized him, and he broke his gaze from the picture. *It was dangled in front of me, mine for the taking. I could have reached out and touched it without leaving my seat, and I turned away.* There was nothing to be guilty of! He'd done *more* than the right thing! This was foolish. *He* was foolish! The galaxy's most beautiful woman already lay waiting for him in his own bed, and he had twelve beautiful children to prove it.

The dread wouldn't ease. He was terrible at hiding things from her. She would know. She always knew when something upset him. How could he tell her? Sasha stepped over to the refrigeration box and opened it. As in every other office in the building, his held ice-cold drinking water. He reached into the back and withdrew a bottle missing its orange label. He removed the cap and took several long swallows before glancing repentantly at the photo. It was cold water. A quarter of it, perhaps.

The rest was vodka.

Forty-three

He'd left work at eight, that much she knew, but every page on his handicom had gone unanswered. Maryana heard the door, ten minutes after she finally went to bed at one. He'd never been this late before. He stomped into the bedroom, piss-eyed drunk.

The blood-red eyes glared at her. "What? You don't wait up for me anymore?"

"It's late." She sat up. Something must have happened. He was never this nasty. Not to her, at least. "I didn't know when you'd be back."

"Well, I'm back now." He stripped off his shirt and threw himself on the bed next to her. "Stay up with me."

"Only if you wash first, Sash. You've been out in the heat all day. You're a bit fragrant. Come, I'll wash you up," she suggested. He'd have settled down by the time she was through. The cool water would relax him, make him sleepy. "Lower your voice, before you wake everybody."

"Why! Why shouldn't they know I love my wife!"

"You're drunk, Sash." She wouldn't hold it against him. He'd had three transfers rejected in the last two weeks. His misery tore at her heart. "You need to sleep some of it off."

"It's not unconsciousness I want." His voice dropped a dangerous octave. He seized her and brought his mouth down forcefully on hers.

"Stop, Sash," she said when he let her up. "You're drunk, and you're hurting me." She coughed at the pungency of his sweat.

"Then don't fight me." He lifted her in his huge hands and kissed her, nipping her on the neck, on the shoulder, on the ear, running his brutal hands over her body, yanking at her dainty nightwear.

Maryana pushed against him. He hadn't been frisky since Alhena. "I'm not fighting you. You're hurting me! *Ow*! Either go easy or stop it!" It was hopeless to fight him – he outweighed her four times over, he was drunk to his feet, and he was far too strong. He'd never been violent to her before; she didn't know whether to be angry or frightened.

"Ouch! *Sasha!*" she cried, trapped in his arms as he nipped her again.

"Oh, for goodness' sake! If it will make you happy and get you to sleep!" Maryana fell back on the bed.

* * *

Twelve-year-old David stirred and turned over in bed. He opened his eyes long enough to find his pillow. In the dim light from the crack under the door, he could make out Dmitri up on his elbows, listening over the faint rush of the enviro fans. David lifted his own head, immediately alert. The other boys breathed softly, deeply in their sleep. Now and then he could hear muffled noises in the room next to theirs.

"Who is it?" he whispered.

"I think it's *Mother*!" Dmitri whispered back. He watched the door, waiting.

"He never touches her! Should we go see? Should we wake Vik?" David would never dream of investigating alone. If there was trouble, Viktor would know what to do. If nothing else, there was safety in numbers. Father couldn't chase three at once.

"No," Dimi said at last, wishing the older, wiser Viktor – now sharing Alexei's room to make space for Nikolai – still shared their bedroom so he could make the decision. "If she needed help, she'd call. We might make things worse. Go back to sleep. No sense in both of us being awake."

David lay down, but he could still hear the low rumbling noises of Father's voice, mixed with the higher-pitched cries of his mother.

* * *

Maryana was dressing when he awoke. He sat on the edge of the bed, holding his head. "What time is it?" he mumbled.

"Ask the clock, not me," she said coldly.

Sasha rubbed his eyes, trying to focus them. "What's with you?"

Maryana took a dress from the closet. "You don't know, do you?" she realized. Not even the Navaran heat thawed her icy stare. She swore for the first time in her marriage. "God damn you. You really don't remember."

"Remember what? Fucking mother, my head hurts."

He reached out a hand. "Sit with me. What am I supposed to remember? Your birthday was last week, wasn't it? Yes it was. We went to dinner. I know it. What the Hell is this?" He pulled her over despite her resistance and brushed his fingers over several fresh bruises on her back and arms. There were more on the sides of her neck, some large ones on her breasts. Some looked like groups of fingerprints. Some looked like teeth marks. "What the Hell happened to you? One of the kids do that? Byeta, that little witch?"

Maryana's eyes filled with tears of anger. She had never been a violent person, but now she almost understood the drive for violence. It boiled up unexpectedly inside her, choking off her words, trampling her elite etiquette into the dust. Her hand raised before she realized it, and she slapped his face as hard as she could, her husband of twenty-two years.

His hand covered the sting. "Tash...!"

"Don't you 'Tash' me, Alexander Kirushenko!" she said, rubbing her throbbing hand. She pulled a loose dress over her head and tied a scarf over the marks on her neck.

Maryana wiped her eyes with trembling fingers, but it didn't help the deluge. "I'm sorry, Sash. I swear to you, if you are ever that rough with me again, I'll... I'll... I don't know what I'll do, but I guarantee you won't like it!"

His eyes widened as he absorbed her words. "*I* did that? Imposs... There's no way... *I* did that to *you*? I would never! Tash! When did I do that? I swear! How would I not remember..." He realized the truth with horror. "I must have been out of my mind!"

"I have no doubt of that."

Sasha threw himself to his knees on the floor before her, one hundred ninety kilos of bloated naked flesh. "By the glory of the universe, Tash! I love you! I would never hurt you! You know that...!"

"I *used* to know that." She wiped her eyes once more, wanting to believe him with her whole heart.

"Never! Never again! I *swear* to you!" Sasha promised. "I had *no idea...* "

* * *

Not a word passed between them at breakfast. Sasha's hair was combed extra-carefully, his clothes unusually neat, as if this were an important day. His eyes never left the floor. Outside of Nikky and Elizabyeta, no one made a sound. The children sensed the tension, disappearing mysteriously to their rooms, readying each other for school without being told, and slipping onto their transports as if invisible. Sasha went to work only an hour late, as meek and jumpy as Vladimir on a bad day.

He arrived home from work exactly fifteen minutes after his class ended, cold sober. His hands shook as he placed his compad bag on the table by the door.

He nodded to Katya, reading with Byeta and Nikky. "Good afternoon, Katerina," he said humbly.

She looked up with a puzzled expression. "Good afternoon, Father."

"David?"

The boy at the commlink ducked, an arm jerking up as if to protect his head. "Yes, sir!"

"How was school?"

The arm came down in confusion. "Okay, I guess."

"No fights today?"

"No, sir."

Sasha nodded. "Good man. Where is your mother?"

"In the kitchen, I think," Katya answered.

He slunk down the hall to the bedroom.

Maryana maintained her silence at dinner. She wasn't rude, she wasn't brooding, just silent. He pretended nothing was wrong, conversing with the children, but he could sense their fear. He knew that look of mistrust. It was a long, long time ago, but the memories were etched too deeply. His food didn't want to go down his throat, and came back to haunt him not long after.

After the majority were in bed, he met her in the hall, holding a shipping box. He said nothing, but handed it to her. Maryana accepted it just as silently. He returned to the bedroom.

In the box were eight bottles of hard liquor, almost a thousand credits' worth, all of them missing quantities. She lugged it outside in the dark, around behind the kitchen where there were no windows, and threw them one by one against the stone ridge, screaming through her tears as they shattered.

It was late when Maryana came in. Her eyes were red, her whole face puffy. She shut down the house and entered the bedroom.

Sasha sat on the side of the bed, fully dressed, hands between his knees. He sat without moving, tears rolling down to disappear in the thick beard.

"I forgive you."

The sound of her voice made his sobbing worse. "I don't deserve it. I'm so sorry, Tash. I tried. I tried so hard. I was born to scum, I thought I could rise above it, but in the end I am still scum."

She sighed with resignation. "Do you really think I would have married scum? Come here." She sat and pulled his teary head onto her shoulder. It didn't take long for her own tears to resurface.

She kissed his hair. "It's this awful planet. It makes people crazy. Humans aren't meant to live like this. Three months, Sash. Just three more, and we're free."

The peace lasted all of a month before Maryana grew irritable. Eight weeks until they'd hoped to leave, and still no transfer had been approved. They'd be stuck for the final eleven months.

"It's only beer, Tash. Exactly one per day, no more," he swore. "You can check my blood. I'm not drinking at work. I went to two support meetings this week. I can make it."

"You're doing well, Sash," she insisted. "I'm not mad about the beer." But she wouldn't say more.

At last Sasha called her on it.

"Five credits cash to the person who can tell me why your mother is mad at me this time," he announced at dinner.

Ten pairs of eyes stared around the table. Father never threw that much money around for fun.

"I'm not mad, Sasha," Maryana said quietly.

"You've been a sour fish for two weeks. Something is wrong."

"Sasha, this is not the time or the place."

"I want to know!"

Maryana wiped her mouth with her napkin and placed it next to her plate. "Very well, then. It will be obvious soon enough. That night you couldn't seem to remember? You'd better try a little harder, because I'm about to remind you of it every day for the next eight months." She rose and brought her half-eaten plate to the kitchen.

Sasha sat while the words sank in. He followed her as a wave of whispers broke out at the table.

Maryana stood near the food recycler, her back to him.

"For real?" he asked, subdued and not a little embarrassed.

She nodded without turning, arms crossed in front of her while she could still do it. "Beginning of March."

"At worst, we'll be out of here in June. Good timing for moving back." He put his hands – very cautiously – on her shoulders and kissed the top of her head.

Maryana shook beneath his hands. "I'm not happy, Sash. I don't want it! Viktor just *graduated*. That gives us *four* in universities! I'm forty years old! Some women my age are *grandmothers*! I've still got a two-year old! I know, I should have put a permanent stop to this when they first advised me. Something always managed to interfere. Now it's too late again. This time I'm not leaving that hospital until there's a complete hysterectomy."

"Then we won't do it. I'll go with you this week and we'll stop it. It's not the best time to be bringing another baby into the house."

Maryana shrugged as he rubbed her shoulders. "When was it ever a good time? When I was eighteen and married one year to the day? When Katya was eleven months? When Vladya was so sick? Hold Nikky and look him in the eye and tell your son he should have been an abortion. I'd have to go off-planet; it's strictly forbidden here. Could you handle them for a week while I'm gone?"

Sasha turned her around to face him. "I'm *sorry*," he said with sincerity. "I'm sorry for bringing you to this awful planet, I'm sorry for hurting you, I'm sorry for that goddamned night, I'm sorry for this baby. These last years have been a... a *nightmare*, and I'm sorry about all of it. I wish we'd never come here. I should have changed my mind those first few days and pulled out of the contract. I probably could still have gone back to Kiev. Probably with a pay cut, but I would have had a job. I'm counting the days until we can leave. *I love you*, Tash! I don't want you to leave me." Any other woman would have, long before now.

Maryana leaned on the broad chest. "Shhh. You know I'll never leave you. What are we going to do, Sash?"

Sasha cuddled her close, kissing the top of her blonde head. "Like you say. We'll take it one day at a time."

Forty-four

Maryana and Sasha always thought the months following their fallout to be the strongest of their marriage. Whatever had divided them before had been replaced by a new maturity. They had one goal together and one goal only: getting the hell off the planet. Maryana walked around with a new sense of calm, organizing and eliminating every unnecessary item with the objective of having less to move. She liquidated the last of her stocks and placed the credits into secured savings accounts, ready to purchase their tickets out at a moment's notice. She chose several of her less-worn top-label outfits and sold them.

Sasha sent out at least two inquiries a week. He jumped down Anseña's throat the first time he got snide, roaring in his face to act like a professional. To his great surprise, two colleagues present backed him up. Sasha found himself dragged before the director of personnel, but threatened to file charges if the harassment didn't stop. Anseña didn't speak to him at all for a week, and then only when unavoidable and began with an apology. Sasha spent his evenings on the sofa before the holovision, Tash curled against his side, the glass beside him containing only a carbonated citrus drink. The children sensed something different, and the level of conflict dropped for a few weeks.

Maryana took no chances. The doctor agreed; the last one would be born by cesarian, and she would be sterilized then and there. No forgetting. No crisis taking precedence. Done, over. No more. Sasha surprised her, making his own appointment and having himself sterilized as well. He wasn't taking chances again, either.

Maryana had been pregnant in every season of the year. She'd been pregnant in Russia, in Israel, in Greece, in a dozen places they'd traveled to briefly. But she'd never been pregnant on Navara. For the first time, she broke out in rashes, sweaty, hot, and miserable. The horrid thin air left her breathless with minor exertions. Her legs swelled.

"Stay off your feet as much as possible," the doctor advised her. "Keep them up. It will help the swelling."

Maryana stared at him with a sense of incredulity. "Did you even look at my chart? I have *twelve children*, including a two-year old. How do you expect me to stay off my feet?" She did a minimum of household tasks, delegating the rest to various children. Her days were spent lying on the sofa, watching Nikky play or readying him for preschool. He would be three when the baby arrived, a perfect age to start him. Nikky had an excess of energy and a fearless, outgoing personality. He would thrive in preschool.

She was proud of Sash, rising to the challenge without his usual crutch. Beer crept back into his routine, but not the happy hours, and not the heavy drinking. Even when a transfer failed to materialize by their early-leave date, he held himself up. Each night they would cross off another day, one more day closer to their goal.

"We're going to make it, Sash," she promised him. "You and me. We always have, and we always will."

"We will make it, if I have to build a ship myself to get us there," he swore.

August began the new semester. Alexei continued his studies in chemistry; Viktor began classes at the Space Academy as well, Dmitri moved up to the high school, and Byeta became the fourth Kirushenko in attendance at Public School Number 4. In October Sarah turned eight, received her blue belt in karate, and she and Vlad persisted in telling strangers they were twins for the ten weeks before he would turn nine. October was also the first time Vlad went an entire month without wetting his bed once. Maryana's optimism bloomed once more as good days won out over bad ones.

Until the end of November.

On her baby check, the doctor took a long time with the scanner. "Mrs. Kirushenko, I'm unable to get a good reading with my equipment. I'd like you to go over to the scanning room; they can do a 360 over there and get a better image. Nothing to worry about; the baby's getting bigger and I just want a better view. You've got a healthy little girl in there and she's doing just fine."

Maryana did so with annoyance. Some doctors were extremely fussy. The scan was painless, but it wasted another half hour of her time. The technicians bounced her back to the doctor.

"Have you ever had a complication with a pregnancy before?"

"I had two preterm labors; my twins were thirty-six weeks, and my tenth was born at twenty-one weeks. Other than that, no. Is there a problem?" Maryana didn't like the sound of the question. For a crazy moment she worried the doctor was going to tell her she was doubly pregnant, the original plus a second younger one. That would be her kind of luck.

The doctor frowned. "I'm concerned you might be experiencing an abruption of the placenta, a condition where the placenta tears away from the uterus."

Maryana felt the color drain from her face. *No. No more half-dead babies.* She was twenty-seven weeks, give or take. "What do you mean? Is the baby okay?"

"Right now everything's fine," the doctor insisted. "The problem is if it worsens. It can possibly lead to internal bleeding, which puts you and your baby at risk. I want you to go on bed rest, and I mean resting in bed. Twenty-three hours a day. If you don't think you can do that at home, I'll put you in the hospital, where we can monitor you closer."

The logistics of such a threat would be catastrophic to the household. "I'll stay in bed."

Maryana went home and lay down, then relayed the news to Sasha. She composed pages of schedules and lists of duties. Nikky would have to start in a toddler program during the day, ahead of schedule. Viktor would be in charge of Dmitri, David, and Sergei. Katya would be responsible for Elizabyeta, Sarah and Vlad, and Sarah and Vlad were already very good at watching Nikky, with Katya to oversee them. Alexei would have to do a little more, but not around his siblings. Everyone would have to pull together for a little while.

By January, Maryana relaxed. Her placenta had remained stable. The baby was due in eight weeks; if it was born now, it had a good chance of being healthy, with none of Sarah's woes. She tiptoed around the house when no one was home, sitting at the table for a glass of iced tea or to answer calls – anything to get out of that bed. Maybe, just maybe, she could convince the doctor to do the cesarian earlier, get her back on her feet. At worst, they had just six months until Sasha's contract was fulfilled, and they would be gone. Anywhere, anywhere, as long as it wasn't here.

January turned to February, and she spent her hour out of bed, maybe a little more, celebrating Nikky's third birthday. It felt good to be up with the family like this. Normal. She was so tired of directing activities from the other room. Her last baby check was still holding okay, but the doctor thought the early delivery might be a good idea, and they planned the birth for 23 February, ten days early.

"Sarah, are you using your inhalers?" she asked as the child coughed for what seemed like the tenth time in half as many minutes.

"Yeah!" Sarah nodded, but Maryana wasn't convinced.

Medicine or not, Maryana woke up to Katya's gentle shaking of her arm.

"Mother? I'm sorry to wake you, but Sarah's coughing really bad. You might want to check on her. I don't know if she should go to school or not. I don't think she's running a fever, but she's breathing really hard."

"Okay." Maryana struggled to roll over and sit up. Her back ached something fierce, and her belly was sore. Maybe, just maybe? *Please, please, let this be it. Get me out of this bed. Let this be early labor.*

She could hear the tell-tale wheeze from the doorway, feel the rattle when she touched the girl's chest. "That's that. You're stuck in bed today, too. I don't want that to worsen."

"But I have so-tau-kam practice today!"

Maryana tipped her head and gave her best look of disbelief. "You can't stop coughing lying still. How do you plan to manage an hour of hard exercise?"

"It could stop!" Sarah bent in half as a strangling cough seized her entire body.

"Bed today. We'll see about tomorrow." Maryana waddled toward the kitchen. "Good catch, Katya. I'll be back with medicine."

After everyone else had left, Maryana ate some breakfast and returned to bed. She watched the local morning news, then caught up on Earth and galactic headlines. *Oh, to get back home! Mother Russia! Earth!* As the house temperature rose with the heat outside, she fell asleep before lunch and woke around two. The pain in her belly was worse; she had nothing better to do, so she timed the pains. Ten minute waves. *Could it be? Could it really be?!* Three weeks early was nothing, not for her. Nothing was ready yet. There were lists to leave, clothing to pack. She stuffed items in a carry bag and packed a few things for the baby. Babies didn't need much on Navara beyond food.

She went out to the kitchen to leave a list on the wallscreen for Viktor and Katya when a fierce pain made her double over and gasp. Maryana grabbed a chair for support. A familiar warm wetness gushed down her thighs. Her water had broken at home with five of her deliveries; nothing new. She glanced down and froze in terror as Maryana saw not clear fluid, but scarlet blood, past her knees, almost to her ankles, and still it seemed to be dribbling.

Lie down! Lie down! her head screamed. She sank to the kitchen floor, lay on her back, and tried to think. *Put the bleeding part higher than the heart.* There was nothing in reach to stuff under her backside; the best she could do was bend her knees. The earset and microphone for the commlink were on the desk. Her palm-com was in the bedroom. "Computer! Commlink!" she ordered, but there was no response. The voice control was off and set to message so she could rest.

Hell in a supernova! Maryana pushed with her feet and slid backwards thirty centimeters toward the swinging door of the kitchen. A second push, but each movement sent a new wave of blood flowing. The contractions were coming closer. Another fast one. She needed help, and she needed it now. She clamped her thighs together and tried pushing with her hands.

The kitchen door swung open. Sarah stared at her, then at the trail. *"Mat?"*

Thank you, God, Saints, and Heavenly Spirits! "Sar'ina! I forgot you were home," Maryana panted. "Be my smart girl and call for help. The baby's coming. Hurry!"

"Right now?" Sarah's eyes held fear, but she turned and ran for the commlink.

Forty-five

T he message came through on Sasha's handicom three-quarters through his afternoon seminar, fifteen students discussing Archeology of Industrialization. His com beeped once, softly. It was set to message; any voice mail would be converted to silent text. He glanced down at the screen. *The baby arrived at home ten minutes ago. Mother isn't well. They sent her to Kinjar Maternity Hospital. She wants you to meet her there.* Sasha's heart stopped.

He stood up from the table and stacked his materials. "I apologize. I have a family emergency I must deal with at once. Class is dismissed. Please check the syllabus for the next assignment." It took less than thirty seconds for him to flee the building, fifteen minutes for him to arrive at the hospital, anxiety turning his blood to ice.

The security guard would not let him past the entry desk. Sasha debated whether or not to force his way past. The guard was a scrawny little thing, a skinny twenty-something twit Sasha could have lifted and carried in one arm, and the guard had no lethal weapons; Navarans allowed nothing beyond stunners.

"Can I at least speak to someone who knows what's going on?" he said too loudly.

A nurse came out to speak with him. "You have a lovely new daughter," the nurse said. "She's upstairs in Special Care just as a precaution. She seems to be quite healthy, otherwise. You can go upstairs and see her any time."

"My wife?" Sasha said, unable to sit down as requested. He couldn't. He just couldn't sit down right now. "I want to see my wife."

"Your wife, I'm afraid, is in critical condition. She is currently in surgery, but you can see her as soon as she's out. She had a placental separation during labor and she hemorrhaged a large volume of blood. They were unable to stop the bleeding and at present they are performing a hysterectomy in order to save her life. I'm sorry, but she won't be able to have any more children."

Nothing was registering too clearly, but the words didn't make sense to Sasha at all. "It's her thirteenth baby; she didn't want this one, why would she want more? She was planning on being sterilized before she came home."

"Then it's a good thing. If you come with me, I can show you where you can wait."

A week passed before a doctor entered the waiting area to speak with him. The chronometer said only an hour, but Sasha had seen a number of long hours in his lifetime and that hour was the longest he'd ever lived, a week's worth of mind-numbing worry squeezed into just sixty tiny minutes. The doctor appeared to be Centauran, stocky in build with pink jiggly skin. He would have preferred a Navaran. He faced the man, afraid to breathe.

"Mr. Kirushenko? I'm Doctor Siad. I operated on your wife."

"How is she? When can I see her?"

The doctor held up a hand to slow him. "I must warn you, she's in very critical condition. She nearly bled out on us; we replaced about three-quarters of her blood supply, and she's still receiving replacer and medication to boost her blood pressure. She had a placental separation during labor, which caused massive blood loss. If the EMP's got there even ten minutes later, I don't think she'd have made it here alive. I'm going to let you in to see her, but her body's still very much in shock and we're monitoring everything extremely closely."

"I want to see her," Sasha repeated.

"Come with me."

The critical care room overwhelmed Sasha. It wasn't the same as the infant critical care where Sarah started out. There were three patients in the cubicles before the nurse's stations, mothers whose pregnancies were jeopardizing their health; Maryana had the farthest one. She was covered with a sensor sheet; a half-dozen tubes ran underneath it. Every two minutes a green light fanned over her from equipment on the ceiling, the results of the body scan updating on the wallscreen above her head. Her lovely skin, so milky and smooth, had a waxy pallor to it. Shadows circled her closed eyes, made valleys appear under her proud cheekbones. An oxygen mask sat over her nose and mouth. His body refused to cooperate; his joints locked until he couldn't walk, his heart unable to do more than shiver in a chest so tight there wasn't room left to beat.

A nurse brought him a chair and helped him sit on it.

Can I touch her? Is that allowed? Fuck that, let them stop me! "Tash?" he said softly. His hand slipped under the sheet; her hand was there. He held it firmly, but not too tight. "Tash?"

He leaned forward to kiss her, right above her eye. She turned her head, and the beautiful ocean-blue eyes blinked open and focused on his face. She smiled under the mask.

"You made it," she said weakly.

"Of course. Where else would I be?"

"Baby?"

"Over in the nursery. Twenty-eight hundred grams, breathing air and nursing on her own."

"Good." Maryana's eyes closed briefly before opening again. She squeezed his hand with what strength she could spare. "I love you, Sash. Never forget that."

"Not half as much as I love you." He pulled her hand out from under the sheet and kissed it. "My brave warrior. You made it. We can leave for Earth as soon as you're ready."

Maryana lifted her other hand and removed the mask. "Kiss me, Sash." He had just enough time to plant his lips onto hers before a low-oxygen beep sounded, and she replaced the mask.

"Make sure to tell the girls what a good job they did. Sarah found me in the kitchen and called for help. She let the EMP's in and got whatever they needed. Without her, the baby would have died. Katya tried, but she was so upset I made her stay with me."

"Sarah's a trooper," Sasha agreed. "Any ideas for a name?"

Maryana seemed to fade for a moment. "No. Tomorrow. I want to hold her again first. I love you, Sash. Don't leave me."

"Never." Her eyes closed, and she slipped back asleep. Sasha sat, one hand holding hers, the other stroking her head. Every time the green light scanned her he studied the output on the wallscreen, though he didn't have a clue what the indicators meant. He kissed her hand after each, as if congratulating her for passing the scan.

She roused a little two more times, enough to smile at him, and once to tell him again that she loved him. An hour had passed when a piercing alarm went off, sending his adrenaline levels shooting into space. A nurse flew in, shoved him out of the way and double-checked the alarm. She hit another switch and a page sounded outside the cubicle.

"Out!" she ordered him. "She's in cardiac arrest." Several personnel ran into the room. A tiny little nurse who didn't look old enough to have any type of diploma yet took him by the hand.

"Come with me, sir. I'll show you where you can wait. The doctor will speak with you as soon as they get her stabilized again."

Sasha barely heard. "That's my wife. I need to be with her. I need to know what's happening."

The nurse tugged at him. "They'll tell you as soon as they're able."

He waited by their line of back-breaking chairs that were too short for someone his size, but he couldn't sit. He stood, back to the room, forehead to the wall, eyes closed. Sasha wasn't religious, not even an agnostic; he had no idea who his words were directed at, but they came to his lips in a whisper anyway.

Please let her be okay! Please! I can't lose her! I promise, I promise I'll do better. I can do it. Tash, stay with me!

Tears oozed upwards. Every so often one would escape, and he'd choke the second or third back down. This was a first-rate hospital on a first-rate world. They knew what they were doing. She would be fine.

He did not know how long it was before a doctor appeared; certainly, entire universes were born in less time. A nurse accompanied him. Sasha spun around to face him.

"Mr. Kirushenko? Please, sit."

Sasha forced himself to fold onto a chair. The doctor sat next to him. "How is she?"

"Your wife lost a tremendous amount of blood this afternoon. We performed an emergency operation to stop it. Her blood pressure was very low, and we were trying to bring that up. Because of the hemorrhage and the surgery, we did not want to take a risk of putting her on blood thinners, anything that might increase her risk of bleeding again. Because of her low heart rate, the medications, and the surgery, I'm afraid a blood clot formed. It broke loose and lodged in an artery, cutting off her blood supply. We put her on a cardiac pump and a ventilator, but we couldn't clear the clot fast enough. By the time we reached it, there was too much organ damage. I am tremendously sorry, Mr. Kirushenko. We did everything we possibly could, longer than we knew there was hope, but your wife died a few minutes ago at 17:11 hours."

The room closed in. His vision went black. Time seemed to stop. Sasha had no idea if he was still breathing, if the doctor was still there, if the man had just told him he himself had died. His brain had stopped functioning. All the little background noises to the world seemed to have disappeared, as if his ears had suddenly filled with wax. He was moving down a silent, hazy tunnel, without ever standing up. The man's words made no sense.

He couldn't feel it, didn't see it, but somehow he knew the doctor was holding his hand. "Is there anyone we can call to be with you? A family member, or a friend?"

Sasha heard his voice answer from deep in the tunnel, but he swore his mouth never moved. "No. We have no family here. We never made close friends. I have to see her. I need to see her." Some odd little piece of his brain said, *I need to hear it from her.*

"By all means," the nurse said. "Come with me."

It was all he could do not to run back to the room; it took just as much strength not to run away. She looked the same, sleeping there on the bed, but the monitors were all dark, and the green light was gone. Someone had removed the tubes and mask. They were wrong, that's what. It was all a mistake.

The chair had been removed; the nurse retrieved it. "Take as long as you need." She patted his shoulder.

"Tash? Tash?" It couldn't be true. It couldn't. He picked up her hand and kissed it. Her hand was limp, more flaccid than when she was asleep, more lifeless than when she'd come out of surgery after Sergei.

Lifeless.

Life-less.

It couldn't be true. It couldn't. He stroked her colorless cheek, still faintly warm. *There! She can't be gone, she's warm!*

"Tash? You can't leave me, Tash. You can't. I don't know what to do without you."

"Tash, don't. Don't go. I can't do anything alone. You know that. I need you."

He slid his arm under her shoulders. He'd held her so many times while she slept; he loved when she cuddled close, content, but this time she drooped like a wet shower rag. He held her, hugged her, and he began to shake. He didn't care who saw his tears, didn't try to stop them. "Tash! You promised. You promised you'd never leave me.

"Tash? It's my fault, Tash! It's *my* fault. I'm sorry! I'm so sorry! Tash, forgive me. Please stay!"

Ninety minutes had passed before a nurse touched his arm and asked if he was okay. Maryana's warmth had gone, replaced by a strange coldness so out of place with her.

"How can I be okay?" he asked. "My wife is dead."

"I'm so sorry, sir. Is there anything I can do for you? Anything I can get for you?"

Sasha started to shake his head, then said, "A hairbrush. I need a hairbrush. Her hair's a mess, and she wouldn't want anyone seeing her like that. Her hair is always perfect."

"Of course. I'll be right back."

With the nurse's help, he brushed her hair one final time, braiding the tresses as precisely as he could, the way she would want. The nurse straightened the sheet and folded her hands over it. Her coloring was off, the cheeks a little slack, but Tash looked as if she'd laid down for a quick nap, that's all.

He kissed the cold lips one last time, an unnatural feeling, as if she'd actually gone somewhere and left herself behind. "They want me to go, Tash. I have to deal with the children. I love you."

For the first time, Tash didn't say it back.

"She's a lady of high class," he told the nurse. "Make sure you treat her that way."

"We treat everyone like that, sir."

"Thank you."

Sasha walked out without looking back. He took the lift up to the sixth floor and stopped at the special-care nursery.

A nurse led him across the room. "She's right over here. She's doing fine. We'll keep her under observation for a day or so, then she should be ready to go. Do you want to hold her?"

Sasha stared down at the baby with a leaden face. A decent size, not big, not small, with brownish hair. All of the other girls were born with pale hair. She didn't look like Tash, but she didn't look exactly like him, either. "No. I just wanted to see her. Her mother just died."

"I am so sorry, sir."

Sasha nodded, and left.

He made it out to the hallway before collapsing against a wall. Sasha took a deep breath and wiped his face with shaking hands. He hadn't been this scared in... longer than he could think. He fought his emotions down, smaller, smaller, small, until he could box them up inside. He would have to be strong. He had a family to care for. They would need him to be strong, in charge, on top of things, set the example. He had no idea what to do, how to plan a funeral, who to call, who to talk to, what to say. Tash would know. Should he even bother to notify her family? He knew what she would want him to do. Take care of his children, stay sober, clean his nails, mind his manners, no farting at the table. He couldn't let her down.

He *wouldn't* let her down. He owed her that much.

He would have to tell the children, somehow, but to say the words aloud would make them real, and he wasn't ready to hear that yet. He took another deep breath, steadied himself, and locked his immediate thoughts away so his legs would work again.

Sasha Kirushenko, widower, walked out to his flyer and went home alone.

End

Susan Staneslow Olesen is a graduate of Chase Collegiate School and studied psychology and writing at Wells College. She is a special-needs foster parent with more than 25 years' experience in autism. In addition to working at her public library, she is holding steady at seven kids, six cats, three dogs, and a yard full of very clumsy squirrels. *Ancient History* is her fifth novel.

For info and trivia, follow along at
Best Intentions book series on Facebook.com

www.ingramcontent.com/pod-product-compliance
Lightning Source LLC
Chambersburg PA
CBHW062027170626
46813CB00001B/318